Hope, Tears, and Dreams on the Way West

An Overland Trail Novel

T. Lynne Jackson

Manastash Books

This book is a work of fiction. Names, characters, places, and incidents are products of the author's imagination. Any resemblance to actual events, locales, organizations, or persons, living or dead, is entirely coincidental.

Copyright © 2025 by T. Lynne Jackson

All rights reserved.

No portion of this book may be reproduced in any form without written permission from the publisher or author, except as permitted by U.S. copyright law.

Cover design by Getcovers

In loving memory of Mom.

Prologue

Meghan held her breath as she tiptoed through the cozy living room toward the front door. Only inches to go. *Creak.* She froze. *Argh.* How could she have forgotten to step around the loose floorboard?

Her twin brother nudged her from behind. "Hurry up."

"Shh." She wrapped her palm around the knob and twisted. The rusty hinge groaned as she cracked the door open a slit. She peered through the gap and frowned. Steel-gray clouds hung heavy over the neighborhood rooftops, and fat raindrops splashed into puddles on the sidewalk. "It's raining."

"Of course it's raining. What do you expect in Oregon?"

"But it's summer. It's supposed to be sunny." She eased the door open enough to squeeze through.

"And just where do you think you two are going?"

"Uh-oh." She stopped midstep, pivoted, and cringed at her mother's squinted eyes glaring at them. "To the mall," Meghan said, with a questioning lilt on the word *mall*.

"At seven thirty in the morning? The mall doesn't open until ten. And why are two fourteen-year-olds up this early on summer break?"

"Uh." How was she going to weasel her way out of this one?

"We're going to meet Mark and April at the coffeeshop first."

Saved by the nerdy brother. She almost reached to tousle his wavy brown hair. But Mom's hands planted on her hips, and her furrowed brow stifled the tease.

"Close the door."

Meghan shut the door and tipped her forehead into the jamb.

Jason leaned against the wall and stared at his sneakers. "Well?"

Meghan winced at the tone of Mom's voice—the "don't mess with me, young lady" tinge that had been all too familiar lately. She clenched her fists and turned to face her mother, who was dressed for her office job in a navy pencil skirt, white blouse, and low-heeled pumps.

"Are the two of you so absentminded that you already forgot the discussion we had last night?" Mom glared from Meghan to Jason back to Meghan. "You know the Realtor is coming tomorrow morning to appraise the house."

Meghan studied a scuff that marred her black ankle boot as her mother unleashed the reprimand.

"You two know you're supposed to clean the attic today. Are you going to tell me you *both* forgot? Don't force me to ground you for the summer."

Jason stubbed the toe of his sneaker into the entry rug. "Sorry, Mom."

"Don't you *sorry* me, young man." Mom reached her hand out, palm up. "Phones."

"What?" Meghan raised her eyebrows, aghast.

"Your phones. Hand them over." Mom pursed her lips and narrowed her eyes, like a cat poised to pounce on a cornered mouse.

"But we need them. I need to let April know we're going to ditch them."

"You have thirty seconds to text her. Then the phones are mine until the attic is spotless."

Meghan slipped the phone from the bulky denim handbag that she had slung over her shoulder and thumbed off a quick text.

"What if we promise not to use them until we're done in the attic?" Jason suggested.

"Not a chance. If I can't trust you not to sneak out, then how am I going to trust you with your phones all day? Meghan will be sharing TikToks with April, and you'll be playing games all day." She wiggled the fingers on her extended hand. "The phones. Now!"

"Ah, Mom." Jason slid his phone from the hip pocket of his jeans and plopped it onto her palm.

Meghan followed and slithered out of the way. Mom slipped the phones into her purse, snatched an umbrella from the stand in the corner, and traipsed through the door.

In the upstairs hallway, Jason tugged the cord that lowered the stair ladder to the attic. The hinges moaned.

"I don't see why we have to do this. None of the stuff up there is ours." Meghan fisted her hands and stared into the dark hole in the ceiling.

"You're right. Dad should have cleaned it out before he left us. It's probably all his stuff up there."

"Is it just me, or is Mom even more irritable lately?"

"It's not just you. In her defense, she does have a lot on her mind, with Dad gone, the demanding boss she complains about, the fact that she has to sell the house."

"It will be nice to get out of this creepy old house." Meghan hugged her arms around her chest.

"You'll take that back when we're crammed into a tiny apartment. Besides, the house has been in the family for generations. I can see why it would be hard for her to part with. Kinda like the end of an era. After you." Jason made a dramatic sweep of his arm to motion for Meghan to ascend the ladder.

The wooden rungs creaked under Meghan's clunky boots. She poked her head through the opening. "It's really dark up here. Did you bring a flashlight?"

"There's a light right above your head. Reach around and find the chain."

Meghan hoisted herself up the last step and flailed her hand in the air. Her knuckle whacked the chain that dangled from the ceiling. She tugged the cord. The bare bulb emitted a smoky amber glow that cast eerie shadows on the walls. She startled at the scrape on the floorboard as Jason came up beside her. "It's really creepy up here."

"And noisy." Jason gazed at the ceiling, as if he could see the rain pounding the roof above their heads.

"Look at all this stuff." Meghan turned a 360. "And all the dust. And cobwebs."

Jason scratched his head and glanced around the room. "It's going to take a year to get this cleaned out."

Fuzzy objects clarified as Meghan's eyes adjusted to the grainy dimness. Stacks of cardboard boxes sagged against the wall near the trapdoor. Folding chairs and a card table leaned against the boxes. Suitcases, one with a broken handle, lay piled adjacent to the table.

"Look, there's our cribs." Meghan pointed to the wooden frames that were collapsed together like a broken accordion and snuggled between two stacks of leaning boxes. "And the old baby furniture that was in our room." She clomped over to a scratched and peeling bureau. "Do you remember this powder-blue dresser? Hey look"—she pointed to a crooked drawer—"it still has the crayon marks on it from when we tried to be mini-Picassos." She rubbed an index finger along the surface. "Yuck! It's filthy."

"Good thing Mom left us a whole box of dust rags."

"Eek!" Meghan yanked her hand from the dresser. "Spider!"

"I can't believe you're still afraid of spiders."

"I'm not afraid of them. It just startled me."

"Spider, spider." Jason pinched his fingers in front of Meghan's face.

"Get away from me!" She shielded her face with her hands.

"Wait until Mark finds out you're afraid of spiders."

"You wouldn't dare tell him." She lifted her shoulders and balled her hands at her sides.

"Try me."

"If you do, I'll tell Mom you're gay."

"And I'll squeal that you're secretly dating Mark."

"You wouldn't dare."

"Nor would you."

She relaxed her hands. "You know you're going to have to tell her sometime. Better she hears it from you."

Jason rolled his lips under his teeth. "I know. I'll tell her when she's ready." He turned toward the stairs. "Let's get to work. I'll get the buckets and cleaning supplies that Mom left in the hall."

As Jason descended the ladder, Meghan surveyed the cramped space. An object, wedged between sagging stacks of boxes abutting the far wall, caught her attention. She heard Jason clank up the stairs and drop the buckets on the floor as she shuffled into the shadow. "Jason, come look at this."

"What is it?" His sneakers squeaked as he crossed the room to stand next to her. "It's just a big trunk. What's the big deal?"

"I don't know. It looks like it could be an old treasure chest or something."

"Well, it's certainly old, that's for sure."

"Let's see what's in it."

"Come on, Meghan—we need to get to work. I don't want to spend the whole day up here. Who cares what's in it?" He returned to the waiting buckets.

"Let's just take a quick peek. If there is a treasure, then we'll be rich and can hire someone to clean this disaster for us." She knelt, facing the trunk, her bare knee rubbing on the floor through one of the many fashionable tears in her faded jeans.

"Don't be absurd. You've been reading too many fantasy novels." He reached down and swiped a rag and stepped toward the dresser.

"Don't be silly. April reads them and tells me about them."

"Whatever." Jason rolled his eyes and started dusting the dresser. "It's probably just full of old ratty clothes and rags."

"Good. We can use more rags to clean up this dump." She reached for the latch. "Eww!" She jerked her hand away. "Speaking of rags, toss me one so I can wipe off these sticky cobwebs. Gross!"

Jason dropped his cloth onto the trunk and plopped to his knees next to Meghan.

Meghan cleaned the grime away from the latch and tossed the rag over her shoulder.

Jason reached out and fumbled with the latch. "This sucker is jammed. I can't get it opened."

"We need a screwdriver."

"Well, we're in luck. Mom put a screwdriver and a toothbrush and a flashlight in the bucket of supplies."

"I hope she left some toothpaste also, because your breath stinks."

He glared at her. "It does not. I brushed this morning."

"So that you can have minty fresh breath before you kiss Jeremy."

"Shut up."

"Just get the screwdriver, okay?"

"Yes, Your Majesty." He rose and emoted a bow and then returned with the tool. He knelt in front of the chest and started to pry the latch.

"Wonder when the last time this thing was opened." She rubbed her hand on the lid. .

"Judging from how stuck this sucker is, probably not for at least a century." Jason grunted as he heaved his weight into the tool. The latch popped open, spitting up a puff of dust.

They jimmied the trunk from between the stacked boxes and lifted the lid. The hinges groaned.

"See, just a bunch of old rags." Jason stood and shoved his hands into his pockets.

"How can you tell? It's too dark to see what's in there. Grab the flashlight."

"Am I your servant?"

"Do you want to get this over with so that we can get this job done and get our phones back?"

Jason spun toward the buckets of supplies.

Meghan lifted out a dress and held it up in front of her.

Jason aimed the light at it. "See, a mess of old, moth-eaten clothes."

Meghan set the dress aside and removed a stack of folded garments and laid them on top of the dress. She reached her hands into the chest. "Shine the light in there so I can see."

"You're being extra-bossy today."

"Just point the light down. Is that so difficult?"

Jason aimed the beam into the trunk.

"Look at all this old stuff. Why would anybody keep this junk? Dented tin cups. Chipped plates." She shifted the dishes to one side. "Wonder what's in this?" She lifted a burlap sack and crinkled her nose. "This is really musty." She untied the string at the top and reached inside.

"Careful—there's probably a rat's nest in there."

She jerked her hand out of the bag. "Shine the light in there." She widened the bag's opening as Jason aimed the beam. She peered inside. "No rats."

"Could be mice. They're smaller."

"I don't think even they could squeeze into this trunk." She tilted the bag and spilled the contents onto the floor and sat cross-legged in front of the pile. She picked up a pair of moccasins. "Look at these."

Jason sat on the floor opposite the pile. "Why would someone keep those? They're totally falling apart."

"But look at this beadwork. These must have been made by a Native American."

"There goes that imagination again."

Meghan set the shoes aside and picked up a small gunny sack, untied the string, and jiggled out a piece of jewelry.

"What's that?" Jason asked.

"It looks like a pin."

"A pin?"

"Yeah, you know, like a . . . what do you call it?"

"I don't know. What do you call it?"

"Like a brooch. You know, something a rich person would wear pinned on her gown. Like when she went to the ball."

"And Prince Charming slips a glass slipper on her foot."

"Cute." She rubbed her thumb over the stone. "I wonder what kind of gem this is. Maybe it's valuable."

"If it were valuable, it wouldn't be hidden in a trunk in the attic. Mom would have sold it already."

"Not if she didn't know it was here."

Jason reached for the last item, which was wrapped in a cloth. "This feels like a book." He lifted it into his lap and unrolled the fabric. He set the cloth aside and blew a stream of dust from the cover. He reached for the flashlight and shone it on the book. "'My Diary.'"

"Give that to me." Meghan reached for the book, but he whisked it away from her grasp.

He untied the ribbon wrapped around the leather and opened the cover. "'To my darling Margaret. Happy fourteenth birthday. Love, Mother.'" He paused. "Must be some stuffy rich lady to sign a gift 'Love, Mother.'"

"Let me have it."

"Here." He set the diary and flashlight on the floor, plodded to the heap of cleaning supplies, and grabbed a broom. "I don't want to read some sappy diary." He gagged on the swirling dust as he swept.

Meghan snatched the flashlight and opened the diary to the first entry. "May 15, 1849."

"1849?"

"Quit interrupting. You said you weren't interested."

Jason set the broom aside and sat beside her.

She returned to the book. "'Dear Diary. My life has been shattered, as if a tornado has ripped out my soul and left it scattered like a wasteland of broken matchsticks.'"

Chapter 1

May 15, 1849

Dear Diary,

My life has been shattered, as if a tornado has ripped out my soul and left it scattered like a wasteland of broken matchsticks. A river of tears has streamed down my cheeks and spilled from my chin like a roaring waterfall since yesterday morning. I brushed away a stray tear and slumped like a discarded marionette between my pa and twin brother in the northeast corner of the Calvary Baptist cemetery.

"In your hands, Dear Lord, we humbly entrust Mary Elizabeth, loving wife, mother, daughter, and friend. In this life you embraced her with your tender love. Deliver her now from evil and bid her eternal rest."

A pine box rested askew on two planks above a freshly dug hole, which was to be my mother's eternal resting place. My mind was muddled like a kettle of thick porridge, unable to process the world around me, my heart empty and cold, like the frozen tundra, and my body numb, unable to feel, as if life had bled from my soul. A knothole that marred a side plank in the hastily constructed casket drew my focus from the preacher's prayer. I inhaled a deep breath, bit my lower lip, and focused on the blemish. I was not going to cry in Pa's presence. My twin sniveled beside me. Pa grunted a reprimand at my sibling's childish weakness. A sprinkle of townsfolk clustered at our backs, heads bowed, bearded men holding their hats in their hands. The dangling leaves of an aged oak tree that shadowed the hallow plot quivered in the spring breeze.

"Ashes to ashes, dust to dust . . ." The preacher continued his humble request to God to grant my beloved mother eternal salvation.

A sniffle escaped from my grandmother's handkerchief, which I knew she held pressed to her clenched mouth as she stood behind me. She rested a trembling hand on my shoulder.

I twitched. I hoped she hadn't noticed. Her presence and her touch were so foreign that I had to suppress the urge to shrug it off. Practically a stranger to me, I did not recognize her when she emerged from the St. Louis stage that morning. Not even a wrinkle or speck of dust marred her black mourning suit, black leather gloves, and black crape veil pinned to her ebony bonnet. I was sure she didn't mean to, but she'd scrunched her nose when she'd eyed my patched-up gingham dress—a proper mourning suit was not one of the two rag garments that hung from the hook above my bed, which comprised my wardrobe—the tousled auburn hair that spilled from my braid, and the dingy, threadbare gray bonnet I'd worn to town to greet her arrival. Her milky skin was unblemished by the harsh elements and the daily grind of hard living.

Her scarlet-painted lips pressed taut, as if the cosmetic had pasted them together in a permanent scowl. I almost melted into a puddle of grief, though, when her soft green eyes, which were a mirror image of my mother's—and according to Ma, mine as well—gazed at me.

My focus zeroed in on the knothole. I grimaced at my mind's vision of the underground creatures slithering through the crevasse and crawling over my mother's corpse. My beautiful mother. My teacher, my confidante, my best friend, my protector . . . lying lifeless under six feet of cold clay, defenseless against the slimy critters that would devour her flesh. I shuddered and whispered a silent plea to the tree to watch over her.

"In the name of our blessed Lord. Amen." The preacher closed his Bible and held it to his chest.

Four men, one of whom was the schoolmaster, Mr. Jones, stepped from the crowd and moved to the grave, two on each side. They each bent and took an end of the two canvas straps that straddled the grave atop the planks that cradled the casket.

"Gentleman." The preacher nodded to the quartet.

The undertaker slid the planks from beneath the pine box, and the men used the straps to lower the coffin into the dark hole. The thud of dirt clods hammering the pine box signaled the crowd to disperse. Pa guided me away from the grave, but he couldn't shield me from the thundering clunks of the shovelfuls of damp clay that pounded my mother's coffin.

The schoolmaster approached us. "I'm sorry for your loss, Elijah." The buttons on Mr. Jones's vest stretched as he gazed up at my pa and extended a pudgy hand.

"Thank you, Amos." Pa's coal-black eyes scanned the spattering of conversing mourners and landed on the grave as he clasped the outstretched hand. "I don't know how I'm going to manage without her."

I almost smirked at the juxtaposition of Pa, tall and wiry with his rumpled brown hair and scraggly beard, next to my portly, clean-shaven instructor. It had never occurred to me that they were acquainted.

"It must be a double heartache, losing a second wife to a fall like that. It appears that your Margaret is the woman of your house now." He winked at me and returned his gaze to Pa. "I'll miss her inquisitive mind and help as a monitor, but I imagine she has a bigger job now, taking care of you and Jacob, than learning about conjunctions and contractions and such nonsense."

I gasped. The thought of leaving school to manage the household for my father and brother rammed me like a punch in the stomach. Unlike most of my classmates, I liked school, even though I was the rare—and oldest—girl among a classroom filled with boys. Somehow, Ma had scraped together enough money to send me and Jacob to school long after most children our age had dropped out. Most parents didn't see a need for an education beyond learning basic reading and writing skills. I, on the other hand, had ambitions of becoming a schoolmarm and running my own schoolhouse one day. Although, my secret dream was to be a doctor because I admired Doc Jackson and the way he helped folks around town. But a girl could never be a doctor, or anything other than a schoolmarm. But a hag who did the cooking and washing and sewing and cleaning up after a sloppy drunk and an absentminded brother—no!

The teacher took his leave, and Pa turned toward my grandmother, who was standing near the grave, watching the workers cover my mother's casket one shovelful at a time. Thud. Thud. Thud.

"You go on. I have some business with your grandmother." Pa strode toward the grieving woman.

I inched nearer so that I could listen while pretending to read a neglected tombstone. I wondered whether Pa would spare the expense of a grave marker for Ma. Probably not. The only monument to memorialize my mother's time on earth was likely to be a crude cross constructed of dead tree limbs, with her name etched with a jackknife.

"Esther, it's so good of you to come, especially on such short notice." Pa stood by my grandmother and stared into the hole.

She didn't raise her eyes from the grave. "I don't recall ever granting you permission to address me by my first name, Elijah. I didn't come for you."

Pa shoved his hands into his pockets. "I'm sorry, Mrs. Peterson. I hoped we could put aside our differences and become more civil. For the children's sake."

She shot him a wicked sideways glance, then returned her attention to the grave. "When have you ever done anything for the children's sake?" She crossed her arms around her chest and exhaled a deep breath. "You know, Elijah, I never could figure out what she saw in you. Why she would leave a lovely, comfortable home to live in some filthy shack with a hard-up loser who could never catch that elusive 'big break' that was always dangling at his fingertips. She didn't see the starry-eyed drunk who was too lazy to earn an honest living until it was too late."

Wow! I stifled a gasp. I'd never heard of a woman who would dare to speak to a man with such a scorching tone. Pa's hands must have been fisted in his pockets, and he must have garnered every morsel of restraint he possessed to stifle the impulse to slap her across the face for the affront.

"Her time was runnin' out, Esther. She didn't want to end up an old spinster living under your wing. She had starry-eyed dreams of her own. And that big break"—he removed a hand from his pocket and rubbed his fingers in front of him—"it's so close that I'm just about to wrap my hand around it."

"You never learn, do you?"

"I mean it. I just need a few hundred dollars—a small investment. Jacob, Maggie, and I are about to step into the good life."

"Are you asking me for money?" She glared at him.

"Just a small loan. I'm so confident that I will pay you back by the end of the year—with interest."

"Go to hell, Elijah!"

My jaw dropped, and I flung my hand to my mouth, shocked at my grandmother's bold use of such offensive language. Not just unladylike but unacceptable in mixed company.

My grandmother spun lynd stomped from the church cemetery, nose pointed to the steeple. The stragglers in the graveyard lowered their eyes as she passed, then whispered behind her back as she made her exit through the open gate.

I wrung my hands together. I could see why Ma would want to escape from the clutches of the stern, stuffy woman. But my stomach tingled in admiration for her audacity to speak her mind—and to give Pa a good dressing down.

I returned my gaze to Pa. He stared into the hole that, judging from the height of the pile of fresh dirt behind the workmen, must have been half-filled. Then he turned and walked toward me. "I have some business to tend to. I'll see you and Jacob at home later."

I watched him stride away, head down, shoulders bowed, as if crushed by the weight of the dirt pile that the workmen spilled over my mother's pine box. I assumed his business was with the bartender at the local saloon and that Jacob and I would be snuggled under the covers when he returned, long after our little cabin was cloaked in darkness. I trailed him as he exited the cemetery, then I stopped in the churchyard and watched him cross the street. The sheriff sidled up to him. I hadn't noticed the lawman at the service. I wished I could have heard their conversation, but it didn't appear the lawman was offering his condolences. Pa's fiery glower could have burned a hole in the sheriff's back when the lawman strode away.

"Hey, runt, where do you think you're going?"

I spun and raced toward a group of boys who were harassing my brother on the other side of the church grounds. The biggest one palmed Jacob in the chest, trying to provoke a fight. My brother stumbled backward a few steps but steadied himself and faced the bully.

"What's the mama's boy going to do now without a mama to run home to?"

"Leave me alone." My brother's cheeks beamed as scarlet red as the begonias that adorned Ma's garden.

"Why don't you be a man and stand up for yourself, you useless piker?"

Luke had harassed my brother for as long as I could remember. But lately, as Luke, a year older than Jacob and me, had sprouted taller and Jacob's growth had stagnated, the scuffles had intensified.

"Hey, what's going on?" I stomped toward the gaggle of tormentors.

"Mind your own business, Maggie." Luke spit at my sibling's feet. "This is between Jacob and us."

My brother stood rigid, shoulders nearly bunched to his ears, fists clenched and red faced. But I knew he wouldn't throw a punch. It was suicide either way. If he tried to fight, the flock of bigger boys would pounce on him. And if he didn't, they would beat him up anyway. Although Jacob and I had recently celebrated our fourteenth birthdays, his wavy brown tufts barely reached my eyebrows. I was also stronger and faster and begrudged the fact that I had to constantly bail him out of jams—like this one. "Come on, Luke—leave him alone!"

"Big sister coming to rescue the little punk. You stupid backward hicks should go drown in that swamp you came from." He puffed his chest as he hurled the insult.

"You're the one who's stupid and belongs in a swamp." All my pent-up rage erupted. I rushed up to the bully and punched him in the jaw.

Shocked, he stumbled backward. I pounced. His breath smacked me in the face when he struck the ground beneath me.

"Maggie, Maggie, stop!"

The schoolmaster's shouts were muffled by the fog of my rage. I tried to shake off his plump hands when they gripped my shoulders as I pummeled the gasping bully.

Mr. Jones hoisted me to my feet. "That's enough, Maggie."

I tried to calm my trembling limbs and shook the pebbles from between my ears.

"I think you need to apologize to Luke."

I turned and glared at him. "What! He started it. I'm not going to apologize to that . . ."

"Watch what you're about to say, miss. Why don't you and Jacob go on home."

The gang of bullies scattered.

"I'm sorry about your ma." Mr. Jones laced his sausage-like fingers in front of his chest. "She was a good woman."

Unable to speak, I nodded and watched him waddle toward his waiting wife.

***

I lay awake, curled up on the straw bed that I shared with my twin and our mutt, Scout, and stared into the darkness. Creepy shadows skated across the conical walls of the cramped loft that was our bedroom. The attic wasn't really a room at all, and for that matter, neither was the bed really a bed. I didn't know where Pa had found the flimsy mattress—a flea-infested glob of musty straw sewn into a frayed blanket—that he'd squeezed into the cramped space. The loft was not only our sleeping space but our private place, our refuge to escape the fights and arguments of our incompatible parents. Although Jacob and I shared just about everything, we had an unspoken rule about the bed. He claimed the third on the left, I was entitled to the third on the right, and Scout owned the middle. Scout, however, was a habitual violator of the space rule. I often woke with a paw, a slobbery nose, a floppy ear, or a tail in my face. Or a kick to my ribs while he scratched a pesky flea. There were a lot of fleas. But we didn't care. Besides each other, Scout was our best friend, and either of us would have gladly given up our corner of the bed for him.

Pa's footsteps thundered up the rickety ladder to our room. I tensed, and my heart pounded. He and Ma usually argued when he came home drunk. Then Ma would try to hide a bruised eye or swollen lip the next day, which she claimed was from an absentminded bump into a doorjamb or a trip over a rug. I'd never witnessed any of her clumsy moments. They only seemed to occur after she and Pa had quarreled. Who would he quarrel with now? I slinked against the wall, wishing it would open to a concealed compartment where I could hide.

"Jacob, Maggie." Pa's words slithered on his tongue, as if he were slurping a bowl of soup while hollering as he stumbled up the steps. "Get some good rest 'cause we're gonna pull foot for California in the morn'." His gruff voice carried an unusual lilt, and he pronounced California as Cal-ee-forn-ee. "There's gooold in Cal-ee-forn-ee, and we're gonna be rich!"

Jacob, who had been feigning sleep, sat up and muttered, "Huh?"

"Be up before the rooster to pack so we'll be on the road to St. Joe by noon. We're gonna strike it rich in Cal-ee-forn-ee! May the good Lord sprinkle gold dust into your dreams."

Pa tumbled from the ladder. I cringed. He cursed and staggered toward his bed.

I rolled to my side to face Jacob. "California? He can't be serious. Can he?"

"Someone at the saloon was probably talking nonsense. He won't even remember it come morning. Get some sleep."

I lay on my back and stared at the ghoulish faces the sinister shadows painted on the walls. "Jacob," I whispered, "how are we going to get by without Ma?"

"I don't know, Maggs. I just don't know."

Scout snuggled up to me and licked an escaped tear from my cheek.

Chapter 2

Dear Diary,

I can't believe it! Pa didn't forget about the California gold. He roused us before dawn by clanking a cast-iron skillet on the stove, demanding breakfast. It took a few breaths for the hazy morning fog to clear between my ears before I remembered Ma was not there to fix his morning meal. A hollow ache burrowed into my core. An emptiness, like a tree eaten away from the inside by millions of tunneling insects, ready to topple with the next whispered breeze. I fried some eggs, which he inhaled while barking orders. Then we tossed just about everything we owned into his covered farm wagon. Pa had acquired the cart years ago from Old Man Jamison, the widower who lived down the lane. He had died one day, and the next, Pa was the new owner of his wagon, which was already crippled from decades of heavy use and neglect. Pa used the wagon to support his vocation, which was collecting discarded odds and ends, or rather junk, that he found along the roads or off-fall pilfered from unsuspecting merchants, thinking, usually incorrectly, that he could repair them—or exploit parts to repair other junk he'd collected—and sell them for a large profit. Most of the junk still *littered the yard and cluttered the barn, which left barely any room for our aged horse, Nellie, or the band of roaming chickens that supplied the eggs for our morning meals. If there ever was any profit, it's no doubt lining the saloon owner's pockets.*

Pa dragged Ma's travel trunk from the bedroom to the center of our little cabin and lifted the lid.

I inhaled a nervous breath. "How about I do that, while you and Jacob get the tools from the barn."

Pa grunted something incomprehensible and stomped out of the house. Jacob glared at me and followed him.

Whew! I knelt in front of the open trunk and lifted out Ma's fabrics, patterns, and sewing supplies and set them aside. I reached for a tattered book that a client had given her as payment for a new dress. I peered at the cover. *Jayne Eyre*, by Charlotte Bronte. I returned the tome to the trunk. Then my palm wrapped around the pouch that contained the last vestige of her life before she'd married Pa. I scanned the cabin to make sure that Pa and Jacob were both outside before I untied the string and fingered out the piece of jewelry. A tear slid down my cheek as I gazed at the heirloom—a silver brooch shaped like a rose, trimmed in gold flakes, with a ruby set in the eye of the flower. Ma had warned me never to let Pa know she still had it. She said she had planned on gifting it to me for my sixteenth birthday, as her mother, my grandmother, had given it to her at sixteen. I rubbed my thumb over the gem, closed my eyes, and pictured her sweet face at the memory of her telling me how she wore it to her stepping-out party and, years later, on her wedding day. I returned the brooch to the pouch, picked up a needle and thread from Ma's sewing basket, and secured the bag to the inside of the waistband of my apron.

I wiped a tear with the back of my hand. *Ma, your secret is safe with me.*

A crippled Nellie lugged the four-by-ten box on wheels, our temporary mobile home crammed with our essential possessions, her final steps to the outskirts of St. Joseph the following afternoon. I imagined the shocked expression of our ruddy-faced landlord when he discovered the inessential remnants of our existence, including the chickens, Ma's vegetable garden, and who knows how many months of back rent that were left in his care.

We settled under a copse of trees among a swarm of white tops. As Pa and Jacob unhitched the wagon, I walked up to Nellie, stroked the side of her neck, and kissed her nose. "I'm going to miss you girl." She snorted and snuggled her snout into my chest. I turned so Pa wouldn't see the tear that seeped from the corner of my eye. The sweet mare had been interwoven with my earliest memories. First Ma, and now Nellie. My heart ached.

Pa unsheathed the pistol from his waistband and led the limping nag from the cluster of wagons.

I flinched when the shot reverberated through the quivering trees.

Jacob dropped to his knees and lowered his head.

"How are we going to get to California without Nellie?" Jacob sniffed back a snivel when Pa returned to camp.

I raked a tangle of underbrush that had been trampled by previous campers to clear a spot for a fire, while Jacob mourned the loss of Nellie, who, besides Scout, had been his best friend and companion.

"We'll get an oxen team and supplies in town before we head out." Pa stroked his tangled beard. "Thank goodness the nag got us this far."

"Still wish you didn't have to shoot her." For Jacob, God's creatures were to be loved and protected, contrary to Pa's opinion that an animal's only value was to serve a purpose and when no longer useful was expendable, like poor Nellie.

In the morning, Pa, Jacob, and I trekked to town to purchase an oxen team and provisions. I pressed myself beside Jacob as we wove through the masses of people, horses, mules, oxen, and dogs that crowded the dusty street. A roar of laughter exploded from the saloon we passed on the way to the stockyard. Glass shattered, and a brawl spilled onto the boardwalk. I shook my head—it was only midmorning.

We joined a boodle of bearded men outside the stockyard gate. A grizzled man standing next to us, gnawing on a twig, turned to Pa. "Mules or oxen?"

"Excuse me?" Pa quirked an eyebrow at the stranger.

"You goin' with mules or oxen?" His words jumbled as he spit them out between the bobbing twig.

"Oxen." Pa crossed his arms and squinted at the stranger. "Why would you choose anything else?"

"Pros and cons either way. Damn mules are temperamental beasts, but they's more surefooted and quicker. And if they's broke, can be ridden if needed for scoutin' or huntin'. Oxen, on the other hand, are sturdier, eat just about anything, cheaper, and less likely to be stolen by shifty Injans."

"Mules are faster, eh?" Pa stoked his beard as he pondered the stranger's useful information. He didn't flinch at the tidbit about the Indians, which had burned my ears. "Which are you goin' with?"

"Oxen, I reckon. If they get me there, I can use em to plow my fertile Oregon fields."

"Where'd you get the money?" I asked Pa after we'd exited the stockyard with two strapping brown mules in tow.

"Your grandmother. She wanted us to have a fresh start, so she lent us some money." He spat a chaw of chew into the dusty street.

"Oh, I thought . . ." I bit my lip and studied the dust on my shoes. I wasn't supposed to have heard their graveside discussion.

"She had a change of heart when I bumped into her later." He fingered a fresh slug of tobacco from his pouch and tucked it between his gum and cheek.

I knew my grandmother was too stubborn and proud to ever change her mind. Pa must have stolen the money from her.

We stopped at the mercantile and purchased three slabs of tinned bacon, sacks of flour, cornmeal, rice and beans, two bags of green coffee beans, and some lard. Then to the saloon for a keg of whiskey. Fortunately, the melee had subsided, although the saloon was noisy, smoky, and reeked of tobacco, whiskey, and vomit. Yuck!

Back at camp, Pa filled his flask from the keg and stored the barrel in the wagon near the rear gate for easy access. I stowed the remaining goods in a pair of crates while Pa and Jacob sorted through a tangle of harnesses. Then they worked to hitch the mules to the wagon for a test drive.

"What are their names?" Jacob asked.

"Don't think they got names." Pa grunted as he wrestled the heavy wagon tongue.

"We need to name them then. What do you think, Maggie? I'll name the boy, and you can name the girl."

I strode over to the mules. "Molly. Doesn't she look like a Molly to you? Those sweet eyes and soft muzzle." I stroked the steed's velvety nose. As if agreeing to her new moniker, she shook her head and then nuzzled her snout into my ear.

"Then this big guy is Jack. Hey, Jack, welcome to the family." He patted the mule on the side of the neck.

"Quit horsin' around and help me with this harness."

Pa's growl made my skin crawl, as if a colony of ants labored beneath its surface. At least his words weren't slurred, so he wasn't drunk—yet. A woman tending a fire at a nearby campsite glanced at us. I lowered my eyes. Pa didn't talk—he growled. Like a bear. It made people uneasy, including me. Most of my childhood was spent trying to stay out of his way. But there was no attic to hide in out here.

When the team was hitched, a man and woman from a neighboring campsite came to check out our rig. The same woman who had eyed us earlier.

"Nice-looking mules," the man said in greeting.

He was one of the few clean-shaven men that I'd seen since arriving in St. Joseph. I guessed he was a few years older than Pa, shorter and stockier, with kind hazel eyes that seemed to smile on their own.

"Name's Charles McNeil." He extended a hand, which Pa ignored.

Mr. McNeil lowered his hand. "This is my wife, Betty." He tilted his head toward the woman who stood like a plank by his side. Her brown hair was coiled in a neat bun under her bonnet, and her square jaw was set so tight that it looked chiseled in marble. Although her green dress was simple, it was clean and unwrinkled. Even the apron tied around her waist was unstained.

"Good to know ya." Pa didn't lift his eyes from the hitch. Nor did he introduce himself or us.

"Are they an experienced team?" Mr. McNeil eyed our new mules. "I'm no expert, but they look pretty green to me."

"Stockman said they're a fine pair. Guaranteed to make the trip."

The nosy neighbor scrunched his forehead. "Only two?"

"Only two what?" Pa didn't mask his irritation.

"Only two mules? Most teams have four to six head. Some more. Two might be sufficient on the flat plains, but the mountains . . ." He shook his head.

"Charles has been studying the guidebooks." Mrs. McNeil must have noticed Pa's annoyance. "He's only trying to be helpful."

As Mrs. McNeil was explaining the source of her husband's expertise, a boy, perhaps jackround seven, sped past.

"William, slow down!" Mrs. McNeil scolded.

The boy skidded to a stop and teetered. Mrs. McNeil clasped his arm to steady him. "Sorry, Mrs. McNeil. I'm looking for my brothers." William bounced on his toes and flapped his hands like a baby chickadee learning to fly. "Ma says it's time for supper."

"I haven't seen your brothers. Let's not run around all these animals. You might spook them, and someone could get hurt."

"Yes, ma'am." He raced away.

"William! Please walk."

I watched the boy race-walk toward a group of wagons nestled in a grove of trees.

Pa turned his back on the annoying Mr. McNeil and feigned adjusting the chain. His lips pursed, and his cheeks turned a deeper shade of crimson. "Besides, we're headed to California."

I bit my lip and rubbed Molly's nose.

"For the gold, I imagine," Mrs. McNeil said to her husband.

"Which train are you traveling with?" The nosy camp neighbor wouldn't take Pa's not-so-subtle hint to mind his own business.

"No train. We're just gonna follow the trail."

"I would strongly advise against that. Most companies have professional guides who know the route and the terrain. Where the water is. Places to graze the animals. Also, the community traveling together provides protection from wild Indian bands. Hate to see one of these young people get kidnapped or scalped."

My eyes widened, and my mouth popped open.

Mrs. McNeil must have noticed my panic, because she quickly offered, "Why don't you join our party. The captain's fare is only five dollars a wagon. Best be safe, and these young people"—she tipped her head toward me—"will enjoy the company of their peers in the caravan." Before Pa could protest, she said, "Oh, there's the captain's son now." She nodded toward an older boy riding a horse through the throng of campers and waved him over.

The boy reined the mare toward us.

"Ethan, this is"—she looked over to Pa—"I'm sorry. I didn't catch your name."

"Hanley," Pa growled.

Mrs. McNeil peered up at Ethan, a scrawny young man perhaps a year older than me and Jacob, who sat slumped in the saddle atop a palomino mare. "Ethan, this is the Hanley family. Will you let your pa know that they'll be joining our company?"

Ethan's foxlike eyes squinted at me while he addressed Mrs. McNeil. "Happy to, ma'am. Pa's hopin' to have at least fifty wagons. This will make forty-eight." He touched his finger to his hat, and a row of jagged front teeth—that reminded me of a shark—jutted between his thin lips when he grinned. Then he nudged his horse with his knees and steered her back the way he had come, presumably to inform his Pa that his coffers had just been enriched by five dollars.

Chapter 3

Dear Diary,

What has Pa gotten us into? I trembled like a leaf in a windstorm before we had even crossed the Missouri River. We had packed up the morning after we'd purchased the mules. Mr. McNeil was right. Those onery mules didn't take to pulling a heavy cart. They played along while Pa and Jacob hitched them up, but as soon as Pa climbed aboard and flicked the reins, they raised the biggest ruckus—rearin' and kickin'. At one point they nearly toppled the wagon. Thankfully, Jacob was able to intervene and calm them down. So long as Jacob led them, they didn't seem to mind the work. Perhaps they thought he was helping.

Midday we neared the Missouri River ferry crossing—and waited. I gazed at the bluffs that loomed on the other side. The gateway to the vast frontier. The wilderness. The edge of the earth as far as I knew. Indian country. I shuddered. A steamboat drifted toward the dock.

"This is going to be exciting," I said to Jacob as we stood near our wagon. "We've never been on a steamboat before."

"You're going to have to rein in your excitement for another day."

"Huh?" The line of waiting wagons crept forward—chains clanking, axles squeaking, mules and oxen snorting.

"There are two lines forming out of this chaos. The one on the left is for the steamboat. We're queuing up for the flatboat."

I plopped my hand on Jacob's shoulder for balance and rose to my toes. I couldn't see the boat over the throng of white tops clustered ahead of us. I lowered my heels and crossed my arms in frustration.

As the afternoon wore on, we finally approached the ramp. We watched two men coax the team of the rig ahead of us onto the craft—a rickety structure that was merely a raft, adorned with a flimsy rail, that looked like it would capsize in even a mild breeze. The beasts stomped and clawed the wobbly boat as the men cracked their whips and cursed. While the boatsman secured the wheels, the wagon owner and driver led four additional cows on board. The boatsman rose and waved his hands at one of the men, obviously not happy with the additional cargo. I couldn't hear the ensuing argument, but the boatsman flung his hands in the air and returned to his task of securing the vehicle. The wagon owner slammed the gate closed behind his boarded livestock. The remaining eight cows were tied to the back of the craft, relegated to swimming behind. A dog yapped from inside the loaded wagon. The boarded oxen stomped and clambered, rocking the craft as the oarsmen rowed and the boatsman guided the craft along the cable that was strung across the river. As if spooked by a cannon blast, the beasts shifted in unison to the starboard side of the boat. The craft bobbed and listed. Water gushed over the edge. One ox crashed through the railing and tumbled over the side, and one by one the remaining frightened beasts splashed behind the leader. A torrent of whitecaps erupted amid a melee of ears, horns, and hooves.

I gasped in horror when a man was swept overboard in the chaos.

A woman behind me screamed.

I flung my hand to my mouth.

Relieved of the weight of the herd, the rebalanced ferry continued its path to the western shore. The oxen swam and sputtered their way to rejoin the landed craft. My eyes froze on the spot where the man had tumbled overboard. He never resurfaced.

"Why don't they try to rescue him?" I shouted to Jacob.

"They'll never find him in that muddy water."

My jaw quivered.

The empty ferry returned to the eastern ramp for the next passengers. Us. Pa grumbled as he leaned from the wagon seat and handed the boatsman two dollars. The boatsman spat a stream of tobacco slurry as he waddled to the craft and opened the gate.

Jacob tugged Jack's bridle to lead the team on board. Jack snorted and pawed the ground. Molly's front legs locked tight, like a pair of iron rails. "It's okay, Jack. There's nothing to worry about. I'll be with you the whole way." Jacob rubbed Jack's nose while he comforted the skittish mule.

I didn't know how Jacob could be so reassuring after witnessing the chaos of the previous crossing. There was a lot to worry about.

"Maggie, come stand by me on the ferry. If they see that we're not afraid, they won't be afraid."

Scout sat at Jacob's heels, looked at me, and yipped a single shrill bark, as if echoing Jacob's order.

I opened my mouth to say that I was afraid, but no sound spilled out. I closed my eyes and inhaled a deep breath, but the image of the doomed man tumbling into a torrent of flailing hooves and horns burned into my eyelids.

"Hurry up, Maggs!" Jacob yelled.

"Hey, you pikers. Get on the boat or get out of the way so the rest of us can cross."

I didn't turn my head to see the angry man behind me. I couldn't. My body was as rigid as a fence post cemented into the ground.

Pa jumped off the wagon, stomped over, and slapped me across the cheek. "Margaret, get on the ferry."

The boatsman and an oarsmen trudged off the craft, lifted me off the ground, and planted me on the boat. My eyes flew open, and I shrieked. I didn't know if it was the shock of the filthy hands on my waist, the foul odor of tobacco and whiskey that tainted their breath, or the scratchy whiskers that scraped against my cheek, but once on the boat, I snapped out of my trance and shook off my disgust. I stepped up to Molly, rubbed her nose, and reached for her bridle. "Come on, girl. Let's go to California." I hoped she didn't sense the fear in my voice.

The team followed me and Jacob onto the wobbly craft and dragged the creaky wagon aboard.

On the Kansas side of the river, excitement reverberated among the four dozen wagons that made up our train. When the last wagon cleared the landing, the captain, who had been supervising the crossing, rode along the caravan on his chestnut horse and shouted, "Move out. Move out."

"Manifest Destiny! Whoo-hoo!" a man hollered.

One by one the wagons crept forward. Pa flicked the reins. Jacob tugged Jack's bridle, and the cart jerked to a start. As I walked next to Jacob, I looked to the east and gazed across the river at the rolling Missouri hills. My heart ached. We were leaving behind everything I knew. My home, my school, my friends, the chickens that roamed the yard. My mother's grave. My stomach churned. God, I missed her. I clutched my palm around the brooch under my apron. Her brooch. My brooch now. All that I had left of her. I wiped my damp eyes with the back of my other hand.

"I miss her too," Jacob whispered.

Deep in sorrow, we walked side by side in silence. Scout trotted at our heels. Wagons creaked, axles squeaked, wheels crunched over the compacted earth, mules and oxen snorted, hooves pounded, whips cracked, children squealed.

"What's that?" I furrowed my brow as Scout raced ahead and sniffed a bacon tin lying on the ground. "Did that fall out of someone's wagon?"

"Why would someone throw out good bacon? Look at that." Jacob pointed to a heap of splintered furniture. A three-legged chair straddled across a fractured table.

Two other chairs were strewn alongside. As we trundled through the late afternoon, we wove around a melee of discarded items—more bacon, sacks of flour, beans, a stove, a spare wagon wheel, wagon jacks, books, clothing, you name it. Perfectly good stuff! I was tempted to scavenge the castoffs for treasures, but our wagon was already stuffed beyond its capacity.

"Hey, isn't that the shopkeeper from the mercantile?" I pointed to a man tossing some discarded tools into a horse-drawn cart. Then he bent to pick up a bacon tin. Then a sack of flour.

"That's just wrong!" Jacob cried. "I bet he's taking all this stuff that he oversold to us pioneers back to his store to sell again."

"I wonder how many times he's resold the same merchandise."

"Or how much of the stuff we bought from him had been previously discarded."

The sun was slinking into the horizon when the wagons in front of us stopped. The captain trotted his horse through the caravan and shouted orders that were swallowed by the wind, clanking hooves, squeaking axles, and anxious voices. Somehow he coached all the wagons into a circle, tongue to stern. I was so exhausted that all I wanted to do was curl up on our straw mattress and sleep for a week. While Pa and Jacob unhitched the team, I snatched the *Jane Eyre* book from the wagon and plopped to the ground next to a wheel.

I hadn't even lifted the cover when Pa snatched the book from my hand and flung it into the dirt. "You got chores to do." He stomped off.

I hadn't even scrambled to my feet when Molly snorted in my ear and Jacob dangled her lead in front of my nose. "We need to take them to the stream so that they can get a drink. We'll also need to bring back some water to refill the barrels, so grab a couple of pails."

I struggled to lug the heavy buckets of sloshing water back to camp. The handles bored painful ridges into my palms, and the jostling pails banged against my shin. There'd be a lump and bruise for sure in the morning.

Water lapped over the sides of the buckets as I plopped them on the ground near our wagon. Pa took a swig from his flask, wiped his mouth with his sleeve, and barked, "Where's my supper? I'm starved."

I glared at him, stunned. Beneath the brim of his tattered straw hat, his coal-black eyes squinted, like a fire breathing dragon about to spew its flaming weapon. Sunburn colored his cheeks a rosy pink, and the blowing prairie dust had lightened his beard.

"I was watering the mules."

He slapped me across the jaw. "Now get supper." He clomped to the front of the wagon and reached onto the seat for his shotgun.

I touched my stinging chin. How could he expect me to do two chores at once? I scanned the scene around me. Men lazed against wagon wheels or around fires, sharpening knives, cleaning weapons, or smoking pipes. The women stooped over makeshift tables, kneading bread dough, slicing bacon, preparing stews in dutch ovens, or tending sizzling frying pans. Children ran amok, screaming while they played tag and hide-and-seek.

I spied Mrs. McNeil two wagons over, carrying an iron skillet toward a crackling fire. I peeked over my shoulder at Pa, who was sitting on the tongue and fiddling with his flintlock. I swallowed the lump of anger bubbling in my gut and rushed over to her.

"Uh, hi, Mrs. McNeil," I whispered.

"Oh, hello, Margaret." Her tone was probably conversational but sounded like a shout.

"Shh." I pressed a finger to my lips and sneaked a peek over my shoulder to make sure Pa hadn't heard. "I'm sorry to bother you, but Pa wants his supper and, well"—I eyed the wad of bread dough in the skillet she held in her hand—"can you tell me how you're going to bake that bread?"

"You don't know how to make bread?"

"I do, sort of. I helped Ma make bread all the time. It's just, how do you bake it without an oven?"

"Margaret"—she sighed—"we're just going to have to figure it out as we go along. Since we can't bake it, we're going to have to fry it in a pan and hope for the best. Instead of bread, I suggest biscuits." She peered over my shoulder toward our camp. "I'll tell you what—I've got a little extra dough. I mixed it yesterday so it would have time to rise. Hold on a minute." She set her skillet on a grate over the fire and then went to the tailgate of her wagon. She soon emerged with a clump of dough wrapped in a cloth. "Take this and fry it up with some bacon and you'll have your first camp meal."

Jacob had a small fire ready when I returned to our campsite. I fetched our only cast-iron skillet from the wagon, scooped in a glob of lard, and gritted my teeth as

I carried it to the fire. Pa was not going to like my camp cooking.

⸺⸺◆⸺⸺

Tensions ran high as the mass of wagons spread across the prairie converged into a traffic jam behind the bridge at Wolf Creek the following afternoon. Molly pawed the dirt, and Jack swished his tail at the pesky flies.

"Why are the mules edgy?" I smashed a mosquito on the back of my hand and squinted at Jacob.

"Because they can sense the anxiety in the air from whatever is causing the holdup."

Pa sat on the wagon seat with his elbows planted on his knees and his bearded chin resting in the heels of his hands. His shotgun lay splayed across his lap. Jacob rubbed the mules' snouts and talked softly in their ears to quell their unease. I stood, arms wrapped around my ribs, and watched—stumped. I let the mules nuzzle my chest, and I whispered sweet nothings in their ears, same as Jacob, but only he could settle the pair when they were agitated.

The congestion mystery was revealed when a gaggle of squawky kids, who must have gone to investigate the holdup, darted past shouting, "Indians! Indians are blocking the bridge." I recognized William, the hyperactive child we'd met days ago, trailing the group, arms flapping, as if he could catch a breeze to propel him into the lead.

The captain, mounted on his horse far ahead, waved the next wagon in line onto the crossing. The string of white tops crept forward.

Finally we reached the bridge. My heart thundered as an Indian approached the wagon. I had never been this close to an Indian. The silky hair that flowed to the middle of his back matched his inky-black eyes. He was dressed in buckskin pants and a white man's shirt, which he wore unbuttoned, revealing his gleaming bronze chest. He extended his hand, palm up. "Two bits."

"What?" Pa growled. "I ain't payin' no Indian two bits to cross a stinkin' bridge."

"Two bits." The Indian shook his fist and reextended his hand for payment.

"Go to hell, savage. I'm takin' this wagon across the bridge, and you ain't stoppin' me. Out of my way, or I'll run ya over." Pa raised his weapon and used the barrel to motion the Indian to step aside.

Two other Indians hopped onto the bridge and poised axes above their heads, waiting for the signal to chop a hole in the center of the span.

"Two bits!" the Indian demanded again.

Pa aimed the gun at the Indian's chest.

The captain trotted over on his horse to investigate the holdup. "Hanley, put the gun down and pay the Indian the twenty-five-cent toll."

"I ain't forkin' over a cent to no Indian. What makes him think he can extort money from me?"

"Hanley, pay the man or turn that wagon back to Missouri—or I'll shoot you myself."

"Pay him for what?"

"Indian Affairs says they can charge us white folk the toll for abusing their lands. Claim we overgraze their prairies, cut down their trees, scare off their game. Government says they have a right, and even if we don't agree, if we're goin' to use the bridge, we pay the toll."

Pa remained rigid as a statue, gun pointed at the Indian. He spat his chew at the Indian's feet, bit down on his lower lip, and squinted at his adversary with a flinty glare that froze my blood.

The Indian didn't flinch.

"Hanley, if you shoot him, I'll put a bullet through your heart before this man hits the dirt." The captain unsheathed his rifle and aimed it at Pa. "Killin' him will cause a massacre that will get us all killed, and you'll be the first."

Pa held his ground for another few breaths, then lowered his weapon. He fished a two-bit coin from his pocket and tossed it at the toll taker's feet. I hoped we wouldn't cross paths with another Indian for some time, because Pa's stubbornness would likely get us scalped.

Chapter 4

D*ear Diary,*

Pioneering is hard! Hard and boring. My feet are so blistered and swollen, I can hardly pull my shoes on in the mornings. My legs ache. My eyes burn from the blowing dust and glaring sun. It's as cold as the North Pole in the mornings and as hot as the fiery underworld in the afternoons. And the mosquitoes . . . argh! I walk with an awkward gait, with one hand on my sunbonnet, or the incessant wind will blow it right back to Missouri, and the other on my skirt, or it will billow up to my knees. Even if I keep my scarf wrapped around my face, my nose is full of dirty snot at the end of the day. Yuck!

I visioned trail life as a lonely existence. Wrong! It's like a little town on wheels fanned across the prairie, creeping at a snail's pace and trailed by herds of cattle and horses. Forget about privacy. During the day we all walk because the wagons are stuffed full of belongings and the teams can't take on any additional weight. Even if we could ride in the wagon, we'd be tossed around like popcorn in a sizzling skillet and our insides would be, well, never mind. In the evenings, with the wagons circled tongue to tail, we practically bump into neighbors while fixing supper and doing chores. And the chores—don't get me started. At night, just let me say, I know which men snore the loudest and which children are the naughtiest.

I couldn't stand it any longer. The monotony of watching the trampled grass and baked dirt pass beneath my feet was mind numbing. Jacob and I walked alongside the wagon. It swayed and moaned as the wheels hobbled over the lumpy earth. Pa hunched in the wagon seat, pretending to drive the team. There was no need to drive. The mules knew the routine. Lean into the harness and put one hoof in front of the other, kick up a whiff of dust, repeat. Jacob hovered close though, as if a hiccup could disrupt the flow at any moment and require his intervention. The thought was probably prudent. I surmised that another reason that Pa chose mules over oxen back at the stockyard in St. Joseph was that mules were harnessed and driven from the wagon. Oxen were yoked and led by walking alongside them and directing them with a pole. In fact, most oxen rigs didn't even have seats, to reduce weight.

I sneaked a peek at Pa. His head bobbed. He wouldn't be able to catch a catnap if he were walking instead of seated in the wagon. He was likely to tumble off the perch if he fell asleep. That would be ugly. I shook the gory image from my fallow brain. He had been slated for guard duty the previous night, but I'd heard him sneak back to the wagon shortly after his shift had started, so his drowsiness couldn't be blamed on a lack of sleep.

I huffed a frustrated breath and jog-walked up to Mrs. McNeil, who was marching by herself near her wagon ahead of us. "Hi, Mrs. McNeil. Do you mind if I walk with you for a bit?"

"Good morning, Margaret." She smiled. "What a beautiful day the Lord has blessed us with today."

"Humph!" I wrapped my arms around my chest. "I don't mean to be disrespectful, but this isn't my idea of a beautiful day. I would rather be stuck at our little cottage in Missouri than walking endlessly in the middle of nowhere."

"You'll think differently when you get to Oregon."

"We're going to California, not Oregon." I lowered my head and frowned.

"Oh yes. Of course. For the gold."

"Why are you going to Oregon? Seems like there's plenty of good farming land in the States."

"Well, Margaret, if you believe all the talk, everything's better in Oregon. The soil is richer, the rain purer, the stars brighter, the nights cooler. I've even heard there's not even a single mosquito in Oregon."

"How could there not be any mosquitoes? They're everywhere." I scratched at the welts that speckled the back of my hand.

"Well, that's what I heard, for what it's worth."

"How long do you think until we get there? We've been walking for days now." I peered into the distance in search of a sign displaying an arrow and a timeline.

"According to the guidebooks, it depends on how often we stop, what sort of weather we run into, but on average, about five months."

"Five months!" I stumbled over a clump of grass.

Mrs. McNeil reached out a hand to steady me. "More or less. Since we got such a late start, we're only observing two hours for the Sabbath, much to our dismay, so that should help us make up some time."

Ethan trotted toward us on his palomino. I stifled a giggle as I watched him jiggle in the saddle. He gripped the reins tightly in his left hand, and his right hand hovered near the saddle horn, like a nervous toddler atop his first pony ride. I lowered my eyes, hoping he would pass by.

He didn't.

"Good morning, Mrs. McNeil." He reined in his ride to follow alongside us. "Maggie." He lifted his index finger to his hat and flashed his shark grin.

I cringed.

"Good morning, Ethan." Mrs. McNeil squinted as she peered up at him. "What brings you around this morning?"

"Just helping the captain out with a courtesy check."

"A courtesy check?"

I wished Mrs. McNeil would stop talking to him so he could perform his courtesy check on someone else.

"Makin' sure that everyone's okay. That no one broke down or got left behind. Stuff like that." He sat straighter, and I could almost picture him beating his fists to his chest in self-importance. I wanted to puke.

"I'm sure your pa appreciates the help."

Why was Mrs. McNeil being so nice to the creep?

"So"—Ethan leered at me—"I'll be comin' around a couple times a day, so if there is anything you need"—shark smile—"I'm your man."

I tried not to snort. Ma's voice in my head commanded me to be polite. "Thank you, Ethan. If I need anything, I'll come find you." I doubted he took the hint not to come around to check on me.

"Duty calls." He flicked his reins and trotted off to annoy his next unsuspecting victim. Probably Jacob.

"He seems like a nice boy," Mrs. McNeil said after Ethan had gone.

"I think he's a little creepy." Oops! I should probably have censored my thoughts in front of Mrs. McNeil.

"Well, he is a little gangly. But most boys his age are. He'll grow out of it soon enough. He seems to have taken an interest in you."

"I hope not! And I don't need him coming around to check on me either." My stomach churned. Five months of Ethan inquiring as to my welfare. *God, I want to go home.*

"Maybe you'll warm up to him over time. When I first met Charles, marrying him was the furthest thing from my mind."

I'd die a spinster before marrying Ethan. I kept that thought stitched behind my sealed lips.

"Why is your wagon painted green?" I wanted to steer the conversation away from Ethan. "And why do you have your name painted on the canvas?"

Her eyes followed my gaze to her wagon, as if to confirm it was indeed green. "Charles and I and five other families that we were planning on traveling with were supposed to depart with a different company a week prior. Two of Charles's brothers and their wives, one of his cousins and his family, and two of our neighbors, who were brothers, and their families. We all painted our wagons green so that we could identify each other from a distance when we got separated. At the time they left, there were over eighty wagons in that company. And Charles painted our name of the canvas so that he could spot our wagon when he came back to camp from hunting."

"Why didn't you go with the other train?"

"The wife of one of Charles's brothers took ill. We decided to wait with them until she was able to travel so they wouldn't have to travel alone. Unfortunately, she still wasn't well enough to go, and it was too late to wait any longer. They are going to have to come next year instead."

"That's too bad."

"The Lord must have a reason."

We both stopped and turned when a mule brayed behind us. Jack and Molly fidgeted in their harness. Pa jerked on the reins. Jacob rushed over and grabbed Jack's bridle. His lips moved, but I couldn't hear the soothing words that he must have said to settle the mules while he stroked Jack's snout. Molly shook her head. Jack snorted, and they resumed their slog along the prairie.

I stumbled over a clump of grass when Mrs. McNeil and I returned to our walk. "I wonder what spooked them."

"Could have been anything. Your brother does have a knack with your mules."

"Yeah, animals seem to take to Jacob. Sometimes I think even Scout likes him better."

"It's none of my business, but Charles is a little concerned about them."

"Concerned about who? Jack and Molly?" I furrowed my brow.

"He thinks your pa is working them too hard. That you should discard at least half the weight in your wagon. Two mules are not enough horsepower to haul a heavy load all the way to Oregon. Or rather, California. They're going to struggle just to get to Fort Kearney."

She was right. It was none of her business. But she was also right about the mules. They were covered in foamy lather by midmorning, long before other teams started to tire. "Pa thinks we'll need everything in California. Especially the tools he purchased for prospecting. And he'll never give up the whiskey." Whisky was a basic need for Pa, like food and shelter, necessary to quell his insatiable thirst. But other men in our caravan seem to do fine with water as their primary thirst quencher. Hmm.

"He does have quite an affection for the whiskey." She scratched the back of her neck. "The company we had originally signed on to had strict rules against drinking and gambling. Anyone caught violating them would be forced to leave the train on the spot."

I crossed my arms and studied the trampled grass. Perhaps it was best that we stumbled onto this train. Otherwise, Pa would have set out on our own and we would have been slaughtered back at Wolf Creek.

"May I inquire about your mother?" Her tone was somber.

I kept my gaze to the ground and stepped around a manure pile. "She died."

"I'm very sorry. How did she die?"

I hadn't talked to anyone other than Jacob about Ma since the gravedigger hurled the dirt clods onto her casket, the echoes of which still rang in my ears. "She fell and hit her head." I scrunched my eyes shut to stifle a threatening tear. "Just before we left home. Buried her one day and headed for St. Joe the next." I sealed my lips. Pa wouldn't want me discussing Ma, especially the circumstances of her unfortunate death. I changed the subject. "Do you and Mr. McNeil have any children?"

I stole a sideways glance to see her gaze fall to the ground. We took a few quiet steps. "We had a daughter, Beverly. She died from a fever when she was only a year old." She sighed. "We were never blessed with another child."

I didn't know what to say. I'd never heard of children referred to as blessings. They just happened whether a mother wanted them or not. Had Ma considered me and Jacob a blessing? Or something to be endured, like frigid winters and houseflies? How would I think of future children of my own—a blessing or a burden? I thought back to my role as a school monitor, helping Mr. Jones teach the younger children. I enjoyed instructing the little ones who behaved and were eager to learn, but the others . . . But if I had little ones of my own, I couldn't be a schoolmarm—or anything outside the confines of the household. Too much to think about.

We walked in silence, each pining our respective losses, enveloped in a cacophony of groaning wagons, snooting, bleating, mooing, and canvas wagon tops snapping in the wind.

"At least we haven't seen any more Indians." I squinted through the dust to scan the horizon ahead of us.

"They're out there. Probably watching us right now."

"I hope not! I really don't want to get scalped."

"As long as you don't wander off on your own, you're not going to get scalped. Most Indians are friendly. Charles even brought some trinkets to trade with them. Coins and beads and buttons. When we get closer to Oregon, he wants to purchase some horses from them. He's heard that there's no finer horse than an Indian horse."

"I just hope Pa doesn't shoot 'em first." *Why did I say that? Urgh!* Why did his outbursts shrink me to the size of a pea? I should have kept my emotions buried instead of airing our family drama to an outsider. Ma had taught me better.

"Your pa does have a temper. I'm afraid it's going to get him in a heap of trouble one day."

It probably already had. And it would drag me into a hole along with him.

The rolling town ahead of us slowed to a stop. I squinted into the dust. "What's going on?"

"It looks like we're about to cross the Big Blue River."

"I better get back to our wagon and help Jacob." *And keep Pa constrained.*

Pa eased the team down the steep bank to the river from the wagon seat. Jacob gripped Jack's bridle, and I walked next to Molly. The mules halted at the river's edge, ears forward as they assessed the danger before them. The swift current lapped at the bank.

"It's okay, big boy." Jacob rubbed the steed's nose. "Just think of this as a big stream. Just a little deeper and wider than the ones we've already crossed. Nothing to worry about. I'll be with you the whole time."

I reached for Molly's bridle. She jerked her head to rear up, but the harness constrained her. She panicked and tried to break free, which spooked Jack. In unison they bolted up and nearly toppled the wagon. Pa cursed and swatted Molly with his crop. She bleated and reared up again, flailing her front hoof near my head. Jacob shoved me out of the way and clasped Molly's head gear when she landed.

"Easy girl, easy girl."

Molly snorted and shook her head.

Jacob spied Pa as he cocked his elbow, cowhide gripped in his fist, ready to strike the steed. "No! That will just make it worse."

Pa snapped the whip in the air above his head, rattled off a string of profanities, and lowered the crop. The action must have stunned the mules into submission. They stood like statues while Jacob rubbed their noses. Amid the ensuing stillness, I felt the agitated stares of our fellow travelers burrow through my psyche. I wanted to jump into the river and let it sweep me downstream, far from Pa and his humiliating outbursts.

Jacob waded into the river to his hips. "See, Jack. See, Molly. It's only water." He bent and trickled some liquid through his fingers, then sloshed back to the mules, who stood frozen on the bank. He let them sniff his damp hands, then reached for Jack's bridle.

I clasped Molly's bridle and stepped into the current. "Eek! This is disgusting." Mud seeped into my shoes, and the current swirled around my calves and tugged at my skirt.

The mules lowered their noses and inhaled a long drink. Water dripped from their snouts when they raised their heads. Jack snorted.

Jacob tugged the bridle. "Hup, Jack. Let's get this done."

Pa flicked the reins and grunted something that may have been "Giddup."

The team leaned into their harnesses and stepped into the river. When the water reached my thighs, I wrapped my arms around Molly's neck and let her drag me through the current while the mules pulled the wagon. The steeds huffed and snorted as they struggled to lug the heavy load through the muddy river bottom. Water the color of burnt coffee swirled around my hips. As we neared the other side, I let go of Molly's neck and eased into the knee-deep current. Mud and silt seeped through my shoes and oozed between my toes as we coaxed the team on.

On dry land, the pair grunted and stumbled as they pawed their way up the steep bank. Near the top, Molly faltered when her front knee buckled. The wagon swayed.

Suddenly Jacob was in front of her. He clasped her bridle. "Keep moving . . . keep moving," he shouted. He tugged on the harness, as if his slight frame could pull her forward.

The wagon groaned as it inched up the rise. Jack stumbled. The wheels slid in the soft dirt.

"Oh no!" I flung my hands to my head.

"Giddup! Giddup!" Pa shouted from the wagon seat. The crack of the whip splintered the air.

Molly jerked. The cowhide cracked again. Jack brayed.

"No!" Jacob shouted.

Mr. May and Mr. Dalton rushed over. "Haw! Haw. Giddup! Giddup!" Mr. Dalton flicked his crop on Molly's rump. "Haw! Haw!"

The mules puffed and snorted. The wagon jerked forward an inch.

"Haw! Haw!" The whip snapped. Molly's front legs folded, and her knees burrowed into the soft dirt.

The wagon stopped. The wheels sank into the sand. Jack shook his head and pawed the ground.

"Charles, bring a yoke. Quick!" Mr. May shouted.

Mr. McNeil trudged toward us with two oxen in tow. The three men tied a chain from the yoke to the wagon tongue. Mr. McNeil and Mr. May each clasped an oxen horn and tugged. Pa snapped the whip.

The wagon moaned when it jerked forward. I held my breath as the vehicle crept over the lip of the bluff. My limbs jelled like putty, whether from fatigue or relief, I wasn't sure.

Once on level ground, Jacob led the team out of the path of the other rigs. Hands fisted and jaw clenched, he marched to the front of the wagon and glared up at Pa. "You're killing them!" Then he stomped to the rear and hopped in. Our possessions came flying onto the prairie—three chairs, table, tools, clothes, dishes, pots, a sack of flour, dutch oven, coffee grinder, the *Jane Eyre* book.

Pa hopped from the wagon and stomped toward Jacob. "What are you doin', you crazy-ass kid?"

"You're killing 'em. They're not taking another step until this wagon is lightened up." Our tattered mattress plopped to the ground, spewing up a flurry of dust, like a volcano spitting an ash cloud over a sleeping forest. When Jacob finished and trod away, the only items remaining were Ma's trunk, with my diary safely hidden inside, and the whiskey keg. The trunk was probably too heavy for

Jacob to move, and he did have enough sense not to touch the whiskey.

I rushed to the pile and snatched the book.

Chapter 5

Dear Diary

There is something more frightening for a mule than a river crossing.

"I sure hope we stop soon. My stomach is demanding supper."

Late in the afternoon, our caravan crept along the bank of the Little Blue River, sandwiched between the river and a high bluff. Our pace had slowed to a typical late-day crawl, as the continuous slog bled the strength of both the animals and humans. The river provided marginal relief from the searing afternoon heat. And we didn't have to lug heavy buckets of water as far.

Jacob was quiet beside me as we walked near our wagon. His stomach growled.

"Aha! You're hungry too."

"I'm hungry for something besides your burnt biscuits and bacon. We've eaten so much bacon since we left home that we're going to start oinking like pigs."

"If you want something besides bacon, then why don't you cook it yourself."

He snorted.

I thrust my hands to my hips. "By the time we get the wagon unhitched, the mules watered, the fire started, and Pa's coffee made, I'm so tired that I'm surprised I have the energy to plop a glob of dough into the pan or pick up the knife to slice the bacon."

A commotion ahead interrupted my rant. Ethan loped his palomino along the wagons, shouting, "Storm coming! Get up on the bluff away from the river."

I looked up at the slate-gray clouds that smothered the late-afternoon sun. Molly aimed her ears toward the rumble of distant thunder. We found a suitable path and clambered up the hill. The captain was perched on his horse at the top of the rise, waving his arms. "Move it! Move it! Get the wagons circled and mules corralled."

A flash of lightning streaked across the western sky. The rumbling growled louder. Coal-black clouds bubbled toward the heavens. Darkness deepened as we reached the top of the bluff and fell in line to form the circle. The wind gusted, almost sweeping me from my feet. A lightning bolt illuminated the prairie, and the heavens roared. Pa and Jacob wrestled to unhitch the mules, who fought against their harnesses as the last wagons closed the loop in the lopsided circle. A hat blew past my face and disappeared into the ether. Shouts were blown away by the gale. An angry thunder cap exploded above us, drowning out the shouts, bellowing, whinnying, and crying. Jack and Molly reared up in unison, flailed their front hooves, and flung free of the hitch. The wagon wobbled and tipped on its side. The mules galloped into the night. Like a breached levee, the clouds exploded, hurling curtains of horizontal rain.

"NO!" I screamed into the black.

Pa shouted a stream of profanities.

Jacob stood stone still, agape. A waterfall gushed from the brim of his hat.

Some men slogged through the mud to help right the tipped wagon. Fighting against the raging wind and sucking mud, they looped a pair of ropes around the wagon bed. Pa and three other men yanked the ropes, and another two pulled on the wagon box. Roaring thunder accompanied their grunts, moans, and curses as they fought against the gale's wrath. One man skidded and slipped onto his rump, as if an avalanche had swept him off a pair of those newfangled skis. Another lightning bolt pierced the darkness, and the skies boomed. The thunderous crackling of the wind-whipped canvas tops reverberated in my ears. I trembled with cold as I watched the wagon teeter and then bob upright. The wheels whooshed as the ankle-deep mire sucked them under almost to the hubs. Crash! Another thunderclap roared across the prairie.

Hungry and drenched to the bone, I crawled into the wagon and rummaged in the blackness for a tarp and blanket among our strewed possessions, wishing I could cuddle in the corner and weep in private. But at night the wagon was Pa's private bedroom. Jacob and I were banished to the elements. Jacob and I struggled to spread the canvas tarp on the miry ground on the leeward side of the wagon. The oilcloth had been our bed ever since our mattress lay rotting with the heap of our other discarded possessions miles back. Muck spilled over the edges when we plopped onto it, but at least our weary masses kept the gale from whisking it away. I wrapped my mother's handmade quilt around my quaking body. Scout snuggled between us and rested his chin on my lap. I leaned against the wheel and watched our fellow travelers struggle to erect their tents. But most would spend the night unprotected because the storm's wrath whipped the shelters away.

I draped my arms around my shins and molded myself into a ball to try to control my trembling. Stranded on this godforsaken prairie without any stubborn mules to haul us to California or return us to our humble Missouri cottage. I yearned to be back in our cozy loft, tucked under the covers of our tattered, smelly, flea-infested mattress. *Ma, what are we going to do?* I closed my eyes and imagined her strong arms enveloping me in a warm embrace, her chin nestled in my wet, tangled hair, humming a sweet lullaby, like she did when I was a toddler. But the fierce storm swept the melody into the gloom.

The dawn brushed the eastern sky a dazzling array of purple, pink, and orange when the wake-up shot rever-berated through camp. I crawled from under the blanket, shivering. My soaking, mud-caked dress clung to my skin. My braid, a tangled mess, spilled from my bun. Jacob looked like he had risen from a sludge pit. I was glad I didn't have a looking glass, as my face must have been a fright.

As I stumbled to my feet to find a water bucket to wash up, three mounted Indians rode toward us. The one in the center held a rope with Molly and Jack in tow. The Indian on the left cradled a shotgun, and the one on the right wielded a tightly strung bow armed with a quilled arrow. The trio, dressed in buckskin trousers and vests adorned with shiny buttons and beads, sat erect on their horses. I trembled—from cold or fear, I wasn't sure. Maybe both. But I was also awed by the grace of not only the Natives but the beautiful horses—a bay mare in the center, flanked by two paints.

Pa stepped toward them, his shotgun gripped in his hand, ready to take quick aim.

The Indian in the center nodded to the mules. "Find." Then he aimed a finger at Pa's weapon and uttered, "Trade."

"Hand over my mules." Pa widened his stance.

"Find." The Indian lifted his hand that held the rope, then pointed to Pa's gun again. "Trade."

Pa raised his shotgun and pointed the barrel at the Indian in the center.

The armed Indians aimed their weapons at Pa.

The captain strolled over to within a few feet of Pa, his rifle barrel pointed to the dirt. He squinted at the Indian in the center. "What do you want for 'em?"

The Indian nodded at Pa's shotgun again and uttered, "Trade."

"He wants your shotgun, Elijah."

"He ain't getting' nothin' but a hole between his eyes."

"Elijah, don't be stupid. Give him your weapon and get your mules back, or we're all going to be slaughtered. You'll be the first. There's no other way out of this. I ain't telling you again."

Pa didn't flinch. I knew that old flintlock was his favorite weapon. But he had another flintlock shotgun in the wagon, plus a rifle and a pistol, so he wouldn't be unarmed. That was, if he could swallow his pride and accept the trade. Sweat dampened my palms, and my heart thundered. I didn't want to be scalped.

Chapter 6

—◆○◆—

Dear Diary,

Degrading! Humiliating! Mortifying! Demeaning! And to top it all off, gross! But that came later in the day. In the morning I walked with Mrs. McNeil as we climbed to the top of the bluff that hugged the Little Blue River and trekked across the prairie toward Fort Kearney. At least we were near the front of the group and the tip of the dust cloud that engulfed our caravan as we trudged across the grassy expanse.

"Mrs. McNeil, this land is so flat that it looks like a rug of trampled grass that stretches forever. It's almost like we can see to the end of the earth."

"It does look that way, Margaret. However, since the earth is round, we're not seeing the end of the earth."

"Okay. But it's flat enough to see clear into next week."

She chuckled. I didn't think she knew how to laugh.

"We must be gaining on another train." She nodded toward a distant spiraling dust funnel on the horizon.

"I hope it's another train and not a band of Indians." Although the morning was warm, a chill slithered up my spine—the standoff with Pa and the Indians over the mules still burned in my mind. The whole company had exhaled a collective sigh of relief when Pa had finally flung his prized shotgun to the ground in front of the Indian's horse. In a move swifter than a hawk diving for a field mouse, the Native with the bow and arrow had leaned to the side of his horse and swooped up the weapon, and they'd galloped into the glare of the sunrise, leaving Jack and Molly in their dust wake.

"I don't think they're Indians," she said, trying to ease my anxiety. "Indians wouldn't be so obvious."

That didn't help.

"Now, what were we talking about? Oh yes, *Jane Eyre*. You we're telling me about reading the story."

"Well, I've only read a few pages. Ma had recently acquired the book. To earn some extra money to send me and Jacob to school, she made dresses and did some mending for some of the ladies in town." I touched my fingers to my lips. "Oh, please don't tell my pa about that. Anyway, one of the ladies, Mrs. Jenson, gave her the book as payment for a new dress shortly before Ma passed. The woman must have fallen on hard times but still tried to keep up appearances by wearing new dresses. Ma was angrier than a caged lion. The agreed-upon price for the work was eight nickels. How was she going buy food and pay Mr. Jones, the schoolmaster, the enrollment fee with a book?" I fisted my hands. The slight still festered like an open wound. I willed for the lion to escape its enclosure and pounce on Mrs. Jenson. We could have used the nickels.

Mrs. McNeil pursed her lips. "I've never read *Jane Eyre*, but it sounds like the story will provide some entertainment for you until you get to California. Perhaps you can offer it to a school there in exchange for admission."

I clasped my hands together. "Do you think there will be a school in California? One that allows girls to attend?"

"Depending on where your pa decides to settle, there might be a school. I don't know about girls. Perhaps, along with the book, you can charm the schoolmaster into taking you on."

A knot strangled my stomach, and I focused on the trampled grass under my feet. "Never mind. My schooling is over. With Ma gone, Pa and Jacob expect me to take over her domestic responsibilities. Cooking, cleaning, mending. All the chores I detest!" *Why did I add that last part?*

"Maybe your pa will find a new wife so you can return to school."

"Oh." I inhaled a shallow gasp. "I didn't even think of that. I don't really want a new ma. But I would like to go back to school. Maybe in California a girl can be a doctor."

"A doctor? Why would you want to be a doctor?"

"I know it sounds crazy." I rubbed some dust from my eye. "When Jacob and I were around seven, at the end of school one day, some of the bigger boys were fighting on their way out the door. One of them, Luke, pushed another boy into a girl—Anna—and she tumbled down the steps and broke her arm. Doc Jackson was summoned. He set the bone and fixed her up in a cast. A couple months later her arm was well enough that she punched Luke in the jaw for what he did. Ever since then, I've wanted to be a doctor. To help people when they get sick or hurt." I didn't say that Doc Jackson was the most well-liked and respected person in town, which may have had more to do with my ambition than being summoned to make house calls in the middle of the night. "I just don't see why a girl can't be a doctor."

"Hmm. What did your ma think of your aspiration?"

I looked at my feet and frowned. "When I told her, she said something like, 'Oh, that's nice honey,' and went back to her sewing. I could tell she thought it was a crazy dream." I had interpreted the strained look on her face to mean that she had pinched pennies to send me to school so that I would be educated enough to attract a good husband so I wouldn't be destined to dress in rags and live in a dilapidated shack, like her. Not to chase some silly, unobtainable fantasy.

"Well, Margaret, it never hurts to dream. Maybe someday a girl can be a doctor. You'd be the best doctor this side of the Missouri."

I smiled at the image of a stethoscope pressed against my ear, listening to the heartbeat of a child on an examination table.

The outline of a wagon and then human figures followed by more wagons emerged through the dust, like ships drifting out of a fog bank—traveling east.

The captain rode over to them and dismounted his horse. Mrs. McNeil and I stopped to listen. The caravan consisted of about a half dozen wagons and weary men and women, plus only one child, that I could see.

Ethan trotted over and slithered off his palomino. He sidled up to his pa.

I gritted my teeth and cast my eyes to the ground when his shark mouth grinned at me.

"Took the spirit right out of us," one of the men said to the captain. "Cholera took half our company. Then the Indians attacked. Killed our captain and stole our livestock. Don't have a prayer of makin' it to Oregon now."

Mrs. McNeil directed me away from the downtrodden party, and we hustled to her wagon. "Stop for a minute, Charles."

Mr. McNeil halted his team, and Mrs. McNeil disappeared into the back of her wagon. "Help me with this, will you please, Margaret?"

She handed me a tin of bacon, then scooted out of the wagon and reached for a half-filled sack of flour. With the bacon in hand, I followed her to the go-backs—what Mrs. McNeil called them.

She handed the flour to one of the women. "It's not much, but it might help."

One of the men took the bacon from me.

"Bless you, ma'am," the man conversing with the captain said to her.

Mr. McNeil gave his lead ox a slight tug on the horn to get his team rolling again. Mrs. McNeil and I resumed our walk.

I scratched my head. "Why did you give them your food?"

"They need it more than we do right now."

"But what if you need it before you get to Oregon?"

"And what if we don't? And if we do, the good Lord will provide somehow."

The plight of the disheveled and disheartened go-backs weighed on me.

"What are you thinking about, Margaret?" she prodded. "It's not like you to be so quiet."

"What if those same Indians attack us?"

"They might. But most likely they won't. Doesn't do any good to worry about it. Also, it may or may not have happened like they said."

I glanced at her. "They looked like they had been through quite an ordeal. Why would they lie?"

"It's possible they may have exaggerated their plight so it would appear worse than it was in order to justify turning back."

"I wish we would turn back." I studied my tattered shoes as I ranted. "I'm tired of walking all day, and hitching and unhitching the team every day, and not having a real bed to sleep in or a roof over my head at night. And this blustering wind in my face, and the dust in my teeth, and biscuits filled with bugs and dirt, which are crusty black on the outside and doughy on the inside, and . . . and . . . I just want to go home!"

"I'll tell you a secret."

"What?" I peered at her. She kept her focus on her husband, who was leading his team slightly ahead of us.

"I want to go home also. But your pa and my Charles saw the elephant."

I furrowed my brow. "They saw an elephant?"

"It's just a saying. They have big dreams in Oregon and California, and we're obligated to go with them. And who knows—maybe we'll be happy there."

"If we ever make it."

"We'll make it, Margaret. Have faith."

—— ❦ ——

Salty sweat stung my eyes and dribbled off my chin as Jacob and I worked to unhitch the mules, a hazardous and strenuous job I dreaded more than any other, besides the equally dangerous task of hitching them back up again in the morning. By the third day out of Missouri, Pa would trundle from the wagon seat and disappear as soon as the vehicle stopped. Now, in addition to all my other duties, each morning and evening I gritted my teeth and hoped there would not be a stampede when I untied a harness, or a spooked mule wouldn't kick me when I reached under a belly for a dangling strap, or the heavy wagon tongue wouldn't smash my foot, or . . .

A loud crash boomed as a crate tumbled from a nearby wagon. Molly belted an earsplitting bray and reared up, jerking the wagon tongue and Jack with her, nearly wrenching my arm from the socket before I released the lead rope. I froze in fear as her front hooves flailed near my head. Jacob tackled me from the side, and we both tumbled to the ground and rolled in the dirt. Like greased lightning, he was on his feet, grasping for the steed's halter as she tried to escape from the hitch. Too stunned to stand, I scuttled backward on my rear and watched wide eyed as Jacob calmed the spooked mule.

"Now that's no way to behave." The beasts now stood at attention, like soldiers waiting for the next order, ears twitching and tails swatting flies, as Jacob scolded. "It was only a little bump. Nothing to be concerned about."

I sat and watched, dumbfounded. The mules snorted and nodded while Jacob rubbed their noses, as if they understood his every word. My brother. The wimpy kid, whom I'd rescued from schoolyard bullies since we were six, had just saved me from getting my head smashed in by a skittish mule.

I rose, brushed some dust off my skirt, and returned to help Jacob finish unhitching the team. I tried to be nonchalant about the incident, but my limbs shook as we completed the task.

"Why did we stop early today?" I clasped Molly's lead rope, and we led the mules toward the stream for a drink.

"So that we can go hunting."

"Hunting?"

"The guide saw a herd of antelope. The captain must be hungry for fresh meat, so he stopped early so the men could hunt."

"It would be nice to have something besides beans and bacon. Are you going?" I squinted at him through the afternoon glare.

"Pa said I have to." He rubbed the back of his neck.

"You don't sound very excited. You've gone hunting with Pa before."

"Yeah. But I've just tagged along. He's always done the shooting." He dropped his gaze to the ground.

"So let him. He'll want to show off for all the other men anyway."

"He said that fourteen is too old to not have had a first kill. That he was eight when he shot his first buck and had at least a dozen under his belt by the time he was my age.

He's loaning me his rifle for the rest of the trip and said it's about time I earned my keep."

"I remember last summer when you and Pa were shooting bottles off a fence post behind the barn. You're aim was so terrible that you couldn't hit one of those jugs if you were close enough that the barrel touched the glass."

"Funny."

"You know I'm right." Jacob was so sensitive that he would be content to eat beans and bread for every meal before he would kill an animal. Once he even chased a rat around the house and shooed it out the door instead of whacking it with a skillet, like Ma or I would have done.

At the stream, the mules drank like camels. I rubbed Molly's neck. "It will be nice for some free time. I haven't had a minute to myself since we left home."

"You're going to be busy."

"No." I glared at him. "As soon as I help Mrs. Adkins with her goats so that you and Pa can have butter on your biscuits, I'm going to sit in the shade and read my book and write in my diary."

We started the trek back to the circled wagons.

"How are you going to make a fire?"

"Same way we always make a fire. Why?"

"Look around." He fanned the prairie with his arm. "What do you see?"

"Wagons. Mules. Oxen. People scurrying around."

"I mean beyond the wagons. What do you see."

I squinted into the distance. "Nothing."

"That's just it. Nothing."

"And some children looking for something." Clusters of women and children roamed about scanning the ground. "One of them must have lost a toy."

"I guess I'm going to have to spell it out for you. The reason that you see nothing is that there are no trees."

"So."

"So what do fires burn?"

"Wood."

"And where does wood come from?"

I crossed my arms and drummed my elbows. "Jacob, I'm not stupid. Wood comes from trees."

"Do you see any trees?"

I scanned the landscape. Barren as the moon. "Then how are we going to cook our supper?"

"That's what all the women and children are doing. They're looking for buffalo dung."

"Excuse me!" My eyebrow must have kissed my hairline.

"Since there is no wood for the fires, we're going to have to burn buffalo dung. To make it more appealing, they call it buffalo chips. The women and children have a new job—collect buffalo chips for the fires."

My jaw dropped. "You mean we have to use buffalo dung—or rather, chips—to cook on?"

"Looks that way. And since we are the 'children'"—he used his fingers to imitate quotation marks—"in our family, we get to collect the chips for our fire. And since I'll be off hunting—well, you figure it out."

"You mean I have to scour the prairie and pick up buffalo dung?"

"Chips. And make sure they're dry. Otherwise, that would be gross."

I decided to wait on my new disgusting, degrading chore until later. I snatched a pail and hiked to the Adkins' camp to help milk their goats. I didn't see the Adkins' children, William and his two younger brothers, who sometimes helped with the task. They must have been off with the other young people searching for fuel. At seven, four, and three years old, their "help" typically resulted in more milk in the dirt than in the pails. I was relieved that I didn't have to supervise them. The task took less time when I did it myself.

Mrs. Adkins sat in the shade of her wagon with her three-month-old baby girl, Abigal, cradled in her arms.

"Good evening, Mrs. Adkins." I peeked under the little pink bonnet that covered the infant's face. A pair of sparkling blue eyes ogled me, and a toothless smile exploded between her chubby cheeks.

"I think she likes you, Margaret. Would you like to hold her for a little bit?"

"Uh, I better get these goats milked. And I need to get some washing and some mending and, uh, another chore done before dark." I didn't want to say that I didn't know how to hold a baby and was afraid I would drop the precious bundle.

I knelt beside the goat and placed the bucket under her belly and worked the udder. Milk streamed into the pail. I would never tell Mrs. Adkins that I did not like milking her goats. But the reward was a pint of fresh milk for my help. Mrs. Adkins had shown me how to tie a tin can of milk to the side of the wagon in the morning. The jostling of the wagon would separate the cream. Then by suppertime we would have fresh butter. No need for the butter churn that was lying on the prairie with our mattress.

"Boo!"

I almost kicked over the half-filled pail as I shot upright. "William! Don't spook me like that if you want milk with your supper."

"Scared ya, didn't I." He bobbled on his toes and flapped his hands. "Bet you thought I was a wild Injin after your scalp."

"I could never mistake you for an Indian." Although I felt like a horde of jumping spiders inhabited my stomach since most of the men left camp.

"Where's Jacob?"

"He's out hunting with the men." I dipped back to my knees and resumed milking the goat.

"I wish I could go, but Pa said I needed to stay in camp to help protect the women and search for chips."

I peered up at him. "So you think you can guard us against a raiding band of mounted Indians wielding guns and arrows?"

His eyes widened, and he raced off toward his ma.

After securing a tin of goats milk to the wagon in preparation for its jarring transformation from liquid to cream and completing my new disgusting chore of prying buffalo chips from the grassy prairie, I nabbed *Jane Eyre* from Ma's trunk. I settled into the late afternoon shade of the wagon and leaned against a wheel. Scout curled up next to me and nuzzled his snout under my hand. I absentmindedly stroked his head and exhaled a sigh. I wanted to lash out at the dastardly Mr. Reed for striking Jane for no reason. Was it the fate of all women to suffer at the hand of a controlling male? I opened the book to my dogeared page and hoped to find Jane's revenge in the ensuing pages.

"Whatcha doin', Maggie?"

I dropped the book and flung my palm to my chest. "William! Don't startle me like that."

"Sorry." He swiped the back of his hand across his nose and jutted his lower lip. His two brothers huddled behind him.

I lifted the book so he could see the battered cover. "I'm reading a book."

He squinted at the tome. "I've never read a book. Can I listen."

"Sure, I suppose."

The three boys plopped to the ground on the other side of Scout and buried their fingers in the mutt's fur.

I read out loud, expecting the boys to spring to their feet and race away.

Less than a paragraph in, two other children approached—a stick-thin dark-haired boy who looked a couple years older than William and a brown-eyed girl about William's age, with auburn locks that tumbled from under her tan bonnet.

"Hey, William"—the boy rubbed his eye—"aren't you going to play with us?"

"Maggie's reading a book."

"Books are for sissies." He flared his nostrils and sauntered away.

"Can I listen?" The girl bunched her skirt in her fists and swiveled side to side and strained her eyes at the words on the open page.

"Sure, if you want to. What's your name?"

"Suzie. And that's my brother Tommy." She aimed a finger at her retreating sibling and then plopped to the dirt across from me.

I resumed reading where I had left off, mid-paragraph. William and Suzie sat cross-legged, elbows on their knees, chins plopped in their hands, and stared wide eyed as I read about the defiant Jane being hauled upstairs to the feared red-room.

The sky had dulled to a muted gray when thundering hooves and shouts announced the hunters' return.

I dogeared the page and closed the book. "It looks like it's time to get supper started."

Scout roused from his nap and wriggled from under the miniature fingers and trotted toward the approaching horses. I rose and was startled to see Mrs. Adkins leaning against the wagon, rocking a sleeping Abigal in her arms.

Suzie hopped up and tried to brush the dust from her skirt. "Can you read to us again tomorrow?"

"How about the next time we stop early enough that there is still daylight after supper."

I heard a rustling on the other side of the wagon and turned to see Tommy racing away. I smiled. The little rascal had been listening.

I stepped toward Mrs. Adkins. "I'm sorry if I distracted your children. They wanted to hear the story. It's a little grown-up for them."

She adjusted the sleeping baby in her arms. "I didn't know William could sit still for so long."

"Whoo-hoo!" Pa's yelp interrupted our conversation. He reined Jack to a halt. Poor mules didn't get any rest either. "Ladies, get the fires cracklin'. Fresh antelope steaks all around tonight." His words slurred. He swung his leg around the back of the saddle to dismount. His boot heel snagged a saddlebag, and he tumbled to the ground.

I rolled my eyes. Heat seeped into my cheeks, and I slunk into the shadows. The other hunters either rode or trudged on foot into camp. Jacob brought up the rear, leading Molly, who lumbered under the burden of an antelope carcass slung over her back. Two other men toted kills as well.

I scooped up the bucket of buffalo chips I had collected and flung the fuel into one of the smoldering community firepits. The added fuel hissed and smoked. Someone tossed in a log they must have been hoarding. William and his brothers yipped and clapped as flames shot up around the firewood. The log popped and crackled.

I watched Pa attack the dead animal with a butcher knife. At least he didn't make me dress it. I shifted my gaze to Jacob, who lurked in the shadows, rubbing Jack's nose. I went to the wagon and pulled out a skillet.

"That was my son." Pa plopped a slap of meat into the cast-iron skillet that I held for him. "My son who got the largest kill." He turned his head to the shadows, where Jacob lurked. "Jacob, get your ass over here and help dress this fine animal you shot today."

Jacob skulked to the dead animal, eyes downcast, knelt across from Pa, and slid a knife into the fallen prey.

I salivated as I devoured the succulent fresh meat. Scout licked a trail of juice that dribbled down my chin. He then sat in front of me and stared me down with his hungry puppy eyes. "You have to wait until I'm finished."

He barked.

"Oh, all right." I tossed him a chunk of my steak, which he greedily wolfed down. "Now we're both in antelope heaven."

—◆—

The following morning, antelope meat replaced the bacon that normally accompanied the charred breakfast biscuits. Pa and Jacob harvested some of the remaining meat to dry for jerky. We packed up camp, hitched the mules, and departed for Fort Kearney, leaving the unneeded carcass—hide, bones, and undesirable parts—to rot on the prairie.

I played a silly hopscotch game in my elongated shadow cast by the early morning sun as Jacob and I walked next to our wagon. I jumped into Jacob's stilt-like form tracking along the grass. He jumped out of the way, and I landed in a puff of sunbaked dust. Then I hopped toward his new shadow, and he bounced back to his original position. I giggled like a six-year-old and gave him a sisterly shove in the arm.

"Ow!" He tapped my arm in return.

I reached up to remove his hat and to tussle his wavy brown hair. He swatted my hand away, and we engaged in a playful hand-slapping battle, like when we were toddlers. We giggled. I was so lost in our childish game that I didn't hear the hooves approach.

"Aw, isn't that sweet—the little kiddies playing handsy."

If Ethan wasn't mounted on his palomino, I might have slugged him. It was the first lighthearted moment that Jacob and I'd had since Ma's death and since we'd left home. A brief breath where a dam had plugged my bleeding soul. Leave it to Ethan to burst a hole and release the tide of ache.

"Isn't it a little early for your courtesy check, Ethan?" I didn't hide my annoyance.

Jacob's cheeks flushed cherry red, and he cast his eyes to the trampled ground.

"Never too early to make sure everyone's safe." He flashed his shark grin.

"All safe here."

He didn't take my hint to move on. The palomino's clanking hooves fell in tempo with the mules as he rode alongside us.

"Jacob, thank you for dinner last night. I mean, Pa got an antelope also. I had one in my sights, but someone fired at the herd, and they bolted before I could get my shot off. I didn't have you pegged as a marksman since you don't carry a gun like the rest of us men." He patted the scabbard that held his rifle. "We should go shootin' sometime. I'm a pretty good shot myself. Maybe we could make a wager."

"That's okay, Ethan. I'm not into betting."

"Not like your pa then." He grinned. "Forget about the wager. We can just shoot. It'll be fun. We could use a break from all this walking."

I bit my tongue. We were the ones who walked, while he spent his days lazing in the saddle.

Jacob focused on his footsteps. "Sure, Ethan. If I ever have some idle time, maybe we can go shooting."

"Something to look forward to. I better be off on my rounds then." He kneed his mare and trotted off to annoy another traveler.

"Why are you so sullen today?" I asked after Ethan had parted.

He didn't respond.

"Jacob, what's bothering you? It's not like you not to talk to me."

He swiped the back of his wrist across his nose and sniffed. Must have been the dust. "Maggs, I didn't shoot that antelope."

"What?" I glared at him. "Pa's been bragging like you were the greatest hunter since Danial Boone."

"We were concealed in some brush, away from the others. There were about six antelope in the open. I had the target lined up, finger on the trigger. Pa was beside me, aiming as well. He kept telling me to shoot, that I was sure to hit one of them." He removed his hat and wiped his forehead with his neckerchief and replaced the hat. "I couldn't do it. He yelled, 'Shoot.' His yell spooked them. So he shot, and one dropped."

"Then why did he say you shot it?"

"I don't know. Probably because he'd been bragging that he was raising me to be a great hunter."

"That would have made him look foolish if you returned without a kill."

"And hungry also. I don't know how many more suppers of bacon and biscuits he could handle." A sheepish grin seeped across his face, but it morphed into a sullen pout. "I don't know what's wrong with me. Why I can't be the man he wants me to be."

I didn't have an answer for that.

"Promise me you won't tell anyone. Not Ethan or Mrs. McNeil or anybody."

"Of course I won't. We've always been able to trust each other with our secrets. Why would that change?"

"I don't know, Maggs. It seems like a lot has changed since Ma died."

"Yeah, a lot has changed. And sometimes I want to wring your neck. But with Ma gone, we only have each other."

A memory of Ma bubbled to the surface of my conscience. I must have been eleven or twelve. We had been kneading bread dough when out of the blue she had said, *"Margaret, I hope you know how much I am counting on you to watch out for Jacob."*

"What do you mean?"

"Well, he's special"—*she had paused as she searched for the right word*—*"different from other boys. People won't understand."*

I didn't know why the recollection popped into my head. But she was right. People wouldn't understand.

Chapter 7

Dear Diary,

Little wings flutter in my belly. My palms are clammy, I'm tongue tied, and my feet haven't touched the ground since we left Fort Kearney. Aah. But I'm getting ahead of myself. Fort Kearney itself was a letdown. I don't know how it could even be called a fort. I had expected a walled compound surrounded by a moat with armed guards keeping a keen watch from lookout towers. But what do I know about forts? A pathetic sprinkling of unpainted wooden and adobe structures in various stages of completion surrounded an empty square that is slated to be a future parade ground. I learned that the fort is to serve as a resupply point for us overlanders, to protect travelers like us from Indian attacks, as well as to protect the Indians from attacks from white folk as well as other Indians. People also whispered about a new threat—white Indians. I didn't understand until Jacob explained it to me. White Indians are white men who paint their faces and dress up as Indians. They raid wagon trains and steal and plunder. The victims would blame the attack on the Indians. Now I not only fear real Indians but fake ones as well!

Pa used some of Grandmother's money to top off his whiskey barrel. I wanted to ask him for money to buy some fabric for a new dress and for a new pair of shoes, but I knew the request was likely to be replied with a grunt at best or a slap across the face at worst. It was nice to have a couple days of rest, although the only ones who rested were Pa and the mules. I spent two whole days mending and washing and mixing up bread dough and concocting a paste of flour and water to bake hardtack and grinding coffee beans with Mrs. McNeil's grinder and cooking our meals and more mending and tending to the mules. I did get a chance to read to the children. Mrs. Adkins had brought Mrs. May with her. The woman perched on overturned washtubs and darned socks while listening along with the children about the harsh treatment Jane endured at her new boarding school. Tommy and Jacob sat by the wagon, whittling on sticks and pretending not to listen. Then Pa appeared and growled at the children. Mrs. Adkins and Mrs. May hustled them away.

In the evenings after supper, the men who brought along instruments strike up a tune. One fellow serves as a caller, and people dance until late into the night. Not me. I am too tired and angry with Pa and have no desire to join in the festivities. And who would I have danced with anyway—Ethan? I did see him look my way a few times, like he might ask me. Each time, I pretended not to notice and walked off in a different direction. Then we hit the trail, and my heart has been dancing since.

Within sight of our caravan, which crawled westward in the late afternoon, Mrs. McNeil and I scoured the prairie for dandelions and fresh herbs to add to our respective stews that we planned on making that evening. I stooped to snap a stem of one of the yellow flowering weeds from the ground near the root. "Who are the people who joined with us?" I rose and slipped the flower into my gunny sack.

"They're from another company ahead of us. Someone said they were from Indiana. Their train left Fort Kearney yesterday, but a couple families laid over an extra day." She fingered her handkerchief from under her sleeve and dabbed perspiration from her forehead.

"Why wouldn't they all go together?"

"Could be several reasons. They may have had some livestock that needed extra rest, or maybe someone was sick and needed an extra day to recover, or perhaps a wagon needed a repair. So the captain is letting them travel with us. It's much safer to be part of a larger train."

"And for an extra fee per wagon, I imagine." In an undignified manner that would have been met with a scowl from Ma, I wiped my brow with my sleeve.

"I wouldn't know about that. Though I did hear that there was a doctor among them. It will be good to have a doctor with us. Maybe he would take you on as an apprentice."

I rolled my lips between my teeth. It was a nice thought, but what doctor would be willing to teach a girl?

I was hungry and exhausted when we noticed the white tops snaking into the evening circle. I said goodbye to Mrs. McNeil and returned to our wagon.

"Where's my supper? I'm starving." Pa spat a stream of disgusting tobacco slurry into a puddle by the wagon right next to where Jacob and I normally sleep.

I stepped around the muck and crawled into the wagon and snatched a pail for my disgusting nightly duty of gathering fuel for the fire. Yuck!

"Hey, Maggie!"

I almost dropped the bucket. "William. You startled me again."

William and his two brothers, each with a pail gripped in their fists, stared up at me. "Sorry. Can we go chip hunting with you?"

"Sure. Let's hurry so we can beat everyone to the closest chips so we can get supper started sooner."

"And then can you read to us."

"Only if you promise not to pelt me with your ammo when you and your brothers have your nightly buffalo chip fight." I winked at him.

"But Tommy always starts it."

Pa stepped around the wagon and sneered at the children.

"Uh, never mind." The boys scattered toward the open prairie, pails banging their shins as they raced from Pa's menacing glare.

I leered at Pa and then stomped off after the children. How dare he intimidate those sweet youngsters. I'd have to find somewhere else to read to the children. Perhaps the Adkins' camp.

When the stew was warm, I dished up a plate for Pa, and he carried it to the front of the wagon so he could sit on the tongue to eat. Since our chairs were days back on the prairie, Jacob and I sat on the ground to consume our meal.

I was washing the plates in a bucket of water when Mrs. Adkins's shout reverberated through the camp. "Doctor! Help, Doctor."

Mrs. McNeil and Mrs. May rushed through the horde of campers. Mrs. May hollered "Doctor, where's the doctor?" as they ran.

The women returned a few moments later, leading a hatless man, one woman attached to each of his elbows.

"Careful, ladies. I'm perfectly capable of walking on my own." The doctor—Doctor Samuelson, or Doc Sam, as everyone called him—was a stout man. The waning sun reflected off a bald patch on the crown of his head. Sprinkles of gray dotted the strands of hair that arced around his ears. Unlike most of the men in our train, his beard was neatly trimmed. "Just point to where you want me to go."

They didn't need to point. "Doctor, please! Please help my baby."

I folded into the crowd that followed the doctor toward the Adkins' wagon. Although we kept a respectable distance, Abigal's wailing screams cut through the whipping wind, crackling fires, chomping animals, and concerned whispers.

The doctor's face was molded into a scowl when he hopped out of the wagon a short time later. I looked to my side when I heard a child snivel.

William wiped his nose with his sleeve. "Did the doctor make Abigal better?"

The doctor paced away, his back arced into a frown. I didn't tell the boy what I suspected. "I don't know, William. Why don't you say a special prayer for your sister tonight." The painful baby wails cut through the air like daggers.

At sunrise two men dug a small grave right in the middle of the trail to the west of our camp. Mrs. Adkins clutched the small bundle to her bosom, while William and his two younger brothers nestled into her skirt. We all bowed our heads while Reverend Danials prayed for the baby's eternal salvation. At "Amen," I raised my head. Mr. Adkins wrestled the baby, wrapped in a pink blanket, from Mrs. Adkins and placed the tiny bundle into a miniature coffin that someone had constructed. Mr. Adkins escorted his weeping wife from the grave. Two men who'd been leaning on their shovels during the prayer began to cover the little lifeless body. I whispered a silent request to Ma to look after baby Abigail in heaven.

Mrs. McNeil and I walked toward our wagons to break camp. "Why did they bury her right in the middle of the trail, where all the wagons will run over top of her?"

"The oxen and heavy wagons will pack down the earth, so hopefully, the wolves and coyotes won't dig her up and drag her off."

"She didn't even get a grave marker," I whispered. Just like Ma. At least Ma got a proper grave in a real cemetery, with a tree to shade her from the scorching sun. I hoped the oak that watched over her would keep the wild animals at bay.

Jacob and I finished hitching the mules. He went to douse the fire while I stowed the skillet I had set aside to cool.

"Aargh!" The anguished cry that pierced through camp halted the wind from howling, the grass from swishing, the cows from lowing, and chains from clanking. I rushed to where the scream originated and weaseled my way through the small crowd that had gathered around a new member of our train. A young man sat on the ground near a team of eight mules, clutching his right hand to his left shoulder. One mule snorted and stomped on a hat lying on the ground.

Doc Sam raced through the gathering and knelt next to the injured boy. "What's the matter, son?"

"Damn!" the boy screamed. "Damn mule tried to rip my arm off."

"Watch your language, son."

"Sorry, Doc, but it hurts like hell. Damn mule."

"If you want me to fix that arm, you better tame the foul language that spews from your mouth."

The patient clenched his teeth. My heart fluttered as I watched the injured boy. He looked maybe a little older than me and Jacob. His sandy hair was plastered to his head by a layer of dirt and sweat. A halo-like hat ring circled his crown. A sparkle flickered from his aqua-blue eyes as his face contorted into a grimace. And the cutest dimple, like a polka dot, formed a cavity in his chin. Doc Sam helped the young man to his feet, escorted him to their wagon, and eased him onto a crate. I noticed that the wagon was painted the same color blue as the boy's eyes.

I picked up the trampled hat, brushed off some of the dust, and tried to punch out the hoof-shaped dent. I hovered near where the doctor examined the injury.

"Slip out of that shirtsleeve so that I can see what kind of damage you did." The doctor's gruff order was unsympathetic.

"I didn't do it. It was that da—I mean, stupid mule." He struggled one armed with the top button on his shirt.

His pa slid the sleeve from his shoulder and pressed his thumb and fingers around the joint.

"Ow, Doc." The young man grimaced.

"Looks like a dislocated shoulder. Nothing broken. I just need to pop it back into place and you'll be wrangling those mules in no time." He slid the shirtsleeve back over the boy's shoulder. "Lie on the ground."

"What?" The boy's eyes widened like a frightened owl's.

"Are you deaf also? If you want your shoulder fixed, I need you to lie flat on your back."

The boy glowered at the doctor, slid off the crate, and settled on the ground.

The doc leaned over and clasped the injured arm by the wrist with both hands. Then he planted his prairie-dusted boot in the patient's armpit.

"Ouch. What are you doing, Doc?"

The doctor leaned his weight into his planted foot and yanked the arm with so much force that I thought he would rip it off and toss it away.

"Damn! Doc." The patient's face glowed beet red.

"I didn't say it wasn't going to hurt." The doctor eased the injured arm to the boy's side. "I'll forgive the profanity this one time, but no more swearing. There's ladies and children around who don't need to hear that trash talk."

The doc left his son lying on the ground. The boy sat up and winced. Then he scooched to his knees, rested the palm of his good arm on the crate, and hoisted himself onto the box. He clasped his right hand to his injured shoulder and inhaled a string of deep breaths.

I clutched the hat in both hands in front of me and approached him. "Ah, this must be your hat." I hoped he didn't notice my hand quiver as I held it out to him.

He peered up at me and squinted. Flecks of silver danced in his blue eyes as the morning sun brightened his face. He tried to smile, but it came out as a contorted scowl. From the pain, I assumed. Or hoped.

"Oh, uh, thank you, ah . . ."

"Margaret. My name is Margaret, but my friends call me Maggie."

He took the hat and tried to punch it back into shape.

"One of your mules stepped on it."

"Stupid mule. Probably the same one that tried to rip my arm off. I'm Eliot." His marine eyes glinted when he smiled.

My palms felt clammy, my heart raced, and heat seeped into my cheeks. "It's nice to meet you, uh, Eliot. I hope your arm gets better."

"Me too. And thank you for returning my hat." He used his good arm to slip the hat onto his head and flashed a smile that made my heart flicker.

I wrung my hands and tried to think of something witty or intelligent to say, but my mind was as empty as an overturned bucket. "I better go." I spun and raced to our wagon, cursing myself for being such a dimwit.

Chapter 8

Dear Diary,

Eliot, Eliot. The sweet name sings on my lips, or in my head, when Pa or Jacab are near. Eliot's blue eyes and warm smile have washed away all my other thoughts since I'd returned his hat and acted like a childish schoolgirl. Why was I such an idiot? And why am I so enamored with someone I had only briefly met? It's not like there is even a remote chance he would ever speak to me again. His pa is a doctor. And I am riffraff. A nobody. A worthless piker. The kind of lowlife that families of his stature look down their noses on. Or pretend we don't exist. If I were alone, I would have curled up in a ball and cried. But he jumbles my thoughts nonetheless, like a frayed rope tangled in wheel spoke.

We have left the Little Blue River near Fort Kearney and are traveling west along the Platte River. The muddy current drifts like a sea of sewage meandering through the prairie. Gross! I hope we don't have to cross it. I don't even want to stick a toe in that sludgy muck. It's too muddy for drinking or washing. For potable water, if you could call it that, we dig holes in the sand and use the water that fills them or, when we can, the streams that we cross. Even then we filter out the dirt and film. An impossible task since the filth just seeps through the sieves like rain through a screen.

"Mrs. McNeil told me that it will take about five months to reach California."

While Pa drove, Jacob and I resumed our normal after-lunch slog across the grassy pancake flat prairie near the wagon. Pa's irritation had bubbled to a boil after I'd handed him a plate of cold bacon and burnt biscuits for the nooning meal. How he could expect better grub to sprout from the dusty prairie was beyond my comprehension. So instead of walking by the mules, we trekked slightly behind and to the side of the wagon, out of Pa's line of sight.

I gagged on the dust the mules billowed up as they hoofed over the sandy prairie. No use. My throat would be forever coated in a layer of grime. "I sure hope she's wrong. I'm fed up with all this walking and pioneering life."

"I don't care much for it either. But she's right. I heard the same."

"That means we're not even"—I paused to do some math in my head. I couldn't calculate the percentage of the five months that we had traveled. Frustrated, I flung my hands in the air. "We still have an eternity to go."

"A little over four months. We haven't even reached the twenty percent mark yet."

He was always better at calculations.

I turned at the sound of footsteps jogging up behind us. I flung my hand to my chest as Eliot fell in step beside me. I hope he didn't hear my startled gasp.

"Good afternoon, Maggie." He huffed a ragged breath as he lifted a finger to his deformed hat. "I hope it's okay if I call you Maggie. Since you were so kind to return my hat, I hope that we can be friends."

"Oh, ah, hi, Eliot." I felt my cheeks burn. "Your shoulder must be feeling better. And of course you can call me Maggie."

"Actually, it hurts like the dickens. But I'm trying to ignore it. I just wanted to thank you again for returning my hat. It's an old crummy hat, but at least it keeps the sun out of my eyes. It did look better before that ornery mule mangled it." He removed the hat and tried to stretch out the dent that marred the crown.

"It was my pleasure. I think the hoofprint adds character." I wanted to say that he'd look like a prince in even the filthiest, tattered rags.

He slipped the hat onto his head. "Well, if that blasted mule even sniffs at my hat again, I'll whip his ass and teach him whose boss."

Jacob grunted beside me.

"Eliot, this is my brother, Jacob."

Eliot peered around me at Jacob. "It's nice to meet you, Jacob. Your sister saved the day for me this morning."

"Whippin' that mule won't show him who's boss." Jacob tensed his shoulders and balled his hands. "It will only teach him who to be afraid of and who not to trust. Lose the trust of your team and they won't work for you."

"Who are you to tell me . . ." Eliot's hands tightened into fists also.

"Jacob, speaking of teams and trust, don't you think it's time to check on ours?"

Jacob snarled and then trotted ahead to walk next to Jack.

I looked at Eliot. "Are you headed for Oregon or California?" I hoped he'd say California.

"Oregon. I wish we were going to California. I'd like to get my hands on some of that gold." He grabbed at the air with his hand, as if plucking a gold nugget out of the billowing dust. "Folks say that it's just lying around waiting to be picked up."

"That's what Pa heard too."

"I take it your headed for the gold then." He hooked his thumbs through his suspender straps.

"Unfortunately. I wish we were going to Oregon. Much nobler to be a farmer than a gold digger." *Why did I say that?* It sounded like something that Mrs. McNeil would think.

"It sounds like you're a good person, Maggie. Me, I'd rather be rich than noble. But why couldn't we be both? Stike it rich in the gold fields and then go to Oregon and homestead on fertile ground by the river. I could hire a whole crew of farmhands to do the work and reap the benefits of a bountiful harvest." He looped his arms in a giant circle, as if he could envision pots of gold and wagonloads of crops before him.

"You must be a dreamer. And that's a nice dream."

"What do you dream about?"

I sealed my lips and watched the trampled grass pass beneath me. Without Ma and a home and nothing to look forward to, my dreams had all dried up. I took a deep breath. "I'm not sure I have a dream anymore."

"Why not? Everybody has something they want out of life."

"I used to have one, well, actually two, but they were stupid." I almost said that the only dream a girl was allowed was to find a husband and be held captive to a life of servitude.

"We'll, come on. Tell me. There is no such thing as a stupid dream."

I bit my lip. I kept my gaze on my feet, and quietly confessed, "When I was younger, I thought I wanted to be a doctor."

"A doctor?"

"Yeah, like your pa. So that I could help people when they got sick."

"You are a good person, Maggie."

At least he didn't say it was a stupid dream for a girl to be a doctor.

"What was your second dream?"

"Well, since the only employment a woman is allowed is to be a schoolmarm, that was my other dream."

"I bet every school in California will be fighting over you to be their schoolmarm."

But if I was held captive as the personal slave to Pa and Jacob, I wouldn't be able to get the proper education to be a schoolmarm. Not wanting to dwell on my dismal future any longer, I asked, "How come you call you pa Doc Sam instead of Pa or Dad or Father?"

"Everybody calls him Doc Sam. Doesn't make sense to call him anything else."

"There's another grave." I pointed to a stick cross wedged into a rock-covered mound several yards ahead and to the side.

"Let's go look. Just to make sure it's not someone from our company."

My stomach dropped. The rest of Eliot's train was ahead of ours. Did that mean he wasn't going to travel with us? He trotted toward the cross, and I followed.

"Looks like three graves," he said when we reached the site where a trio of freshly turned mounds rested at the foot of the cross.

I wiped some dampness from my eye with the back of my wrist. The hole in my heart from Ma's absence widened with every grave we passed. How could so many people die out here? "I wonder what they died of."

"Could be anything. Because there are three together, my guess is cholera. Likely from the same family."

"There are no names carved on the marker. The people from the train of go-backs that we met a while back mentioned cholera. What is it?"

"Don't know. Because people seem to catch it near the river, Doc Sam thinks it could have something to do with the dirty water. Other folks think it must be something in the air. It strikes so fast that a person could be fine in the morning and dead by suppertime."

"He is a doctor. Wouldn't he know?" I studied his profile as he stared at the mounds.

"He said it's not something that he studied in his medical books. We'll probably never know. But to be on the safe side, we're making the extra effort to avoid the river and get our water farther upstream from the creeks we pass." He looked at me. "You should do the same."

As I stared at the graves, I wondered if cholera had plagued little Abigail. I scrutinized the desolate landscape that surrounded us. When the wagons and horses and livestock and screaming children had passed through, the three mounds would rest abandoned on the windswept plain, the prairie dogs and mosquitoes the only witnesses to their presence.

"Eliot," a dainty voice called from behind us.

We turned to see a girl about my age trotting toward us. The wagons creaked and groaned as they trundled behind her. She scurried over the uneven ground with one hand pressed against her bonnet, while the other clutched a fistful of her skirt so she wouldn't trip.

"What do you want, Sissy? Can't you see I'm busy?"

Eliot's sister, I presumed. They looked more like siblings than me and Jacob. Her golden curls bounced from under her bonnet when she ran. Her hazel eyes lacked the sparkle of her brother's aqua blues, and her lips were plastered together in a scowl that vaguely reminded me of my grandmother. "You don't look busy. Looks like you're just trying to impress another girl."

"Sissy, what do you want?" He planted his hands on his hips and squinted at her.

"Doc needs you to come right away. A rider came looking for him from a train behind us, and he has to go quick. Mama's not feeling well, so he needs you to manage the team until he gets back."

Sissy spun and dashed back toward the creeping wagons, her curls bobbing behind her in the breeze.

"Would you like to come help keep my onery mules pointed in the right direction?" He winked at me.

My eyes widened, and I said, too eagerly, "I would love to. You might need me to keep them from eating your hat."

He chuckled, and we jogged back to the slow-moving caravan.

"What took you so long?" Doc Sam barked as he heaved a saddlebag onto the back of his sorrel gelding, which stood at attention near their stopped blue wagon.

"Sorry, Doc. Came as soon as Sissy summoned me. How long are you going to be gone this time?"

"I should be back before dark. The train is not far behind us."

"That's what you said last time."

"Couldn't be helped. Your mother is resting, so try to drive as smooth as you can so she can get some sleep."

"Someone needs to smooth out the lumps on this prairie then."

The doc glared at Eliot.

"Who's going with you since Mama's laid up?" He scanned around him, as if searching for a helper ready for the cue to mount a saddled horse.

"I'm going to have to be both doctor and assistant this time."

"What kind of help do you need?" I squeezed my palms together.

"Being a doctor sometimes requires three hands."

"I can help." My eyes widened. "I've always wanted to be a doctor."

Eliot gave me a quizzical look.

I assumed it was because I had implied that I had given up on that silly dream. I thought I had, but it must have burrowed up from the cavern where I had buried it.

Doc Sam looked up from the cinch strap that he was tightening around the sorrel's belly. "Are you sure you want to help?"

I nodded.

"Then hustle and let your pa know. Wasted minutes could mean the difference between life and death some-times."

"He won't even know I'm gone. Let's go save a life." I swung my fisted hand across my hip.

"I only have one horse saddled, so you're going to have to ride double." He tightened the cinch and lowered the stirrup. He mounted and then reached a hand down to me.

"How am I going to ride side saddle with two of us?"

"No room for modesty as a doctor's helper. Put your left foot into the stirrup."

I slipped my foot into the stirrup and reached for his hand. A little screech slipped from my lips as Eliot put his hands around my waist and hoisted me up as the doc pulled me onto the horse. I was barely balanced with my arms wrapped around his waist when the doctor flicked the reins and spurred the gelding into a gallop.

My raw bum screamed in pain when we reached the stopped caravan. I clasped onto Doc Sam's arm with both hands as he swung me off the horse. My legs wobbled. I stumbled, then fell on my derriere in the most unladylike fashion. My cheeks burned. I rose and brushed the dust off my skirt. A group of children of various ages raced toward us, yelling and screaming so loud that we couldn't understand a single word. I jumped with a start when Doc Sam belted out a shrill whistle. The crowd froze. Then the rumbling voices erupted in unison. Doc Sam whistled again, and it turned as quiet as the arctic tundra.

"We'll start with you." The doc pointed to a freckle-faced girl in pigtails.

"Ma's real sick. Can't keep anything in. Please help her."

"What about you?" He nodded to a boy, a little younger than me, wearing a torn shirt.

"Baby's sick. Fever and cryin' constantly. Ma's scared out of her wits."

"You?" Doc asked a taller boy.

"Uncle Billy got his arm crushed when the wagon jack slipped. Folks got him loose, but he's bleeding bad. Our captain sent the rider for you."

"Let's go." He untied the saddle bag, and we trotted after the boy. The gaggle of children followed.

The injured man lay supine on the ground, next to a wagon with the front wheel askew. Concerned whispers filtered from the somber crowd gathered close by.

"Let the doc through," a voice boomed. The crowd parted like the Red Sea for Moses. I followed the doc as he slipped through the gap.

Two women, one sobbing into a scarf, knelt by the injured man. Doc Sam shooed them aside.

"He's unconscious," the other woman whispered. She rose and led the weeping woman away.

Doc Sam picked up one of the bloodied rags that covered the wound and tied it around the man's arm just above the elbow. "Someone get me a wrench. And start a fire next to me."

I pondered why the doc would need a wrench, when someone slipped an iron tool in his hand. And it was much too hot for a fire. Then my gaze froze on the puddle of blood that oozed into the baked dirt. Deep red when it dripped from the gash in the man's arm and rust-brown when it seeped into the earth. From the corner of my eye, I saw Doc Sam slip the wrench into the knot of the rag that he had tied around the contorted arm. The nub of the broken bone jutted through the bloodied gash. The blood in my veins stopped flowing.

The doc twisted the wrench, strangling the life out of the limb.

The cold bacon I'd gnawed on at lunch turned rancid in my stomach as I knelt and stared at the crimson blood dripping from the severed bone.

Doc Sam gave the wrench a final twist with a grunt. "Maggie, I need you to hold this wrench tight so that it doesn't move. Use two hands."

His words sounded garbled and far away, like he was talking from the depths of a scummy pond.

"Maggie, are you with me?" He nudged me with his elbow. "Take hold of the wrench. Close your eyes if you need to."

I squished my eyes shut, then opened the left one just a slit and peered at the tool glinting in the sun. I clasped the wrench with both hands. Through my squinted eye, I watched the doctor use two fingers to pry the man's eyelids open, first the left, then the right. He pressed his fingers to the man's neck to feel for a pulse, then lowered his ear to the patient's chest.

He unrolled a satchel of shiny surgical tools. He set aside a knife and another instrument that resembled a cleaver with teeth like a saw, removed his neckerchief, and used it to wipe some rust-colored dirt from the implements. I closed my eyes when I realized the dirt was dried blood.

"Now, everyone please back away." He looked at me. Sweat dripped from his chin. "Maggie, please escort these folks to the other side of camp. You can let go on the wrench."

I was about to protest, but his grave expression, and the sharp knife clasped in his hand, convinced me to follow his order.

"How are we goin' to get on without Billy?" one young man asked as we meandered away from Doc Sam and his patient. "He's the best there is at fixin' things."

"The doc's going to take care of him," a woman said as she looped her arm around his. "Billy will be fixin' our broken axles again in no time."

"But he wasn't moving," the young man argued. "What if he's already dead?"

"No talking like that. Especially in front of the children." A boy about William's age rushed up and nuzzled his face in the women's skirt. She wrapped her other arm around him.

"AAARGH!"

The crowd froze at the blood curdling scream.

A sob wafted through the huddled bodies.

A man with a handlebar mustache removed his hat and wrapped his arms around a petite woman. She nestled her head under his chin.

Soon Doc Sam strolled over, his saddlebag slung over his shoulder and his hands shoved into his pockets. "Might be best if he went back to Fort Kearney. I gave his wife instructions on how to keep the wound bandaged and dry. She is pretty distraught, as you can imagine, so I'm not sure how much she understood. If you decide to push on, she's going to need a lot of help."

"You mean he's going to live?" the young man asked, his eyes brightening.

"I'll be honest. His chances are slim. He's lost a lot of blood, and even though I cauterized the stump, gangrene's likely to set in. I've seen some amazing recoveries, so pray for him." He held the young man's eye for a moment. "Now who's next?"

Doc Sam tended to the sick baby and then the woman with dysentery. As the assistant, I fetched water, wiped the woman's forehead with a damp cloth, and tossed soiled laundry into the fire. Not the glamorous work I had envisioned.

On the ride back to our train I asked, "Are the baby and the woman going to be okay?"

"That's for God to decide. The best I could do is administer laudanum for the pain. Some make it. Most don't."

I decided then that I didn't want to be a doctor anymore. Not if most of the patients died despite a doctor's best efforts. And the blood . . .

The western sky exploded in a vibrant pastel canvas as Doc Sam's horse loped into the dying day. But the dazzling display was in sharp contrast to my dour mood. The meandering water of the nearby Platte danced in the glow of the rising moon as we jostled into camp. My bum hurt, my feet were numb, my stomach begged for food, and I wanted to crawl under my blanket, close my eyes, and forget about the poor armless man. Crackling fires and a strumming banjo greeted us as we approached our camp. The greeting from Pa was not so warm.

"Where have you been!" he yelled after I limped to our wagon.

"I was helping Doc Sam." I didn't get to finish before he slapped me hard across my cheek. Behind the tears festering in my eyes, I spied Eliot, his mouth agape. Pa raised his hand to strike me again.

"That's enough, Elijah." Doc Sam clasped Pa's wrist midswing. "It was my fault. I promised to have her back before dark, and we got delayed."

Jacob and Scout emerged from behind the wagon. The pooch sprang up to my side and growled at Pa.

"Your responsibility is here with us." Pa ignored Doc Sam and the eyes of the other campers as he ranted. "Jacob had to do your chores, and Mrs. McNeil was kind enough to feed us, since you ran off and neglected your duties." He wrestled his arm free from Doc Sam's clutch and slapped me again. "Now get me some coffee!"

I tromped to the wagon knowing that I would go to bed hungry—again.

Chapter 9

Dear Diary,

"Just a couple of hurdles." Mrs. McNeil's idea of a hurdle is more like a mountain. This whole journey has been one giant hurdle, with a bar that keeps rising. Somehow we manage to claw over them, but each one chips away at our spirit. Ma's little voice in my head tells me it develops grit. Makes us stronger. I don't feel stronger. Just tired. And sad. Cholera took two more members of our company. Mr. and Mrs. Martin. I had seen Mrs. Martin and some of the other women filtering water from a mud hole they had dug by the river. The next day, the Martin's adult sons dug their graves. Perhaps Eliot was right about the water.

Ah Eliot. If only I could spend more time with him. The snippets that we can be together are delightful. But the responsibilities that tether us to our respective wagons and families don't allow much time for socializing.

"Blessed morning to you, Margaret." Mrs. McNeil greeted me in her usual joyful tone when I trotted up to walk with her. Walking with Mrs. McNeil had become a morning ritual. Lately Jacob had become somewhat of a stick-in-the-mud, unusually quiet and brooding and not good company. Eliot was typically tied to the Samuelsons' wagon while the doc was off on his "rounds." And I certainly wasn't going to interact with Pa. That left Mrs. McNeil, who, besides Eliot of course, had become my only friend and confidant in the company.

"Mrs. McNeil, how can you be so chirk on such a miserable morning?"

"There is a lot to be cheerful about, Margaret. The sun is shining, the grass is swaying, the late spring flowers are blooming, we're alive and healthy, and we're a day closer to Oregon."

"Hmph," I responded. Again. Although the morning sun was at our backs, by midday the fireball would burn my cheeks, glare in my eyes, and siphon the energy from my being. The swaying grass, at least the tufts that weren't trampled, leaned, as if bowing to the eastern wind gods. The wildflowers lay crushed and broken, the fragrant beauty stomped out by the unyielding parade of prairie traffic. I did feel alive on those rare occasions that I could spend with Eliot. And the sporadic evenings I could break away to read to the children. But I wasn't sure that any of us were healthy. The dust and bugs that filled our stomachs and lungs couldn't be good for us. But she was right in that we were not injured or had succumbed to cholera or dysentery or any of the other sicknesses that had plagued some of our fellow travelers. But I didn't say any of that to Mrs. McNeil. Let her bask in her joy.

"We do have something to look forward to." She slipped out a rag that she had tucked into the strap of her apron at the small of her back, stooped, and with the cloth, pried a buffalo chip from the grass. She stepped close to her wagon and deposited the fuel into a pail that was secured to the side of her wagon for that purpose, replaced the rag, and resumed her walk.

"That we're turning around and going home?" I hop-skipped a step.

"We can only look forward, Margaret. Charles reminded me that we'll reach Ash Hollow in a few days."

"Ash Hollow?" I envisioned a pit of smoldering buffalo dung.

"The guidebook describes it as paradise. Like an oasis in the middle of the prairie. Although there are a couple of hurdles in the way."

I squinted into the vast emptiness that stretched for days. Not a single tree sprouted from the monotonous landscape that would suggest even a spot of shade, let alone a paradise. "What kind of hurdles?"

"First the Platte, and then something called California Hill."

"You mean we're close to California?" I clasped my hands together.

"No, I don't believe that we are. I don't know why it's called California Hill."

"Oh." I dropped my hands to my side. "And why is the Platte a hurdle? We've been following it for an eternity."

"Paradise is on the other side of the river."

"Hmm." I frowned. "Paradise better be better than the garden of Eden if I'm going even put a toe in that water."

"To us, Margaret, a tree or clear water will seem better than the garden of Eden."

I gazed into the cloudless sky and tried to imagine our descent into paradise. The image wouldn't focus.

After a pause that was filled with the din of wind-whipped canvas tops, clanking hooves, shrieking children, and mothers' reprimands, she said, "I've noticed that you've been spending a lot of time with Eliot."

I smiled. "Well, yeah. Besides you and Jacob, there really isn't anyone else to talk to. And walking by myself is boring." I focused on my footsteps. "Although it hasn't been very much time. Since Doc is away so much, Eliot has to drive their wagon and is always busy tending to his Ma. Then there are all the other chores that need done. And it seems like he draws guard duty almost every night, so he's always plum tired."

"I did expect there would be more older children, or rather younger adults, in our company. I gather that you and Eliot don't just chat about the weather."

"We talk about that too. And about Jacob and Sissy. And he shares some of Doc Sam's stories about his injured and sick patients. Just stuff like that."

"It sounds like you've developed a fondness for him."

Understatement! "Yeah, sort of. I mean, I do get these weird sensations in my belly when I'm with him. And then I get tongue tied, which embarrasses me. I can't believe the stupid things I say when I'm with him."

"Ah, the thrill of young love." She paused for a few steps. "I'm not your mother, and I should probably mind my own business, but if she were here, I think she would caution you to be careful around that boy."

"Why?"

"He's a spirited young man."

"Some people would say that I'm spirited also." I flexed my fingers and balled my hands into fists. "Maybe that's why we get along so well."

"Margaret, you are the definition of spirited. I'm not saying that you shouldn't be friends. Just keep your wits about you."

Hmph! I almost stomped away, but my angst dissipated when the wagons ahead of us slowed. "Why are we stopping?" I shielded my eyes with my hand and squinted at the mass of bunched white tops.

"It looks like we're about to cross the river."

"I still don't understand why we have to cross it."

"Charles showed me the map in his guidebook. The river splits in two. Like the letter Y. We have to cross the south fork so that we can follow the north fork. The north fork leads to Oregon."

"What about California?"

"California also."

"I better go help Jacob." I wove through the wagons, oxen, and mules back to our rig.

I was sure my eyes were as wide as plumbs as I stood next to Molly at the river's edge and watched the travelers ahead slog through what looked like an endless sludge trough. "It must be a mile wide," I shouted to Jacob under the mules' snouts.

"It is. But it's not supposed to be very deep here. That's why the captain chose this place to cross." He clasped his palm around Jack's bridle. "Just don't stop, because the captain said that the bottom is like quicksand. He claims it can swallow a mule up to its ears, so keep moving."

I rubbed Molly's nose and reached for her bridle. "Here goes, girl. And please don't stop."

Scout, whom Jacob had earlier put in the wagon box, poked his head through the canvas over Pa's shoulder and yapped an encouraging bark.

Jacob and I stepped forward in unison. The mules didn't budge. Scout barked again. "Quiet, Scout," I scolded. "We don't want Pa's help," I whispered under my breath. I knew the crop was resting across Pa's lap, along with his shotgun.

Jacob took another step into the sludge, squatted, and filtered some of the water through his fingers. "It's just water, boy. See all those other mules and oxen already crossing? It's only as deep as their knees."

Another gentle tug, and a flick of the reins by Pa, the team followed us into the muck. I squirmed as the cold, soppy mud seeped into my shoes and oozed between my toes. The muddy bottom tried to suck the shoes off my feet. The mule's hooves slurped as they lifted from the goop, like the sound Pa makes when he inhales the dregs of coffee from his tin cup—only a thousand times louder. The crossing seemed to take hours.

When safely on the other side, I plopped to the ground and tried to clean the gunk from my shoes and toes. Hopeless.

I was cleaning the breakfast dishes the next morning when Ethan circled the camp on his palomino, summoning us to an all-train meeting. Usually only the men attended the morning briefings. I glued my gaze to the ground and sidestepped around Pa, who leaned against the wagon sipping his coffee, hoping that he wouldn't divert me away to do some unnecessary chore.

I stowed the skillet and joined the crowd congregating in the middle of the circle near the captain. I wriggled through the mass of chitchatting women and giggling children and tried to find a spot where I could see between the boodle of bearded men. I thought it was unfair that the women and children were relegated to stand behind the taller and broader men. The women were better trusted to remember and follow the captain's instructions.

The captain stepped onto a crate and removed a pipe from between his lips and stashed it in a pocket. Ethan stood off to the side, holding the reins of his palomino and the captain's chestnut. He winked at me. I ignored him and cast my eyes on the captain.

The captain cleared his throat. "Later this morning . . ." He paused. The audience noise only slightly abated. A child's gleeful shriek splintered the rumble. A woman, I think Mrs. Adkins, whispered, "You children settle down."

"Attention please," the captain yelled over the buzz.

A shrill whistle sliced the air. The flock of bodies froze. A pair of chickadees that had been engaging in a morning conversation in the distance fluttered away.

The captain removed his hat, wiped his brow with a neckerchief, and recovered his greasy mop. "Now, as I was saying . . ." His eyes drifted over the heads of the audience and stopped behind me. "Hanley, this is an all-hands meeting. Get over here so that you know what's in store for today."

I didn't dare turn my head to look where the captain squinted. I assumed he was watching Pa meander over to join the group.

The captain hacked a hoarse cough and restarted the briefing. "As I was saying, it's just a few hours to California Hill. This will be the first of many steep climbs between here and Oregon. It takes a village, so to speak, to get a wagon two thousand miles from Missouri to Oregon."

"What about California?" a man yelled.

"Quit interrupting." He glared at the disruptive man across the arc from me, then turned back to the assembly. "As I was saying, getting up and down these steep grades requires extra hands and horsepower. That means we help each other out. The wagons need to be unloaded and your belongings carried up the hill. The women and children can do most of that. Then some of the wagons need to be double or even triple teamed. Two measly mules won't haul even an empty wagon up the hill." He glared over the heads around me. I assumed it was a warning to Pa. "Some of ya will need to be generous and bring your teams back down to help others."

He paused and waited for the grumbling to subside.

"The next thing, and this is important, once you start moving, do not stop for any reason. Your teams will not be able to get going from a dead stop on a steep grade. Do whatever you need to coax the animals on. Work it out among yourselves, as I'm not goin' to play traffic marshal." He scanned the crowd. "Any questions?"

"How many oxen per wagon will it take?" a man shouted from the center of the mass of bodies.

"Henry, you've only got four on your team. If they're fresh, they might make it. Likely they're worn by now, so I wouldn't try it. Six at the least. Eight to ten would be better." He scanned the crowd. "Any more questions?"

The horde shuffled, but nobody spoke up.

"Let's get moving."

We nooned early at the base of California Hill. Then Jacob and I unloaded the contents of the wagon into a heap beside the rig. He had to fetch Pa to help with the trunk. After the chest plopped to the ground and kicked up a puff of dust, I watched Pa roam through the throng of wagons. He approached Mr. Adkins. As soon as William's pa saw my pa, he slid under his wagon and inspected an axle. Pa threw up his hands in frustration. I wanted to giggle. The rebuff served him right, since Pa would be the last person to help a neighbor in need. On the other hand, how would our wagon get up the hill?

The McNeils were busy unloading their wagon near us. I noticed that Mrs. McNeil stopped her work to watch Pa. Then she looked at me. I quickly turned away and bent over to reposition a tool. I overheard her ask, "Charles, why don't you offer our team to help the Hanleys."

He glared at her.

"Do it for the children."

Mr. McNeil glanced our way.

"All right, hon. For the children."

Thank you, Mrs. McNeil.

My abused limbs shook from ache and exhaustion as Jacob and I descended the steep slope for the umpteenth time. The hill wasn't like the hills back home. The route to the top was a mile long, with false ridges that tricked us into thinking the summit was near. As soon as we reached the crest, another steep grade mockingly loomed before us. Only the trunk remained at the bottom, looking lonely and forgotten. Why didn't we take that first? Pa had disappeared again, so if the chest was getting up the hill, Jacob and I would have to drag it. I wiped the sweat from my forehead with a hankie and plopped down onto the trunk, wedged my feet to the ground for support, and leaned onto the arched lid. "Jacob, I don't think I can do this. My arms feel like they've been yanked from their sockets, and my legs feel like a glob of Ma's elderberry jam." I puffed an exasperated breath.

He looked up the hill and then back to the chest. "Somehow, Maggie, we need to get this trunk up the hill. Unless we want to leave it behind."

"But it was Ma's. We can't leave it behind."

"It's the only thing of hers that we have left." He wiped a rivulet of sweat from his chin with the cuff of his shirt-sleeve.

I didn't tell him about the brooch. But I did want to keep the trunk also. I stood and wrung my hands together and shook out my arms. "All right, let's do this." I bent and grabbed a handle.

"Let me help you with that."

I dropped the handle, sprung upright, and flung my hands to my chest. "Eliot. I, ah, sorry. You startled me."

"I've been learning from William." His eyes sparkled when he smiled.

"Don't even . . ."

"We've got this, Eliot." Jacob stood on his side of the trunk, folded his arms across his chest, and glared at Eliot.

Eliot straightened, crossed his arms also and stared back at Jacob. "I know how heavy these things are. Doc and I hauled one up this mountain already. I'm sure you don't want your sis to be his next patient."

My stomach flipped a summersault. Why couldn't they get along? "Here, Jacob, why don't you and I take one end and Eliot can take the other. The faster we get this beast up the hill, the sooner we can take a rest."

The metal handles clanked against the side of the chest as we dropped it near our heap of belongings at the top of the rise. The three of us hunched over, hands on knees, and wheezed, like we had just run with Filippides from Marathon to Athens with news of the victorious Greeks.

Eliot stood and stretched his back.

I rose and looked down the hill at the grooves the trunk had carved into the path where we had dragged it. Sissy was slogging up the hill, struggling with a handful of tools. "Jacob, why don't you be a gentleman and help Sissy."

He sneered at me, understanding my motive was to get him out of the way so I could be alone with Eliot, and then turned toward Sissy halfway down the slope. She dropped a shovel. When she bent to pick it up, a pickax slipped from her grip. I knew Jacob couldn't pass on an opportunity to help someone in distress, no matter who she was. He unfolded himself, brushed some dust off his trousers, and scuttled down the hill.

"He doesn't like me very much." Eliot watched Jacob trundle down the slope.

"He'll get over it. Come to think of it, Sissy doesn't like me much either."

"She'll get over it." He smiled.

My heart fluttered. *If only I could rub the dirt off his cheek.* "I wonder . . ." I paused.

"What do you wonder?"

"What if we could get them together?"

"Why would we want to do that?" He furrowed his brow.

"Well, if they were focused on each other, they wouldn't bother us all the time. Would they?"

He grinned. "Maggie, under that beautiful, good-natured facade harbors a devious streak."

I felt my cheeks flush. He said I was beautiful. I wanted to melt.

Chapter 10

*D*ear Diary,

If a horrible thing and a wonderful thing both happen on the same day, are you a bad person if the wonderful thing makes you forget about the horrible thing?

Mrs. McNeil hadn't lied after all. After ascending California Hill two days prior, we had trekked along the grassy plateau wedged between the north and south forks of the Platte. I had silently cursed her for tricking me into believing there was something other than barren prairie in our path. Astounded, I stood at the top of Windlass Hill and gaped at the green expanse of Ash Hollow at the bottom of the steep slope. Clusters of white tops blanketed the floor beneath the smattering of trees. Oxen, mules, and horses grazed in the surrounding meadows. Screeches from playful children floated up the slope with the breeze. I inhaled a deep breath and drank it all in.

Eliot sauntered over and stood beside me. Our arms brushed. I breathed in his presence along with the paradise at the bottom of the hill. He carried the prairie odors of dirt, sweat, and mule dander. I must have been coated with the same stink.

A commotion to my right drew my attention from the idealistic moment. Hooves clattered. Men shouted. Over the din, the captain's voice boomed. "Easy, fellas."

"How did all those wagons get down there?" I raised my hand above my eyes to shield the glare.

"I think we're about to find out."

"Eliot!"

Sissy again. Ruining another perfect moment.

She galloped toward us, breathing heavy from the exertion of her effort to break us apart.

"Doc says you need to get over to the wagons and help. They need all the men, including you, for some reason"—she leered—"to be brakemen."

"Tell Doc I'm on my way." Eliot sighed.

Sissy ran back to the commotion on the ridge.

"Duty calls." He turned to face me. "I'll see you later in paradise."

I smiled as he jogged off toward the jumble of activity.

I marched to our wagon, where Jacob was comforting Jack and Molly. Our possessions were piled nearby, waiting to be hand carried down the grade. My muscles ached just thinking of the arduous task. The jittery mules shook their heads, twitched their ears, and kicked up dust as they pawed the ground. Scout trotted to me and sat near my heels, wisely keeping me between him and the twitchy mules. I bent and scratched behind his ears.

Pa slid his flask into his pocket as he stepped around the wagon. He patted Jack on the rump. The mule stomped his back hoof in protest.

Scout followed me as I stepped a few paces closer to the edge of the ridge, where some men were preparing a wagon to descend the hill. Shouts of "Hup, hup" and "Easy" cut through the cacophony. The wagon jerked and then eased down the lip of the slope. Six oxen led the wagon, and four burly men, heels dug into the earth, clutched on to the back. "Easy, easy!" The shout cut through the din. The wagon picked up speed. Like a volcano spewing ash, a dust cloud mushroomed around the rig and engulfed it as the wagon bobbled like a toboggin down the incline.

Clanking hooves pinged on the loose stones. I turned toward the captain, who guided his horse toward our wagon, his face contorted into a scowl. "Hanley, get your ass over and help with the next wagon."

Pa feigned making an adjustment to Jack's harness. "Got my own wagon to tend to."

"Hanely, you're starting to annoy me to no end. That's not how things work in this company. If you want your wagon to the bottom of the hill in one piece, then I suggest you help the Johnsons with theirs, and then maybe someone will be bighearted enough to help with yours. Trust me, you'll never make it down this hill on your own." The captain glanced at Jacob and nodded. "Looks like things are under control here." He turned his horse and trotted toward the commotion near the Johnson wagon.

Pa uttered a string of profanities, spat a stream of tobacco slurry, and stomped after the captain.

I pressed through a group of women who were watching the descent, to join Mrs. McNeil. "Why don't they hoist them down with ropes and chains? That's what Jacob thought they were going to do."

"I don't know, Margaret. Perhaps the captain thought this would be quicker. I think the chains would be safer though."

"If it were me, I would choose safer." I raised my hand to my forehead to shield my eyes from the glare as I gazed into the oasis at the bottom of the hill.

"I agree with you. Unfortunately, we don't get to make the decisions."

"Where's Mr. McNeil?"

"Our wagon was one of the first to descend. He's down there somewhere." She swept her hand in a wide motion over the valley below us. "After he gets the team settled, he'll climb back up to help other wagons. You know Charles, always the first in line to assist when needed." Unlike Pa. The unspoken dig burrowed in the uncurrent of her tone. "Then we need to lug all our belongings down the hill."

"Don't remind me." I frowned. "I wonder how many times we're going to have to do this."

"I imagine this is just the start of many before we reach Oregon."

"Or California."

I turned my attention to the next wagon preparing to descend.

"Looks like we're up." Mrs. Johnson, who stood on the other side of Mrs. McNeil, wrung her hands. "Benjamin has fretted about this for the last two days."

"It'll be fine," Mrs. McNeil reassured her. "Half our train has already made it without incident. The men know what they're doing. Think instead about sitting in the shade under one of those trees, sipping a nice cold cup of clear water." She sighed in anticipation.

Someone shouted, "Giddup. Giddup. Here we go." The Johnsons' wagon, led by six sturdy oxen, started down the hill. The white canvas swayed as the wheels lumbered over rocks and clods. The quartet of brakemen, Pa on the flank, clasped either the wagon box or a rope looped through the undercarriage. The wagon picked up speed as the grade steepened. Shouts were swallowed by the cacophony and dust cloud. The wagon tongue pressed into the oxen. The brakemen burrowed their heels into the earth as the wagon plunged down the incline. Their slanted bodies gyrated against the pull of the wagon, like the prairie grasses bowed in the wind. Pa stumbled and rolled away from the melee. The wagon box plowed into the oxen, and the wagon flipped on its side.

A woman screamed.

Mrs. McNeil gasped and flung her hand to her mouth.

The box separated from the bolsters. The wagon box, bolsters, and axle tree tumbled down the hill, dragging the oxen with it. A hat flung into the air. A twisted body was wedged in a wheel spoke, scissor kicking. The axle tree crashed onto the crushed canvas top. The three pieces smashed into a tree at the bottom of the hill, one after another, and splinted like a tumbled pile of pickup sticks scattered on the floor.

"Benjamin!" Mrs. Johnson screamed. Mrs. McNeil and Mrs. May restrained her.

Pa rose and brushed dust from his trousers, scoured the ground around his feet, and lifted his hat from a nearby bush, where it had been snagged, seemingly as unruffled as if he'd bent over to pick up a stone to skip across a placid pond. He sauntered down the hill. The other two men leaped from the ground and raced to the destroyed wagon.

"Benjamin! NO!" Mrs. Johnson wrenched free of the grasps of the women who tried to restrain her and flew down the hill. "Benjamin!" She tripped and fell forward and rolled partway down the slope before getting trapped in some brush. She scrambled to her feet, clutched a wad of her skirt in her hand, and continued down the grade. The two men who were inspecting the wreckage intervened and carried her away from the carnage.

I couldn't shake the vision of the Johnson wagon splintering to pieces as Jacob and I hauled our belongings down the steep slope. Mr. Johnson was such a good-hearted man. And Mrs. Johnson, a widow at such a young age. I whispered a plea to Ma to help welcome Mr. Johnson to heaven.

The sun glided into the horizon when Jacob and I dragged the trunk to camp and finished repacking the wagon. Exhausted, I snatched an empty bucket and a washrag and headed to the nearby stream. I fantasized about stripping naked and letting the cool water wash the filth from my body. The downside of paradise—too crowded. I overheard some women plotting about taking turns bathing while the others would hold a screen of skirts and blankets for privacy. I planned on joining them.

I knelt in the grass on the bank of the stream and scrubbed my face with the wet cloth. Dirt bled into the clear water as I submerged the rag and wrung it out. I wished that I had a looking glass to see if my face were still bathed in a layer of prairie dust. My cheeks might never be clean again.

"Mind if I share your little patch of paradise?"

I peered up at Eliot's grimy face gazing down at me. I felt a blush seep into my cheeks when he smiled. Maybe it would be better if my face remained dirty.

He knelt next to me, leaned over the stream, cupped his hands in the water, and splashed it onto his face. Rust-colored liquid streamed through his fingers and ran down his wrists.

"Here"—I handed him my washrag—"this might work better."

"Thanks." He winked and proceeded to scrub the muck from his cheeks.

He rinsed and wrung out the rag and handed it back to me. "Maggie, you saved the day for me again."

I wanted to hand it back and tell him to wash his neck and ears also. "Your wagon must have made it down the hill without any mishaps?" I tried to smother the image of the Johnson wagon shattering to pieces. "Poor Mr. Johnson." Fingers of guilt strangled my heart. Would Mr. Johnson still be breathing if Pa hadn't let go? Did anyone else notice? I tucked my chin into my chest and stared into the meandering stream, wishing its waters would wash away my shame and bring Mr. Johnson back.

"I wonder what Mrs. Johnson is going to do now, without a husband or a wagon." He lifted his hat and threaded his fingers though his hair. "Fortunately, we made it safe and sound. Although not without some collateral damage." He dropped the hat back to his head and opened his hand. A raw gash burned across his palm. "Darn rope cut right through my glove."

"You should get that cleaned up." I rewet my wash rag. He held his hand out, palm up, and I scrubbed the wound.

"Ouch!"

I pulled the cloth away. "Sorry. Don't be such a baby."

He submerged the injured hand into the creek. "I'm the one who should be sorry. It's not that bad of a wound."

"Sometimes it's the small ones that hurt the most. You should ask your pa, uh, I mean, Doc Sam for some balm to put on it."

"Yes, Doctor. I'll do my best to get the prescription filled." He smirked.

I wagged a finger in front of his nose. "Don't make fun of me. I never should have told you I wanted to be a doctor."

"Maggie, I would never make fun of you. And if you want to be a doctor, I will support you all the way."

"Really?" I quirked my eyebrows.

"Yeah, really. Why wouldn't I?"

"Because I'm a girl and girls can't be doctors."

"Well, I don't see why you couldn't be a doctor."

I lowered my head. "After what I saw that day I rode with Doc Sam, I don't want to be a doctor anymore."

"Then you'll be the most beloved schoolmarm in California."

I looked up expecting to see a taunting smirk on his face, but his expression was as serious as a stone. I smiled, recalling the children's relief when we reached the passage in *Jane Eyre* where Brocklehurst was removed from

Lowood. Each gasp or sigh reinforced my desire to become a schoolmarm above all else.

Giggling voices interrupted our private moment—again. Two young women rustled through the brush and approached the stream. "Oh, so sorry," one of them said. "We'll find another spot to wash up."

"Uh, no. It's okay. We're just getting some water and heading back to camp. The stream is all yours." Why had I offered up our private sanctuary?

We stood. Eliot reached for the bucket with his uninjured hand and filled it with stream water.

"I've never seen so many wild roses in one place." We walked along the narrow path through the thick brush toward our camp. I leaned into a bush and inhaled the sweet aroma of the fragrant pink flowers.

Eliot reached his hand over my shoulder to pick one. "Ooh," he cried and retracted his hand.

"A beautiful rose has to protect itself with nasty thorns." I smiled.

"Ah, but a beautiful girl like you should have a beautiful flower." He set down the bucket and slid his hand into the bush and plucked a rose off the vine. He twirled the blossom between his thumb and forefinger by the short stem. Then he slid the flower into my hair above my ear. "Perfect."

He stepped closer. He fingered a tendril of wet hair that had escaped from my bonnet and slid it from my cheek. I gazed into his aqua-marine eyes. My heart thundered. My belly felt like it was filled with a million baby sparrows happily fluttering their tiny wings. He reached his injured hand around the small of my back and pulled me closer.

Salt, sweat, and prairie wafted on his breath. His lips were soft when they touched mine. I closed my eyes and absorbed his essence.

"Eliot. Eliot, where are you?"

We parted in a flash as Sissy stomped through the brush toward us.

"Sissy, what do you want now?"

"Mama needs you back at camp."

Urgh!

Chapter 11

Dear Diary,

The fluttering baby sparrow wings frolicked in my belly as I lay on my tarp and stared into the dark. I'd pressed Eliot's rose between two blank pages in my diary and slid the book under a rolled-up blanket that served as my pillow. With my quilt pulled under my chin and arms folded across my chest, I gazed at the stars and imagined Eliot gazing at the same stars and thinking of me. I fantasized about the road ahead. Me and Eliot walking side by side, holding hands. Stopping for a kiss. Being alone after dark. Aah.

In stark contrast to the terrain that we had traveled the past hundred miles or so, Ash Hollow was pioneer heaven. Under the canopy of ash trees that flourished along the creek and springs, thick brush bursting with roses, jasmine, currants, and other lush flora sprouted in abundance. The captain informed us that we would stay an extra day so the livestock could rest, the men could make wagon repairs, and Mr. Johnson could have a proper burial. I wondered how they would ever repair the Johnson wagon. The extra time meant that I'd spend the day cooking and mending and washing and, ugh!—all the work that needed *done while Pa got his rest. But somehow I'd find the time to sneak off with Eliot.*

After lunch Pa lay stretched out in the shade, his hat tilted over his eyes, snoring. The laundry hung on a line stretched between the wagon and a tree. The lunch dishes were washed and stowed. The mending could wait until later. Jacob was off helping to rebuild the Johnson wagon. I brushed and braided my hair and pinned it into a low bun at the nape of my neck, washed my face, pinched my cheeks to add some color, like I'd seen some of the ladies back home do, and popped a sprig of mint into my mouth to freshen my breath. I grabbed *Jane Eyre* and tucked it under my arm. "Wake up, Scout—we're going for a walk."

The dog sprang to his feet. I glanced over my shoulder to make sure Pa hadn't stirred. "Now, Scout"—I pressed my finger against my lips and whispered to the mutt—"we need to be coy. Don't let on that our objective is to find Eliot. If anyone asks, we're just looking for a shady spot by the stream to read. Got it?"

The pooch lifted his floppy ears, cocked his head, and wagged his tail.

"Good. Let's go."

"Good afternoon, Margaret." Mrs. McNeil looked up from the dress she was mending as we passed by her campsite. "Would you care to join me for a cup of tea?"

"Eh, thank you for the offer, Mrs. McNeil. Maybe later. Scout and I are taking a walk."

"Well, the pot will be warm if you change your mind. Have an enjoyable walk, and I hope you find who you're looking for." She tipped her head in a knowing nod.

"I told you not to let on what our mission is," I whispered to Scout when we were past the McNeils' camp.

The pooch slid his tail between his legs and peered up at me with his big brown eyes.

We paused when I spotted the Adkins' goats nibbling on the leaves of a jasmine bush near their shaded wagon.

"Boo!"

I almost dropped the book. "William. How many times have I told you not to sneak up and scare me like that."

He shoved his hands into his pockets and jutted his lower lip. "Sorry."

"That's okay. Tell your ma I'll be back later to milk her goats."

He eyed the book snuggled under my arm. "But you're going to read to us first, right?"

"Uh . . ."

William's brothers, Adam and Joshua, raced toward us. The younger boy, Joshua, clapped his miniature hands as he stumbled through the dirt. "Maggie read. Maggie read."

My plan had been thwarted. How could I refuse those sweet, dirty faces? "Okay, but just one chapter today."

I followed the boys to their wagon, and we settled into a circle on the ground around Scout, who had already made himself comfortable. Before I had the book open, the boys scooched around to make room for Suzie, who seemed to emerge from the ether. Mrs. Adkins dragged an overturned washtub from behind the wagon, eased onto it, and picked up a hand loom and began weaving. This is the first time Mrs. Adkins had joined us since her husband had wrestled her dead child from her arms and placed the little body in the tiny coffin. Her grief hovered over her like a warped halo.

I eased onto the ground and rubbed a spec of sadness from my eyes. "William, I seem to have some dust in my eyes. Could you start us off by reading the first few sentences until my vision clears?" I held the book out to him.

He lowered his eyes. "Uh, I don't know my letters."

"Oh. Suzie, how about you start us off then?"

Suzie plopped her chin in her hands and studied the dirt. Apparently she couldn't read either. I looked at Mrs. Adkins, who focused on her hands spinning around the loom. No wonder she hadn't taught William to read.

I set the book in my lap. "I have an idea. How about before I start to read, I teach you the alphabet. That way we can discover Jane Eyre's fate together."

I heard a shuffle and noticed Tommy hovering near the Adkins' wagon. "Tommy, could you bring me a stick from that kindling pile over there?" I tilted my head toward a heap of twigs near the fire pit.

Tommy brought the twig and lingered as I sketched an "A" in the dirt. "Can everyone say 'apple'?"

I clasped my hands to my ears as the kids shouted the word in unison. "Very good. The word apple starts with the letter 'A.'"

After working through the letter "G," the children giggling over each other's goat imitations, and reading a chapter of *Jane Eyre*, I closed the book. "Enough for today. Scout and I are going to finish our walk."

The little ones sprang to their feet and scattered. I stood and brushed dust from my skirt. "Let's go Scout." The rested pooch sprang to his feet and wagged his tail.

William followed me for a few paces. "You're not going to find him."

"I'm not going to find who?" I squinted at the boy.

"Your boyfriend."

"What boyfriend?"

"Your boyfriend, Eliot."

"What makes you think he's my boyfriend?" I adjusted a hairpin on my bun. "And why do you say I'm not going to find him?"

"Everybody knows he's your boyfriend." He shrugged. "You can't look at each other without goo-goo eyes."

"William, you're too young to know about such things. And what are goo-goo eyes anyway?"

"Well, goo-goo eyes left this morning, so you won't find him."

"What do you mean he left?" My hand flew to my chest.

"The people who joined us at Fort Kearney. They left early this morning with the other train."

"Are you sure?"

"They were camped over there." He aimed his finger to his left. "See, they're gone. Except some new people have been taking up their spots."

My gut felt like it had been crushed by a wagon wheel. My limbs quivered, and tears pricked the back of my eyes. I sniffed. "Come on, Scout. Let's finish our walk."

A hazy numbness enveloped me as I walked with Jacob next to the clomping mules as our train snaked along the trail out of Ash Hollow the following morning. Pa loosely held the reins as he drove the team, his hat tilted over his droopy eyes, his shotgun resting on the perch beside him. Whenever I peeked over my shoulder to check on him, I couldn't discern whether his shaded eyes were open or closed. A good child would have joined him to ensure he stayed alert. Neither Jacob nor I felt compelled to do so. Perhaps Jacob hadn't noticed. My world had been shattered. I hardly cared. I mindlessly put one foot in front of the other, like a wooden toy soldier blindly marching into a futile battle. Mrs. McNeil was right—I should have been wary of Eliot. He didn't even have the courtesy to say goodbye! I wiped some moisture from my eyes with the back of my hand. I couldn't even blame the tears on the dust.

At least there was something to see besides fog-like grime billowing on the horizon. The copses of trees provided pockets of welcome shade, the fragrant roses sweetened the air, and lush green hills cast long shadows over the sandy valley. But the pleasant scenery was eclipsed by my solemn mood. I mindlessly snacked on some wild strawberries I had picked the previous afternoon while walking with Scout. I had planned on sharing them with Eliot. At least I discovered he wasn't worthy of my generosity before I parted with the sweet treats.

Molly nuzzled my pouch. "Sorry, girl. I love you, but you're not getting any of these tiny treasures." I popped another berry into my mouth and pouted.

I sidled closer to Jacob as the trail jagged around some bends and wove through an Indian camp. A splattering of coned tepees—like mini volcanoes—reached skyward, ashes smoldered in unattended firepits, and bored horses pawed the dirt behind a rope fence. Some children chased each other in circles squealing with delight. Two women sat cross-legged in front of a tepee flap, mending. I admired the intricate beadwork that adorned their deerskin dresses. I didn't see any men.

"Sioux," Jacob said, as if that would allay my fear. "They won't bother us if we leave them alone."

"How do you know that?"

"The captain negotiated our passage. I don't know what he traded, but we should be safe so long as nobody does anything stupid."

I snuck a peek at Pa and cringed.

Chapter 12

Dear Diary,

My mood has been as grimy as the murky North Platte that we've been following since leaving Ash Hollow days ago—a wide, slimy mass of sludge, sometimes as placid as a giant mud puddle, and other times hunks of driftwood tumbled in the swift current in a race to reach the Missouri. The ash and cottonwood trees that lined the muddy banks shimmered in the morning breeze, a welcome relief from the weeks of slogging under the scorching sun on the monotonous empty prairie. But the reprieve was short-lived.

Late morning I watched Mrs. McNeil tromp near her wagon ahead of us. I'd been avoiding her, afraid she would ask me about Eliot. Jacob must have noticed that Eliot and his family were no longer traveling with our caravan. He was surprisingly mum about it. Although he had never been a windbag, like Mr. Jones used to call me, he'd been even more reserved than his normal quiet self. It was not like him to forgo an opportunity to badger me.

The boredom was more than I could take. I inhaled a deep breath. Scout and I scuttled up to walk with Mrs. McNeil.

"Good morning, Margaret," she greeted me in her normal upbeat tone.

"Good morning, Mrs. McNeil. How come you're always so chirpy?" I didn't know why I always asked that.

"Margaret, the Lord has provided us with another beautiful day. The sun is shining, the birds are singing, the wind is calm for a change, our bellies are sated from a hearty breakfast, and we're a day closer to Oregon, and California than we were yesterday."

Like most mornings after her upbeat greeting, I internally rephrased each of her comments to reflect my psyche. It was hotter than buffalo dung sizzling in the fire; the chorus of singing birds was swallowed by the clanking hooves, creaky wagons, and livestock cackles; and the unappetizing breakfast of charred, gooey biscuits and cold bacon sat like rocks in my stomach. And the boy of my dreams had abandoned me. But I didn't say any of that to Mrs. McNeil. She would just try to cheer me up. I was content to wallow in my sorrow.

"But we do need to be careful."

"Why?" I smashed a mosquito on the side of my neck.

"Someone left a message beside the trail, alerting us to alkali in the water. Some livestock drank it and died."

"Oh dear. It's a good thing they left a note."

"The warning was carved into a buffalo scull. Wasn't that clever? It's a good thing it didn't get crushed or dragged off. The good Lord is watching out for us. Be sure to keep your dog away from the water."

"Scout, no swimming, okay, boy?" The mutt prancing at my heels looked up at me and barked.

Ethan trotted his horse against the current of wagons toward us, waving something above his head.

"A courtesy check again? Didn't he already come by this morning?" The last thing I needed was for Ethan to harass me about Eliot's abandonment. I'd never be able to live that down.

Ethen reined in his palomino. "Maggie Hanley, Maggie Hanley."

Was he going to broadcast my misery to the whole caravan?

"Is there a Maggie amongst us?" He glared down at me as if he were a king atop his throne, and I a measly peasant about to be sacrificed. "Oh, of course. You must be the infamous Maggie Hanley, sister of Jacob."

"What do you want, Ethan?" I crossed my arms and drummed my elbows and ignored Ma's little voice nagging me to be polite. I was in no mood.

"Oh yes, of course. Special delivery for one Maggie Hanley." He waved a piece of paper in an arc above his head.

"What are you talking about?"

"Ethan," Mrs. McNeil interrupted, "if you have something for Margaret, why don't you be a gentleman and deliver it to her."

"Of course, Mrs. McNeil." He leaned over the neck of his horse and lowered his hand that clutched a piece of paper just beyond my reach.

I hopped and tried to snatch it from his grasp.

He jerked his arm back. "Maybe I should read it for you." He started to unfold the page.

"Ethan, I believe that Margaret can read it herself."

I had no doubt that Ethan had already read the note.

"Of course, Mrs. McNeil. Not everybody on this train knows how to read. I was only trying to help." He handed the note to Mrs. McNeil.

"You've helped plenty by delivering the message. It looks like you have some additional deliveries to make." She nodded to the crumpled papers clutched in his other hand.

"Have a good day, ma'am." He lifted his index finger to his hat and spurred his mare.

Mrs. McNeil handed me the paper and resumed walking. I delayed a few steps so that I could read the note in private. The little birdies slapped around in my stomach again, but their wings flapped like a murder of angry crows. I inhaled a deep breath and braced myself for heartbreaking news and unfolded the note. The writing was sloppy, and the crumpled page smudged.

Dear Maggie, I hope you got my last note. In case you didn't, I'll tell you again. I'm sorry I couldn't tell you goodbye before we left Ash Hollow. Doc didn't tell me we were leaving until we were pulling out. I'll spare you the details, but I couldn't break away to find you. I hope you'll forgive me. I'll find you, even if it means going to Caleforna. If you'll have me, we can continue the discussion we were having by the rose bush. Yours, E.

Of course I'll have you, Eliot! I hugged the letter to my chest and skipped up to join Mrs. McNeil. "You are right, Mrs. McNeil. It is a lovely day today."

"I take it the note was from Eliot."

"He didn't desert me after all."

"Desert you?"

"He left ahead of us to join their original train without letting me know. I assumed he didn't tell me on purpose. Turns out, he didn't know he was leaving either."

"Ah, so that is why you've been moping around like you lost a new puppy."

I reached down and patted Scout on the head. "Scout, he didn't forsake me."

⸻◆⸻

Jacob and I muddled though the erratic shifting sand that the trail morphed into later that afternoon. I wabbled when my foot sank into a quicksand-like depression. Jacob clasped my elbow. "Careful."

"Thanks. Somebody is going to twist an ankle wading through this stuff. I just hope it's not one of our mules."

Jack snorted in agreement.

"I heard about your love note."

I hadn't planned on telling Jacob about the message. And I definitely wasn't going to tell him about the flower or the kiss. Thanks to Ethan, everyone in our company must have known about Eliot's note—which I had no doubt he'd read and likely embellished in the retelling. "No big deal. It was just a note. He just let me know that he and Sissy are okay." I hugged my arms around my chest and smiled at the memory. If I were alone, I would have danced a jig. *He didn't desert me after all!*

"Nobody else got notes."

"There were other notes. Ethan had a fistful of them."

"Okay, there were other notes. There was a note about the alkali water, a note for the captain about a washout ahead and a detour route, and someone left a note because they were excited about some giant rocks ahead of us. But you got the only love letter."

"Are you jealous I got a private note?" I patted my apron, over the pouch with Ma's brooch, where I had stashed the note.

"What! That's crazy. Why would I be jealous about that jerk?"

"Just because you don't like him doesn't mean he's a jerk."

"He's a mammoth jerk." He spread his arms out. "He's arrogant, he's selfish, and he has no respect for animals."

I threaded my fingers and nestled them under my chin. "He has the most exquisite aquamarine eyes and a heart-stopping smile. He's sweet, considerate, and funny. And when I'm with him"—I sucked in a breath as the awareness jolted me like one of Pa's smacks across the cheek—"I don't think about Ma so much." I whispered that last part.

My revelation was gut wrenching. Was I being unfaithful to Ma's memory, that Eliot's presence could patch the fissure her absence had chiseled into my heart? Jacob must have thought so, because his lips sealed tight, as if my confession were a vise that clamped them shut.

The trail wound around some boulders and up a rise. "Easy, boy," Jacob said when Jack stumbled on the uneven terrain. The mule snorted.

"What do you think about Sissy?" I asked after we both had ample time to commiserate over our late mother.

"What do you mean?"

I laced my fingers in front of my chest. "What do you think I mean? She's a girl. You're a boy. Do you like her?"

"That obnoxious twit?"

"Jacob, that's not a very nice thing to say." My hands flung to my hips.

"Well, you asked me what I thought." He shrugged.

"Okay, so she can be annoying at times. Do you think she's pretty?"

"I haven't noticed."

"You're a boy. You're supposed to notice things like that." I snatched a sideways glance, but his eyes concentrated on his footing. "Maybe you and Sissy can join me and Eliot on a date sometime. Then you could take the opportunity to notice."

I watched him study his footsteps. Then I looked down to his feet. His boots and lower trouser legs were dusted in the silty beige sand that we slogged through. His trousers that had dragged on the ground when we'd left Missouri had risen to his ankles. The tip of his big toe snuck through the splintered seam in the toe box of his boot. I was going to have to darn his socks again.

"I don't think so. Have you forgotten we're not traveling with them anymore?"

I sighed. I could only hope we'd catch up. Or that he'd be delayed. I gazed at the cloudless sky and inhaled the memory of our kiss. Would Eliot really seek me out in California like he said in his note? And then what? Marry him and give up my dream to be a schoolmarm? Although he said he would support my desire, a married woman saddled with children and a household to keep would not be able, or allowed, to be a schoolmarm. The light in the children's eyes when they'd drawn letters in the dirt with sticks back at Ash Hollow ignited a fire in my core to want to teach them more than their ABCs. How could I ever choose?

Jacob returned to the wagon to relieve Pa. Scout and I scampered up to bother Mrs. McNeil again. Did we bother her, or did she welcome the company? It was hard to tell, since she was always so polite and so composed. Ma would have approved of her. Grandmother also. I wondered if Ma had colluded with the angels in heaven to convince God to cause the McNeils' delay back in Missouri and insert them into our lives. My legs felt like porridge as I lifted my aching feet through the dense sand. Every few steps required an extra tug, like I needed to extricate it from a sucking quagmire.

"Look up ahead." Mrs. McNeil aimed her finger toward the horizon.

I squinted through the dusty haze. "Are those mountains?" Two colossal stone masses towered in the distance, like they had bubbled up from the center of the earth to pierce the monotony of the grassy expanse.

"According to Charles's guidebook, the Rockies are still weeks away, although those must be the mountains that were mentioned in the note from the train ahead of us."

Ethan rode along the caravan, waving the signal to circle the wagons. "It looks like we're stopping for the night."

Thank goodness, as my wobbly legs needed a break. "Maybe we can noon in the shadow of those monoliths tomorrow."

Chapter 13

Dear Diary,

The mammoth rocks taunted us like a mirage in a scorching desert. With each haggard step forward we took, it seemed like the boulders receded a leap, mocking us, making us believe we weren't making any progress at all. That the Eden we were striving to reach would never be within our grasp.

The aspens that had shadowed the riverbank were replaced by spindly bitterbrush that snagged my dress and scratched my hands as the trail veered from the river earlier that morning—only a couple of miles, but it might as well have been a hundred. The air was hot and dry. Sparse clumps of wilted grass limped through cracks in the parched earth, depriving the livestock of needed nourishment. Shade was scarce. So was fresh water.

Jacob and I led the team to a flat spot with a tuft of trampled grass for the mules to munch on while we nooned. Within seconds they started pawing the earth, trying to excavate a feast of tasty treats. They would be disappointed. I was disappointed. Cold bacon and dry biscuits again. Pa must have found someone who could rustle up better grub, because he'd been scarce lately.

Not that I was complaining. A heaviness vaporized from my shoulders when he was gone, like pressure seeping from a stirring geyser. But in his presence, the steam vent remained plugged, and the pressure would build, forcing me to raise my guard, since the slightest misstep would blow the cap off his boiling cauldron.

Jacob leaned against a boulder, untangling a harness while I scrubbed the lunch dishes with dirt so as not to spare a drop of precious water. Snorting and rustling oxen from a nearby rig interrupted my work. "What are the Ericksons doing?" Mr. Erickson had unyoked two emaciated oxen from his eight-head team and led them away from the camp.

Jacob's eyes followed my gaze. "I don't know, but it can't be good."

Two shots splintered the air. I shuddered. Jacob dropped to his knees and bowed his head. Mr. Erickson returned to camp, head down, his weapon held limply in his hand, barrel sagging.

Back on the road, we plodded past a cast-iron stove, a table, a rocking chair, and a trunk not unlike Ma's—no doubt possessions jettisoned from the Ericksons' wagon.

Later that afternoon, Jacob and I hiked by the team in silence. Talking took too much energy, especially late in the day, when we were hot, tired, and thirsty. I stole a glance at him. His gaze probed the horizon. I still pondered his moroseness. He never was a chatterbox like me. Ma had always called me a chatterbox. To Mr. Jones, I was a windbag. To Ma, I was a chatterbox. And to Pa, I was a nuisance—except when he wanted something. Then I became a bungling servant. Ma had said that once I learned the word "Ma," the words had spewed constantly from my mouth. But Jacob and I had always been gabby when we were alone. Now it seemed like I had to yank the words through his teeth. He had become more introspective, even gloomy. But we'd all been changed by this journey. Maybe it was just a phase.

I daydreamed about lounging in the shade at the base of one of the two towering structures we had finally reached and were about to pass to the north of, when Ethan clomped up on his palomino. "Maggie Hanley, Maggie Hanley. Another delivery for Maggie Hanley." He reined in and waved a crumpled paper in front of his face. His fox eyes squinting, as if to pounce, and shark teeth keen to snap off my head.

"Hi, Ethan." Jacob shielded his eyes from the sun with his hand, tilted his head, and smiled at the letter bearer. "Thanks for bringing the note. I know Maggie appreciates it." I glared at my brother as he took a step toward Ethan's mount and reached out his hand. "I'll take it for her."

"I don't know, Jacob. Being postmaster is a big responsibility. How do I know the important message will reach the intended recipient."

"Since this is not an official post and you're not a government official, I don't think you'll be tossed in jail over it."

Was he serious? "Ethan, I can vouch that Jacob will deliver the note to the proper addressee, so please give it to him."

Ethan handed Jacob the note. "You better read it first. Make sure the gentleman's intentions are honorable. She looks like she needs a man to protect her from evil desert predators." He sneered at me, then returned his gaze to Jacob. "And, Jacob, whenever you want to go shootin', let me know." He lifted his forefinger to his hat and urged his horse into a gallop.

I snatched the paper from Jacob's hand while he watched Ethan's bobbling figure gallop into the dust.

Dear Maggie, I hope you are well. Courthouse Rock and Jail Rock are amazing. I felt like a mouse standing beneath the towering peaks. I climbed to the top of Courthouse Rock and could almost see clear back to Indiana. I looked for you, but all I could see were white tops and dust. After I got down, I chiseled our names in the rock. Eliot and Maggie, side by side forever. I hope you can take the side trip to see my handiwork up close. Looking forward to when we can be side by side for real again! E.

"Jacob, it looks like we're about to stop for the night. Let's go see Courthouse Rock. We can make it there and back before Pa even knows were gone."

"Maggie, it's two miles each way. Once we get camp set up and supper, it will be too late. We'd never get there before dark, let alone there and back."

"Hmph!"

Chapter 14

Dear Diary,

Fort Laramie at last! Although the official name is still Fort John. I heard that the compound was recently acquired by the military and the name will officially change to Fort Laramie, which is what everyone already calls it. Regardless, what chaos. A bustling white-top city surrounded the fort. A crowded and dirty city. Heaps of scuttled belongings littered the ground. Women pilfered through piles of discarded clothes, furniture, utensils, and other odds and ends in search of treasures. Children pried siding from abandoned wagons and hauled them to their campsites for firewood. A pleasant relief from buffalo chips! A sprawling Indian village sprouted into the scrub on the north side of the river. Emigrants grumbled that the possessions they had hauled from Missouri to sell at the fort were not needed or the price offered was offensively low. But all that ebbed into a background nuisance when I followed Pa to the trading post shortly after our arrival.

"Eliot!"

Eliot dropped the burlap bag he carried when I raced up to him and flung my arms around his neck. He smothered me in a tight embrace, hoisted me off the ground, and twirled in a circle.

Pa stomped up to us. "Get your hands off my daughter!"

My feet still hovered over the ground when Pa's fist thrust into Eliot's jaw. Startled and off balance, Eliot tripped over his heel and tumbled to the dirt. He shook the shock from his head and dragged himself onto his knees. He wobbled halfway to his feet only to be flattened by Pa's knuckle punch to his eye.

"Pa, NO!" I shouted and clasped his elbow when he wound up his fist for another blow.

He flung me to the ground like a sack of oats.

Doc Sam and Mr. McNeil rushed over. They each grabbed one of Pa's arms.

"Easy, Elijah." Doc Sam wrestled Pa's arm with two hands. "He wasn't doing any harm."

"She's my property and ain't nobody gonna touch her."

I crawled onto my hands and knees and wobbled to my feet, mouth agape.

"Whoa." Doc Sam tightened his grip on Pa's forearm as Pa tried to wrestle his limb free. "Appears to me she's an independent young lady with a mind of her own."

Pa spat a stream of slimy chaw at Eliot's feet. "Her mind is me and my needs. Not gallivanting with some misfit." He glared at Eliot. "If I see you within a mile of Maggie, your pa's goin' to have a grave to dig."

Eliot stared at Pa, gaping.

"Get your ass out of my sight."

Eliot looked too stunned to move.

"NOW!" Pa wrenched his arm free of Doc Sam's grip.

Eliot spun and disappeared into the sea of wagons.

The crowd that had gathered around the commotion dissipated, murmuring as they shuffled into the hazy dusk. My limbs quivered, and I tried to snuff out the tears that threatened to burst from behind my eyes. I would not cry in front of Pa. But underneath the hurt and shame, my heart fluttered. Eliot was happy to see me.

I followed Pa to the Post Trading Store, which also held the post office. I spied the pile of letters stuffed into a slot behind the counter. Correspondence that had been carried by travelers for miles with news to be sent back to family and friends in the States. I debated whether to pen a letter to my grandmother informing her of our whereabouts. Would she care? Did I care? I wouldn't write a letter. Maybe when we got to California.

Pa sauntered toward a barrel-shaped man stocking a shelf behind a counter. "Tobacco, whiskey, and . . ." Pa turned toward me. "What else do we need?"

"Salt, lard, and sugar. And bacon," I added as an afterthought. I couldn't remember how much bacon we had left. My eyes paused on a jar of hard candy on the counter. A rainbow of sweet morsels glistened like gems. Edible gems. Calling me. Waiting to rest on my tongue, the flavor on the verge of bursting into an array of sugary sensations about to trickle down my throat. I thought of the children. If I had a nickel, I would have purchased treats to reward them for when they recited the complete alphabet. We were up to the letter "P," so it should be soon. I frowned and turned from the container.

"Fifteen dollars, thirty-five cents." The shopkeeper slapped a tin of bacon on the counter.

"What!" Pa's eyebrows shot up to his forehead. "You must be mistaken."

"Fifteen thirty-five. You hard of hearing?"

"That's five times what it would cost in St. Joe."

"Then why don't you just mosey on back to St. Joe and stock up." He lifted his eyes over Pa's shoulder. "Next."

We left without the bacon and the sugar.

By the light of crackling campfires, I scrounged through heaps of travelers' cast-offs searching for treasures that Pa was either too stingy or too broke to purchase at the post. I lugged a near-empty sack of sugar to our wagon and headed back into the shadows to continue plundering.

Someone nearby plucked a banjo. "Oh! Susanna." I hummed along as I combed through a mess of discarded garments, looking for a dress and a pair of shoes that might fit me. The pile was mostly men's and children's clothes. I set aside two shirts and a pair of trousers for Jacob. I thrust my hand back into the heap. A pair of boots. I held them out at arm's length, utilizing the glow of a nearby fire to assess their worth. "Another find for Jacob," I mumbled under my breath. The pile tumbled into the gap where the boots had been revealing the spine of a tattered book. I shimmied the book from the pile, rubbed dirt from the cover, held it up to the fire's glow and squinted at the marred jacket. *iss F mily Robin.* Huh? I set it next to the boots. I would need another book to read to the children once we finished *Jane Eyre.* At the last reading, the children, as well as Mrs. Adkins and Mrs. May, were bewildered by the mysterious Mr. Rochester.

"Psst."

I jumped at the whisper, like I had been caught red handed in a bank heist.

"Psst. Maggie."

I turned toward the figure crouched in the shadow of a nearby wagon. "Eliot?"

"Shh." He lifted a finger to his lips. "Where's your pa?"

"Probably off playing cards somewhere." *And probably losing the rest of his money.* "I think it's safe for you to come out."

He shuffled over and knelt beside me. "Doing a little shopping?"

"I can't believe that people are just throwing all this stuff away."

"Our captain instructed us to only carry what we absolutely need. We're only a third of the way to Oregon, the easiest third."

"You mean it gets harder?" My eyes widened.

"Yep. And not just a little." He glanced at the items I had set aside. "Good idea to pick up some extra boots. You're likely going to need them."

"I wish I could find some that fit me. These are for Jacob. He's growing right out of the ones he has. Plus, they're also falling apart. He's patched them up with scraps of leather and tar. Doesn't work."

"You're a good sister. Sissy wouldn't care a hooter about my boots."

He stood and extended a hand to help me up.

I clasped his hand, and he pulled me from the ground. We stood facing each other, inches apart. The glow from a flickering campfire shimmied off his cheek as he gazed into my eyes. I felt as if he were peering into my soul. I thought he might kiss me. Instead, he bent and picked up the boots and garments. "I'll help you carry these back to your wagon."

I snatched up the book. I balanced it in my hand to try to judge its weight. The rational voice in my head warned that it was an unnecessary burden to add to our load. But then, the scale shifted toward the children's hunger for another story once we closed the cover on *Jane Eyre.*

I pondered the discarded items as we wove back to our camp. "I wonder why someone would throw out perfectly good clothes and boots. You told me that everyone should lighten their loads, but you would think that whoever they belonged to would need them."

"Well"—he answered slowly—"it's possible that the feet the boots belonged to are buried in a grave along the trail."

"We did pass a lot of graves." I had whispered to Ma to help God and the angels protect the souls of each lifeless occupant.

"It's unlikely the owner will need them now."

"Let's not tell Jacab that theory. Maybe he'll think the owner just outgrew them, like he outgrew his."

Jacob had a crackling fire blazing when we reached our camp. Scout lay curled up in a ball, sleeping next to a wheel. The pooch raised his head, opened one eye to acknowledge our presence, then lowered his chin into his paws and resumed his nap. Some watchdog. Jacob tossed a slab of wood, which must have been a piece of an abandoned wagon, into the fire. The plank hissed and crackled as the flames leaped around it. The brightness danced across Eliot's face, magnifying the swollen eye and bruised jaw.

"Wow, Pa really dealt you a good blow." Jacob squinted at Eliot. "You're pretty brave to come around here."

"It'll take more than a lump on the chin to keep me away from Maggie." He handed me the garments.

I listened to them talk while I carried the clothes to the wagon and set them on the tailgate. I made sure to conceal the book under the garments. I decided that I would give it to William in the morning for safekeeping, in case Pa or Jacob found it and tossed it out.

"I'm sorry he did that. You didn't deserve it."

"At least it's good to know that he loves his daughter enough to defend her honor. Even though I'm harmless. At least so far." He winked at me as I returned to his side.

"He's protective, that's for sure." Jacob stoked the coals with a stick. The embers sparked and drifted into the darkness. He had arranged sticks into a spit holder on two edges of the firepit. He rose and walked to a table, or rather an overturned crate, near the wagon and returned with a spit strung with strips of meat which he fitted into the holder over the fire. The coals sizzled from the dripping fat.

"What kind of meat is that and where did you get it?" I laced my fingers behind my back.

"Buffalo. Mr. Erickson and Mr. May downed one earlier today and are sharing it with our train."

"That's nice of them. Lord knows we'd have to exist on bread and bacon if the hunting was left to you."

He glared at me.

"How is it that we haven't seen a buffalo, yet the prairie is littered with buffalo dung, and we have buffalo steaks cooking over the fire?"

"Dunno?" He plopped to the ground and sat cross-legged in front of the fire.

"Are you making jerky?"

"Yep. Captain says we've got a long haul before we get another layover, so we need to be prepared. Did you get some salt at the post?"

"Not just any salt. Based on what Pa paid for it, it must be an exotic spice from some foreign land fit to season the most royal of tables."

Jacob rolled his eyes.

Eliot winked at me, then looked at Jacob. "You know, uh, Jacob, Sissy is back at our camp trying to get our fire going. Doc's tending to some sick folk, as usual, and Mama's not feeling well. This is such a grand fire you've got blazing. Maybe you could share some of your pyrotechnic skills with her. I'll watch over your meat while you're gone."

Jacob hesitated, then rose. He opened his mouth, likely to protest, then clamped his lips into a scowl. He tossed his stick into the fire and stomped away. Scout lumbered to his feet and watched Jacob disappear into the maze of wagons, then plopped down to resume his nap. Or maybe he stayed to chaperone.

"That was genius." I grinned.

"Thanks. I thought that appealing to his soft and generous side might keep him out of our hair for a while." He snatched two nearby empty buckets, flipped them upside down, set them near the fire, and motioned for me to sit on one of them.

He sat on the other and scooched it close to me and wrapped his arm around my shoulders. I leaned into him. His warmth enveloped me like a feathered duvet. He kissed the top of my head.

"We'll have to think of something to keep him busy tomorrow also," I whispered.

"Uh-oh. We're headed out at the crack of dawn. I was hoping your train would be joining us."

"Oh." I watched the flames flicker around Jacob's crispening meat. "We're not leaving until the day after."

"I wish we could hold back another day. Our guide is worried that if we don't pick up the pace, we won't make it over the Blues before the snow falls."

"That doesn't bode well for us then." I looked at him and frowned.

"I assume you'll catch up. Then we can scheme about more ways to ditch your brother."

"And Sissy."

We chuckled.

A clanking sound rang from behind our wagon, like someone kicked over a tin pail. Then a thud. "Dang blasted."

"Pa," I whispered.

"Gotta run." Eliot kissed me on the cheek, leaped to his feet, and vanished into the night.

Chapter 15

Dear Diary,

My hand is trembling like a quivering leaf in a late-autumn windstorm as I try to write this. My pencil may never ink another legible letter. Maybe that's a good thing. If I can't read it, maybe I won't relive it. But every time I close my eyes . . . Eliot was right—it does get harder after Fort Laramie. And terrifying!

West of Fort Laramie, the trail entered the high desert plains and the rolling foothills of the Rockies. Jack and Molly strained under the uneven terrain, stubby clumps of grass, spindly sage, arid heat, and heavy load. Jacob was worried about them. I was too. And then, of all days, on the Sabbath . . .

I scrubbed the breakfast dishes in a pail of soapy water while debating whether to attend Reverend Danials's Sunday sermon. Ma's scolding voice in my head reminded me that I'd skipped most of the reverend's services. But the inner whisper was always trounced by Pa's shouts demanding more coffee, or a clean shirt, or darned socks. The imminent sting from a slap across the face for disobedience was a more powerful deterrent than my unredeemed soul.

Ethan trotted up on his mare. I hid behind the wagon. I was in no mood for his condescending leers or sour jabs.

"Good morning, Ethan," I heard Jacob say. "What brings you around so early on the Sabbath?"

I wish Jacob wouldn't talk to him, so Ethan would leave and bother someone else. I shook my head. Why was Jacob so nice to him anyway?

"Captain sent me around to tell folks to hustle up."

"How come?"

"We're losing too much time. Darn hills and sand are slowing us down more than he'd expected."

"But today's the Sabbath. Reverend Danials is getting ready to start his sermon, and folks take extra time for prayers on Sunday mornings. In fact, most folks think we're going to be condemned to hell for traveling on the Sabbath at all."

"Well, the reverend will need to save our souls some other time. Anyone not ready to head out in twenty minutes will be left behind."

I slipped from the behind the wagon when I heard Ethan shout in the distance, "Mr. McNeil, Mr. May, time to head out. Pass the word down. We need to make up time today."

Pa drove the wagon. Jacob and I walked next to the team as we trailed behind the McNeils' rig, thankfully near the front of the train, so we wouldn't have to eat so much dust. Jacob wore his new trousers and boots. He faltered when he stubbed a rock that snuck out from the earth. He bent and grabbed his bootstrap and thrust his heel back into the loose boot.

"When we stop to noon, let's find something to stuff into those boots so they're not so wobbly. Last thing we need is for you to twist an ankle."

"The boots are fine. At least they don't have holes and I don't have to stop and dump the dirt out of them all the time."

"You're welcome, by the way."

"Sorry. I did forget to say thank you. And for the clothes as well." He wobbled as he stepped around a clump of grass. "Why didn't you snag a pair for yourself? Yours look as bad as mine did. Maybe worse."

"Couldn't find any. Except for Sissy, I haven't seen any girls my age. And she needs her shoes."

"There must be more girls on the other trains. And there are plenty of women. They must not be dying at the same rate as the men and boys."

I watched the grass and loose stones pass beneath my tattered shoes. "I wasn't going to mention that the owner of the garments that I pilfered for you is probably in one of the graves we passed."

"You'd have to be an idiot not to assume that."

We navigated around a cluster of sage and through a ravine. A prickly limb from a brittle sagebrush scratched the back of my hand. "Ow." A drop of blood oozed through the break in the skin. I fingered out my handkerchief that was tucked up my sleeve and pressed it against the wound. The hanky was dotted with rust-colored stains from previous scrapes and cuts that scarred my cheeks and hands.

Molly stumbled in a soft patch of sand. She recovered, shook her head, and resumed her lumbering slog beside Jack.

"I don't know how much more they can take." Jacob reached his arm out and patted Molly on the neck. "They need a rest. Rest and reinforcements."

Jack snorted, as if agreeing with Jacob's assessment.

I glanced at Molly. The path where the harness rubbed her neck was lathered in sweat. She puffed a snorty breath with each step. "I still don't get why Pa only got two mules."

"Remember that man he talked to at the stockyard? The one who said mules are faster? Mules are also more expensive. My guess is that the stockman wanted to sell Pa the mules so he wouldn't take his business elsewhere. Pa believed him."

"Because he wanted to believe him. Even though other folks tried to warn him."

"They're edgy today also."

"The mules?"

"Look at them. Even though they're tired, their ears are pointed forward, like they're listening for something that they can't quite make out."

I looked at Molly's bobbing head and twitching ears. "You mean like when we used to hear Ma and Pa talking downstairs, and as hard as we pressed our ears to the floor, we couldn't make out what they were saying?"

"Exactly like that. And they keep lifting their heads and sniffing, like they smell danger."

Jack cocked his head. Molly faltered a step. The wagon moaned. The chains clanked. I scanned the horizon. "I hope it's not Indians."

"Whatever it is, I hope we don't find out."

I wrapped my arms around my ribs and shuddered.

After a long silence fretting about the possible impending danger, I couldn't resist asking, "So how was your evening with Sissy back at Fort Laramie? Did you get her fire blazing?"

"Please don't do that to me again." Jacob shoved his hands into his pockets.

"Do what? We were just trying to give you a little nudge. Now that you've had more time with her, don't you think she's cute? If I were a male, I would think she was cute."

"Well, you're not a male. And I really don't care if she's cute or not." He bit his lip and studied his boots as we walked.

"Okay, okay. If you don't like Sissy, we'll find someone else for you."

He jerked his hands from his pockets and clenched his fists. "Maggie, I am not interested. Not in Sissy, nor anyone else. So quit trying to play matchmaker."

"Okay. Be that way then."

Fed up with Jacob's moodiness, I skipped up to walk with Mrs. McNeil. Her typical squared shoulders slumped, as if she were carrying the weight of her wagon on her back. Her feet shuffled in the sand. Streaks of gray that I hadn't noticed before threaded tendrils of hair that escaped from her normally tightly wound bun.

"Good morning, Mrs. McNeil." I tried to sound chipper.

"Oh, good morning, Margaret." Her voice cracked as she uttered the greeting.

"Gee, Mrs. McNeil, you look tired this morning. Are you okay?" I wished I hadn't said that out loud. Ma would have chastised me for my rudeness.

"I imagine I look like a fright this morning, Margaret. I feel like an old rag doll dragging through the sand and scrub up this hill. It's hotter than the dickens, and it's not even noon yet."

"Eliot did say it gets harder after Fort Laramie."

"Charles said the same. They were right. If only it weren't so hot." She dabbed the back of her neck with a handkerchief.

"At least we're near the front of the train, so we're not engulfed in a cloud of dust." I was perplexed by the role reversal. Usually Mrs. McNeil tried to cheer me up. "It looks like we're near the top of the rise, so it should be easier going down."

We crested the hill. Finally! The captain motioned us to halt.

"Why'd we stop?"

"Look, Margaret." She pointed to the valley. "There must be a million of them."

"Wow!" Between the hill we were stopped on and the one looming in the near distance, a sea of chocolate-colored humps carpeted the valley floor. "Buffalo! How are we going to get past them?"

"Charles read about the buffalo herds in his guidebook. We don't want to spook them, or they might stampede. The book said to wait until they mosey out of the way."

"We could be here for hours. Or days. They don't look like they're in a hurry to go anywhere. I'd better get back to our wagon."

"Whoo-hoo!" Pa shouted as he hopped from the wagon seat. "Jacob, grab a gun. We're goin' to bag us some beeffalo. Let's see how many we can drop."

Jacob tightened his grip on Jack's bridle.

"Come on, get movin', boy."

"Someone needs to stay with the team while their hitched."

"I ain't waitin'. Whoo-hoo!" Pa's yelps wafted up the hill as he scuttled toward his prey, his shotgun swinging in the air above his head. Two other armed men in the company raced after him.

"NOOOO!" the captain screamed.

The warning was ignored as shots reverberated through the valley. The captain faced the onlookers who had gathered to witness the spectacle. "Those fools are goin' to start a stampede. Three of you men grab a rifle and follow me. Everyone else, get the wagons in as straight of line as you can, front to back, and take cover."

Jacob rushed to our wagon and emerged with Pa's rifle.

"What are you doing? You need to help with the team."

"Our wagon is already in line. If those beasts turn our way, it won't matter. We'll all be trampled."

He clutched the weapon in both hands and raced toward the front of the train, where the captain, Mr. McNeil, and Mr. Dalton hovered with rifles in hand. I was close enough that I could hear the captain shouting instructions. "Likely they'll go the other way. If they do turn and charge up the hill, our only hope is to split the herd. When I give the order, shoot straight ahead, directly over the heads of the leaders. Don't hit any of 'em. That'll make it worse."

An eerie moan reverberated from the dell. I peeked around the McNeils' wagon. The mass of black humps bobbled to the left along the valley floor, like the swift current of the Platte after a storm—only darker. I released a thankful breath that we were going to be spared. The herd dissolved into a cloud of dust. The moan crescendoed to a rumble and then an earsplitting roar. The earth vibrated. The mules brayed and fought against their harnesses, heads bobbing, hooves stomping. I reached for Jack's lead rope. He jerked his head and rammed me in the jaw. Off balance, I tumbled. I rose and peered at the thundering herd. As if spinning on a dime, they changed direction and stormed up the hill—toward us.

The captain's shouts were swallowed by the roar. "Steady. Hold fire until my order."

I opened my mouth to scream, but no sound escaped. A child shrieked. A woman behind me shouted, "Shoot! Shoot!"

I thought the lead beasts were going to plow into the riflemen, including Jacob, when the captain shouted, "FIRE!"

I leaped under the wagon and pressed my palms against my ears. Scout burrowed under the crook of my armpit and trembled. We both quivered. The earth shook like Mount Sinai before God's revelation of the Ten Commandments to Moses, jostling us like pebbles trapped in a bubbling caldera. To the left and the right, thundering hooves pounded, flinging rocks and clods in every direction. The juddered wagon creaked and moaned overhead, and our possessions clanked and crashed.

I closed my eyes and pleaded, "Ma. Please, Ma. I don't want to die." Rocks and dirt clods pinged the wagon. The mules brayed and wrestled in their harnesses. The wagon listed, then plopped upright, then jostled, as the trampling hurricane raged past.

"Stop! Stop! Please stop."

It seemed like an eternity when the thunder tapered to a roar and then a distant rumble. The earth stilled, as if the stampede had trampled out its heartbeat. I lay like a toppled statue, my heart hammering, ears ringing. *I'm alive.* "I'm alive," I whispered. A mule snorted. Scout raised his head and nudged my chin. I tightened my arm around the mutt and hugged him. "We're alive, Scout. We're alive."

Voices filtered through the silence. I slithered from my shelter and gaped as I stood. Except for the line of wagons, a cratered moonscape stretched before me—the high prairie transformed into a gorged, barren wasteland. A knot tightened in my gut, and I wrapped my arms around myself and trembled.

"Jacob," I whispered. "Jacob!" I shouted. I looked to where the riflemen had assembled at the head of the train. "Jacob. Thank God." My brother shambled toward our wagon, head down, shoulders bowed, rifle barrel sagging to the uprooted earth. I rushed toward him. I was about to fling my arms around him, but his ashen face and blank, hollow eyes froze me in place.

He acted as if he didn't see me, although I was directly in his path. "Jacob? Jacob, are you okay? Are you hurt? What happened?"

He slunk past me, tossed the gun into the wagon, and then ambled to Jack and stroked the mule's nose. Jack snorted and snuggled his snout into Jacob's chest. Molly, feeling neglected, nudged closer to him. Jacob moved between the pair and wrapped an arm around each of their necks and buried his fingers in their manes.

I walked up behind him and rested a hand on his shoulder.

He shrugged it away.

"Jacob?"

"Fine. I'm fine, Maggie. Just leave me alone."

"Okay." I backed away. "Okay. I'll just check the wagon."

The captain and Ethan rode up to us. "Everything okay here?" the captain asked from atop his horse.

"I think so." I sneaked a glance at Jacob.

The captain followed my gaze. "Your sibling is a brave young man."

"Huh?" I furrowed my brow. A lot of words could be used to describe Jacob, but brave would not be on the list.

"When I asked if he was sure that he wanted to help, do you know what he said?"

"No idea." I watched Jacob out of the corner of my eye.

"He said he had to save his sis."

"He said that?" I quirked an eyebrow while squinting up at him.

"Yep. And when I gave the order to fire, his gun rang the loudest. You and your pa should be proud of him."

Jacob stole a peek at us talking, and the captain touched his finger to his hat in an appreciative salute.

Ethan lowered his eyes and flicked his reins to steer his horse down the line.

The captain started to follow, but he halted in front of a sea of stunned faces that emerged in front of him. He removed his hat and wiped his forehead with his neckerchief. He returned the hat and addressed the assembly. "This has been quite an unsettling ordeal for all of us. I see there are damaged wagons at the back of the train. Hopefully, no casualties, but I wouldn't be surprised if there were. We have no time to spare. We move out in one hour. Get any needed repairs done. Any graves that need dug and funeral prayers said. Help each other out. I know this sounds cruel, and I'm sorry. But we'll all be sorry if we don't get more ground covered." He squeezed his horse with his knees, and he and Ethan rode toward the destruction at the end of the caravan.

My eyes followed them. It looked like a tornado had touched down and torn across the plain. An assortment of wagon parts, broken furniture, clothes, tools, pans, and utensils cluttered the ground, as if they had spewed from a volcano. Bludgeoned carcasses of mules, oxen, and livestock mingled with the debris. My stomach churned. I prayed there were no human graves that needed dug, but…

Jack and Molly sucked the dregs from the buckets of water that I filled from our barrel. We'd checked the harnesses, inspected the wagon for damage, and were tidying up when the captain approached on foot. He gripped the reins of his horse and two mules in one hand, and the other was clasped around William's wrist. Tears streamed down the boy's mud-caked face. He held a death grip on the book that I had given hm for safe keeping under his other arm. The captain stopped and asked Jacob to hold the reins for a moment. Then he and William proceeded to the McNeils' wagon.

"Mrs. McNeil." He nodded. "Charles. I'm sorry to have to ask this."

Mrs. McNeil rose from her wash bucket, and Mr. McNeil patted the cow he was tending to and walked over to the captain.

"What is it, George?" The grave look in Mr. McNeil's eyes made me think he already knew.

"The, uh"—the captain diverted his eyes to the ground and then looked back to Mrs. McNeil—"the, uh, some of the folks at the end of the line didn't make it. The Adkins. William is the only one who survived."

Mrs. McNeil gasped and flung her hand to her mouth. So did I.

"I hate to ask this, but could you look after for the boy? At least until things settle and I can determine whether he has other kin on the train."

"Of course, Captain. We'll take care of him." Mrs. McNeil rushed to the boy and wrapped her arms around him. William's free arm hung limp at his side as Mrs. McNeil nestled his face into her belly.

"Thank you, ma'am." The captain nodded.

He turned and approached us. He took the reins from Jacob, sorted out the set that belonged to his horse, and handed the mules' leads to Jacob. "I don't know what your pa was thinking trying to haul a wagon two thousand miles with only two mules. Based on what he did today, I should expel him from the company. But you're good kids and don't deserve that. The Campbells won't be needing them anymore." He tilted his head toward the mules. "We don't have time for you to get them rigged up today, but when we stop tonight, you can figure it out. You might want to pilfer through the wreckage and see if you can find enough scraps to repair the broken harnesses. Otherwise, you'll just have to rotate them in so your team can get some rest."

Jacob and I both stared at the captain, mouths open as he made the offer. He was right. After what Pa did, we didn't deserve it.

"Thank you, Captain." Jacob sniffed back his emotion.

The captain didn't respond. He mounted his horse and rode back to the carnage.

We led the mules to the back of the wagon and tied them off.

"Thank you," I said to Jacob as he ran his hand along the flank of one of the mules.

"For what?"

"For being my hero."

His hand stilled. "Don't mention it. And I mean that. Especially don't mention it to Pa." He bent to examine the hooves of the new team.

"You don't have to worry about that. And speaking of Pa, he's headed our way." I squinted at Pa trudging up the crest of the hill toward us.

"Jacob, Maggie," he shouted through haggard breaths as he tromped through the moonscape. He stopped and eyed the carnage. "What happened here? Did the buffalo do this? Who would have thought those beasts could cause such a ruckus."

Jacob shot straight up and stomped up to him, his hands clamped into fists at his side. "A ruckus? Is that what you call this?"

"Looks that way. Boy, you missed all the fun. I got four, maybe five of 'em. It was hard to tell through all the chaos."

Jacob rose on his toes and tilted his chin up, his chest inches from Pa's ribs. Snakelike veins stretched the skin on his neck, and his cheeks flashed scarlet. If Jacob were taller, they would have stood nose to nose. "Fun. You think this is fun! You and your fun nearly got us killed. It did get people killed. William lost his family. Wagons are destroyed. Livestock trampled like they were field mice. Your fun did this!" He fanned the wasteland with his arm.

"Seems to me the buffalo did this." Pa removed his hat and scratched his head. "We're okay though."

Jacob threw his hands in the air and stomped off toward the wreckage, I assumed to not only escape Pa's insensitivity but also to search for rigging for our additional team.

"I'm plumb tired from that trek up the hill. I'm gonna sit on the wagon seat so I'll be ready when it's time to pull out."

I turned my back on Pa and took over for Jacob, inspecting the new mules. One johnny, one molly. They were going to need a good brushing tonight and some salve for a cut on the molly's leg.

A short time later, the captain trotted up the line on his chestnut, shouting, "Time to roll out. Let's move."

Jacob jogged up and tossed some leather straps in the wagon just as Pa yelled "Hup, hup, giddup" to the team and flicked the reins.

Jacob was sullen as we descended the hill. I shuffled up to Mrs. McNeil, who held a firm grasp on William's wrist. The boy still clutched the book to his chest with his other arm. "Do you mind if I walk with you for a while?"

"I suppose you can walk wherever you want."

The curt response cut, as if she'd wedged a dagger into my gut. "William, I'm really sorry about your family."

William didn't raise his eyes from his feet. If it weren't for Mrs. McNeil's firm grip around his wrist, I imagine he would have tumbled facedown and been trampled by the caravan.

"When my ma died, I was sad for a long time." I knew there was nothing I could have said to bring him out of his gloom and that I should probably have kept my mouth shut. But I'd never been comfortable with silence, and my mouth seemed to have a mind of its own.

He sniffed and wiped his nose with his sleeve. His clothes were filthy, and his trousers torn. I wondered where he'd been when his family was trampled. Did he hear their screams, see the fear in their eyes? Or had he been huddled under a wagon with his eyes closed and his hands pressed against his ears, like I was?

Mr. McNeil walked a few feet ahead alongside the lead oxen in his team, his guiding stick slung over his shoulder. The oxen didn't need a guide. They knew what to do. A monotonous game of follow the leader—day after day after day. Mr. McNeil glanced over his shoulder and scowled, then turned his attention to the ox he was leading.

Hurt boiled from my core and scalded my cheeks. "You blame me, don't you?"

Mrs. McNeil didn't acknowledge me. Like the silent treatment Ma used to dish out when I'd made a transgression.

"You can't blame me. I didn't do anything wrong!" The bubbling hurt flooded behind my eyes, threatening to erupt into a lava flow of boiling tears.

"He's your pa." Her icy tone froze the fire in my core.

"He wasn't the only one." I balled my hands.

"You're right, Margaret. He wasn't the only one. But he was the instigator, and as far as I'm concerned, he murdered William's family."

"But you can't blame me!"

"You're his kin."

I froze. I watched her plod beside her wagon, her hand clasped around the grieving boy's, the lifeline that pulled him forward.

"Get out of the way, Maggie, or you'll get run over," Jacob shouted as the team clomped up behind me.

I stepped to the side and let them pass, my gaze focused on Mrs. McNeil and William fading in the horizon.

Jacob loped to me and looped his arm around my elbow and led me forward. "What's gotten into you?"

"Rough day."

"Understatement. We don't need any more days like this." He let go of my arm and asked, "How's William?"

I didn't respond.

"Poor child. Losing his whole family in a flash like that."

"And to witness the gory details. At least when Ma died, we weren't there to see it or know it was happening."

Jacob rolled his lips under his teeth, shoved his hands into his pockets, and studied his footsteps.

Chapter 16

*D*ear Diary,

Please, Ma, let this be just a nightmare and I'll wake up on our flea-infested mattress in our stuffy loft to the wafting aroma of bacon that you're frying on the stove. If only . . . At camp the night of the stampede, Pa and Jacob repaired the harnesses for our new mules. I don't know how Jacob could even hold the leather strips in his hands. Mine still trembled so much that I spilled Pa's coffee when I carried the cup to him. He reprimanded me for my incompetence with a slap across the cheek. Since we didn't know the names or our new mules, and based on their color, we're calling them Penny and Buckskin (Buck for short) for now. Maybe someone will let us know their real names. That is, if anyone will ever talk to us again. On the trail and at camp, our fellow travelers kept their distance, including the McNeils. Occasionally, someone would look our way, then quickly turn when I caught their gaze. After supper, Suzie walked toward me and Tommy hovered not far behind her, but their ma intervened and shooed them back to their camp. I didn't have the heart, or the energy, to open the book to learn of Jane Eyre's fate without the children. A tear slid down my cheek. Mrs. Adkins and her little sweet, inquisitive boys. I hoped a giant library overflowing with the world's greatest literature awaited them in heaven. And then, as if the stampede weren't enough to deter us from pressing on, God issued another warning that the wild west was not to be trespassed.

"I'm so hungry I could eat a buffalo." Jacob and I trudged up another hill that mirrored the rise we had slogged up the previous morning before the stampede. The stiff wind molded my face into a contorted scrunch. I kept my burning eyes open a slit so I wouldn't stumble over the clumps of scrub that tangled the ground. "My legs feel like they're going to crumble underneath me, and my aching feet are screaming for a soak in a cold stream. I don't see why we can't take even a short nooning break."

"I'm hungry too. And these new boots are giving me blisters. But you know the captain said we can't stop. We were too far behind even before the buffalo delayed us yesterday."

"Don't remind me. I'm trying to forget about the buffalo. I couldn't sleep last night because every time I closed my eyes, I would see those beasts charging at us." I tried to shake the memory from my brain.

"We'll probably be haunted by buffalo nightmares for the rest of our lives." He wrung his hands together and then wiped them on his trousers. "The mules are edgy again today."

"Better not be more buffalo. I don't think I could live through that again."

A wind gust slammed me off balance. I grasped Jacob's sleeve to steady myself.

As we crested the hill, I tensed, afraid that the valley floor ahead would be clogged by a sea of black humps. I gasped. It wasn't buffalo. A cauldron of steaming mush billowed to the sky—a giant bubbling dust bowl. The murk swallowed the wagons ahead of us, one by one, as they descended the hill, as if sinking into a raging, grimy sea.

"Here goes." Jacob sighed and gripped Jack's bridle.

The wind howled. A tumbleweed scuttled past. We were smothered in the blinding dust hurricane. The wind-whipped particles that pummeled the thin scarf I had wrapped around my head stung my cheeks. Jacob looked like a mummy with his neckerchief wrapped around his nose and his hat strapped under his chin. Another tumbleweed rolled past. Then one slammed into the wagon wheel and disintegrated. The wind-whipped wagon tops beat like kettledrums.

"Jacob, this gale is blowing me backward. And I can't see a thing." I didn't know if he could hear my shout over the howling wind.

"Just keep your head down and put one foot in front of the other."

Easy for him to say. I felt like a twig bobbing in a raging sea about to be snapped by a breaking wave. Thwomp! My face slammed into the earth. The breath whooshed from my lungs, as if a cannonball had slammed me in the gut. Flat on my stomach, nose wedged in a clump of scrub, I lay paralyzed, gasping for air that wouldn't slip through my strangled windpipe.

"Maggie! Maggie!"

Jacob. The plea trapped in my throat. *Jacob.* I couldn't see through the swirling murk when I lifted my head. A tumbleweed bounded past my nose.

"Maggie, where are you?" His shout was swept away with the dust.

"Here." I whispered a throaty groan. "I'm here." My plea died in my throat. "Can't breathe." He couldn't have heard me. I couldn't hear me.

"Maggie!" The shout blew farther away.

"Jacob." The groan croaked through my lips and was whipped back down my throat. "Jacob."

Hooves plodded to my left. Horses, mules, oxen—I couldn't discern. Suddenly my mind had me cowering under the wagon with millions of buffalo thundering past.

A metal shoe pinged against a rock. A horse whinnied.

"Hey!" The shout came from the rider. Ethan.

"Maggie, where are you?" Jacob's cries were muted wisps in the dust.

"Jacob, don't leave me." The grunted whisper evaporated behind my lips.

"Jacob, she's over here." Ethan's yell boomed, as if he were right on top of me.

The palomino's shoes clinked on nearby stones.

"Ethan, I can't see you."

"Jacob. This way. Follow my voice. She's over here."

The horse's hoofs stomped near my head. Dangerously close.

"Maggie, get up!" Ethan screeched. "Wagon behind you. You're going to get trampled."

"Maggie, move." Jacob clasped my arm and tugged.

I flopped to my knees. My head hurt. A drop of blood slid off my cheek and seeped into my apron. I gasped haunting breaths, scratchy ghost beaths. I shook my head to rattle the dust webs from between my ears.

Jacob clasped his other hand on my arm and swung me toward him. We rolled like one of the skipping tumbleweeds out of the way of an oxen team that trampled the spot where I had just been splayed like a wounded puppet.

"Jeez, Maggie, you need to be more careful. Hurry and get up before we both get run over."

Jacob clutched my arm, and I lumbered to my feet and wobbled. He steadied me. I inhaled a wisp of air. Then another. I gagged on the grime that coated my throat.

"What happened?"

"I. . . I, ah, don't know." My voice croaked like a sick toad. "I think I tripped."

He bent and picked up my scarf. He started to hand it to me and stopped when he looked at my face. "You have a nasty gash on your forehead." He slipped his hand into his trouser pocket and slid out a soiled handkerchief. "Hold this over your cut to stop the bleeding." He passed me the scarf, then led me by the elbow. "Come on, we need to get moving. We'll never find Pa and our wagon in this mess."

I pressed the cloth against my forehead and clutched my scarf in the other hand—the tails flapping in the gusts—and let Jacob lead me through the tempest.

After I regained my voice I asked, or rather shouted, through the gale, "Since when did you start carrying a handkerchief?"

"Ma gave it to me. She said that a gentleman always has a clean handkerchief handy. So I always kept one in my pocket. I never knew why. Sorry, it's, ah, a little dirty."

"We'll, I'm sorry you had to sacrifice it on your sister instead of a cute damsel in distress."

I stole a sideways glance and saw him bite his lip. He must have lost his neckerchief when he helped me up. I suddenly wished that it were Eliot who had rescued me. I wondered where he was and if he was fighting the same storm. My stomach soured at the thought of him rescuing someone else—someone prettier, wittier, more experienced at kissing.

I lifted my eyes for a quick peek ahead. A steely gray tint intertwined with the murky brown dust. Plop. A raindrop splashed on my cheek. Plop. That one hit my shoulder. Plop. Plop. Plop. Then, as if we'd stepped through a wall, we were assaulted by a barrage of water, an army of rain guns blasting a deluge of stinging liquid bullets, raging a battle to keep us from the promised land.

The ground became a soupy concoction of tar and grease-like mud that clung to our feet like glue. Nearby livestock slopped and slurped as they plodded through the slick muck. We trudged, shielding our faces from the wind-whipped torrent, our legs heaving, like we were crossing the quicksand-like river bottom of the Platte again. The rain turned to hail, like the heavens parted and pummeled us with icy stones. I trembled with ache and cold.

"Jacob, I can't see anything," I shouted through the whistling wind and pounding ice balls.

He looped his arm through mine. "I've got you. Just keep moving forward."

"Can't we stop? I need to stop. I'm soooo cold."

"You'll get colder if we stop. Keep moving."

How could I be any colder?

The pounding hail that hammered the wagon tops flooded my mind with images of thundering buffalo hooves. At least we were near the train. I lowered my head against the deluge and trudged onward as best as my cold, shivering, aching body would allow.

What seemed like hours later, the hail waned to a gentle rain. Then it stopped. The air was clear and fresh. The storm had pounded the dust deep into the earth and buried it under a rug of soppy mud. A sunray slithered through a break in the clouds and streaked to the earth like a golden rod. The charcoal clouds dissolved into light pewter puffs. I clasped my hands in front of my chest and gaped in awe at a double rainbow that arced across the sky in the distance. A full range of colors, from red to orange to yellow all the way to a vibrant violet in the inside strips. I inhaled a sweet, lung-cleansing breath and whispered a thankful prayer.

Below the bluff we had been traveling on, the North Platte, which had been a gentle muddy flow meandering through the high prairie that morning, was a raging torrent as wide as the Missouri, roaring through the canyon like a spooked buffalo herd. Interspersed with the tree trunks, limbs, and branches swept in the deluge, a tattered white top bobbed in the current.

Chapter 17

—◄○►—

Dear Diary,

Sweet! Sweet! Sweet! I never thought that word would pass through my lips again. Although the road to sweet was laden with days of hard traveling through the barren, windswept grass and sage lands. Each buffalo that blotted the horizon sent a ripple of fear up my spine, but the beasts kept their distance and let us pass in peace. Phew! The hunters would bring one back to camp every few days, and we were glad of the supply of fresh meat. Pa was itchin' to go with them, but the captain had banned him from getting within shooting range of one of the beasts. We plodded through barren, powdery, alkali-laden passages where even the buffalo wouldn't tread. Many hot, arid days were void of fresh water and grass for the animals. Or buffalo chips for fires. We forded the North Platte without incident. But the grim reaper of the underworld reminded us, sometimes brutally, that we were not welcome in this desolate terrain. The foul odor of rotting carcasses and the skeletons and bone fragments that littered our path served as omens to those who dared to cross the unforgiving land. Our company lost four oxen, two cows, and one mule. And one human. Mr. Smith was cleaning his rifle one evening and—boom—he shot himself in the chin. The bullet lodged in his skull. Folks had to drag Mrs. Smith off his shallow grave when we broke camp the following morning. But then . . . sweetness.

"Why is everyone in such a hurry?" Jacob and I trundled near the wagon, when the typical late-afternoon sluggish pace of the animals picked up a notch. My parched throat was sandpaper dry, my chapped lips were cracked and sore, my legs wobbled like globs of mashed potatoes, and the grit and glare made my eyes feel like they were being attacked by prickly needles. I was in no condition to pick up the pace.

"We must be getting close to the Sweetwater."

"The Sweetwater?" I quirked an eyebrow.

"The Sweetwater River. The captain said in the briefing this morning that we should reach it sometime today. Then instead of following the North Platte, we're going to follow the Sweetwater all the way to South Pass."

"That doesn't explain why we're speeding up. Usually we slow down this late in the day because everyone's worn out. Even the animals have perked up."

"They can smell it."

I tilted my head and sniffed the dry air. It reeked of dust, animal dander, and sage. "Smell what?"

"The Sweetwater."

"What's so special about another river?"

"Think about it. Why do you think it's called the Sweet-water?"

"Because it's sugar water?" I licked my chapped lips. "I can see it now—snow-white crystals meandering down a hill just waiting to land on our tongues. Or maybe it's made of molasses, since the only white around here is salt and alkali dust."

"Don't be stupid." He rolled his eyes. "It's because it's clean, fresh water from the mountains. The water is supposed to be clear and cold and safe to drink. Legend has it that a trapper once accidentally spilled a load of sugar in the river."

"Sweet! Let's hurry." I balled my hands and pumped my arms to propel me toward the sweetness.

We stopped for a short rest at the bank of the winding river. Scout barked, then sprang from the shallow ridge on the shore and splash landed with a belly flop. He surfaced and shook his head, spraying a rain shower from his flapping ears. He swam in a circle, yipping. I imagined his submerged tail wagged under the surface.

Jacob and I sat in the grass and watched. This would have been an idyllic spot to read to the children. If only their parents would let them near me again. I'd become an ogre ever since the day of the stampede. Did they think I was going to sic a herd of trampling buffalo on their precious youngsters? Or maul them myself? I plopped my chin into my hands. Maybe in California, where no one would know our history, parents would trust me with their children.

Scout swam up to us and yipped. Then he paddled back into the middle of the river and then back to us again and barked.

"He wants us to swim with him." Jacob tugged off his dusty boots, then his filthy socks, which he stuffed into the boots. Without rolling up his trouser legs, he waded into the river. Soon he was hip deep, splashing the pooch as if he were a toddler. Scout tried to bite the streams of water that Jacob tossed his way.

If only I weren't a girl and I could join in their fun. "Unbefitting a lady," Ma would say. A wave of sadness washed over me that she wasn't there to share the moment of joy.

"Hey, you jackass, quit acting like a child and get the mules watered and the barrels filled so we can get moving."

Another idyllic moment ruined by Pa.

"Another mammoth rock," I commented to Jacob after we hit the trail. "It's almost like God plops them in the middle of nowhere just to break up the monotony of this desolate landscape."

"This one is called Independence Rock."

"It looks like a colossal stone whale breaching out of the earth." I squinted at the massive formation through the afternoon glare.

"Nah. More like a giant space monster gagged on some of your mush and slammed the overturned bowl into the ground so he wouldn't have to smell it any-more."

"Funny." I slapped his shoulder. "See if I make mush for you again. Why would someone name a giant rock after a holiday?"

"Dunno. Might be some fur trapper discovered it on Independence Day. Although I did hear that to reach the Blues before the snows, it's best to pass Indepen-dence Rock by the Fourth of July."

"It's a week past the Fourth, I think." I scratched my head. "I thought that since we're going to California, we don't go over the Blues."

"We don't. But we go over the Sierras. Just as bad."

"Or worse. Remember the Donner party?" I frowned.

"Yeah. I remember. That's why the captain has been pushing us so hard."

Dusk was snuffing out the daylight when we reached the base of the giant granite rock to set up camp. I was famished. Thankfully, the river was close, so watering the mules and filling the barrels wouldn't take long.

Jacob and I unhitched the team. As I carried the rigging to the wagon, I spied Pa steal a swig from his flask and then slip the pouch of tobacco from his pocket before settling to the ground by the wagon wheel. The other men were busy tending to their animals or starting fires or repairing harnesses or other "men" chores, while the women scurried with dinner preparations.

The injustice angered me. I flung the harnesses by the tailgate, stomped back to the team, and grabbed Molly's and Penny's lead ropes and headed for the river. Jacob followed, toting Jack and Buck.

A gaggle of shrieking children sped toward the rock, where pings from clanking chisels reverberated between my ears. I felt the onset of a headache creep up the back of my neck into the base of my skull. "What are they doing—trying to dig a cavern into that rock?"

"They're carving their names and hometowns to immortalize their presence. Then everyone throughout eternity will know that they were here."

I smiled at the memory of Eliot carving our names in Courthouse Rock miles back. "Are we going to do that?"

"Nah. Who cares that we were here."

"Hmph." Both Molly and Penny echoed my dismay with a snort. I wanted everyone to know that we were here.

Then my anger, and my headache, abated—for a single chisel clink.

"Eliot!" I screeched when I spied him to the side of our path with his back to me, talking with . . . I wanted to sink into an alkali pond when the girl he was conversing with peered around his shoulder and glared at me. Tall and slender, perhaps a year older than me, her clean and pressed dress looked as if it had just been purchased from an expensive boutique. Not a tendril of her silky chestnut hair escaped from the chignon secured at the nape of her neck. The peach-shaped face that peered from under the bonnet was clean and pale, with full lips that that weren't cracked and bleeding.

Eliot pivoted toward me. "Maggie." He wrung his hands together. "Maggie, what a surprise." His eyebrows shot up under his hat brim.

"I, uh, I didn't mean to interrupt."

"Hey, don't be sorry. It's always nice to see a friendly face." He touched the elbow of his companion. "Maggie, this is Constance."

So now I was just a friendly face. *Where was that alkali pond?*

Constance lifted the corners of her lips into a faux smile that only another woman would recognize as a disguised sneer. The witch.

Jacob continued toward the river with Jack and Buck. Molly brayed. Penny stomped her hoof.

"I, uh, I just want to say hi. Nice to, ah, meet you, Constance." I lowered my head and made a beeline for the river.

"I'll see you around," Eliot called to my back.

I wanted to run, but I tried to appear dignified. I peered over my shoulder and uttered, "Uh, sure, Eliot. See ya around."

I snuffed a tear as I joined Jacob at the riverbank, ensuring that the mules were between us so he wouldn't notice my foul mood. *How could he do that to me?* Mrs. McNeil's warning crashed like cymbals in my pounding head.

Pa stirred from his catnap when Jacob and I returned with the mules and buckets of sloshing water. "What took ya so long? Where's supper? A man could starve to death around here. You better be fixin' something other than burnt biscuits and bacon again." He stomped off to refill his flask.

I began our nightly ritual of cooking, cleaning, and preparing for the day ahead, and most importantly, staying out of Pa's way.

After the unappetizing meal, I sat cross-legged by the dying fire and watched the flames flitter around the charred logs. Thankfully, real wood instead of smoky buffalo chips. The fire's glow warmed my cheeks, but even an inferno couldn't melt the iceberg in my heart. Jacob sat against the nearby wagon wheel, whittling on a stick. Pa had wandered off, like he did most evenings, probably in search of a card game, or Mrs. Johnson. He'd been spending most of his time "helping" Mrs. Johnson lately. A fiddler and banjo struck up a tune on the other side of the circle. "Sweet Chariot." If I weren't in such a foul mood, I would have hummed along. Couples lined up to dance.

I opened *Jane Eyre* and rested it on my lap. I longed to know whether Jane accepted St. John's proposal and sacrificed love for security. Why must there always be a choice? I closed the book, set it aside, and plopped my chin into my hands. I couldn't bear to learn of her fate ahead of the children.

"Psst. Maggie."

I cringed at Eliot's whisper behind me.

"Mind if I share your fire?"

Before I could answer, he plopped to the ground next to me.

"Nice night, isn't it?"

"Uh, sure. Nice night." *Why had he come?* Every muscle in my body tensed in anticipation of his shattering confession. I picked up a nearby stick that served as a fire poker and scribbled in the dirt. His silence unnerved me. "I thought you would be dancing with your friend tonight."

"My friend? Oh, you mean Constance."

I studied my artwork. "She's pretty."

"Oh. I guess. I hadn't really noticed."

"How could you not notice?"

"Maybe I noticed a little. Although she's not as pretty as you. And she certainly doesn't have your spunk."

I felt my cheeks flush, and not from the fire. "Don't tease me."

"Maggie, I wouldn't tease you. At least not about this."

I studied my scribbles like I was creating a masterpiece to rival the great da Vinci.

"Maggie, Constance's parents and my parents are friends. They live, or lived, I guess, down the lane from us. We grew up together. I think of her more like a cousin."

"A cousin." The cynicism oozed in my skepticism.

"And I would much rather dance with you."

I turned and peered at him. The glow from the fire flickered in his eyes. The passion in his gaze bled into my soul. My heart raced. His face leaned into mine. My lips parted.

Jacob coughed, and Eliot jerked away.

We sat, arms brushing, and stared into the fire. Eliot reached for my stick and poked the embers. Sparks rose and flitted away in the darkness.

"You stopped writing me notes."

"I, uh, I stole the paper from Sissy's diary. She caught me and hid the diary. Now I don't have any paper. She also hid the pencil."

I smiled and bumped him with my shoulder. He returned the gesture.

"Where's your pa?"

"Probably out looking for trouble."

"Just want to make sure he's not going to sneak up and stab me in the back."

"He doesn't sneak." I didn't say it was because he couldn't tiptoe when he was drunk. "He would probably just shoot you instead. Stabbing would take too much effort."

"Good point. I'll be fast then." He sneaked a quick peek at Jacob and then kissed me quick on the lips.

I looked at Jacob to make sure he didn't see. He had stopped his whittling and sat cross-legged with his elbows on his knees and his chin resting in his palms starting at the next campsite. My eyes followed his gaze. Ethan. Great. The last thing I needed was for Ethan to have witnessed the kiss. The whole camp would know by morning—including Pa.

Eliot's gaze followed Jacob's as well. "Why is Jacob watching Ethan like that?"

"Like what?"

"Like, you know. Like"—he flipped his wrist and pointed his limp fingers toward the ground—"he's hopelessly in love."

"But that's Ethan."

"Disgusting. I know. He isn't one of those deviant types, is he?"

"Deviant?" I scrunched my forehead. Jacob was a little odd, or "different," as Ma had inferred. But there was no one more obedient, helpful, honest, respectful, and a host of other good qualities. I couldn't even recall a time when Mr. Jones had reprimanded him.

Eliot must have sensed my confusion. "You know, men who are attracted to other men instead of women."

"That's sickening!" I stole another peek at Jacob, who hadn't taken his eyes off Ethan.

"Like I said, disgusting." He inhaled a deep breath and swallowed. "Back home there were these two men who lived in the same house. They claimed it was to save money since they were both unwed. Folks called them perverts. Said that their 'ways' went against the laws of God and nature. Mothers warned their children to stay away from them. Then one night, a posse of men burst into their house and dragged them outside in their nightshirts. The mob strung them up and hanged them from an oak tree in their front yard as punishment for their sins."

I opened my mouth, but no words tumbled out. There were no words. For the two men, nor for the men who hanged them. Disgusted, I shook my head. "Did they find the men who did it?"

"I don't think anyone tried. Everyone knew the perverts got what they deserved."

I studied Jacob studying Ethan. "Jacob's not like that." I tapped my fingers together. "Ethan's a creep. He's condescending to Jacob. Jacob is probably seething because Ethan insulted him again."

"I hope you're right. For your sake as well as his."

I tensed at a rustling sound in the darkness behind the wagon. Then a thud. Then "Damn!"

"Pa," I whispered.

"My cue to flee." Like a felon dodging an armed lawman, Eliot disappeared into the night.

"Coffee."

"Huh?"

Pa tripped over a twig as he stumbled into camp. "Coffee."

"Uh. I'll have to make some."

"I said coffee. Now!" He stomped toward me and slapped me across the jaw.

I touched my stinging chin. "I said I'll make some coffee." I tromped to the wagon and rummaged for the coffeepot and sack of beans that, thankfully, I had ground earlier, and returned to the fire.

"What's this?" He bent over and picked up the book, surprisingly without tumbling into a heap in the dirt.

"It's my book. Can you please set it down and I'll get your coffee ready." I poured water from a bucket into the pot and gripped it in my hand.

"You needn't fill your little head with nonsense. I never shoulda let your ma send you to school. No good comes from a woman readin'." He wobbled.

Huh?

He tossed the book into the flames.

"No!" I lunged toward the fire, but the blaze had engulfed the book. Flecks of singed pages fluttered in the air.

Pa grabbed me by the waist with both hands, spun me around, and punched me in the eye. I tumbled into a heap.

He stomped to the wagon, without his coffee.

Chapter 18

Dear Diary,

The Sweetwater isn't always so sweet. And neither are some people. The rough road, rugged terrain, steep climbs, river crossings, heat, wagon breakdowns, and fatigue bleed the spirit from our bones. Tempers simmer. Women scold unruly children. Husbands are short with their wives. Tensions are frayed, like an old rope stretched taut, ready to snap. The slightest provocation can lead a man (it's always a man) to lose control. But I'll get to that. First, the Sweetwater. Have I mentioned that river crossings are right up there with Indians and buffalo on my fear meter?

The current flowed swift as I stood on the riverbank with my palm clasped around Molly's lead rope and watched the rigs ahead of us splash across. Jacob was on the other side of the team next to Jack. Pa lazed in the wagon seat—his usual spot for river crossings. Heaven forbid he should get his feet wet. Although never voiced out loud, ever since the scene on the Big Blue River in what seemed like a lifetime ago, he has left the management of river crossings to Jacob. "We've crossed this river twice already. Why do we have to cross it again?"

"Only six more to go after this one."

"What? That makes nine crossings. Of the same river." Even I could do that simple math.

"Yep. Supposedly there is a way to avoid them, but that requires a detour that would add days."

"Which, I know, we can't afford." I frowned.

"Here goes." Jacob gave Jack's bridle a slight tug, and we stepped into the icy current.

"William, you be careful!"

I turned toward Mrs. McNeil's warning. The McNeils were preparing to cross to the right and slightly behind us. Mrs. McNeil knelt in her wagon and watched from the front as Mr. McNeil hoisted William onto his shoulders and then reached for the yoke of the lead ox.

I returned my focus to my footing on the slippery, rocky bottom and gripped Molly's bridle for balance. Halfway across, the chilly water lapped around my waist and the current tugged at my skirt. Molly stumbled and fell to her knee. I lost my grip on her bridle and splashed facedown in the water. I recovered, staggered upright, and clasped onto Molly's mane.

"Charles!"

I spun toward Mrs. McNeil's scream just as Mr. McNeil tumbled into the water and William toppled backward off his shoulders. Mr. McNeil looked dazed as he struggled to his feet and clasped the horn of one of his oxen to steady himself. Blood oozed from his forehead.

"William," I whispered.

"William! William!" Mrs. McNeil's frantic cries swirled in the cacophony of splashing animals, bleating and mooing livestock, and shouting teamsters.

I pushed myself away from Molly and sloshed through the current toward where William had hit the water. I squinted through the spray and the sun's blinding glare. "William." My gasp was swallowed by my panic as I waddled to the spot where he went under—precariously close to the plodding oxen hooves. The ripples splashed against my ribs, and I held my arms out for balance while struggling over the uneven riverbed.

"William!" I cried. I dove under the surface and flailed my hands. Nothing. My lungs burned. I stood and sucked in a gulp of air and dove into the water again. The melee of hooves and wagon wheels whipped the normally clear river into a blinding underwater dust storm. An object drifted into my hand. I grasped it. A twig. Air. I needed air. I thrust my head and shoulders out of the water just as something bumped against my calf. I reached down and clutched a fistful of fabric. I yanked Willam by his collar to the surface with strength I didn't know I had.

Mr. McNeil appeared beside me. He snatched the boy, hugged him to his chest, and carried him to shore. I wobbled behind them, gagging and gasping. My limbs wilted like flower stems breathing their last whisps of life at the end of the summer, and I shook from cold and exhaustion. I slipped and fell to my knees, then staggered to my feet. Three more steps and I stumbled. The bank was just a stone's throw, yet miles, away. My legs gave out, and I crawled to the shore on my hands and knees and collapsed on the flattened grass.

"Get up, Maggs. Get up. You're going to get trampled." Jacob tugged my arm.

Through a squinted eye, I peered behind me at the herd of cattle charging across the river toward us. Jacob helped me scamper to my feet. He hustled me out of the path of the splashing herd, which were being goaded by whistling, hollering, and lasso-twirling mounted cowboys.

"Geez, Maggs. You almost got yourself killed."

"William." I hunched and planted my hands on my knees and gasped. "Did William make it?"

"I didn't see William. Just you lounging in the path of a wild band of livestock. Why did you let go of Molly?"

"I, ah. . ." I realized that he couldn't have seen Mr. McNeil or William from the other side of the team. "Never mind." I crumpled to the ground and buried my face in my hands. *How can this land be so cruel?* William was just an innocent child. A simple misstep nearly snatched him away in the blink of an eye. I muttered a quick prayer of thanks that a grave didn't need to be dug for William. *Too many graves.*

We nooned in a barren clearing that looked like a disrupted rock garden. I was still shaken by William's close call with the grim reaper. That one was too close. Even with all the graves we'd passed, and all those that have been lost from our train, William's near miss shook me the most. It could have been Jacob. Or Pa. Or me. My limbs felt like melting butter. I eased against a boulder and tried to massage life back into my legs. The baking sun hadn't yet dried my dress and underthings, which clung to my back and ribs. Six more Sweetwater crossings to go. I wanted to curl up under the rock and hibernate.

"What are you doing sitting on your ass when I haven't had my lunch?" Pa lifted his hat and ran his fingers through his sweat-soaked hair. I wondered who had cut and tamed his tangled mop. And trimmed his beard. Must have been Mrs. Johnson. Grief for her late husband must have blinded her sensibilities if she had succumbed to Pa's advances. Poor woman. I wondered about Pa's intentions.

Ethan trotted past on his palomino, shouting, "Half hour. We head out in half hour."

Why couldn't we ever get a proper nooning break? I hoisted my depleted self from the rock and fixed Pa a bacon and biscuit sandwich. He grunted and snatched it from my hand and wandered off. I fixed another one for Jacob, and he ate it one handed while he greased the axles. I took the last biscuit and a slice of bacon and returned to the rock. Its warmth felt good on the back of my legs. The slab of granite was the closest thing to a chair that I'd rested on since leaving home ages ago. I closed my eyes and pictured Ma's rocker gently swaying near the fire back in our Missouri cottage. Before the chair was smashed into a splintered pile of sticks miles back on the prairie with our mattress. If only I could sink my weary bones into the seat and rock myself into a blissful slumber.

I gagged on the last bite of burnt biscuit when Mrs. Mc-Neil and William approached. I wanted to evaporate and dissipate under the rock. Although I missed her company, I was still hurt by her accusatory association. I didn't choose to be related to Pa.

"Good afternoon, Margaret."

Jacob stepped closer.

"Mrs. McNeil." I nodded while I studied the fluttering leaves in a copse of trees beyond the clustered wagons. A wren flew from its perch concealed within the greenery and disappeared behind the grove.

"Margaret, I need to apologize."

I meet her gaze without rising from my perch. William hunched beside her, studying the pebbles that littered the ground around his feet, his hands clasped behind his back.

"First, Charles and I want to thank you from the bottom of our hearts for rescuing William. That was a brave thing you did."

I wanted to say something flippant, like "Don't mention it" or "It was nothing," but my voice was trapped in my throat. Perhaps Ma had reached her hands down from heaven and clasped them around my neck to keep my insensitive and impolite remarks strangled inside me. I nodded and studied the split seam in my shoe.

"And about the stampede. I'm sorry. I shouldn't have lashed out at you. It was un-Christian of me to hold something your pa did against you. You are your own person, and I know that." She looked over at Jacob, who was pretending not to eavesdrop. "And, Jacob, I never did thank you for your bravery. You have my utmost admiration and appreciation."

Jacob nodded and returned to inspect his grease job. I didn't have any words. Or Ma still had my throat gagged.

"If you could ever forgive me, I hope that we can be friends again. I miss our talks."

Not knowing whether I could forgive her or not, I studied the pebbles along with William.

"William, do you have something for Margaret?"

William whisked his hand from behind his back and held out, straight armed, a bouquet of wilted wildflowers.

"William, they're lovely." I took the flowers and held them to my nose and inhaled their sweet fragrance. "Where on earth did you get these?"

He cocked his head to the side. "Down the river a little way. Mrs. McNeil helped me find them." He stubbed his toe in the dirt. "They looked better when we picked them."

"They're beautiful. That was very sweet of you. These are the most special flowers I've ever received." I bent and kissed him on the cheek.

He blushed and lowered his head. He fidgeted. "Do you think that maybe you could read to us again?"

"Of course, William. I would love to read to you some more. Do you still have the book I gave you? *The Swiss Family Robinson?*"

He nodded.

"Then tonight after super, we'll read it together. Maybe Suzie and Tommy will want to come as well."

"And Jimmy?"

"And Jimmy also." I tried to remember who Jimmy was. One of the Erickson children perhaps.

"Whenever you want some company, come seek me out. William might also like to walk with Jacob so they can talk boy talk while we have some girl talk." She smiled at the boy. "William, let's go help Mr. McNeil get ready to head out."

"Move out! Move out!" Ethan trotted his horse through the wagons, whipping his hand in circles above his head.

He leered at me and then kicked into a gallop. I eyed Jacob, who watched Ethan get swallowed by the horse's dust wake.

Pa appeared, snatched the reins from Jacob's hand, climbed onto the wagon seat, and flicked the straps. "Hup, Hup."

Jack snorted, Buck shook his head in protest, and Molly and Penny leaned into the harness ready to get to work. Scout sprung to his feet and trotted to his normal position at Jacob's heels.

I spied the McNeil wagon two rigs ahead of us. William shadowed Mrs. McNeil as they walked, his head down, body slumped into a frown, hands shoved into his pockets, feet dragging, like he was going to dissolve into a mound of sand to be scattered by the wind. I suspected that Mrs. McNeil had an ulterior motive when she suggested that William might want to spend time with Jacob. The boy had been appended to her side, as if they were yoked together like the oxen that powered their wagon, since he'd lost his family that horrible day of the stampede. I scrunched my eyes closed to erase the nightmare. Didn't work. I felt William's sorrow. He needed a distraction from his grief. And I suspected Mrs. McNeil needed a short reprieve from the tether.

My thoughts drifted to the night at Independence Rock with Eliot, sitting close by the fire, arms brushing. I imagined him draping his arm around my shoulder and snuggling my head under his chin. Anticipating another kiss. The unsettling story he told me about the men who were hanged nudged the idyllic vision aside. What had he called them? Deviants? Sinners? Perverts? I couldn't wrap my mind around the concept. And how could he think that of Jacob? Jacob had a multitude of annoying habits, and he was different, as Ma had said, but a sinner? Not Jacob. I wished Ma were here to help me understand. A stew of anger and betrayal simmered in my core. How could she leave me so alone when there were so many questions that I needed her help to sort out?

I watched William stagger by Mrs. McNeil. I couldn't imagine the ache in his heart. Well, I could imagine it. At least Jacob and I had each other. And we were old enough to take care of ourselves. Willam had no one left. Thank goodness for Mrs. McNeil. She had to be an angel. But I was still angry with her. But maybe angels had their faults like everyone else. She did apologize. Was I a good enough person to forgive her? I was bored, and I did want to talk to someone about what Eliot had said. I strolled up to her.

"Good afternoon, Margaret." She peeked over her shoulder and smiled when she heard me.

"Hi, Mrs. McNeil. I hope I'm not disturbing you."

"Heavens no, Margaret. William and I have run out of things to talk about. And I imagine he would much rather spend time with Jacob than with and old lady like me." She looked at the boy and smiled. "Right, William?"

William stared at his tattered shoes as he scuffled through the sand.

I decided to try. "Hey, William. I know you miss your ma and pa a lot. And your brothers also. I miss my ma so much it rips my heart apart. Every morning when I wake up, I think she is still here, fixing me breakfast and trying to hustle me to get ready for school. And then I remember she is with the angels in heaven. But I also know she is here"—I curled my hand into a fist and tapped my chest—"inside. I talk to her. Especially when I'm sad or scared. And you know, if I listen very carefully, I can hear her answer."

"What does she say?" he asked through a snivel.

"She tells me that she loves me and that if I look hard enough, I will find my way. And then she still reminds me that as annoying as Jacob is sometimes, that as his big sister, I still need to watch out for him."

"I thought you were twins."

"We are. But since I was born ten minutes before him, I get the job of big sister." I smiled at him. There was a hint of a smirk in the filthy face that looked up at me.

"Could you do me a favor through?"

He studied his footsteps again.

"I'm tired of protecting Jacob right now. Could you take over for me for a little bit? You could also ask him how he's getting on without his ma."

Mrs. McNeil smiled at me and then said to William, "Why don't you go and help Jacob. He's likely tired of his big sister bothering him and would like to engage in some man talk." She winked at him.

William lowered his head and uttered, "Yes ma'am." He abruptly stopped his forward motion and waited for Jacob to catch up.

"That was a nice thing you did, Margaret. I hope he takes your comments to heart."

A twinge of guilt kicked me in the gut. My ulterior motive was to get him out of the way so that I could talk to Mrs. McNeil. "I really am sorry about his family."

"I know you are, Margaret."

I gazed at the cloudless sky and tried to determine a tactic to broach my agenda. I opted to start with a different topic and devise a way to weave in my touchy question. "Do you think what people are whispering about demons is true?"

"I haven't heard any whispers."

"All the troubles we've had since leaving Independence Rock. Wagon breakdowns, oxen collapsing, William almost drowning, the fight that broke out after supper last night."

"I don't think it's demons, Margaret. But you are right—folks are tense. It's quite the juxtaposition that God has put on this place."

"What do you mean?"

"Look around us." She fanned her arm in an arc. "Who could have imagined scenery like this back home? These stunning granite cliffs and rock formations, the crystal-clear water, the interesting flora. Not many people get to experience this rugged beauty."

"And the jagged trail that causes wagon breakdowns and wears on the animals, the heat that saps our energy, the swift water of the river crossings, the steep climbs."

"Hence the juxtaposition. The good and the bad. Unfortunately, the bad seems to be putting an extra strain on some folks."

"I've heard Reverend Danials say that it's God's punishment because we're not observing the Sabbath." I peeked at her out of the corner of my eye.

"I don't know about that either. You know that Charles and I believe we should rest on the Sabbath. However, I don't think God wants us stranded in the Blues either. So I imagine He'll forgive us until we reach Oregon."

"Or California," I added with a frown.

"The way your pa's been courting Mrs. Johnson, you may have a new ma by the time you reach California."

I gasped. Pa had been spending most of his time with Mrs. Johnson, but he claimed he was just helping her out since she'd lost her husband. But then, when had Pa helped someone only from the goodness of his heart? I wondered whether Mrs. Johnson had any idea that Pa might have had a hand in her husband's death. And if he did marry her, wouldn't he at least wait until after we'd reached California? Out of respect for Ma? Although, if he had a new wife, then maybe I wouldn't have to be his slave anymore. And if there was a school in California, perhaps I could train to be a schoolmarm. Surely they'd take into account the time I spent as a monitor back home helping Mr. Jones teach the younger children. And I would need to double down and work harder with the children in our caravan—at least the ones whose parents would let me near them—to add to my résumé. Maybe Mrs. McNeil would even write me a letter of recommendation before we part ways.

Shouts behind us interrupted my pondering.

"Jeffries!"

Mrs. McNeil and I turned toward the commotion.

It was Mr. Bacon who shouted. "Jeffries, you thief! Give me back my cows."

"What's that about?" I asked.

"No idea." She resumed walking. After a few steps she said, "Margaret, I have a sense that there is something you want to discuss."

I watched my frayed dress swish with the rhythm of my steps and my dusty, tattered shoes trod over the uneven ground. I stepped on an unseen pebble, hop-skipped, and winced in pain.

Mrs. McNeil watched my feet as I tiptoed through a cluster of jagged stones. "Perhaps your pa can get a new pair of shoes for you when we reach Fort Bridger."

Unlikely.

"Jeffries, I'm warning you." The shout cut through the cacophony of trail noise.

"See what I mean about the demons."

"It's not demons, Margaret. Mr. Bacon is just a little hot under the collar. It'll pass."

"Go to hell, Bacon—we ain't got your cows." This was a new voice. I assumed Mr. Jeffries's hired man. Since the cowboys mostly trailed the caravan with the herd and rarely socialized with the rest of the company, I didn't know his name.

We stopped and watched the altercation, along with some of our other nearby caravan mates.

Mr. Bacon rushed up, grabbed Mr. Jeffries by the elbow, whipped him around, and punched him in the jaw. Mr. Jeffries spun and tumbled to the ground.

"Leave him alone," Mr. Jeffries's employee repeated. "We ain't got your cows." He stomped up to Mr. Bacon, hands fisted, and slugged him in the gut.

Mr. Bacon stumbled backward. When he had regained his footing, he wielded a pistol. Bang! Mr. Jeffries's partner's knees buckled, and he crumpled to the ground. Blood oozed from his chest.

I scrunched my eyes closed.

"Don't look." Mrs. McNeil wrapped her arm around my shoulder and tried to lead me away. But my feet wedged into the dirt, and I froze in place.

"Someone get the captain," a man shouted.

Another man answered, "He must have heard the shot, because he's headed this way."

"I didn't mean to. I didn't mean to," Mr. Bacon mumbled as he backed away from his victim, who lay splayed on the ground, unmoving. His hand shook, and he dropped the pistol.

"Come on, Margaret," Mrs. McNeil said. "Let's move out of the way so the men can sort this out."

"He's cold as a wagon tire," a man grunted.

Mrs. McNeil hugged my shoulder and led me away. *Cold as a wagon tire. Dead.* In the blink of an eye. I swallowed a lump of bile rising in my throat. One minute the man was minding his own business, herding cows, and the next he was shot in the chest. Dead for no reason. Not sickness or an accident . . . *When does it stop?*

A short distance from the commotion, we turned and watched the crowd of men congregate around the fallen cowhand. Two men restrained Mr. Bacon a few feet beyond them. William scuttled up and buried his face in Mrs. McNeil's skirt. Jacob and Scout appeared behind us. Murmurs filtered through the growing congregants. Mrs. May jostled through the crowd, stood next to Mrs. McNeil, planted her hands on her hips, and exclaimed, "Of all the cockamamie things. Mr. Bacon was such a proper gentleman. Looks like we're going to have a trial."

"Seems like a waste of time. Half the train witnessed the crime," a woman behind me said.

"It appears that Mr. Bacon saw his own elephant," another woman muttered.

"Demons," I whispered under my breath.

"The captain says that a man is entitled to a fair trial with a jury of his peers. It's the law."

I didn't turn my head to see which woman knew of the captain's statement. The men in Eliot's tale who didn't get a fair trial flashed in my mind.

I followed Mrs. McNeil's gaze to a clanking sound. Two men, one with a pickax and the other with a shovel, were digging a grave. Another two men were stringing a rope over a tree branch. "Looks like Mr. Bacon is expected to be found guilty."

The captain scanned the assembled men. "Doug Tompkins, Jedediah Olsen, Jonah May."

"Uh-oh." Mrs. May gasped. "Looks like hubby pulled jury duty."

"Charles"—the captain nodded to Mr. McNeil—"we're gonna need you."

"Oh dear." Mrs. McNeil flung her hand to her chest.

The captain eyed the men. "That's five. Need one more." He looked to the gravediggers, who kept their focus on their task, then at the men fashioning the rope. He shook his head. "Hanley, congratulations. You're juror number six."

"Guilty." Mr. May, the man who had been selected foreman, announced the verdict after the jury deliberated for a short five minutes.

Another man was going to die. An otherwise good man who'd momentarily lost control in a spat of anger. The biscuit I ate for lunch soured in my stomach. Senseless.

Mr. May and Mr. Olsen tied Mr. Bacon's hands behind his back and led him to the tree where the noose swayed in the breeze.

Mrs. May wiped her forehead with a hankie. "Looks like Mr. Bacon got what he deserved."

Mrs. McNeil clasped her palms together and bowed her head. Her lips moved, but she kept her prayer private. Knowing Mrs. McNeil, I imagined she was praying for the souls of both men.

The caravan pulled out a short time later, leaving Mr. Bacon and his victim side by side, head to toe, in the same shallow grave to rest for eternity.

Chapter 19

*D*ear Diary,

There's hard. And then there's harder. And then there's just plain brutal. I had thought the hard was behind us, but it was only a teaser, like a nice day in early spring that is swept away by a biting storm. We had made the ninth and final crossing of the Sweet—not-so-Sweet—water River and wound our way to South Pass and the Continental Divide. I remembered Mr. Jones's lesson on the Continental Divide. All the water on the east side of the divide eventually flows to the Atlantic Ocean and all the water on the west side flows to the Pacific. I was anxious to see the notorious fissure and had a fleeting notion to tell Ma about it. But then, like a wrenching gut punch, I realized I couldn't share anything with her—ever. I'd made a mental note to teach the children about the Divide after our recital of the alphabet at our next lesson. The granite canyons had opened to a wide high-altitude grass-and-scrub plain that was framed by distant snowcapped peaks. Except for the biting wind, it was a pleasant reprieve while it lasted.

I was beyond bored. I wished Eliot were here to keep me company. Time had whizzed by like a band of wild horses the afternoons we had spent together traveling on the prairie before he had abandoned me at Ash Hollow. Pa was off with Mrs. Johnson, Jacob was driving the team, and I walked alone near our rig. Bored out of my mind. As usual. The McNeil wagon lumbered ahead of ours. I still hadn't had an opportunity to ask Mrs. McNeil about the men Eliot had told me about. I hadn't been able catch her alone. The topic was so uncomfortable that I wanted to keep the conversation private, and especially far from William's ears. I also needed to muster the courage to broach the delicate subject and the deft to not reveal my motive or my source. Tricky.

The stars and moon must have aligned. William sprinted ahead to help Mr. McNeil lead their oxen team. Mr. McNeil relinquished his poking stick to William. The boy was assiduous in keeping the cows moving along,

I jogged up to Mrs. McNeil while clutching a clump of skirt in my fist to keep from tripping. "Good morning, Mrs. McNeil. Do you mind if I walk with you for a while?"

"Good morning, Margaret. Isn't it nice to have some easier traveling instead of having to squeeze through ravines and wind around cliffs and boulders?"

"I thought you liked that scenery. I remember your delight when we passed all those landmarks like Scott's Bluff, Devil's Gate, and Split Rock."

"I did think they were marvelous sights. How blessed we are to witness God's magnificent creations."

"But you're right. This is much easier." I hugged my arms around my chest. "Although it's colder at this high altitude."

"This wind does have a bite to it." She tightened her shawl around her shoulders.

I fisted my hands and inhaled a deep breath. How to begin?

"I've sensed, Margaret, that there has been something on your mind that you've wanted to talk about."

Thank you, Mrs. McNeil, for the segue. "Well"—I weaved around a scruff of brush—"there sort of is. I mean, well, I heard something that I'm trying to understand."

"What did you hear?"

I tried not to stumble over my tongue as I fabricated a plausible scenario for the source. "There were some men talking. It must have been after some whiskey and a card game, because they were talking rather loudly, almost shouting. So even though I tried not to listen, I couldn't help it."

"Was your pa among them?"

"Uh, no. Not this time anyway. He may have been with Mrs. Johnson. Anyway, one of the men was telling a story about something that happened in the town where he was from. Maybe I heard wrong and am just confused, and well, it's . . ."

"Why don't you just tell me what you heard."

I focused on my footsteps, took a deep breath, and repeated the story Eliot had told me.

She was quiet for what seemed like an eternity but was probably only a minute or two. I stole a sideways glance as she tiptoed around a glob of cow dung. Her face was as stiff as a brick. I wished I could have erased what I'd told her.

Finally she inhaled a shallow breath. "God created men and women for a reason, Margaret. The only romantic relationships that are sanctioned by God are between a married couple—a man and a woman. The family created by that union is sacred. Anything else is unnatural, immoral, and a sin in the eyes of God."

I tried to digest what she said. "Then it was right for that posse to hang those men? Because they had engaged in sinful acts?"

"No, that wasn't right either. Those men probably thought they were doing the right thing—protecting the innocence of the women and children in the community from the immoral activities those men were engaging in."

I wanted to ask her more questions because I still didn't understand. And then she almost bumped into William, who was suddenly in her path.

"William, you should be more careful," I scolded.

"Sorry. Mr. McNeil sent me to tell you that we crossed the Conti.. ah, Conti something…" He touched his finger to his chin and scrunched his forehead. "Ah, some kind of Divide."

"The Continental Divide. William, I think you may be right." Mrs. McNeil panned the landscape "It looks like we're easing down the slope."

"Really?" I glanced over my shoulder at our wagon behind us. It was indeed higher. I stumbled over a clump of grass and teetered before regaining my balance. Best to watch where I was walking. "I expected South Pass to be a narrow canyon surrounded by jagged peaks. The way everybody's talked about it, there should be a giant monument to mark the Continental Divide."

"Maybe someday there will be. According to the guidebooks, if it weren't for South Pass, a wagon wouldn't be able to cross the Rockies to get to Oregon."

"Or California."

Maybe it was the cooler weather or the gentle grade, or perhaps malevolent spirits had dwelled among the granite crags east of South Pass, but since crossing the Continental Divide, the trail drama had subsided. I hadn't witnessed any serious altercations, or fights, or murders—thankfully. Wagon breakdowns were fewer, the animals less ragged. We enjoyed a short rest while camped in a lovely place called Pacific Springs, where two additional children joined in story time. Fortunately at ages seven and nine, they knew the alphabet and could spell simple words, so I was able to keep the class on track. After the lesson, Mrs. May brought two other women, Mrs. Erickson and Mrs. Dalton, to listen along with the children while I read a chapter of *The Swiss Family Robinson.* The pupils squawked a collective gasp when I got to the part where the ship capsized and the family became marooned on the mysterious island.

The following morning, we broke camp and descended the western slope of the Rockies to the Big Sandy River with our eyes set on Fort Bridger, the next opportunity for rest and resupply.

"What?" Jacob and I were preparing the team to break camp the morning after we'd crossed the Big Sandy River. "What do you mean we're not going to Fort Bridger?"

"We're taking a shortcut. It's called Sublette Cutoff. Before we head out, we need to top off every barrel and pail and cup and dish that will hold water." He bent and lifted one of Buck's front feet and used a hooked pick to clean the mule's hoof.

"Why?"

"Because we have about fifty miles of hot, dry country to cover before we reach the Green River." He released the hoof, rose, and patted the mule on the side of the neck.

"But surely there will be streams where we can get water."

"No streams. Not even a puddle." He slipped a bridle over Buck's ears and rubbed the steed's nose.

I stamped my foot. "But fifty miles—that will take over three days. Jacob, we can't go three days without water, especially in this heat. Neither can the team." I wiped the sweat from my forehead with my sleeve. The chilly South Pass weather hung in the high country, while we descended the Rockies into the scorching high desert.

"I haven't told you the best part yet." He grinned.

"How could it get any better?" I glared at him.

"Not only isn't there water, but there also isn't grass for the animals. So we're traveling straight through. No stopping."

"No nooning breaks?"

"You're not following. We're going to travel day and night. We'll get a mini break in the mornings and evenings, and that's it."

"Yippee." I rubbed Penny's nose. "Did you hear that, girl? No stopping, no nooning, and no water." And no *Swiss Family Robinson.* I frowned.

"Pa's likely going to be with Mrs. Johnson, so I'll have to drive our wagon. It might be best if you walk with Mrs. McNeil."

The inky dark night was creepy. The moon refused to show its presence to illuminate our path or arc across the sky to mark the passage of time. I tried to pry my eyelids open with my thumb and forefinger. Didn't work. I yawned and shook my head and pinched my shawl tighter around my shoulders. I envied William, fast asleep in the McNeil's wagon, wedged between a crate and a sack of flour. After a grueling day ascending the steep hill in the arid heat, my strength, and my patience, was sapped. I feared we were lost. It was challenging enough to blindly follow the creaks and moans of the wagons ahead of us. Even with the lantern that I knew our guide had strapped to his saddle, how could he possibly navigate through this pitch-black wasteland? Hours must have passed since the dark smothered out the last breath of dusk. I hovered close to Mrs. McNeil. She walked near her husband, who kept a hand on the horn of his lead ox. Ragged breaths communicated her exhaustion.

"Mrs. McNeil, I don't think I can do this anymore. I can't keep my eyes open. My feet hurt. My head is throbbing. My throat is so parched that I can't even swallow. I'm shaking with cold. And it stinks to high heaven."

"I hear you, Margaret. What I wouldn't give for a sip of water and a warm fire. And to think that just hours ago we struggled with the oppressive heat. The good Lord is certainly challenging us tonight. But at least He provided a cloudless sky. Have you ever seen so many stars?"

I tilted my head to the heavens. Stars splashed across the sky as if God had splattered the dark with a flick of a colossal, holy paintbrush. Big stars, little stars, twinkling stars. "It would have been nice if He would have given us a full moon also so we could at least see the ground beneath our feet."

"There you go again. Always focusing on the negative."

"Well, maybe it's best that we can't see all the stinking, rotting carcasses that are fouling the air." I pinched my nostrils closed. Thwonk. I was facedown on the ground. Not on the ground. I shrieked. It was cold and hairy and stinky and . . . "Get me away!"

Mrs. McNeil bent and clasped my arm. I reached a hand down to push myself up. "Ewe! Disgusting! Get me off it."

With Mrs. McNeil's help, I scrambled to my feet. I trembled as she wrapped an arm around my shoulder and led me away from whatever dead animal I had stumbled over. I was tired of dead animals. Tired of their stink. I was tired of the dark. And tired of being thirsty. Tired of being tired. I wanted time to roll back, to before Ma's passing, before Pa's reckless quest for gold, and be back in our little cottage, for Ma to snuggle me in a tight embrace and kiss my forehead like she did when I was six and crying over a skinned knee.

Mrs. McNeil and I walked the rest of the night arm in arm, supporting each other as we stumbled and slumbered through the dark. Silhouettes of wagons began to leech through the haze as the charcoal din of the pending dawn edged out the inky-black night. Then a soft glow warmed the horizon behind us and radiated an orange aura over the scrappy sage land. I peered over my shoulder and squinted at a streak of reddish-orange that nudged the dark night from the awakening earth. I inhaled the scent of morning. Then coughed up the stink of rot.

Chapter 20

*D*ear Diary,

Are some people born cruel? Or is it a trait acquired somewhere in their life journey before they are thrust in my path? By God's grace, we survived the final miles of the Sublette Cutoff and stumbled down the steep ridge to the Green River. My pasty tongue had swelled in my mouth, and my raw throat prickled like it was plugged with crushed glass. The scorching inferno that the sun rained down on us sapped our will. Including the teams. They had leaned on each other for support, the way Mrs. McNeil and I had clung to each other during the long, dark night. They dragged our wagon as if it were made of lead and overloaded with iron bars. The animals smelled the Green River from a mile away and threatened to stampede down the ridge to the water. The captain had the sense to hold the cattle herd at bay until all the wagons were safely out of the way. Aah, sweet water. I'll never take a sip of cold water for granted again! But the sweetness was tainted by a bitter gulp of nastiness

"Why are we breaking camp early?" I looked up from my pail of soapy water when Jacob returned from the captain's morning briefing.

He tossed a bucket of water on the fire. The coals hissed, and smoke coiled into the air and fluttered away in the breeze. "The ferry crossing is just up the river. Captain wants to get moving so that we can all get across before dark."

I glanced at the Green River flowing near our camp—a wide and swift current racing toward the Pacific. And deep, so I'd been told. "At least we don't have to ford it."

Jacob maneuvered our wagon midway in the squiggly queue for the ferry behind the McNeils. At the dock far ahead, Pa and the ferryman were loading Mrs. Johnson's wagon. The flimsy raft, which was constructed of planks bolted onto cross logs, wobbled as two of the six-oxen team pulled the rig onto the craft. A cable strung across the river looped through a hook on the raft so the swift current wouldn't sweep it downstream.

Jacob hopped from the wagon seat and watched the scene beside me. "Do you think he even remembers who we are?"

"I can't imagine what she sees in him." I wiped my sweaty hands on my apron.

"Well, she probably needs his help since she lost her husband."

It occurred to me that Jacob hadn't witnessed Pa jettison the Johnson wagon before it crashed. "But still, Ma hasn't been buried very long. You would think he would have more respect for her memory and observe a proper mourning period."

"Mr. Johnson has been in the ground even less. But a woman needs someone to take care of her."

Hmph. *A woman should be able to take care of herself.* "But still, you know Pa. I never could figure why Ma married him."

Jacob stubbed his toe in the dirt and slipped his thumb into the waistband of his trousers. "I do remember one time, after she and Pa had quarreled and he had stomped out of the house—probably to the saloon—she had told me that he had been a perfect gentleman while they were courting. He would take her on picnics. He would buy her little things. Nothing expensive, just little trinkets to show that he cared. It wasn't until after she said 'I do' and he slipped a ring on her finger that he turned into someone she didn't recognize."

"Like waking a hibernating grizzly." I hugged my arms around my chest and huffed a breath.

"Exactly. And then he sold the ring."

The ferryman untied the line and shoved the craft into the current with a long pole. "Mrs. Johnson probably has no idea what he's like. Or maybe all men turn into monsters after they marry." I'd never considered how other husbands treated their wives, when the woman became the personal property of a man to do with as he pleased. The concept simmered in my bones. Was it the fate of all women to be subjected to the whims of men simply by being born female? I thought of Eliot. How would he treat his future wife? Would he value her as a life partner and treat her with kindness and respect? Or like a mule that he would whip if it stomped on his hat? "What if he does marry her? Do you want a new ma?"

"Whether he marries again or not, as soon as we get to California, I'm heading out on my own."

"And leave me with him?" I glared at him. Pa would chain me up like a dog, never allowing me the freedom to teach young children to read or count. The *Jane Eyre* book perishing in flames flashed through my mind. I'd never be able to wrap my hands around the pages of another book, to have my horizons broadened by stories of exotic lands, or my heart filled with the joy of love.

He shrugged. "I suppose you can come with me."

"And wait on you hand and foot? I don't think so." I crossed my arms and stared at the lone puffy cloud dangling in the sky. Why must a woman be subservient to a man—if not her husband, then a brother, or an uncle, or the next closest male relative? Unable to discover her own identity? Must I be destined to live in the shadow of a man—whether Pa or Jacob or my future husband—for the rest of my life? I thought of Ma. Did she foresee the miserable life that laid before her when she married Pa? The thought fermented like sour milk in my stomach.

Finally at the dock, I inhaled a shaky breath as we led the team to the ferry upon its return from dropping the McNeils safely on the other side.

The bearded ferryman extended his hand and growled, "Eight dollars."

"What?" Jacob quirked an eyebrow.

"The crossing fee. Eight dollars."

"But we don't have any money."

"No money, no crossing."

"But our pa's on the other side. After we get across, we'll get the money and pay you."

"Do I look like a trusting sort?" He squinted and spat a stream of chew over the side. "If ya ain't got the fare, then move out of the way. You're holdin' everyone up."

I stared at his weathered face in disbelief. Clumps of oily hair dangled beneath his torn and soiled hat. Tattered gloves covered his hands, and his rolled-up shirt sleeves were wet and muddy. He reeked like he needed a soak in the river with a cake of soap. He must not have had any soap. At eight dollars a wagon, he should have been able to buy soap.

Jacob looked at me. "I guess we'll have to ford instead."

"If ya try, do it downstream from me so when the current sweeps ya away, ya don't damage my boat. Then the rest of these payin' folks'll be stranded. Out of the way so I can get on with my business."

I fingered the pouch that contained the brooch as we led the wagon away from the crossing. I rubbed my thumb over the gem in the center of the rose, closed my eyes, and visualized the pin. Ma's pin. Would the greedy ferryman accept it as payment? It must have been worth far more than eight dollars. I decided to wait until the rest of the wagons were across before making the offer. Surely Pa would notice we hadn't crossed and would come pay the fee. It was his wagon, filled with his belongings, including his whiskey.

Out of the way of the crossing, I plopped onto the ground in the shadow of the wagon and sat cross-legged, elbows on my knees, chin in my hands, and watched the next wagon load onto the ferry—with nothing to do. I wished I hadn't given the *Swiss Family Robinson* book to

William. It was tucked away in the McNeils' wagon, on the other side of the river. Along with most of the children.

"Jacob. Hey, Jacob." Mr. Jeffries rode up on his roan horse, leading another saddled mare.

"Mr. Jeffries. What can I do for you?" Jacob squinted at the mounted cattleman, who was silhouetted by the late-morning sun.

"A few of my cows wandered off. I've been shorthanded since I lost my cowhand back along the Sweetwater. Do you think you could help me round them up? I want to be sure they all get across before dark."

Jacob looked at the team. Then at the ferry. Then at me.

"Go help Mr. Jeffries. Beats just sitting here."

Not long after Jacob had galloped off with Mr. Jeffries in search of his wayward cattle, Mrs. May and Mrs. May's mother-in-law, also Mrs. May, approached. The elder Mrs. May carried a bundle with her. I stood to greet them.

"Good day, Margaret," the younger Mrs. May said.

"Mrs. May." I nodded. "Mrs. May." I nodded to the elder.

"Margaret, I hope that you can help my mother-in-law. She has some mending that needs done, and I don't have the time to help her. Her eyesight isn't so good, so she can't do it on her own anymore."

"Can hardly see a thing these days," the elder Mrs. May said in a raspy voice, "and my arthritis has been acting up."

I had not been this close to the older Mrs. May before. The hair that peeped from her bonnet was the color of clouds on an overcast day—the same color of the filmy cataracts that dulled her eyes. Weblike creases sprouted from the corners of her shriveled lips. "I'm so tired of poking my fingers every time I try to thread a needle. Lord knows where my thimble might be. I swear, that little eye shrinks every time I pick the darn thing up."

I reached for the bundle. "Mrs. May, I will be happy to help with your mending."

She lifted her palms to her chest. "Thank you, dear. I've seen you patching your dress and darning your Pa's socks, so I know you'll do a good job."

I took the bundle and sat in the shade of the wagon and threaded a needle. I would never let on to Mrs. May that I didn't like mending all that much. But I cherished the memories of helping Ma turn bolts of cloth into beautiful dresses for her clients. And I loved running my fingers over the intricate designs and textures of the soft fabrics. The memory warmed me. But then I would gaze at the ferry and watch another wagon cross, and seethe at the selfishness of the grubby ferryman and my pa too. Was our entire train going to abandon us on the wrong side of an un-fordable river?

Chapter 21

Dear Diary,

The Bear River meanders through the Bear Valley. The valley is a paradise, except for the bears. And supposedly there are a lot of them. Brown, black, grizzly. They like to nap in the lush grass swathed by the shade of the cottonwood trees that hug the river. A river teeming with fish. Bear food. The country between the Green River and the Bear River, however, was far from paradise. "Hellish" some of the men called it.

The Green River ferryman had snarled at us when Jacob presented eight dollars—five dollars that Jacob earned from helping Mr. Jeffries with his cattle and three dollars that Mrs. May gave me for doing her mending. I tried to tell Mrs. May that it was too much money for the simple job, but she insisted. The ferryman raised his fee to nine dollars on account that the sun was about to set. How could he be so evil? Jacob bartered some of Pa's tobacco and whiskey for the increased fare. The ferryman still made the mules swim behind. I'm surprised he didn't make us swim behind—even though we don't know how to swim.

And then Dempsy Ridge, the obstacle between the Green River and the Bear Valley. A fifteen-mile hot, exhausting, steep climb. At night the twinkling stars that filled the inky-black sky radiated ice crystals that even the thickest blankets and quilts wouldn't shield. Brr. But the worst part was the two-mile descent into the valley. Nearly straight down. Makes me dizzy thinking about it. Unload the wagon and carry the belongings down the ridge—again. I wanted to abandon everything we owned and travel with an empty wagon. But then we'd have no food. The men lowered the wagons with ropes and chains. Fortunately, no mishaps. This time. But then all the struggles fizzled into a fuzzy memory.

"Eliot!" I shrieked. Molly and Penny tromped behind me on a narrow path through the thicket, which opened to a clearing by the river. The mules' leads slipped from my hand as I rushed toward him.

Eliot rose from the riverbank and sprinted toward me. Silty water dripped from his chin, leaving furrows of tanned skin through the layers of caked dust and salty sweat. "Maggie!" He wrapped me in a tight embrace. I felt his lips press against my forehead. I tilted my head and met his eyes.

"Eliot! Eliot!"

We parted at Sissy's squeaky voice.

I turned and glared at her.

Eliot fisted his hands. "Sissy, what do you want now?"

"Oh, hi, uh . . ."

"Sissy, you remember Maggie."

I furrowed my brow in anger and dismay. How could she not have remembered my name?

"I didn't mean to interrupt." She flicked a wayward golden curl from her cheek with the back of her hand.

"Of course you did. What's so important that you had to barge down here looking for me?"

"Mama wants you to gather some firewood and then get a chair out of the wagon so she can sit to mend Doc's torn trousers. You know she's too weak to be on her feet much longer. It's jammed behind a trunk again, and I can't get it out. The chair, not the trousers."

"You've delivered the message. Tell Mama I'll be there shortly."

Sissy sneered at me and skuttled away.

"I'm sorry. I swear her mission in life is to try to ruin mine."

"Maybe I can help you gather wood? We'll need some as well."

"You might want to round up your wayward mules first." He grinned and tilted his head downstream to where Molly and Penny were chomping on the tall grass.

"Say, I have an idea." He picked up a stick and added it to the assortment of twigs and branches cradled in his other arm.

"What kind of idea?" I plucked a twig from the grass.

"I was thinking that, since it's such a nice day, it would be a shame to waste it. If it's anything like yesterday, it should be a nice evening also. Perhaps we can pilfer some grub from camp and eat together. There's a nice, quiet spot by the river that I found earlier. That is, if you can break away from your pa."

My palms turned clammy, and my heart thundered. "It's not Pa I'm worried about. He's been spending most of his time with Mrs. Johnson. As soon as I get his supper, he'll disappear until bedtime. It's Jacob who may be a challenge."

"Good point. Sissy has also been hovering like a swarm of mosquitoes."

I didn't ask him if Constance also hovered. "Hmm." Molly snorted in my ear. She and Penny would have rather grazed than collect firewood.

"Okay then, let's bring them with us."

"What? Why would we want to do that?" I stooped and gathered another stick.

"You bring Jacob and I'll bring Sissy. We can meet at the spot where we met a little while ago. Where you caught me trying to make myself presentable."

I couldn't see his face as he knelt to reach for another branch, but I felt the smile that I knew emanated from his sparkling eyes.

"Then we can find a way to give them the slip."
Devious.

"If we play our cards right, maybe we can encourage them to like each other so they'll pretend not to notice when we slip away."

Could we?

⸻ ◆ ⸻

"Pa!" I screeched as I approached our wagon, carrying a berry pie that Mrs. McNeil had helped me make. Somehow word had seeped through camp that Eliot and I were having a "date" that evening. I kept telling Mrs. McNeil that it wasn't a real date. That we were just going on a picnic by the river and that it couldn't possibly be a date if Jacob and Sissy were coming also. She said that it sounded like both Jacob and I had dates then. I secretly hoped she was right. She had "coincidentally" passed by our camp when I'd returned from picking some berries earlier in the afternoon. She swore that she didn't know the source of the sugar and butter that were waiting by our wagon. I grabbed some flour and lard, and we hauled the ingredients to her camp and made the pie in her dutch oven. I hoped Eliot would like it.

"It's about time you showed up to fix supper. I'm half starved to death."

He didn't look starved to me.

"What's that ya got there?" He feathered his beard with his fingers and eyed the dessert I carried.

"It's uh, it's not for you. I mean, it's not for us."

"Are you hiding something from me?" He furrowed his brow.

"No, I . . ." I couldn't get the words out before he stomped over and slapped them down my throat. He snatched the dish from my hands and took it to the wagon. My mouth hung open as I watched him scoop a glob of the treat with his fingers and stuff it into his mouth. A trickle of blood seeped between my teeth. The metallic drips burned rancid on my tongue.

Jacob sneaked around the wagon, hands deep in his pockets and jaw clenched, and glared at Pa as he flopped onto the wagon tongue and took another bite of Eliot's pie.

Later, Eliot hopped up from the blanket he and Sissy were sitting on when Jacob and I arrived at our picnic spot by the river. "You're here." He smiled. "I was afraid you might not show up." He scrunched his forehead. "What happened to your lip? Are you okay?" The nearby fire that they had started popped.

I touched my sore lip with my finger. "Oh, ah, it's nothing. I just wasn't paying attention to where I was going and bumped into the corner of the wagon. I'm so clumsy sometimes." I tried to make light of it, but my stiff laugh sounded like a sick goat.

Jacob quirked an eyebrow.

"Then it took a while to convince this clown"—I tilted my head toward Jacob beside me—"that if he was going to get anything to eat tonight, he had to come with me. I'm sorry, but there was a little mishap and the only food we brought is some bacon and bread."

"Hey, I didn't expect you to bring anything. Sissy and I have everything covered." He swung his arm toward the fire. "There's venison steaks and trout on the grill, a pot of beans and rice warming, and for dessert"—he glanced at his sister—"Sissy made a pie." He rubbed his belly.

"Wow!" Jacob's eyes lit up. "We'll come eat with you every night." He looked at me. "The only grub Maggie serves is cold bacon and blackened bread."

I scowled at him.

The meal was heavenly. Eliot and I sat side by side on the blanket, facing the river, arms and hips brushing as we ate. Scout sprawled between Jacob and Sissy, who sat opposite from us, as far from each other as possible while still on the blanket, like they were trying to anchor the corners so the wind wouldn't sweep them up and overturn the repast.

Only, the air was still, except for the mini breeze Jacob stirred up by swatting the pesky mosquitoes.

Eliot licked some pie juice from his fingers in an exaggerated gesture. "Um, um. Sissy, this is one of the best pies I've ever eaten."

It was a decent pie, for a camp pie. Although not nearly as good as the pies Ma used to make.

"What do you think, Jacob? Doesn't Sissy make a mighty fine pie?" Eliot winked at me.

I took the cue. "It's one thing to make a good pie in a real oven with all the necessary ingredients at your fingertips. But to make a pie this good in the middle of nowhere, with ingredients concocted from thin air"—I snapped my fingers—"now that's an impressive feat."

Eliot smiled at me. "Hey, Maggie, I saw something upstream I want to show you." He looked at Sissy and then Jacob. "Could you two tend the fire and keep the blanket warm for us? We'll be back in a little bit."

Before either one of them could object, Eliot leaped to his feet, extended a hand to me, and pulled me up. He led me down a narrow animal trail through the underbrush.

We stopped in a clearing by a bend in the river. The water gurgled as it lapped against the rocky bank. Eliot raised his arms above his head and stretched.

"What did you want to show me?"

"This." He swung his arm in an arc along the river. "Isn't this the most beautiful spot you've ever seen? The river. The cliffs hovering on the other side. I thought this would be a good place to watch the sunset."

I listened to the quiet. The swishing of the current as it lapped against the rocks, the crickets announcing the pending dusk, murmurs from the camp through the trees—muffled laughter, livestock chomping, cattle bellowing. The fiddler and the banjo struck up a tune to start the dance. The baritone voice of the caller bellowed "Bow to your partner." Hands slapped and boots stomped.

The sun slipped behind the bluff, casting long shadows over the day. Eliot faced me and reached for my hand. His fingers were rough and callused. He rubbed his thumb over my knuckles. I felt heat seep into my cheeks as he gazed into my eyes. My palms dampened, and my stomach churned. Not from the pie. I didn't want the day, or the moment, to end.

"You're not watching the sunset," I whispered. Did he notice the wobble in my voice?

"I've seen every sunset between Indiana and here. I thought I'd look at something more lovely for a change."

My cheeks were on fire. I looked down at his feet. He touched his finger under my chin and lifted my face to his. I closed my eyes when his lips touched mine.

"I think they went this way."

Sissy. The brush rustled.

Eliot sighed and stepped away.

"Here they are." Sissy stepped into the clearing followed by Jacob and Scout. "Eliot, it's getting late. We need to get back and help Mama."

The orange glow that had burnt the sky had grayed as dusk nudged the idyllic evening to a close.

"Last time. Swing your partner, do-si-do," the caller bellowed in the distance. The banjo strummed, and the fiddler bowed.

"She's right," I said. "We should get back before Pa returns from his carousing."

Eliot clasped my hand, and we followed Jacob and Sissy to camp. The music quieted. The dancers had bid their good nights and taken their leave. A din of our fellow travelers as they performed their nightly rituals hummed in the air. Jacob and Sissy separated as soon as we stepped into camp and hustled to their respective wagons. Eliot kissed me on the forehead.

"Will I see you tomorrow?" I asked.

"We're heading out at first light. Here is a carryover until we see each other again." He pulled me into the shadows and kissed me. Then he disappeared. Again.

"Where have you been?" Pa's hand slapped across my cheek before I registered that he was at our camp.

"I, uh, I went for a walk."

"I was looking for you." The shout thundered through the cluster of white tops.

"Pa, please." I sniffed. "People are trying to sleep."

I didn't see his hand until it connected with my jaw. I stumbled backward.

"You don't go for walks when I need something. I wanted coffee."

Coffee?

I crossed my arms in front of my face and ducked when I caught a glimpse of his fist swinging at me from the corner of my eye. I wasn't fast enough. The blow landed on my ear.

"It was my fault." Jacob stomped to my side. "I wanted to go to the river and watch the sunset. Since we shouldn't be away from camp alone, I asked her to come with me."

Pa backhanded Jacob on the side of the head and stomped to the wagon and climbed in. I wasn't about to disturb him to dig out my toothbrush and blanket.

Chapter 22

*D*ear Diary,

I have disowned my brother.

Pa grunted and climbed onto the wagon seat and flicked the reins when we broke camp after lunch the day after my date with Eliot. He had hovered near the wagon all morning. I did my best to stay out of his way. He was in an unusually foul mood. The coffee was too cold, the biscuits too burnt, bacon—again—and why hadn't I made him another pie? Oh, and clean his boots, and fetch his other gun out of the wagon, and wash the shirt that he wore the previous day, and his sock had another hole that needed darned. Urgh! He was like a firecracker with a lit fuse. William had come near our wagon with the book tucked under his arm and the other children trailing at his heels. But they quickly scattered when Pa growled at them.

"I thought we were going to camp an extra day so the animals could get some rest." I walked next to Jacob, near, but not too close to, our wagon. "And why did we wait until after lunch?" Although the lush grass swayed and the tree leaves fluttered in the midday breeze as we followed the Bear River north through the Bear Valley, the sun beamed its fiery heat rays between the surrounding hills. I would rather have traveled in the morning to take advantage of pockets of shade.

"Too congested. Two other trains needed to move out first. And we need to make up some time since we're so far behind."

"I think Eliot's company left first. I wish we could travel with their train."

"So the lovebirds can be together," he mocked.

I closed my eyes and reminisced about our kiss. I tripped over a root. Best to keep my eyes open. I looked at the wagon slightly ahead of us. "Pa and Mrs. Johnson must have had a row."

"Looks that way." He followed my gaze to the wagon as if he could see Pa through the canvas top.

"What do you think about him marrying someone else?"

"Seems like a moot question now. Why would you ask?"

"I don't know. It would be nice to have someone to help with the cooking and the cleaning and the washing and the mending. I'm just really tired of being his servant." I puffed an exasperated breath.

"Doesn't matter to me who does it."

I thrust my hands to my hips and clenched my jaw. "Sure, as long as it's not you! You men think you work so hard." The pitch and volume of my voice rose. "In the evenings when you and Pa and all the other men in camp sit on your rumps and clean your guns and smoke your pipes, us women are busy picking up gross buffalo turds and cooking your supper and cleaning your dishes and rubbing our fingers to the bone doing your laundry and darning your smelly socks and waiting on you hand and foot!"

Jacob looked up at the cloudless sky, and I imagined he was rolling his eyes.

"And on Sundays! When you *men* get to observe the Sabbath, who do you think is doing your cooking and your washing and your mending and milking Mrs. Adkins's goat so you can have butter on your biscuits and…"

"Are you done yet? You can scratch the goat milking off your gripe list because Mrs. Adkins and her goats are no longer with us. And it appears that we are out of buffalo country, so no more chips to harvest."

"No, I'm not done yet." I stomped my foot. "I'm just as tired as you and Pa are when we stop, maybe more because you both get to rest on the wagon seat and pretend to drive. And then you get to sit on your derriere in the evenings while I'm still up working. Maybe I should run away and live with the Indians and let you and Pa fend for yourselves." *Hmph.* Maybe living with the Indians wasn't a good idea. But I refused to believe that women were put on earth solely to serve the whims of men. Maybe it would be different in California. If only I could find a way to escape Pa's clutches.

Jacob snorted. "Can you picture Pa doing the wash?"

If I weren't so angry, I would have laughed.

In almost a whisper he said, "So you want a new ma to make your life easier."

"No." I lowered my head and my voice. "I want mine back." As much as I missed her, I imagined Jacob's hurt was even deeper. As a scrawny, awkward kid, he didn't have any friends. Luke, the bully back home, was right about one thing—Jacob was a mama's boy.

"Tag, you're it!" William slapped my arm, then pivoted and raced back toward the McNeils' wagon, which was following ours.

"William?" I gasped and clasped my hand to my chest. I turned and chased after the rascal.

"Easy, William," Mrs. McNeil scolded as he rushed past her.

I halted and fell in stride alongside Mrs. McNeil.

"William!" she yelled.

The boy peeked through the brush he had crouched behind. He rose, shoved his hands into his pockets, and lumbered toward us.

"He seems perkier now." I stole a glance at the sulking child.

"Yes. It's nice to see him act like a boy again."

I nodded as William weaseled between us.

"Sorry, ma'am." He studied his shoes as he stubbed his toes in the dirt, kicking up puffs of silt as he scuttled along.

Mr. McNeil turned his head and glanced at us. He slung his poking stick over his shoulder, like a soldier would carry a rifle while on parade, and returned to his task piloting his team.

Mrs. McNeil placed a hand on William's shoulder. "Let's make a deal."

William concentrated on the mini dust volcanoes he kicked up as he shuffled.

"While the train is moving, it's work time. Even though we're just walking, we're still working—keeping the teams moving along. When we're stopped, then it can be play-time, but away from the animals. So when we stop tonight, you can play tag or hide and seek with Margaret and Jacob until you wear them out." She winked at me. "Deal?" She smiled at him.

"Deal," he mumbled.

"It looks like Mr. McNeil is getting tired. Maybe you could use some of your youthful energy to help him with the team."

I tapped his arm. "Tag. You're it for later."

He raced ahead to join Mr. McNeil. He waved his arms while he jabbered with, or rather at, Mr. McNeil, who handed the boy his poking stick.

Mrs. McNeil fanned her arm through the air. "Isn't this such a lovely valley the Lord has created for us to travel through?"

"At least the wind isn't trying to blow us back to Missouri and the trail isn't so sandy or rugged."

"Plenty of lush grass for the animals to graze, a clear river with cold, fresh water, trees for shade, game for the men to hunt. Charles thinks this would be good farming land if only it were closer to civilization."

A cluster of Indian women were gathered aside the trail ahead. Baskets overflowing with dried fish, fresh root vegetables, moccasins, and buffalo hides cluttered the ground around them. This was the third group we'd seen since breaking camp earlier in the day.

"Well, I just wish there weren't so many Indians trying to sell us fish. I don't even like fish!" Not that I had anything to trade. I doubted they would take what little bacon we had left. But I didn't say that to Mrs. McNeil. She knew we were poor. I didn't want her to know just how destitute we were. I braced myself for the upcoming barrage of high-pressure bartering in gibberish that I didn't understand. Although I would like to snag some footwear. If only I had something of value to barter with.

"They're just trying to survive the best they can. Just like we are. Charles told me that since the fur trade dried up and the trappers have gone back to the States, they've lost their trading partners."

"Why did the fur trappers leave?"

"I've heard there are two reasons. One is that fashion trends have changed, and that the city folk don't want beaver hats anymore. Which is probably good, because the trappers have largely depleted the beaver population."

"Hmm." I scratched the back of my neck. "I don't know why anyone would want to wear a beaver fur on their head anyway."

"I imagine they would keep one's head warm. Have you noticed how cold the water is on this side of the Rockies?"

"Oh yes, I've noticed." I shivered at the memory of the frigid bath I'd taken in the river the previous afternoon.

Mrs. McNeil smiled and said hello to the Indian women as we passed them.

I kept my eyes forward and ignored their attempt to compel me into a trade I couldn't afford.

"Can I ask how your date was last night? Did Eliot like the pie?" Mrs. McNeil asked when the woman could be heard bartering with the travelers behind us.

I wasn't about to tell her that Pa ate the pie she'd helped me make for Eliot. "It was nice. Except for the mosquitoes. They ate me alive! Eliot and Sissy brought venison and trout and beans and a pie. Another pie," I added, hoping she wouldn't catch my slip. "Eliot and Sissy talked about Indiana. And we watched the river and the sunset." I didn't tell her about me and Eliot slipping away. Or the kiss.

"It sounds like you had a lovely time. You and Eliot seem to be getting along well."

"I think so. I mean, I really like him. And I think he likes me too. But there's this other girl." Why did I mention Constance?

"Another girl?"

"Yeah. He says they grew up together. That they're just friends, but . . ."

"But?"

"But, well, she's pretty. And sophisticated. Their families are traveling together. Which means they're together all the time. And, well, I know that he's going to Oregon and I'm going to California, and we'll probably never see each other again. I sensed from Sissy that it's expected that Eliot will marry her. And, well, never mind. I guess it doesn't matter." I studied the split seam in my shoe. It had sprouted in the last few days.

"But it was you that he wanted to take on a picnic. Not this other girl. And you are quite pretty yourself. I can see why he would have eyes for you."

I wanted to believe her, but . . .

"The Lord works in mysterious ways, Margaret. Even if Eliot is not your intended match, He will put someone in your path."

"No disrespect, but I don't think I want someone else dropped in my path. I mean, on one hand, I can picture being married to Eliot, but on the other, I really don't want to be bound to him, or any man, for the rest of my life."

"Margaret, marriage is a partnership. A woman needs a man to take care of her, and in exchange, she takes care of him. That's the way God created us."

"But that's not what I want for myself. Why can't I be a doctor or a schoolmarm or a shopkeeper or something—anything—and earn my own way?" I wrung my hands together. I wanted to hit something or someone. "I watched my ma work so hard that her hands were raw and her fingers would bleed. And nothing she did ever pleased Pa. And I could tell she wasn't happy." I felt like a golden rod had touched my shoulder and crystalized my life purpose. "Reading to the children and teaching them their letters and seeing their faces light up when they discover something new—that makes me happy. Not cooking and cleaning and washing and mending." And getting smacked around for my incompetence.

Mrs. McNeil inhaled a deep breath. "Margaret, I don't have a good answer for you. Sometimes we just have to do the best we can under the circumstances we are dealt."

I wished God had shuffled the cards differently and dealt me a better hand. If the only reason I was put on this earth was to serve a husband, why did He give me the ability to think for myself and a desire for something different? But I couldn't say that to Mrs. McNeil.

"Looks like we're going to cross another stream. I better go help Jacob." Without saying goodbye, I walk-jogged up to our rig.

The stream was shallow and easy to ford. On the other side, I patted Molly on the nose. She snorted in my ear and tried to rub her snout on my shoulder. "Love time later, girl. After the work is done."

"Out of the way." Pa flicked the reins. "Hup, hup, giddup."

Jacob and I skirted to the side and marched a safe distance from Pa and the wagon. "Up another mountain." I sighed as I eyed the climb looming ahead of us. Mountains, mountains, mountains. This whole journey had been a continuous slog up a single rugged mountain—a mountain without a summit.

"But not like some of the other slopes that we've pulled. Easy as Pa eating your pie." He looped his thumbs through his suspenders.

"Hey! Don't rub it in." I blew an angry puff and stomped my foot. I then filled my lungs with a calming breath. It didn't quell my angst. "Speaking of pie, what did you think of the pie that Sissy made?"

"What's the big deal about the pie. It was a pie. It tasted like pie."

"Have you ever made a pie? I thought that maybe it tasted special since Sissy made it."

He scrunched his forehead. "Why would that make a difference?"

"I don't know. If Eliot did something special for me, I would think it was the best thing ever." I clasped my hands in front of my chest.

"I doubt Sissy gave me a second thought when she made the pie. It was just a pie. We all shared it."

I clenched my fists. "Do you know how much effort goes in to making a pie? Especially out here in the middle of nowhere, without the right ingredients, or an oven."

"You said that yesterday. It wouldn't surprise me if the Samuelsons had an oven. They've got a team of ten mules, eight working at a time and two that they rotate in. Plenty of strength to pull an oven. Even uphill."

"Boy, you are so dense." I stepped on a pebble and hop-skipped and winced.

I stewed for a few minutes before I prodded him some more. "So what did you and Sissy do while Eliot and I went for our walk?"

"You mean when you went off to smooch?"

I looked at the ground so he wouldn't see my cheeks turn pink. "Okay, so there may have been a little kiss. What about you? Did you kiss her?"

"Sissy?"

"Of course, Sissy."

"Why would I kiss her?"

"Because she's a girl. You were alone with her in a romantic spot by the river—at sunset."

He studied his footsteps.

"You didn't do it, did you? You had the perfect opportunity. When do you think you'll get another chance?"

"Hopefully never. Why are you being so pushy about something I don't want to do?"

My mind flashed back to the story Eliot had told me about the two men who were hanged . . . and the way Jacob was watching Ethan.

"If it were Ethan instead of Sissy, would you have wanted to kiss him?" How could I even think that, let alone say it out loud?

His eyes remained focused on his dusty boots.

"Oh my God!" I shrieked. "Say something. Tell me it isn't true! Tell me I'm crazy to even think something so disgusting."

He rubbed his eye with the back of his hand and sniffed.

"It's true! It's really true! How could you do this? To me? To Pa? To our mother's memory? You're not my brother—you're some kind of freak!"

I stopped midstep. My insides sizzled like bacon grease over an open fire. My life was ruined. Any future I could have imagined for myself had just been swept away, like a toppled tree hurling down the Platte after a fierce storm. Tears spewed down my cheeks as I watched the slumped figure of my brother, my ex-brother, disappear around a bend.

Chapter 23

———◆○◆———

*D*ear Diary,

A different brand of fear rammed its way into my growing list of fears as we traveled from the Bear Valley to Fort Hall. Not a transient fear, like river crossings or Indians or buffalo. But a fear that simmers like burning coal in my gut that no amount of water will extinguish. I feel like a criminal, constantly peering over my shoulder to see who might be whispering behind my back. At camp I sit alone and watch my fellow travelers and wonder—do they suspect? What if they find out? I've even been avoiding Mrs. McNeil, and the children. Mrs. McNeil's keen senses would root it out, and she would be the first to shun me if she suspected. And reading to the children, well, my heart just wasn't into it.

One night we camped at a place called Soda Springs. Literally, springs of warm bubbling water. Some of the boys played in the gurgling ponds. One pool had a geyser that shot foaming water straight up in the air, like a belching volcano. Mrs. McNeil and Mrs. May picked some flowers and ground them with a stone, added some sugar, and mixed them with the soda water to make a sweet bubbly drink. Mrs. McNeil said it was like a lemon soda when she offered me a cup. It was the most marvelous treat. It cheered me up, until the cup was empty.

Usually, I feel a sense of relief when we reach a fort. Since we spend an extra day for rest, repairs, and resupply, folks relax and tensions ease. I didn't feel at ease when we reached Fort Hall. Too many people meant too many roaming eyes, accusing eyes. Why did it have to be my brother? How could he do this to me? And what would I do when we reached California? I would have no future, no family—somehow I would escape from Pa. No husband—no man would have me—no means to support myself, no friends. I'll be a castaway who lives in the shadows and begs on the streets. Or worse.

Ma, help me.

Water sloshed from the buckets I carried in each hand as I wound through a city of wagons back to our camp, head down, wishing I was invisible. I froze at the heartwarming voice that called out.

"Maggie? Hey, Maggie."

I looked up and smiled. "Eliot!" Then the blow pounded the elation into the basalt ground beneath my feet. She was there, right beside him. The witch. "Oh, hi, uh, Constance."

She gave me the look. The subtle slight that only the intended victim would understand. A crinkle of the nose, a furrowed brow, a slight tilt of the chin, a sneer disguised as a smile. "Oh, hi again, uh. I'm sorry . . . what's your name again?"

"Maggie," Eliot reminded her.

Not Maggie, I wanted to say. *Only my friends call me Maggie. You may address me as Margaret.* I bit my tongue.

She patted her shiny hair with her hand. Even her fingernails were clean. I read the scorn in her expressions as her eyes scanned me from head to toe, assessing my grungy, frayed bonnet, my filthy hair that spilled from my mangled plait, my dirty and sunburned face, my cracked lips, my patched-up dress and tattered shoes. I willed the ground to split open and suck me under.

"Oh right, Maggie." She rested her hand on Eliot's forearm and turned to him. "Remember, Eliot, that we're supping with the Nelsons tonight. They're helping us celebrate Cody's fourteenth birthday. We don't want to be late."

"Maggie, Constance is right. It's tradition for the Samuelsons, the Appletons, and the Nelsons to celebrate birthdays together. We need to run. I'll see you around."

Constance looped her arm through his and escorted him away. "Is that what you're wearing?" she nagged. "If you're going to be my dance partner, you could at least put on a clean shirt." She peeked over her shoulder to make sure I heard. "And wash your face and comb..."

I raced back to our wagon, water spilling onto my skirt from the buckets I carried, sank to the ground, and tried to stifle the avalanche of threatening tears.

Footsteps interrupted my despair. Pa. I hopped to my feet and pretended to busy myself with supper preparations.

"I'm headed to the fort. Do we need anything?"

A new dress and shoes without holes. My mushy brain couldn't recall what we were running low on. "We could always use bacon and flour and lard." I probably missed something important but assumed we could make a follow-up trip in the morning.

In the evening after supper, I sat by the fire—alone. Music drifted from the other side of the camp. The dance was in full swing. Women shrieked, and hands slapped in rhythm. A guitar strummed along with the fiddle and the banjo. I didn't know where Pa or Jacob had disappeared to. Pa probably went in search of a card game, and who knew about Jacob. Probably a walk in the dark alone. Fine by me. He could walk all night and wear out the boots I'd snagged for him clear back at Fort Laramie. Before Jacob became a freak. Before Constance. From now on he could scavenge his own boots. And after we reached California, he could fix his own supper, and do his own washing, and darn his own smelly socks.

"Argh!" I reached for a nearby stick and poked the fire.

"I hope that grunt wasn't for me."

Startled, I dropped the stick. "Did you turn into a cat so that you can lurk around in the dark and spy on people?"

"If I were spying, I wouldn't let you know that I was lurking. Mind if I join you?"

Before I could answer, Eliot plopped to the ground by my side. He picked up the fire poker, my weapon, and twirled it in his fingers.

"So how was your sup with the Neilsons?" My tone was so icy it could have frozen the bubbly Soda Springs.

"The Nelsons. And it was fine."

"And did Cory blow out all the candles on his cake?" I dropped my chin into my palms.

"Cody didn't get a cake. Just a pie. And there were no candles."

The caller announced the next dance. The fiddler bowed an intro to the Virgina reel. "I thought you'd still be dancing."

"I wanted better company."

"Hmph."

"Maggie, I told you that the Appletons are family friends. Constance and Cody grew up with me and Sissy. And yes, Mama and Mrs. Appleton have been planning our wedding since we were three. They can plan all they like, but they will need to find a different groom because I will not be the one standing at the altar." He set the stick on the ground in front of him.

I picked it up and started drawing circles in the dirt. "She's pretty."

"And pompous and boring."

"She can't be that boring."

"You can't imagine. If Constance and I were married, she would try to mold me into a stuffy, stiff-necked banker."

I smiled at the image of Eliot dressed in a starched suit and sitting behind a polished desk covered with stacks of money up to his eyebrows. He was right—it wasn't fitting.

"Why do you think I ditched the dance?"

"Because you have two left feet?" I smirked.

"Well, there's that. And I'd much rather dance with you." He stood and reached his hand down to me. "Maggie, dance with me."

I slipped my fingers into his palm, rose, and we stood face to face. The fire reflected off his eyes as he gazed into mine. He slid his arms around my waist.

"I, uh, I don't know how to dance."

"There's nothing to know." He pulled me into him. I wrapped my arms around his neck and nestled my forehead into his shoulder. Our hips swayed to the rhythm of the guitar.

"Dagnab it." The explicative came a split second before the crash. "Who put that crate there?"

"Pa!" Like a log split by an axe, we separated.

"I'll find you." Eliot kissed me on the cheek and disappeared into the dark. Again.

"Who was that?"

I stared into the blackness where Eliot had fled.

"I said, who was that?" His slurred words sounded like a two-year-old learning to talk in a grown man's voice. He grabbed my shoulder, spun me around, and his fist rammed me in the eye before I could blink.

I crossed my forearms in front of my face to block the next pending blow. "No one."

He clasped my wrists in his hands and jerked them away from my face. "I said, who was here?" He shook my arms and then gripped both my wrists into one powerful hand. I gagged on the whiskey and tobacco odor that erupted from his breath. "Was it that boy again?"

Eliot, I wanted to say. *His name is Eliot.* I kept my lips sealed and braced for his fist, which landed on my jaw.

"Pa, stop!"

Jacob.

"It wasn't him, Pa."

"She was with that boy again."

"Pa, there was no one here."

"Stay out of this, Jacob."

"Pa," Jacob yelled. "There wasn't anyone here. It was me. I just got up to check on the team. There was no one else here. Just me and Maggie. Let her go. She didn't do anything." Jacob stomped to my side, fists clenched. "Pa, listen. There was no one here but me and Maggie."

Pa lowered his fist and released my wrists. I expected they'd be bruised, along with my messed-up face, in the morning. I peeked at Jacob and lowered my gaze to the ground. I didn't want to acknowledge that he'd saved me from another blow to the face—or worse.

"Be ready to leave at dawn."

Jacob uncurled his fists and gaped at Pa. "I thought we were staying here another day."

"California train leaves in the morning." Pa clomped to the wagon and climbed inside.

Chapter 24

Dear Diary,

Yet another rung has been added to my fear ladder. A whole different type of fear that merits a new step. And I'm surrounded. Vulnerable. Defenseless. We had departed Fort Hall before sunup. I didn't even get a chance to say goodbye to Eliot or Mrs. McNeil or the children. We had joined a new train with only eight wagons. Eight wagons, ten creepy men, and one woman—Daisy, the wife of Mr. Bennett, one of the creepy men. And me and Jacob. Not nearly enough to ward off an Indian attack, real or white.

The trail out of Fort Hall parallels the Snake River. The river roars like a demon through a steep canyon outlined by sheer rocky cliffs. The water taunts us in the hot, arid climate. Another one of God's jokes. An abundance of fresh water and no way to reach it. The terrain is sandy and rocky—rough, hard, black basalt rock. Someone said it was volcanic rock. Looks to me like a black moonscape sprinkled with spindly bitterbrush and sage that creeps up through the crevices. It's hard on the animals, hard on the wagons, and hard on me. Especially with bad shoes. Two broken wagon wheels in the first two days—the Bennetts' *and Mr. Rawlins', another one of the creepy men—impeded our progress. I learned that the wood spokes and rims shrink in the dry heat, causing the brittle wood to snap, or the iron ring loosens and the wheel collapses. Jacob inspects ours every day, then shakes his head and mumbles to himself. Since I'm not talking to him, I don't ask. But the creepy men…*

I'd just finished stowing the supper dishes in the wagon the second night out of Fort Hall when Daisy jiggled over and draped her arms over my shoulders. Her long, uncovered strawberry hair flowed loose down her back to her hips. Her ample breasts threatened to spill from her low-cut dress, and the hemline of her skirt cut off at midcalf. I'd never known of a woman who dared to wear a dress without a collar that pinched her neck or a hemline that skimmed the ground. She leaned in close while she talked, our foreheads nearly touching, and I tried not to gag on the stale coffee, whiskey, and cigarette smoke that fouled her breath.

"You missed a fine time at the fire last night. We girls, you know, we gotta stick together."

The strained sweetness in her voice, along with her sour breath, made me want to puke.

The men seated around the community fire near the center of the loose wagon circle roared in laughter, probably from a vulgar joke that it was best I hadn't heard. The windblown sagebrush that surrounded the camp rustled, as if joining in on the merriment.

"Stoke that fire nice and hot, would ya, Joey?" Mr. Rawlins, I thought.

"You do like it hot, don't ya, Howard," another man shouted.

Why do men always have to raise their voices when they've had a spot of whiskey? A whisper would have sufficed.

"You'll join us tonight, right, honey?" Daisy rested her palms on my shoulders and gave them a gentle squeeze.

"I'm plum tired from walking all day in this heat." I faked a yawn. "I'm going to try to catch up on some sleep."

"Suit yourself. You'll be missin' out on a heck of a lot a fun." She fluttered her eyelashes and winked.

"You have some fun for me."

"Say . . ." She leaned even closer and whispered.

I stifled a gag.

"I saw you with that boy back at Fort Hall. What was his name again?"

"Eliot." *Why did I tell her that?*

"Yes. Eliot. That's it."

Our noses were separated by the width of a buffalo chip. Buffalo dung would have smelled better.

"He's a doll, that one. Perhaps I can give you some pointers." She stroked her hair with her hand.

"Pointers?"

"You know. About men. I've had some experience—if you know what I mean." She winked. "I could give you a few tips on how to hang on to that gorgeous hunk of flesh."

"Gee, uh, thanks for the offer, uh, Daisy. But Eliot's going to Oregon and we're going to California, so I won't see him again."

"Well, let me tell you, there's hundreds of available men in California just dying to meet someone like you. So if you want some advanced tutoring, I can show you the ropes." Fake sweet smile. "We'll have plenty of opportunities for some lessons before we reach California."

Yippee. I glanced at the scruffy men by the fire. A representation of the available bachelors waiting for me to do their cooking and cleaning and other "chores" that I didn't even want to imagine.

Daisy glanced toward Jacob, who was brushing the mules. "Your brother, though, he's goin' to have a hard time with the ladies. There's gonna be fifty or more fellas for every lady in California. Hey"—she touched her chin with her index finger and widened her eyes, as if she'd just discovered a new moon orbiting the earth—"maybe I can give him some pointers too. You know, teach him what the ladies like. Maybe that'll at least give him a fightin' chance."

I didn't think Jacob wanted any pointers on how to woo a lady.

"Daisy, where the heck are ya?" Mr. Bennet hollered from his perch by the fire. "The fire's cracklin' and the whiskey's pourin'."

"Gotta run. Come join us. It'll be great fun."

I watched her sashay in her heeled shoes toward the gaggle of waiting men. I wondered how she could jiggle like that without spraining an ankle.

"Coming. I'm coming." She aimed her index finger to the sky. "Don't start the fun without me."

"You're the fun, doll."

Was that Pa?

I spread my blanket on the ground by the front wagon wheel on the outside of the circle, as if the wagon would shield me from the leering eyes of the inebriated men. Jacob did the same next to the rear wheel. I think he wanted to stay clear of the creepy men as well, for a different reason. What would happen if his secret were discovered—to him, to me, to Pa? I bit my lip and tried to shake off the thought.

As soon as Jacob's blanket hit the dirt, Scout curled up in a ball in the center. Jacob sprawled out next to the pooch and stroked his head. Scout rolled onto his back for a belly rub. I hadn't thanked Jacob for intervening back at Fort Hall the night Pa caught me with Eliot by the fire. It would have been the right thing to do. I thought back to Ma and the time she asked me, or rather ordered me, to watch out for him. *Ma, you were right—he is different. And people won't understand. I don't understand.* Had she suspected? Would she have accepted him if she knew? No, she couldn't. No one could. Maybe it was for the best that she never knew, so she wouldn't suffer the grief of losing her son. Like I'd lost my brother. My stomach churned. I felt abandoned and alone. Since this caravan of creepy men was devoid of children, I couldn't even escape from my morbid self-pity by reading to them. What if there were no children in California to teach? I hugged my arms around my chest.

I rolled to my side and watched the carousing men by the fire through the wheel spokes. Daisy was perched on her husband's lap. She snatched the tin cup from his hand and drained the contents. Whiskey, I assumed. Some dribbled down her chin.

"Hey, give that back." Mr. Bennett lowered his arm that supported his wife and swooped her onto her back. He leaned over her and covered her mouth with his.

Her feet scissor-kicked the air.

"Can't waste a drop of that," a man shouted.

The group chuckled. Someone whooped. *Pa?*

"Let me go, you scoundrel," Daisy shrieked after their mouths parted, then pounded her fists against his chest. She wrestled to her feet and faced him, leaned over, and kissed him hard on the lips. He reached his arm around her waist to pull her into him, but she slapped his hand away and freed herself. She sauntered over to Mr. Rawlins—who sat on the other side of Pa from Mr. Bennett, with eager eyes and open arms—and slithered onto his lap. She reached for the flask he clutched in his hand, but he extended the container just beyond her grasp.

"Too valuable to be spilled by some broad." His shouted words slurred.

"I'm not just some broad!" Daisy bolted off his knee and slapped the hand that held the flask, knocking the coveted spirit to the dirt.

I couldn't see how much of it spilled, but Mr. Rawlins whisked his hand down and snatched the container before Daisy was swept onto the next lap. Pa's.

"Hey, darlin'." She wrapped her arms around Pa's neck.

I waited for Pa to push her away. He didn't. Of course he didn't. He looped his arms around her waist and snuggled her into his chest. Then his lips engulfed her mouth. She playfully pushed his face away. Then she leaned back against his arm and fluttered her feet. Her dress slid up past her knees. Pa gripped her bare knee with his palm, leaned over her, and kissed her again. His hand drifted up her thigh—under her skirt.

She slapped his wrist and kicked herself upright. She stood, snatched his flask, and kicked back a slug. She gagged and fanned her hand over her mouth. "Woo-wee, there's a good burn."

Pa put his hand on her hips and tried to reel her back onto his lap. She bent over and kissed him on the mouth. Then she swatted his arm and straddled the lap of the next man.

I closed my eyes and pictured Ma up in heaven with her angel wings glaring down at him. *How could he tarnish her memory like that?*

Chapter 25

*D*ear Diary,

    Tragedy.

I watched Daisy glide off the Bennetts' wagon seat when we stopped for the day. We had halted earlier than normal, since we came across a sheltered site near the Raft River with grass for the animals and some trees for shade. Finally. My heart ached when we had passed the fork in the road around midday, where the Oregon and California trails separated. Eliot had probably reached that point not long after us. Except his wagon rolled along the main route westward toward the Willamette Valley, while ours turned south, toward . . . I frowned at the image of Constance walking at his side, plotting their future together.

Pa had disappeared as soon as he hopped off the wagon seat when we pulled into camp and navigated the wagons into a jagged loop. Unlike the circles from our previous train, which were bound together tongue to tail like a tightly coiled chain, our California-bound caravan settled in a more haphazard sphere, like leftover puzzle pieces that weren't meant to snap together. I reflected on the undisciplined, raunchy, and independent temperaments of our gold-seeking caravan mates while Jacob and I watered the mules and set up camp.

I pulled our last, and nearly empty, tin of bacon from the wagon and carried it to an overturned crate, which served as a makeshift table, fuming that Pa hadn't purchased another tin at Fort Hall. Jacob returned from the river, toting a bucket of sloshing water in each hand. Scout trotted at his heels, water dripping from his sopped fur. At least someone had cooled off. And cleaned up. Jacob shuffled his feet and rolled his lips under his teeth as he struggled with the pails. I focused on my task without offering to help. Water splashed over the rims as he plopped the buckets onto the ground beside the wagon.

Scout wiggled up to me, tail wagging and tongue flapping. He braced his front paws and shook the excess water from his coat, soaking me with the spray.

"Scout, knock it off!"

He peered at me with his droopy brown eyes, dropped his tail between his legs, and padded off to the shade of the wagon.

I stomped to the wagon and retrieved the coffeepot and plunked it on the fire grate. Clank. Pa and his coffee. Why couldn't he ever have a meal without coffee? It was too blazing hot to make a fire just for coffee. And just once, couldn't he make his own coffee? Or slice his own bacon, or butter his own biscuit—if only we had butter—or wash his own filthy socks? And Jacob too! Rage exploded from my bones. A tsunami of tears threatened to burst from behind my eyes. I kicked over one of Jacob's buckets with my heel and fled to the river.

I knelt on the grassy riverbank and sobbed. Losing Ma, Eliot on his way to Oregon, Jacob the freak, Pa and his coffee, no children to teach, my filthy, thread-bare patched-up dress and tattered shoes, the creepy men, Daisy. The lit fuse that simmered in my core connected with a keg of gunpowder, and the explosion blasted from my soul. I smeared a tear from my cheek with the back of my hand and reached into the pouch under my apron and pinched out the brooch. I rubbed the gem with my finger, like Aladdin rubbing his magical lamp and summoning his genie. If only there were a genie.

"There you are."

Pa's growl curdled my blood. My hand trembled as I tried to slip the brooch into the sack. But the pin fumbled in my sticky fingers and fell into the grass. I swiped it from the ground and wrapped it in my palm. He'd surely notice if I tried to stash it away.

"I came back to camp looking for supper. Not only weren't it ready, but you weren't there fixin' it neither."

I leaned back on my heels, my back to Pa, and watched the current romp by, wishing it could sweep me with it, far away from Pa and his hunger. The metal petals from the pin dug into my skin.

"Did you hear me? Get off your behind and get my supper before I starve to death." His words slurred. Drunk again.

I wanted to shout that the biscuits and bacon were waiting next to the plates and utensils and that he could serve up his own stupid grub. "I'm coming." I scampered to my feet. "I was just washing up." I turned toward him, head down, avoiding his coal-fired eyes.

"Are you crying?"

"Uh, no. I'm just hot." I sniffed. *Oops.*

He took a step toward me.

"I said I'd get your supper." I expected him to turn and stomp back to camp.

He didn't. He stood rigid as a deep-rooted tree and glared at me—blocking the path to our wagon and his meal.

There was no getting past Pa without brushing against him. The thought of touching him, even just a swish of the elbows, twisted my insides. "Uh, if you let me by, I'll get your supper."

He remained planted between me and the wagon, as if thick tendrils had sprouted from his feet and wedged so deep into the cement-like basalt that even the fiercest hurricane couldn't uproot them. His shotgun dangled in his right hand, barrel pointed down. He furrowed his brow, tightened his lips, and threaded his free hand through his tangled beard. His cheeks burned red, and his eyes glossed. "You got a rebellious streak in you that I won't tolerate. That boy. Fillin' that little head of yours, and them children, with bookish nonsense. Neglectin' your responsibilities." His tongue stumbled over the word "responsibilities."

He leaned his weapon against a nearby tree stump and rushed toward me. "It's time you learned your place."

"No!" I flung my hands to my face to shield the imminent blow.

He grasped my arms and wrestled both of my wrists into his giant hand and punched me in the jaw with his free hand.

I tried to squirm free of his grasp. He knocked my clenched hand loose, and the brooch tumbled into the grass. His fist rammed into my eye. "Stop."

With an iron-like clamp around my wrists, he stooped and picked up the pin. "What's this?"

"It's mine!" I tried to jerk my arms free.

He held the pin close to his eyes. "This was your ma's."

"She gave it to me. It's mine." *Sort of.*

"She told me she sold it."

"Only so you wouldn't gamble or drink it away." *Uh-oh.*

"Why you little . . ." He smacked me so hard that if he hadn't had such a firm grip on my wrists, I would have tumbled backward into the river. My knees buckled, and I collapsed to the ground. The dry grass scraped against my shins. He was over me like a hawk and hoisted me to my feet and punched me in the gut. The breath spilled from my lungs. I tried to suck in fresh air, but it trapped in my throat, as if I were submerged beneath the rapids of a raging river. Drowning.

"Let her go."

The threatening edge in Jacob's command halted Pa's fist midswing. A faint ping splintered the air. Quiet and thunderous. Metal on metal. The cock of a shotgun.

"I said let her go."

A glint flickered in the corner of my eye. I turned my head and gaped at the barrel of Pa's flintlock aimed at us.

"Jacob, put the weapon down." Pa twirled me into a bear hug and positioned me as a shield between him and Jacob.

"I said let her go." Determination and anger spewed from Jacob's squinted eyes and contorted face.

"Jacob, put the gun down before someone gets hurt." *Jacob, please put the gun down.*

"Let her go first." He used the barrel to motion Pa to step aside.

"Jacob, you couldn't hit a herd of buffalo at close range if your life depended on it. Drop the gun."

He's right, Jacob. Please don't shoot me.

"Maggie just needs a reminder of her place."

"Is that why you killed Ma, because she didn't know her place?"

"Whacha talkin' about? Your ma fell and hit her head."

"No. You beat her just like you're beating Maggie. You hit her so hard that you knocked her into the stove. You killed her."

"You don't know what you're talkin' about."

I squirmed and tried to break free. Pa's whiskers scratched my cheeks. He tightened his grip, strangling the breath from my lungs.

"I do know. I saw you. You stumbled into the house drunk as a log and started swinging. She begged you to stop. Said you were hurting her. You always hurt her. I snuck down the ladder to try to stop you. Every time you beat her, I promised myself that it would be the last. That I would make you stop. Make it so you couldn't hurt her anymore." He sniveled. "But I was too late. You shoved her into the kitchen. Before I could get there, you punched her so hard, she went flying into the stove."

"That's not how it happened. She tripped when she went into the kitchen." Whisky and tobacco tainted spittle spewed from his mouth and splattered the side of my neck. I wanted to vomit.

"You may have twisted the facts to suit yourself or to mollify the sheriff, but that's what happened. I saw it. YOU KILLED HER! And I've lived with the guilt of not stopping you ever since. I will not let you do that to Maggie."

Bzzzz. I almost didn't hear it. Bzzzz.

Jacob's eyes bulged like bowling balls. The buzzing, which judging from where Jacob looked and the direction of the sound, was inches from where Pa and I stood. I screamed. Pa clamped his hand over my mouth. "Snake! Snake!" I shouted, but only a muffle filtered through Pa's fingers.

"Pa. Snake!"

"Don't try an' trick me, son. Drop the gun and back away."

Bzzzz. I tilted my head a smidgen and strained my eyes sideways and down at the coiled rattler inches from our feet. Another scream evaporated into Pa's hand. I tried to wrestle free. I accidentally stepped on his foot.

"Maggie, don't move a muscle, or it will strike."

I ignored Jacob and squirmed. *Get me away! Get me away!*

"Quit fighting, Maggie." Pa tightened his grip around my ribs.

"Get me away. Get me away." Only an incomprehensible squeal escaped through Pa's fingers.

Pa squeezed my ribs so tight I was sure they'd cracked. I winced in pain. To brace himself against my struggling, he took a step to widen his stance. To the left, closer to the serpent. He shouted an explicative and released his hold.

A shot boomed.

Off balance, I tumbled to the ground and scurried away from the danger. I scrambled to my feet and dashed to Jacob.

Jacob's face was wagon-top white. The shotgun had fallen to the ground. I followed his line of sight.

Pa sat on the ground, inches from the snake.

"Did it get you?" Jacob asked.

"Yep." Pa's hat rested upturned in the grass near where he sat clutching his calf. Sweat dripped into his eyes from matted hair that hung over his forehead. Next to Pa, the rattler was sprawled in the grass, still as a gnarled stick.

"Maggie, get some help." Jacob's gaze remained focused on the dead snake.

I snatched the brooch from the grass and raced toward the wagons. "Help! Help!"

Daisy toddled up to me as I cleared the brush and stumbled into camp. "What is it, hon?"

"It's Pa"—I gasped for a breath—"a snake."

"I can't believe your pa's scared of a little ol' snake."

"Giant snake." I stretched my arms out full length. "Bit him."

"Joseph"—she yelled over her shoulder—"come quick."

Our caravan mates sat in a circle around the fire in the center of the wagon loop, some in chairs, some on logs, and Mr. Schmitt sprawled on the ground, gnawing on a blade of grass. Mr. Bennett grunted as he pushed himself up from his seat. The chair tumbled backward, but he didn't stop to righten it. "Come on, Jimbo. Let's go see what kinda trouble Hanley got himself into this time." He shoved that last bite of biscuit into his mouth and lumbered toward us.

Mr. James followed.

Back at the river, Pa was upright, hobbling on one foot. He had one arm draped around Jacob's neck, and the other hand was clutched around his shotgun, which he tried to use as a cane. Mr. Bennett rushed over to them, took the weapon from Pa, sidled up to his side opposite Jacob, and scrunched down as Pa wrapped his other arm around Mr. Benett's shoulders.

Mr. James hovered over the dead snake, mouth agape. "I ain't never seen a snake that big." He removed his hat and wiped his brow with the back of his wrist and replaced the hat. "Must be at least a five footer. Maybe six. And as thick as an elephant turd."

Daisy planted her hands on her hips. "Mr. James, that's disgusting." A smirk accompanied the scolding remark.

"Well, my dear lady, come look for yourself."

Daisy tiptoed through the grass and stood by Mr. James. "Ooh!" She covered her mouth with her hand and turned her head away and clamped her eyes closed.

Jacob and Mr. Bennett assisted hopping and hobbling Pa back to camp.

I eavesdropped on the conversation by the snake, as I trailed the human crutches.

"Have you ever ate rattlesnake?" Mr. James asked.

"Eww."

I imagined Daisy scrunching her nose. Her screeching shrills rattled my nerves, along with the image of the snake.

"Bet it tastes like chicken. Let's take it back, and you can fry it up for supper."

"I ain't goin' near that dead snake. If you want it for supper, you can fry it up yourself. And not when I'm anywhere near."

"Come on, doll—you'll love it."

Daisy's response was swallowed in the jumble of brush.

Upon reaching camp, Jacob and Mr. Bennet led Pa to our wagon.

"Maggie, find something for your Pa to lay on," Mr. Bennet ordered.

I crawled inside the wagon and retrieved Pa's bedroll and spread it on the ground near the tailgate.

Jacob and Mr. Bennett eased Pa onto the blanket.

Pa moaned a coarse, groaning sound that froze my blood.

"Anyone know how to treat a snakebite?" Mr. Bennett asked the group of gawking men who had gathered around us.

One of them belched.

"Only way I heard is to whack off the limb so's the poison don't spread."

I leered at the short, stocky, rosy-cheeked man who offered the suggestion. I didn't know his name, nor did I want to.

"No one's choppin' my leg off."

I thought back to the afternoon I helped Doc Sam. My first and last day as a doctor's assistant. He didn't have any snakebite patients that day. I winced at the memory of the horrific wail the injured man had howled when Doc Sam severed his arm. I crept away from the group and sat on the wagon tongue.

Jacob sat near me. We watched in silence.

Daisy knelt next to Pa and reached for his hand. "Someone fetch me a clean, wet cloth."

The hovering men fidgeted.

I grunted under my breath. As the only other female present, it was my duty to get the rag. I walked around the opposite side of the wagon from Pa, Daisy, and the huddled men and climbed in and searched for a towel. I couldn't find one. I grabbed one of Pa's shirts that I had recently laundered, eased from the wagon, and soaked the shirt in the pail of water that Jacob had filled earlier. The bucket that I had kicked over remained askew in a mud puddle. I rang the excess water from the garment and handed it to Daisy.

"Thanks, sweetie."

Don't call me sweetie, I wanted to shout at her. I bit my tongue and scampered back to my seat at the front of the wagon.

"Someone should find a doctor." Daisy rolled up the damp shirt and placed it on Pa's forehead.

"What for?" Rosy Cheeks asked. "You either whack off his leg, or he dies." He shrugged and moved back to the smoldering fire at the center of camp. He picked up a nearby log and tossed it onto the flames. The blaze crackled and hissed.

"None of you is touchin' my leg. Hear? Nobody's coming near me with anything sharp or they'll find their own leg sliced to bits."

Daisy looked up at Mr. Rowlands. "Howard, you've got a horse. We're only a half day past the cutoff. You could find another train and spread the word that we're in need of a doctor."

"For him?" Mr. Rowlands scrunched his face, the way Jacob used to when he was a toddler and Ma tried to feed him mashed peas. He aimed his finger at Pa. "You want me to venture out alone after dark and risk being attacked and scalped by Indians? Not on your life." He turned to join Rosy Cheeks at the fire.

<hr>

Jacob shaking my arm, accompanied by a clanking sound, woke me the following morning. Better than a gunshot, which was the alarm used by our previous train. "Go away." I moaned, and rolled onto my side.

"Maggie, wake up."

I opened my right eye a slit. The morning sun glinted off the dancing leaves of the cottonwood trees that hovered near our campsite. Clank. Clank. The morning fog started to evaporate from between my ears. Digging. Someone was digging in the rocky ground. Two someones. Deep voices wafted in the morning breeze. I tried to open my left eye. It screamed in pain and refused. My face felt like simmering pulp. I touched the tender spot on my cheek with my finger. A firebolt speared through my shoulder and wrist at the movement. The events of the previous evening flooded into my consciousness. I wrapped my arms around my screaming ribs and turned my aching head toward the clanking noise. Mr. Rawlins and Mr. James were digging a hole at the base of one of the quivering cottonwoods. My stomach churned. I looked at Jacob, who knelt beside me.

"He's gone, Maggie."

"Pa?"

"He didn't make it through the night."

The fog rolled back into my head and cluttered my thoughts. I had no thoughts. I was numb. But not a numbness filled with grief, like I felt at Ma's passing. Just plain numb. I rose to a sitting position. Scout scooted up next to me, lay down, and nuzzled his chin into my lap. I absentmindedly patted his head and watched the men work.

"Oh, Maggie, I'm so sorry." Daisy's shrill voice sliced the breeze, like a karate chop through a hunk of wood, as she tiptoed toward us.

She eased onto the ground next to me. Scout raised his head, as if to ask if it were okay for the woman to invade our space.

"It was just so awful. I didn't know what to do. He groaned and moaned. He kept calling me Patty. I kept telling him that my name is Daisy, but he kept saying, 'Patty, make it go away.'"

I was confused, because Ma's name was Mary Elizabeth.

"Then he vomited. Eww!" She pinched her nose with her thumb and index finger. "It was so disgusting."

I wished she would leave. I didn't want to hear about the vomit. Or the snake. Or Patty.

"Then he started choking. He couldn't get the disgusting stuff out of his mouth."

I shut my eyes and tried to blot out the image.

"I think that's what got him. He couldn't breathe. Choked to death on his own puke." She wiped her mouth with the back of her hand, as if some of Pa's vomit contaminated her lips. "The bite would've done him in anyway. So maybe this was better, that he got out of his misery sooner."

"Daisy"—her husband shouted from across the camp—"are you gonna fix up some grub or are you gonna let me starve to death?"

"Look, I gotta get something in the stomach of that big baby husband of mine, or he'll start growling like a grizzly." She staggered back toward her hungry spouse. "Can't you be patient for once in your life? These children need some comfort from a motherly figure."

Please go nourish your famished husband. Did all men act like that? Hopefully not Eliot. *Eliot.*

I turned and watched Mr. Rawlins and Mr. James tamp down the dirt over Pa's fresh grave. Was that his punishment for hurting Ma? For hurting me? Was dying a just punishment for anything? I should have felt sad. But I didn't. My disdain for Pa had always simmered beneath the surface of my consciousness, and since Ma's death had bubbled up like one of the Soda Springs geysers. But as much as I loathed his temper, the beatings, the fact that in Ma's absence I became his servant, he was our support line. How would we get to California now? And when we got there . . . then what?

"They're wasting their time," Jacob whispered. "The wolves and coyotes will dig it up before tomorrow."

I cringed. *Probably serves him right.* I reprimanded myself for the evil thought. Ma taught me long ago not to speak ill of the dead. Or something like that. *Did that include ill thoughts?*

"What do we do now?" Jacob propped his chin in his palms. "I don't want to go to California."

"I don't want to go to California either. Especially with these people. They scare me." I stole a glance at the creepy men huddled around the fire eating breakfast. My gut soured at the thought that I would be forced to marry someone like them. "Maybe we could go back to Missouri." I massaged my throbbing wrist.

Jacob pressed his lips together and stared into space, as if trying to summon the answer to one of Mr. Jones's tough math questions. "Too late, and too dangerous. We'd never make it by ourselves. Our captain was right—it does take a village to get a wagon from Missouri to the West."

Chapter 26

D*ear Diary,*

If fear were a mountain, we had reached the peak. The things that scared me—river crossing, Indians, buffalo, wolves, bears, rattlesnakes, dust storms, hail, the creepy men—were just mounds piling up to the apex of fear: terror. A blood-freezing fright with gut-strangling tentacles that squeezes out your breath and won't let go. And I wasn't alone. While on the trail, Scout hugged my heels like a shadow. I shadowed Jacob. Jacob held a white-knuckled grip on Jack's reins. The mules were also edgy. Four sets of twitching ears pivoting in unison at each sound, real or imagined.

As soon as Mr. Rawlins and Mr. James had tossed the last stone on Pa's grave, Jacob and I packed the wagon, said goodbye to Daisy, and pointed the mules north toward the Oregon cutoff. Mr. Bennet had cautioned us not to travel alone, especially through the territory of the Snake Band of the Shoshones. I wasn't sure which to fear more—hostile Indians or the creepy men. We reached the fork late in the afternoon. Except for the howling wind and rustling sage, everything was quiet. And empty. No parade of white tops swaying in the distance. Not even a far-off dust cloud to hint at the presence of life. Just us, the jackrabbits, the grasshoppers, and the rattlesnakes.

Dawn filtered through the crinkles of the drawstring enclosure of the canvas wagon top, splaying a saw-tooth-like stream of light across the blanket that straddled my lap as I leaned against Ma's trunk in the wagon bed.

We didn't die last night.

Jacob sat against the side rail near the tailgate, legs splayed, boots on, shotgun dangling across his lap, asleep. I wasn't the only one on edge.

Except for Ma's trunk and the little food that we had left, we had set our possessions, including Pa's whiskey keg, outside to make room to sleep in the wagon. Or rather hide in the wagon and wait, like bait, like an injured cottontail in a field of hungry coyotes. I didn't sleep a wink. I tapped Jacob's boot with my foot. My big toe had escaped from my shoe, exposing a hole in my stocking. Dirt and dried blood caked the digit. Another sock to darn. Unless I died first.

Scout lay between us, his chin resting on my lap. I patted his head. He rotated and positioned his ear under my fingers. His favorite spot to be scratched. He moaned with contentment as I massaged the base of his ear. He snuggled closer and rolled on his back, his front legs bent at the elbows. How could he be so relaxed? I rubbed his belly. A mule snorted outside. "Scout," I whispered, "we didn't die last night."

Although I felt half-dead, I mentally scanned my aching body from head to toe. Everything hurt. My cheeks and jaw sizzled like smoking oil in a frying pan, my left eye was swollen closed, and my lip was split. Through my squinted right eye, I examined my bruised wrists. I rested my hand on my sore ribs. It hurt to breathe.

I tapped Jacob's foot again. He stirred. Then his eyes popped open, and he sat erect and clutched the flintlock.

"It's morning,"

"Morning?" He blinked the sleep from his eyes.

"We weren't attacked last night."

"Scout didn't make a sound, so nothing came near." He eased his grip on the weapon.

"No wolves. And no Indians." I exhaled a nervous breath.

Jacob looked at me and cringed. *That bad.* He wriggled to his knees and untied the drawstring above the tailgate. Morning sunshine flooded the wagon bed.

The glare burned my stinging eye.

Jacob hopped out and lowered the tailgate. Then he raised his hand above his eyes to shield the brightness as he scanned the surroundings.

"How does it look?"

His gaze dropped to the ground where we had piled our possessions. He grinned. "You better come out and see for yourself."

I crab walked to the tailgate and eased down. My ribs exploded in pain. I followed Jacob's gaze to the heap of our belongings. An assortment of tools, a crate containing our dinnerware and utensils, another crate stuffed with clothes and blankets. Then I realized—the whiskey barrel was missing. In its place was a pair of moccasins adorned with intricate beadwork. Delicate blue, red, and white beads woven into a nested diamond pattern on the instep

and a blue-and-red braided band around the seam of the
sole.

Jacob peered at me out of the corner of his eye. "They
look like they might be your size."

I knelt and lifted one up as if it were a fragile egg and
caressed the adornments with my thumb, like I rubbed the
gem on Ma's brooch.

"Try them on."

"But how did they get here?" I looked up at him.
"How could someone sneak up to the wagon and take
the whiskey barrel, which isn't exactly light, I might add,
without Scout hearing? Or spooking the mules?"

Jacob shrugged. "Dunno. I've heard that Indians like the
white man's 'fire water,' but I think you got the better end
of the trade."

I wrestled off my mangled shoe and slipped my foot into
the moccasin. The soft leather molded around my instep.
"I've never felt anything so comfortable." I wiggled my
toes. The movement was as free as if I were barefoot. No
pinched toes! I tugged off my other shoe and donned the
other moccasin, rose, and took a tentative step. Then another. Like walking unshod in sand. I hopped and skipped
and giggled. I raised my arms in the air and twirled. I
wanted to dance—with Eliot.

"Let's get this stuff loaded and decide what we're going
to do next."

"Yes, my practical brother." I spun again, like a clumsy
ballerina.

"Good grief." He picked up some tools and slid them
into the wagon.

I had called him brother. *Did I mean it?*

We waited at the cutoff. Even if our train had already passed, another was likely to come by soon. While Jacob and Scout took the mules out to find some grass to graze, I made a fire and dumped some green coffee beans into the skillet to roast. Or rather fry, as we no longer had a roast pan. I didn't know why I craved a cup of steaming coffee. I would have thought that as much as I had detested keeping Pa's caffeine craving sated, I wouldn't want to roast or grind a bean again. I peered at the cloudless blue sky and realized that I'd never have to drop whatever I was doing to make him a hot cup of coffee again—ever. I exhaled a breath. A layer of tension melted away. Did that make me a bad person? Should I feel guilty now that I could relax and savor a warm cup myself after a meal instead of sneaking a quick sip to choke down the dust and bugs that tainted the leftover biscuits and bacon while cleaning up the dishes?

The vision of our coffee grinder abandoned on the prairie with our other unnecessary possessions flashed through my mind as I ground the fried beans with a stone. I grunted. Right then, I thought the appliance was rather necessary. I decided it would be one of our first purchases when we reached Oregon. After boiling some water and straining the grounds, I poured myself a cup. I inhaled the aroma and wondered how long we would be stranded here and who would eventually come by—if anyone.

Scout bounded up to me and nudged my elbow.

"No, Scout. I'm not sharing my coffee with you."

The mutt gave me his sad-puppy-eyes look and rested his chin on my lap.

"Sorry, boy. I'll share my biscuits and bacon and even fresh meat when we have some. But you keep your nose away from my cup."

I inhaled the nutty scent and slurped the liquid through my cut and swollen lip. Ow. Right then the soothing beverage tasted like heaven. Any other day the bitterness would have had me gagging like an old hag and the drink would have been dumped onto the dirt.

Jacob sauntered over and poured himself a cup. "Thanks for making the coffee." He held the tin cup in both hands and plopped to the ground across the dying fire.

"How are the mules?"

"Hungry. They're hobbled, but they need to be moved soon because the grass is scarce."

"How long do you think we're going to have to stay here? What if no one comes by? I don't think my nerves can handle another night alone out here."

"Considering how well it worked out for you, I would think you would want to spend every night out here." He smirked.

"Funny." I took another sip and stared one eyed into the cup.

"At least you're talking to me again. Does that mean I'm not a freak anymore?" He looked at me and then focused on his cup.

I watched the specs of dust that skimmed the surface of my beverage while I pondered his question. "No. You're still a freak. But you did save my life."

"You're welcome."

I looked up at him. "For someone who can't hit the side of a barn while standing right in front of it, your aim was spot on that snake. How did you do that?"

"I don't know. It's like the gun went off by itself. I don't even remember pulling the trigger." He stared into his cup. Then he picked up the stick I had been using as a poker and swirled the ashes. A puff of smoke escaped and evaporated in the breeze. He dropped the stick and took a biscuit from a nearby plate, looked at it, frowned, and then set it back.

"You know, you didn't shoot Pa. So you can't feel guilty about that."

"I don't feel guilty about it. It's just that . . ."

"It's just what?"

"It's just that . . . I don't feel bad that he's dead. I know it's awful to think that." He picked up the stick and resumed mixing the smoldering ashes.

"It probably is an awful way to think. I'm not sad that he's dead either. In fact, I'm kind of relieved."

"At least he can't hurt you anymore."

I touched my sore lip. My face must have been a mangled mess. "Is that what happened to Ma? What you accused Pa of?"

His poker paused in the ashes. Then he resumed his stirring. "Yeah. That's what happened. Every night he came home drunk, he would find some little annoyance and beat her. Sometimes it was just a shove or a slap and others, like the last time . . . It was like he had turned into a monster and couldn't stop."

I lowered my head. "I must sleep like the dead." I bit the inside of my lip. "She always told me that the cuts and bruises and black eyes were because of some clumsy thing she did. I knew he hit her sometimes. A slap across the face, like he would slap you or me. And he would throw things—dishes, cups, whatever was within reach when he went into a rage. It scared me so much that I startle at any crashing noise." I closed my eyes for a moment. "Deep down I think I knew it was more, especially after those nights when their fights managed to wake me up. Looking back, I think I was so consumed with my life and my problems that I was too selfish to be cognizant of hers."

"You were a sound sleeper. I laid awake every night listening for him to come home and tried to find the courage to stop him." His stick froze. "If only I wasn't so afraid of him."

"You had reason to be afraid. I'd never seen him so unhinged and out of control as he was the other day. If he was like that, he would have killed you also."

Jacob resumed his etching in the ashes. "This was worse. Ma's face never looked as bad as yours does right now. He had turned into a maniac."

I squinted at him. "If the snake hadn't bit him, would you have shot him?"

"You were in the way. As you noted, I'm not exactly a marksman." He took a sip from his cup.

"If you had a clean shot though, would you have taken it?"

He inhaled a deep breath and stared into his cup. "I don't know. I just knew that I couldn't let him hurt you anymore."

I took another sip and winced. Tepid. I liked my coffee steaming hot. Too hot to start another fire. "Why would Ma stay with him?"

"What else could she do? She had us to think about. And a woman couldn't be on her own. Especially one saddled with children."

"For better or worse. Till death do them part."

"And death did them part."

The spindly branches of the rustling sage creaked and moaned in the stiffening breeze. I set my cup on the ground and poked my finger through a new tear that marred my patched-up skirt. "Now that I have some new shoes, do you think when we get to the next fort, we could spend some of Pa's money on a new dress? This one is falling apart, and I'm afraid by the time we get to Oregon, it will have completely unraveled and I'll be naked."

"Now there's a gruesome image." He grinned. "And no, there's no money."

"What do you mean there's no money?" I gaped at him.

"If Pa had any money, it was buried with him. Or Mr. Rawlins took it."

"What!" I raised my good eyebrow. "We'll need money before we get to Oregon."

"We'll need money when we get there as well."

"What are we going to do?" I tipped my chin into my palms.

"We'll figure something out. In the meantime, you're pretty good with a needle and thread. Why don't you make a dress out of Pa's clothes. He won't need them anymore."

The thought of even touching Pa's garments, let alone wearing them, was repulsive. But then, so was walking around in my underthings, which were in worse condition than my dress.

I picked up another nearby stick and sketched in the ashes along with Jacob and whispered, "At least Pa never knew that you're a freak."

He cringed and clambered to his feet. "I better check on the mules."

"I'm sorry. I just don't know how to deal with it." I focused on my artwork. What was this bond that Jacob and I shared? Like we were tethered together by a thick cable that even the sturdiest cutters couldn't sever. As much as I wanted to break free and not have to live under a dark cloud threatening to burst when his sin was discovered, the noose at the end of the rope bound us together. We'd always been a team—stronger together. We would need each other more than ever now if we're going to reach Oregon. And then what?

"You don't know how to deal with it." He thrust his stick into the ashes and threw his hands in the air. "Do you think I want to be a freak? Do you think I like looking over my shoulder all the time, wondering what people are whispering behind my back? Do they suspect? What will they do if they find out? Beat me and leave me for dead? Shoot me? Hang me? Do you think I like living with that threat hovering over my head?"

He stomped off toward the mules.

Scout sprang up and bounded after him.

I brought my knees to my chest and wrapped my arms around my shins. Pain erupted from my ribs. My bruised face sizzled under the sun's fiery rays. I touched my swollen eye and tried to open it. No luck. My mind drifted to the promise I had made to Ma a lifetime ago. I assumed she had wanted me to protect Jacob from the school bullies who taunted him and beat him up because he was smart, and awkward, and a runt, and, well, different from the other kids. *Ma, I don't know if I can keep my promise.*

A stiff afternoon gale whisked away the morning breeze. The wagon canvas flapped, and the sage whistled. Not a soul had passed. Not a wagon or a hunter or an Indian—thankfully. I shuddered. I wished I had a book to read. And children to read to. Free from Pa's bondage, I intended to read every book I could get my hands on and fill my head with knowledge and ideas that would have raised the hackles on his neck and spewed smoke from his ears. And I'd teach every child I could reach, as well as their mothers, to dream of a world they could only discover through books.

I dropped my chin into my hands. Books cost money.

I took Jacob's suggestion and spent the time hacking away at Pa's trousers and shirts. Not enough for a complete dress. I ripped open the trouser seams and used the wool fabric to reinforce my skirt. Then I fashioned a new apron, with a clever—if I do say so myself—inside pocket, from his cotton shirt. My underthings would just have to hold together a bit longer.

The sun had arced to the west when a clattering of hooves jerked me from my task. I pierced my finger with the needle. *Ouch.* I eased to my feet and met Jacob at the wagon as he tied off the mules.

"Someone's coming." He gave the slip knot on the mules' leads a tug and reached for the shotgun, which he had leaned against the wagon.

I squinted toward the eastern horizon. A contrail of dust swirled in the wind. I sucked in a breath. "Do you think it's Indians? Or bandits?"

"Dunno. If they are, they might be friendly."

Might be. Mr. Bennet's warning boiled in my gut.

A horse whinnied. My limbs trembled, my heart raced, and a tingle slithered up my spine and attacked the back of my neck. The clanking hooves neared.

Jacob cocked the gun.

Chapter 27

Dear Diary,

I never thought I'd be happy to see Ethan! More like ecstatic. I recognized his bumbling form swaying in the saddle as he and our guide emerged through the sage before they were close enough to determine whether they were Indians, bandits, or emigrants. I flung my hands to my chest and dropped to my knees in relief. Jacob raised his gun in the air and whooped. I'd never heard a sound so loud and shrill escape from his lips before.

Our train welcomed us with a feast of fresh meat, wild onions, and a pie that evening at the cutoff where they stopped for the night. Nobody seemed sad at the news of Pa's death. That didn't surprise me. In fact, I think that some of them, including the captain and Mrs. McNeil, were relieved, although that thought would never escape from their lips. After a warm embrace by Mrs. McNeil, she fussed over my cuts and bruises. I doubted she believed my fib when I told her I fell. I blamed it on my old shoes. I kept the bruises on my wrists hidden under my sleeves.

Grueling, taxing, punishing, harsh. Words can't describe the struggles of traveling the rugged sand and basalt trail that *hovered on the ridge above the Snake River. Mr. Jeffries hired Jacob to help round up his cattle and get them moving in the right direction each morning, so I drive the wagon while he works. A bolt of pain radiates through my aching body with every bump of the volcanic wasteland. I use a folded blanket for a seat cushion, but it doesn't help much. Occasionally some of the men try to scale the steep canyon wall to reach the water, but each time they give up in frustration. The relentless wind and heat and dust are the worst we've encountered. It drains us all. Especially the animals, who grow wearier and more withered each day. The sharp basalt tears their hooves. Jacob wraps the mule's hooves in buffalo hide to help protect them against the sharp rocks. The wrapping needs to be replaced every few days. We're almost out of hide. The McNeils lost an ox, the Daltons lost a mule, and Mr. Jeffries lost three cows. Jacob is worried about Penny. I'm beyond worried. Her ribs and hip bones protrude through her dull coat, her once friendly eyes have become glossy and expressionless, and she has lost interest in nose rubs and neck scratches. I pray that she can hold on until we find better grass.*

Late afternoon, the wagon creaked and moaned beside me while Jacob drove the team. I plowed forward with my chin tucked to my sternum, my bonnet gripped tightly in my fist, and my eyes squinted against the afternoon glare and biting dust. According to Jacob, the bruises on my face had faded from a deep blackish blue to a pale brownish yellow. However, the tiny dust particles felt like giant wasp stingers as they attacked my sensitive skin. An unyielding barrage of insect warriors wielding miniature lances.

The team slowed with the string of wagons ahead of us. "Why are we stopping?" I shouted to Jacob.

He released the reins when the mules stopped. Buck snorted. Molly pawed the ground. "We must be near the crossing."

"Crossing?"

He slid from the wagon so he wouldn't have to shout. "The captain said in his briefing this morning that we're going to stop early this evening so that we can have a fresh start when we cross the Snake tomorrow."

"You mean we have to cross the Snake?" I couldn't see the river from where we stood, but the times I'd peered down the steep canyon wall, it ran swift and deep and menacing.

"The place we're fording is called Three Island Crossing."

"Let me guess—there are three islands."

"Bravo. On the one hand, the islands serve as sort of stepping stones, but all that water still needs to flow past them. So it will be dangerous."

"Yippee." I shook my head.

"After we get the mules settled, we need to inspect the wagon to make sure it's sealed tight." He patted Buck on the neck.

"Do we have any more tar? We've used so much of it to patch our shoes that I'd be surprised if there is any left."

"I hope so. If not, we can probably buy some from someone."

"Without any money." I frowned.

"Maybe we could trade something then."

"Like the last of our food." I crossed my arms around my ribs. *Ow.* Still tender.

As we set up camp, I gathered the snags of sagebrush that I had collected throughout the day for the fire and arranged the larger sticks in a pyramid form over the smaller pieces that served as kindling. Fortunately, the stiff afternoon gale had waned to a mild enough breeze to allow for a fire.

"Maggie!"

My heart skipped a beat. "William, when are you going to learn not to sneak up on me?"

He jutted his lower lip and stared at his shoes. "Sorry. I didn't mean to scare you."

"I know you didn't. But please don't sneak up on me like that anymore."

He shoved his hands in his pockets. "Okay, I'll try not to."

Now I felt bad. "I'm sorry, William. I guess I'm a little edgy this evening." I squatted and peered under the brim of his dirty hat into his sullen eyes. "Forgive me?"

His nod was almost imperceptible.

"Do you want to help me start the fire?"

"Oh." He lifted his head, and his face exploded into a grin. "Now I remember why I snuck up on you." He bounced on his toes. "Mrs. McNeil said to invite you and Jacob to our wagon for supper."

"Gee"—I stood—"that's awfully nice of her."

"She said it's a special dinner."

"What's so special about today?"

"She said it was a surprise. Come in about an hour." He touched his chin with his finger and scrunched his forehead. "Or maybe she said half hour."

"Why don't you let her know we'll be there when Jacob gets the mules settled."

"And, oh, the Fishers are coming too."

"Who are the Fishers?" I raised an eyebrow.

"They're the new people who joined us at Fort Hood."

Two new families were traveling with our train. I had been so absorbed in my own troubles that I hadn't made the effort to meet them. Another black mark, if Ma were keeping track in heaven.

William turned and raced away.

"And, William . . ."

He skidded and teetered when he pivoted to face me.

"Don't startle Mrs. McNeil."

"Okay, I won't." The promise evaporated in the breeze as he sprinted off.

Later, I carried a stack of dirty dishes to a pail of soapy water that Mrs. McNeil had waiting near her wagon for cleanup. "Thank you for having us tonight," I said. "The antelope and fresh bread were a refreshing improvement from the cold bacon and hard biscuits that I was going to feed Jacob." I didn't say that it would be the last of our bacon or that we only had enough flour for one or two more batches of biscuits. "And where did you find fresh onions in this desolate country?"

"The onions are the last from what we gathered back at Bear Valley. I could tell that Jacob enjoyed the meat. Perhaps he would like to accompany Charles the next time he goes hunting. I imagine Jacob misses hunting with his pa." She removed a soapy plate from the wash pail and set it into the rinse bucket.

"Uh . . ." I couldn't tell her that the only thing that Jacob had ever killed was a rattlesnake. "I bet he'd enjoy that." Jacob would have to weasel his own way out of that one. I handed her the last dirty plate.

She washed and rinsed the dish and set it on a stack with the others. She picked them up and handed them to me. "Can you please take these back to the table? We're going to need them for the party."

"Party?"

She winked and turned toward the back of her wagon.

When I returned to the makeshift table near the fire, Mr. and Mrs. Fisher and their two children, seven-year-old Mary Alice and four-year-old Stephen, had joined the celebration. Mr. McNeil made the introductions.

Mrs. McNeil came around the side of her wagon with a cake cradled in both hands as if it were an injured bird she was trying to protect. A cake. A real cake! She set the treat on the table in front of William.

His eyebrows shot up almost to his hairline and his lips formed an O. "How did you know?"

"Friends"—Mrs. McNeil clasped her hands in front of her chest—"today is William's birthday. Happy Birthday, William!"

Happy Birthday wishes were shouted from around the table.

William's grin stretched ear to ear as we clapped.

Stephen, who sat next to William, patted the birthday boy on the back. "How old are you, William?"

"Eight." He thumbed his chest. "I'm eight years old."

"Eight years old." Mr. Fisher feigned amazement. "Soon you'll have a sweetheart and be off on your honeymoon."

Stephen grimaced. "Pa, that's gross!"

I peeked over at Jacob, who studied the pattern on the tablecloth that covered the crate that served as the table. I recall Pa teasing Jacob with a similar comment when Jacob turned eight. Or maybe it was nine or ten.

"Hey, Maggie"—William bobbed in his seat—"after the cake, can you read to us again?"

I'd had no time or energy for reading or lessons since we reunited with our train. "Of course, William. We can continue with *The Swiss Family Robinson* where we left off. I've been dying to know what happened on that deserted island. But you'll need to spell your name for me first."

"W-i-l-l-i-a-m." His grin could have been seen from the moon. "We have to start over from the beginning, for Stephen and Mary Alice." He glanced at his new friends.

"From the beginning it will be. After cake."

Mrs. McNeil wielded a knife and divided the cake into nine wedges, one larger than the rest. She slid the larger slice onto a plate and placed it in front of William. "Happy birthday, William."

William clasped a utensil in his fist and stabbed his treat.

"Hold on a minute, young man. Even though it's your special day, let's mind our manners and wait until everyone is served."

William lowered the fork. "Yes, ma'am."

"Isn't this grand." Mrs. McNeil fanned her arm over the scene before us. "God put this gully right here by these islands so we can get to the river. And look"—she pointed to the bottom of the ridge—"there's even some grass for the animals to graze while waiting to cross."

She was right in that the steep canyon walls parted to form a gentle descent to the riverbank. A line of white tops snaked down the hill and queued along the shore, waiting to cross. A herd of cattle splashed between the third island and the far shore. "Why are people swimming with those animals?"

"They're Indians"

"Indians?"

"Charles told me about it this morning. Since most white folks don't know how to swim, we hire Indians to swim the animals across." Some of the Indians were escorting the herd on horseback, but there were a few heads bobbing in the water.

"Usually the cattle cross last, after the wagons."

"Since there is grass on the islands, they crossed the cattle to the first island last evening to let them graze overnight."

I returned to our wagon, which was in line behind the McNeils'. When we reached the shore, I climbed onto the seat beside Jacob.

"Scout, you ride in the back, buddy." Jacob gave the pooch a nudge, and Scout hopped into the wagon bed. He stood on Ma's trunk and watched over our shoulders.

"Are you sure the wagon is sealed tight?" My heart pounded, and I wiped my sweaty palms on my apron.

"You watched me smear the last of our tar into every crevasse. We should be good to go."

The McNeil wagon rolled into the water ahead of us.

"Here goes." Jacob flicked the reins. Jack and Molly were the lead pair. They didn't move. Jacob flicked the reins again. "Hup, hup." Jack pawed the sand.

"Move out! Move out!" A rider on horseback trotted up to Jack and yanked his bridle.

"Hup, hup, hup!" Jacob flicked the reins harder. "Hup, Jack. Giddup, Molly. Penny, Buck, let's move."

The rider splashed into the water, and the team followed.

I shielded my face from the spray.

Scout yelped.

"Good boy, Jack. Good girl, Molly. Penny, Buck, keep it up. Hup, hup. Keep moving."

The water lapped onto the side of the wagon as we lumbered over the bumpy riverbed.

"So far, so good," Jacob shouted over the cacophony of splashing, braying, creaks, groans, and shouts. His eyes, however, remained deadlocked between the mules' ears.

The current tugged on the wagon as the wheels lifted from the riverbed. The mules lowered their heads, leaned into their harnesses, and huffed and snorted through the flow.

"Come on. Come on." I fisted my hands. My fingernails dug into my palms.

A sigh of relief escaped from my lungs as the mules clawed the solid ground of the first island. We waited until the group ahead of us reached the second island and for the riders to cross back to escort our group.

The mules deserved an extra scoop of oats for their effort, dragging us to the second and third islands. If only we had some oats.

"Three down, one crossing to go," Jacob whispered to himself.

"One to go," I repeated under my breath. Yelling and splashing blew from the far shore. A whip cracked. Livestock snorted and bleated as they labored across. The group ahead snaked out of the water and onto the bank. *They made it. We will too.* But my confidence waned as we neared the water's edge. This section was wider. The current swifter. A head bobbed up next to a cow. I inhaled a gulp of air and tensed. Then I relaxed—a little. It was an Indian guiding the wayward beast toward shore.

Ahead of us, Mr. McNeil shimmied from under his wagon. He approached, uncoiling a chain. "Jacob, hop down and give me a hand, would you?"

Jacob slid to the ground. "What are we doing?"

"We're chaining all the wagons in our group together. The lead rig has twelve oxen. If the wagons are tied together, either the teams in front or the teams in the rear will have good purchase. When the lead team reaches solid ground, they can pull the rest of us out if there's any trouble."

After assisting Mr. McNeil with the chains, Jacob climbed back onto the wagon seat. I handed him the reins, which I had been holding for him. "Who's behind us?"

"The Fishers. You remember, from William's party last night."

"The ones with the two kids. Stephen and Mary, uh, Mary something." I clenched my fist, as if that would squeeze the name from my memory.

"Mary Alice. You never were good with names." He shook his head.

I supposed if I was planning on teaching children, I should devise a method to remember their names.

A mule brayed. Jack kicked up a cloud of dust as he pawed the ground. Hooves clapped down the line of wagons toward us. Ethan. I cringed. The sun glistened off the palomino's wet coat, and Ethan's trousers were soaked.

"Hey, Maggie." He lifted his finger to his hat.

I bit my lip and looked forward.

"Jacob." Ethan nodded. "Just checking to make sure everyone's secure before we cross."

"I think we're good here." I noticed a smile seep from Jacob's lips from the corner of my eye.

"Tell you what, Maggie . . ."

I kept my eyes focused on Molly's ears in front of me.

"After I make sure that everyone is set, I'll come back and cross next to you. That way, if anything happens, I'll be here to rescue you."

My shoulders tensed. "Uh, thanks, Ethan. But I think we'll be okay."

"It's no problem. I'll be back in a few."

I peered over at him just as he winked at me and nudged his horse forward to harass the Fishers behind us.

"The last thing I want is to be rescued by Ethan. I'd never be able to live that down."

Jacob didn't respond. I imagined that he would like to be rescued by Ethan.

Someone whistled ahead of us. Another man shouted, "Move out." The animals snorted, wagons moaned, and chains clanked as the line of wagons crept forward.

"Here goes." Jacob flicked the reins. "I sure hope everyone's sealed tight."

"You said we are."

"We should be. We're about in the middle of our group of about a dozen wagons. If someone starts to sink, they could pull us under since we're all chained together."

"I thought the point of chaining us together is so that we wouldn't get swept away." I wiped perspiration from my forehead with my sleeve.

"We won't get swept away. If we run into trouble, we'll get pulled out. It's just a matter of whether the wheels are under us or not."

My gut sizzled.

The mules splashed in the water. Molly balked.

"Easy, girl. Easy, girl." A nervous edge crept into Jacob's voice that I hoped the mule didn't sense.

The girl must have taken a cue from Jack. She lowered her head and leaned into the harness.

"Good girl, Molly. Good girl." Jacob relaxed his grip on the reins and let the mules do their work.

"Good girl," I whispered. I held a white-knuckled grip on the lip of the wagon seat.

The current pressed at the wagon box when the wheels cleared the bottom. Then I felt a tug, as if a fissure had opened beneath us and the earth's core tried to siphon us under. I peered over the edge. The waterline was halfway up the side of the wagon. "We're sinking."

"We'll be fine." The stony expression and set jaw belied his words. "Hup, Jack. Hup. Molly. Pull, Penny. Give her all you got, Buck. We're almost there."

Poor Penny. I didn't think she had enough heart left in her to pull. And we weren't almost there. Not even halfway.

"Looking good." I turned to Ethan as he bobbed up beside us on his palomino. I felt bad for the mare. Her ears thrust forward, and her eyes crossed, a mixture of angst and determination as she fought against the swift current.

A shrill shriek pierced the cacophony of sounds. "Pa!" Mary Alice. She screamed again.

I twisted my head to try to see the Fisher wagon behind us. The canvas top blocked my view.

"That didn't sound good." Jacob tightened his grip on the reins. "Something's not right."

Another scream.

"I'll go check." I ducked into the wagon bed and crawled over the trunk and squeezed over and around crates of food and supplies and knelt at the tailgate.

"Oh no!" Water lapped over the side of the Fishers' wagon bed. Mr. Fisher was frantically bailing water out with a pail. "Ethan," I shouted around the side of the canvas "The Fishers are sinking."

The six oxen pulling the Fisher wagon puffed and snorted. Only the noses, ears, and horns of the pair nearest the wagon cleared the water.

"Help!" Ethan shouted. "Wagon sinking."

Another rider bobbed up alongside the Fishers' wagon.

Mrs. Fisher stood in the wagon box, fear erupting from her wide eyes as she watched her husband hurl another bucket of water out the front. Mary Alice clung to her waist and screamed. Mrs. Fisher held crying Stephen, his legs looped around her hips and his arms wrapped around her neck, like a boa constrictor.

"Save my children!" Mrs. Fisher cried over the shrieks.

Mr. Fisher tossed another pail of water out of the wagon. It splashed the back of an ox.

The rider wrangled his horse adjacent to the wagon. "Hand me the boy."

Mrs. Fisher scooted toward the front. Mary Alice held a death grip around her waist.

The rider squeezed his knees into his horse for balance. "Lower him down to me and have him grab my waist."

Mrs. Fisher wriggled closer to the lip of the wagon and tried to pry Stephen's grip from her neck. He clung tighter and cried louder.

Mr. Fisher flung another bucket of water.

Hopeless.

"If he won't let go, you'll both have to come. You need to get out of the wagon."

Mr. Fisher dropped his bucket and pried Mary Alice from his wife's waist.

"Mary Alice. I can't go without my girl. Take the children only."

"You need to hurry. Ethan will get the girl."

Between Mr. Fisher pushing while trying to block Mary Alice from her ma and Mrs. Fisher squirming, Mrs. Fisher and a sobbing Stephen landed astride the horse. The rider wrapped one arm around Mrs. Fisher, clutched the reins in his other hand, and steered his ride into the current.

"Mama, Mama," Mary Alice shrieked.

"Get the girl, Ethan," the rider shouted.

Ethan steered his mare to the side of the Fisher wagon. He reached his hand out to grasp the canvas but was swept into the current. He gritted his teeth and reined his horse back into position.

Mr. Fisher lifted his daughter by the waist.

"No, Papa. I'm scared."

Mr. Fisher's whispered something in her ear. He kissed her cheek and lifted her so that her feet dangled at the lip of the wagon box. Their wagon sank lower. Water gushed in.

The tail of our wagon sagged.

"One, two, three," Mr. Fisher shouted, and hurled his daughter into Ethan's outstretched arms.

The force of Mary Alice's body coming at Ethan knocked him askew. The mare whinnied and thrashed, spewing spray like a fountain. Ethan and Mary Alice splashed into the water.

I screamed.

"What happened?" Jacob shouted from the wagon seat.

"Ethan and Mary Alice. They fell in."

A head broke the surface through the melee of flailing hooves and rippling waves. Glossy black hair shimmered in the sun.

The Indian submerged into the churning water.

I held my breath.

Moments later he resurfaced with his arm wrapped around Ethan's chest. He swam toward us, slapped Ethan's hand onto the lip of our tailgate, then disappeared in the swirling current.

I clasped onto Ethan's wrist with both hands.

Ethan coughed and gasped. His wet hair strung over his face. "Ethan's okay," I shouted to Jacob.

"Mary Alice?"

"I don't know. I can't see her."

Ethan hacked some more and clasped his other hand on the wagon. I kept my grip on his wrist. I tried to pull him in, but I wasn't strong enough and there was nothing for him to grasp with his feet.

The wagon sagged lower. The water reached the lip of the wagon box and Ethan's chin. *We're going to sink.* The oxen pulling the Fisher wagon huffed and snorted, eyes crossed and ears back.

I gasped as a head shot out of the water near the lead oxen. The Indian. Then Mary Alice. She gagged and sobbed. The Indian grabbed the oxen's horn while clutching Mary Alice to his side.

"She's safe. Mary Alice is safe." I exhaled a relieved breath. Then I sucked in another. Water lapped over the tailgate and soaked my dress.

Chapter 28

Dear Diary,

Ma used to say that the good and the bad tend to even out over time. Ma, I think you were wrong. The scale is weighted so heavy to the bad that the good can't possibly catch up.

The captain was right in that travel on the north side of the Snake was easier, somewhat. The jagged lava fields that stretched forever on the south side of the river are partially buried under packed earth and sand on the north side. Although evidence that the ancient volcanoes didn't discriminate which side of the river to ooze their molten lava abounded as we lumbered over patches of rough basalt. Jacob said that the river didn't exist then, that the underground volcanoes erupted first, and the river carved a deep gorge through the lava fields. But how would he know? It was eons ago anyway. I'm just thankful that we didn't drown back at Three Island Crossing. Neither did the Fishers. But their wagon suffered damage that took several hours to repair, and most of their food was ruined. While not lush pastures, the north side of the river had patches of grass for the animals to graze. Penny is starting to fill out some and has regained a little of her feistiness, much to Molly's annoyance.

We rolled in to Fort Boise late in the afternoon. Jacob told me that, like Fort Hall, it was built as a trading post for the trappers. However, after the beaver trade dried up, the military did not take over Fort Boise like it had Fort Hall. So the compound had been left to decompose, like the dead animals rotting alongside the trail. The fort does have a small trading post, but the shelves are mostly bare. Those who were planning on restocking were met with disappointment unless they were willing to shell out for overpriced sugar. Then, a bittersweet reunion.

I spied him on the shady side of the fort, sitting on the ground, leaning against the cracked and splintered wall, arms wrapped around his shins. His eyes hid behind his hat brim, and he chewed on a blade of grass. Perhaps I was mistaken. I watched him for a moment, then walked to a few feet from where he sat. "Eliot, is that you?"

He raised his head. "Maggie?" He sprang to his feet. "Maggie!" He rushed over and engulfed me in a passionate embrace. I smothered my face into his shoulder, and his chin rested on mine. "I thought you were on your way to California." He raised his head and glanced over my shoulder. "Where's your pa?"

"Don't worry—he won't hit you anymore." I looked at my dusty moccasins. "He's dead."

He tightened his embrace. I leaned into him. "I'm sorry, Maggie." He released the hug and rested his hands on my shoulders and gazed into my eyes. A moist gloss clouded his aqua-marine orbs, and a somberness veiled his playful grin.

"You look sad. What's happened?"

He reached for my hand. "Come sit with me."

We sat against the adobe wall, shoulder to shoulder. He rubbed his hands on his trousers and leaned his head against the facade and closed his eyes.

"Eliot, what's wrong?"

He didn't answer. Finally he whispered, "Mama died yesterday."

I inhaled a shocked gasp. "Eliot, I'm so sorry." I rested my hand on his forearm, then jerked it away. Was that too intrusive?

He reached for my hand and intertwined his fingers with mine and covered the union with his other hand. I rested my head on his shoulder. I felt his warmth, his breath, his sorrow, his being.

"You know she hadn't been well." I had to strain to hear his muted words. "She spent most of the trip laid up in the wagon. Jostled about by every bump and dip and swerve in the whole damn earth." He sniffed. "As far as I'm concerned, it's Doc's fault. He knew she wasn't well when we left home. Said she would get better. The fresh air and change of scenery would do wonders. Deep down, I think he knew she wasn't well enough to travel, but his determination to get to Oregon to fulfill his own stupid dream clouded his judgement." He curled his lips under his teeth. "We buried her this morning. Her body will be abandoned on this godforsaken desert with not even a spindly tree to shade her from this fiery hellhole."

I thought of the oak that sheltered Ma's grave back home. "I'm sure that Doc Sam loved her. How is he? And Sissy?"

"Haven't seen him except at the funeral. He's off trying to heal some poor soul somewhere. He couldn't even save his own wife."

I squeezed his forearm with my free hand.

"And Sissy's a wreck. Hasn't stopped crying. She and Mama were close. I don't know what she's going to do without her."

The shadow cast by the wall elongated as we sat huddled together, hand in hand, shoulder to shoulder. It felt right. Like we belonged here together. Connected by our struggles and sorrows. And the joyful times that surely must lie ahead.

He released my hand and rested his palm on my knee. "I'm sorry for dumping all my sorrows on you. Thanks for listening."

I nodded. "I know how I felt when Ma died. She was my rock. The fountain where I drew my strength. When she died, it felt like my life's blood had been sucked from my soul. I didn't know how I could ever survive without her. Sometimes I still don't."

He squeezed my knee.

"I know how much pain you and Sissy are going through right now."

"And you just lost your pa. What happened?"

I told him about the snake. I omitted the part about Pa hitting me. And Jacob's accusation. And the vomit.

He was impressed by Jacob's marksmanship. "I had no idea he was that good of a shot."

"He's not. It was a fluke. He could have just as easily hit me, or Pa, or missed us all, including the snake. So if you ever see him with a gun, make sure you're behind him. Better yet, run—in the opposite direction."

He chuckled and reached for my hand. "So does Jacob still have eyes for Ethan?"

"What?" I had hoped that Eliot had forgotten about Jacob's obsession with Ethan—if that was what it was.

"You remember, the night by the fire, before your pa stumbled in and ruined a perfect evening. Where was that?"

"Independence Rock. And Jacob doesn't have a thing." I emphasized "thing" with a one-handed quote mark. "I imagine he was watching Ethan because the only other thing for him to look at that night would have been us. And that would have embarrassed him. And us. He was just staring into space because he was lonely, and Ethan just happened to be there." I hoped I sounded convincing.

"I think Ethan has a thing for you though, because I'd seen him watching you."

Despite the warm afternoon, I shuddered. "Creepy." I didn't say that he, Eliot, was the only person I wanted watching me. "Besides, ever since I witnessed that he almost caused Mary Alice to drown and that he was saved by an Indian at that Three Island Crossing place, he's been avoiding me."

"Good. Then I don't have to worry about him snatching you away before I see you again."

"No chance of that." I shook my head.

"Perhaps you and Jacob could join our train?" He quirked a questioning eyebrow. "We head out in the morning."

My eyes brightened. Then I frowned. "If it were up to me, I would be ready at dawn. However, our mules are so ragged that they've been stumbling over their own feet, so they need some rest. Also, Jacob has been working for Mr. Jeffries every morning, helping with his cattle. So that leaves me managing the team and the wagon while he's away." I didn't tell him that we were penniless and needed the money Jacob was earning, or that I also helped the elder Mrs. May with her mending occasionally, which added a couple of bits to our coffers. And I would be overcome with guilt if I abandoned the children again without finishing *The Swiss Family Robinson.*

"There you are."

I frowned at Constance, who hovered over us with her hands on her hips, with her perfect clothes, and scrubbed face, and shimmering hair, and . . . How had I not noticed her sneak up on us?

"Constance." Eliot released my hand and sprang to his feet. He removed his hat and ran his fingers through his tangled hair. It was longer now and sweat-plastered to his head around his hat ring. I wished I could have washed it and given it a proper trim.

"Oh"—she glared at me—"you again."

I clambered to my feet and stared at her perfectness.

"Uh, Constance, uh, you remember Maggie. Her train just arrived today. We were just catching up."

"I can see how you were catching up."

I could almost see steam spew from her ears.

"Mother is expecting you and Sissy for supper. Perhaps you can offer to help with the fire, and fill the water barrel, and get the table and chairs out of the wagon for her."

I wondered why her brother Cody couldn't help with the chores.

"Coming."

Constance pivoted and stomped away.

"Your Highness," Eliot whispered to her back. "I'm sorry. I did promise Mrs. Appleton that we'd be there for supper. She's trying to be helpful." He looked to make sure Constance was out of sight, then kissed me on the cheek. "I'll try to escape later."

He trotted away. *Ah, Eliot.* How I longed to be close to him. If wed, would he allow me the freedom to be my own person, or would he try to control me to do his bidding, much like Constance was trying to mold him?

⬦

I scrunched my forehead. "You mean we have to cross the Snake again?" Jacob's update on the captain's briefing curdled my stomach. I was already mad. Mad at Jacob because he vanished each morning to work for Mr. Jeffries, leaving me with all the chores. And Eliot . . . argh! He didn't escape the other night. I had kept the fire stoked and bathed in its glow for half the night, then cried alone while the flames evaporated into a mound of smoldering ashes. He had weaseled out with his train early the following morning without saying goodbye.

"The crossing is going to be tricky."

Constance would have roped Eliot into an engagement commitment before I saw him again.

"Maggie, you need to pay attention."

"Huh?"

"I said the crossing is going to be tricky."

"It can't be worse than that Three Island place."

He rolled his eyes. "Let's get moving."

"You're not going back to help Mr. Jeffries again this morning?"

"The cattle are already staged. We'll get the wagon across, and then I'll go back and help him." He climbed onto the wagon seat and took the reins.

Irritation still simmered under my skin when we reached the river a short time later. Jacob hopped from the wagon and stood beside me. We watched four men lift a wagon box off the undercarriage. Two canoes abutted each other on the riverbank, with their noses pointed to the far shore.

"What are they doing?"

"Watch." He nodded toward the men lifting the wagon.

The four men heaved the wagon box crossways so it straddled the two canoes. Two Indians on shore pushed the canoes into the current. The wagon teetered. Then the Indians splashed into the water, and one leaped into each canoe, picked up an oar, and paddled the bound canoes toward the far shore.

"Why don't they make a raft and ferry us across, or just ford across like we did at the other Snake crossing?"

"Captain didn't say. The river looks too swift and deep to ford, even with the wagons chained together. It's also too wide without the islands. And anyway, it is a ferry. A canoe ferry. Pretty ingenious, don't you think?"

I watched the canoe ferry reach the far shore. The men lifted the wagon box off and set it next to the wheels and axle tree to be reassembled.

"It's going to take all day for all of us to cross." I watched Mr. McNeil and Mr. Fisher loosen the wheels of the Fishers' wagon, next in line. "How much is this going to cost us? You know we don't have any money."

"I've earned two dollars." He patted his pocket.

"Is that enough?"

"We'll find out."

Chapter 29

*D*ear Diary,

It started as a murmur. Like the reverberation of a distant drum with a beat too faint for the ear to perceive. The albatross that lurked beneath the surface of our consciousness. No one dared speak of it. During the day, the struggle of putting one foot in front of the other and the grind of setting up and breaking camp kept the scourge at bay. Then it seeped through someone's lips like a breath of fog that rolled in and hovered over us, taunting us, like a dark cloud threatening rain. Then the whispers dripped in, like stray raindrops at the onset of a storm that you mistook for a gnat when it tickled your cheek. But then one evening, in the dark by the fire, someone voiced the demon—will there be snow in the Blues? "Shh" someone shushed. Each night the whispers grew louder. Bolder. Mr. Dalton said, "It's nearly October. Snow's likely." "Quiet," the women would hiss. Then Mr. Tompkins dared to say, "Remember the Donners." Mrs. Fisher would scold, "Hush. You'll scare the children." Mrs. McNeil would press her palms together in front of her chest and face the heavens and exclaim,

"The good Lord will protect us." The scene would repeat the next night. And the next. Different voices, same theme.

But first we had to reach the Blues. We traveled along the south side of the Snake until we reached a place called Farewell Bend, where the river turned north, and we continued west. The sagebrush stayed with us, but loose rock and sand replaced the jagged basalt. We followed the Burnt River through a rugged canyon where a wagon in our train was lost when it slid off the narrow road and plunged down the ridge. The shattered wagon pieces comingled with shattered pieces from other doomed wagons that had passed before us. I hoped one of them wasn't Eliot's. Then we climbed a steep ridge. The reward for the exhausting ascent was a magnificent view of spiky snowcapped mountains. We descended into a long, wide valley framed by a ridge of snowcapped peaks on the right and the left. Jacob said it was called the Powder River Valley. I don't know why—there was no powder. Up another ridge and then down into the Grand Ronde Valley. A lush basin with abundant grass and fresh water for the animals. Then pioneer hell. (Sorry for the language, Ma.) Three grueling days of climbing the steep slopes of the Blues. Unload the wagons. Double or triple team up the steep parts. Reload the wagons. Repeat. Repeat. Repeat. Weaving through the thick timber slowed us considerably. Fortunately, the trains ahead of us cleared the way of rocks and fallen trees. My exhausted limbs quivered as we crested the summit and snaked into a place called Emigrant Springs to camp.

"The captain said we're going to stay here for two nights to let the animals rest," Jacob informed me as we unhitched the team.

"Did you hear that, girls?" I rubbed Molly's nose. "You get an extra day of rest." She snorted in my ear. "Quit trying to be fresh." I nudged her snout away and stepped to Penny. "You deserve a whole week of rest, but you'll have to settle for just a day."

The dense woods made it impossible to maneuver the whole train into a single circle, so we clustered into small groups. Our wagon was in a lopsided ring with the Mc-Neils', the Fishers', the Mays', and the Daltons'. Twilight seeped through the towering trees. The thick canopy of pines that stretched over our camp smothered us in a dingy gray of the looming dusk. Our group had settled farthest from the hub of the other clustered wagons, and our wagon abutted the eerie forest. If someone, or something were to attack, we'd be first in their path. A tingle skittered up my spine.

Someone started a fire in the center of our ring. My eyelids sagged. Judging from the sluggish pace and haggard faces of our camp mates, I wasn't the only one longing for a good night's sleep. Crackers for supper because I didn't have the energy to cook the last of our beans—the bacon long gone. And a badly needed bath in one of the springs would have to wait until tomorrow. Fortunately, even the children were too exhausted for lessons and story time.

Conversation was muted as we lazed around the community fire after supper. Stephen slept in his ma's lap. Mary Alice leaned against her pa, droopy-eyed, as she tried to stay awake like the grown-ups. Then her eyes closed and her head bobbed. Her pa wrapped his arms around her and kissed the top of her head. William sat cross-legged between Mr. and Mrs. McNeil. Content. Like he belonged.

I wondered what that felt like—to belong. I swallowed a lump of envy.

A horse whinnied. I looked up at Ethan chatting with nearby campers. He sagged in the saddle, like his spirit had been wrung from his core, like the rest of us, even though he spent his days atop his ride while we slogged up and down the steep slopes, crawled over and around boulders and felled trees, splashed through icy streams, and lugged belongings up steep ridges. He'd been avoiding me since the mishap at Three Island Crossing. The day he was saved by the Indian. The day he caused Mary Alice to almost drown. I wondered who else knew besides me and the Fishers. His pa, the captain?

Ethan steered his palomino to our group. "Everything okay here?" He directed the question to Mr. May, as if Mr. May were our group spokesman. He was likely too embarrassed to address the Fishers, or the McNeils, or especially me. Thank goodness.

Jacob leaped to his feet and sauntered to Ethan. He rubbed the horse's snout. It occurred to me that I didn't even know the name of Ethan's mare—not that I cared. I strained my ears but couldn't hear their discussion. Ethan was probably passing on important information from the captain that Jacob would update me on later. Mr. Dalton joined the conversation. Jacob's back was to me, so I couldn't see his face, which I hoped held a blank expression so as not to betray his feelings toward Ethan. Jacob never could conceal his emotions. *Will I go through the rest of my life worrying whether Jacob will expose himself?*

After Ethan left, I stowed the dishes in the wagon while gnawing on a bite of hardtack. Then I slid out my tarp and blanket. I didn't have the energy to unload the wagon to make room to sleep inside. I whisked away some stones and twigs from the ground near the wagon tongue and spread out my bed. A mule snorted. "Quiet," I whispered. I wrapped myself in the quilt and stretched out on the tarp. Scout scurried over and curled up beside me. Someone tossed another log onto the fire. It popped and crackled, but my bed was beyond the radius of its warmth. The glow shimmered against the white tops and the sprinkling of nearby tents. Moon rays streaked through the towering pines. *If the moon was out, it couldn't snow.* I tucked the blanket under my chin and shivered.

OWOOOO! I pulled the cover up to my eyes. Wolves. Scout raised his head and growled. HOWL! The screams pierced the darkness.

A sob drifted through the Fishers' tent. "Mama, I'm scared," Mary Alice whimpered.

"Shh," her ma whispered.

I'm scared too, Mary Alice. If a pack of wolves raided our camp, the tent would be shredded in an instant. But I was between the howls and the tent. Their sharp fangs would find me first. My jaw quavered.

OWOOOO! The howls were louder. Closer.

Scout leaped from my side and disappeared into the dark. My eyes flew open. "Scout, no." The mules scuffled. The fire had burned down to a bed of glowing embers. Moonlight slinking through the branches of the towering pines as they swayed in the breeze cast eerie shadows on the wagon tops. Only the shadows morphed into long noses and pointy ears. I scooted to the wagon and leaned against the wheel and folded my knees to my chest. OWOOO! I trembled. "Ma," I whispered, "they're coming."

Scout bounded back to me, licked my cheek, and plopped down beside to me. "Thank goodness, Scout. I thought you were going to be wolf food." I pressed my forehead to his.

A twig snapped. Scout bumped my chin with his head when we both jolted.

"Ouch," someone whispered.

A figure loomed above me, then knelt. "Shh."

"Eliot?" I scrambled to my knees and flung into his arms. "Eliot, you scared me to death." I nestled my face into his neck.

He rested his chin on my head. "I heard that your train pulled in earlier tonight. I got away as soon as I could. I've been looking for you for hours."

"How did you ever find me in the dark? You could have gotten lost in the woods. Or eaten by a wolf. And there's panthers and bears out there also."

"I'd fight off a whole pack of wolves to see you. Or a panther. Or a grizzly. Or all of them at once."

"I hate to think how that battle would end." I tilted my head and peered at the shadows the moon rays painted on his face.

"I just needed to see you again, before we head out in the morning."

He kissed my forehead. Then his lips connected with mine. Soft. Sweet. He tasted of salt and coffee and fear.

"What's going on?"

Eliot and I separated at Jacob's groggy voice from near the wagon tail.

"Nothing, Jacob. Go back to sleep." How could he sleep?

OWOOO!

I lifted the blanket, and Eliot snuggled under and wrapped his arms around me. I leaned into him. I felt safe.

OWOOO!

Chapter 30

D*ear Diary,*

It didn't snow in the Blues. The relief oozed from all our veins like sap from a maple. Hints of smiles escaped from plastered lips. Bowed shoulders straightened, as if the strain of carrying a wagon full of packed snow melted as soon as we reached the floor of the Columbia Plateau. I was still crushed by a burden, although my burden wasn't snow—it was loneliness. The burden had dissipated the night I fell asleep snuggled in Eliot's embrace. A gray haze had filtered through the treetops when the gunner fired the morning wake-up shot. Eliot was gone. Amid a town full of bustling campers slogging through their morning rituals, I felt like I was marooned at sea in a leaky boat without a paddle. But as we descended the steep slopes out of the mountains into the vast valley, the wonderful sight that unfolded before us gave me hope.

"Mount Hood." Jacob nodded toward the pointy, majestic, snow-capped peak that towered over the purple-gray mountain range in the distance.

I hadn't asked him. I walked next to him after he had finished his morning shift with Mr. Jeffries. By now the team was conditioned to the monotonous pioneering routine that on flat terrain they could be driven from the ground while walking by the wagon, which was fine with me because each wheel bump sent a wave of pain through my ribs. Although I must be healing because I could breathe without an inferno exploding in my chest. The familiar tune of clanking hooves, creaking wagons, and rustling bitterbrush provided the background music to my thoughts. I hated that Jacob could read my mind. How was it that I didn't know him anymore, yet he could read me like a favorite well-read book? Sometimes I wished I could just run away so as not to have a freak for a brother. A knot strangled my gut. Then I would have no one. Except, maybe Eliot. If Constance didn't wrangle him first. Would Eliot have me if he knew about Jacob? The knot tightened. Unlikely.

Clanking horse hooves pinged behind us. I tensed. The last mount I wanted to see was Ethan's palomino. Whew. Mr. Jeffries rode up on his roan, leading a saddled dun mare by the reins. "Sorry to bother you, Jacob." Mr. Jeffries peered down at me and touched his finger to his straw hat. "Margaret."

"You must need some help, Mr. Jeffries." Jacob handed me the reins.

"Half a dozen or so wandered off again. Lost so many already . . . can't afford to lose any more. Any chance you can break away and help?"

Jacob was already mounting the dun when he said, "Maggie can manage. Let's go find 'em." He steered the horse around, and they galloped off, kicking up a trail of dust in their wake.

"Jack boy, what am I going to do?" I flicked the reins. The tired wagon moaned when the creaky wheels rotated.

The mule grunted. I patted his rear. "You don't know either, do you? How about you, Scout?" I looked down at the mutt trundling through the grass at my heels. Then he darted off, nose to the ground, after some varmint. "And you don't care either."

"Maggie!"

I gasped. "William. Are you ever going to learn not to sneak up on me?"

He puckered his lips and stared at his shoes as he shuffled on his toes, kicking up dirt as he fell in step beside me. "Sorry." He rubbed his eye with his knuckle.

"I'm sorry, Willaim. I didn't mean to be cross with you. I know you didn't mean to startle me. Again," I added under my breath.

He shoved his hands into his pockets.

"What do you think of that big mountain ahead of us. Isn't it amazing?"

He looked up, and his eyes widened. "It looks like it's poking a hole into heaven."

"It does look like it's piercing the sky."

"Do you think it can see God?"

"I don't know, William. Why do you ask?"

"Mrs. McNeil's been teaching me about God. I wonder if the mountain knows what God looks like." He scratched his cheek. "Maybe that's where He sends the angels down from heaven."

I wondered if she'd been teaching him that people like Jacob were sinners and were condemned to hell. Was Jacob a sinner? Would he spend eternity in hell? How could someone with a heart as pure as Jacob's be condemned to a world of fire and brimstone?

"Oh, I know what I was going to tell you." He hopped like an excited toddler anticipating a piece of candy.

"What's so exciting?"

"Mr. and Mrs. McNeil." He stumbled over his feet and nearly fell.

I clasped his elbow to steady him. "What about Mr. and Mrs. McNeil?"

"They're going to adopt me."

"Really?" I clasped my hands together. "That's fabulous news, William."

He continued to hop-walk beside me.

"Calm down a little before you hurt yourself." I inhaled a deep breath. More dust than fresh air. I coughed. "That must mean that you don't have other relatives then."

"I have an uncle back home. But he's a recluse and won't want me."

"How do you know what a recluse is?"

"It's what Ma always called him. Anyway, Mr. Mc-Neil is going to teach me how to hunt, and skin a deer, and ride a horse, and drive a plow. And Mrs. McNeil said she'd make me a giant cake for my birthday next year in an oven and everything. And they're going to build a big house"—he stretched his arms as wide as he could reach—"and I'll have my own room."

"That sounds grand. Will you invite me to your party? I would love to have a giant piece of Mrs. McNeil's oven-baked cake."

"Maybe you and Jacob could be our neighbors. Then you could be my friends and you could come over all the time." He looked at me with a questioning eye.

"Maybe we could. But you'll have to quit scaring me or I'll be too afraid to visit you."

"Okay, I promise." He stopped bounding and stared at his shoes as his steps melted into a shuffle.

"What's the matter?"

"Well, it's just that . . . when you marry Eliot, you'll probably move away with him."

I raised an eyebrow. "Who said anything about me marrying Eliot?"

"Well, you like him, don't you?"

I smiled and felt heat seep into my cheeks. How could a little runt like William make me blush? "Yes, I do like Eliot. But that doesn't mean that I'm going to marry him."

"But you want to. Right?"

Did I want to? It wasn't like I hadn't pondered the thought—repeatedly. The answer was a puzzle. On the one hand, the thought of spending the rest of my days with Eliot was glorious. But even though, clear back at Ash Hollow, he had said he would support me in whatever I wanted to do, would he really mean it when his shirts were dirty, and his socks needed darned, and supper wasn't on the table? But any other alternative would likely be worse. And I didn't, or rather couldn't, believe that Eliot would ever strike me, or any woman for that matter. So yes, I think I would rather have liked to marry Eliot. But I couldn't admit that to William, or anyone, just yet.

"William, I'm only fourteen. It's going to be a long while before I marry anyone. Eliot or someone else. And by then you'll have your own girl and won't want me around at all."

"Ick!" He scrunched his nose. "I don't like girls."

"You will someday. You just need to learn not to scare them away." I winked at him. I wondered if Ma ever said something like that to Jacob. That he'd have his own girl someday. How would she have dealt with her son being a freak if she were still alive? Would Jacob have confided in her? I thought back to the men Eliot told me about. I wondered if they were decent, kind, hardworking men like Jacob was becoming. Or would Jacob not be a good man because he was a freak? I wished there was someone I could confide in to sort through it all.

"And then . . . hey, Maggie, are you listening to me?"

"What? Oh, I'm sorry, William. My mind took a detour for a moment. What were you saying?"

"I was saying, when you and Jacob are both married…"

"There you go with that marrying talk again."

"Let me finish." He shook his arms, palms up, in front of him. "When you're both married and you and Eliot move away and Jacob and his wife are our neighbors, will you still be my friend?"

I bent and gave him a gentle squeeze. "William, wherever I live, I'll still be your friend. If we live far apart, we can write each other letters."

"Oh." He watched the dust puff up around his shuffling feet.

I smiled at the thought of Mrs. McNeil teaching him to walk like a gentleman. "Don't you want to write to me?"

"It's just that . . . well, I know all my letters now, and I can spell my name, but I don't know how to write a whole letter."

"Well, I'm sure that when you get to your new home, Mr. and Mrs. McNeil will send you to school, where you'll learn how to string letters into sentences. And if we're neighbors, I'll teach you how to write so well that you can send letters to me and Jacob and Suzie and Tommy and Jimmy and Mary Alice and Stephen. You can even send one to your recluse uncle to let him know you have a new family."

"Yeah, maybe. If we ever get there."

"We'll get there. We just need to get past those mountains ahead of us, and we'll be in the Willamette Valley and our new home."

"Oh." He narrowed his eyes.

"I thought you'd be happy that we're so close to the end of our journey."

"Are there wolves in those mountains too? Mountains are scary." He shoved his hands into his pockets and squinted at the jagged peaks jutting through the haze.

He was right. Mountains were scary. Especially without Eliot to hold me. "I heard that we don't have to go over them. We're going to raft through them on the Columbia River."

"Rivers are scary also." He lowered his head.

He was right about that too.

Jacob trotted over to us on Mr. Jeffries's horse.

"Did you find them?" I asked.

"They hadn't gone far. They're all rounded up and pointed west, so I've been released for the time being."

"That's a really big horse." William's eyes bulged like ballons as he gazed at Jacob atop his ride. "What his name?"

"He's a she. And she's about average height for a horse. Her name is Ginger."

"You're so lucky that you get to ride a horse. I've never been on a horse."

"Do you want to ride her?"

"Can I? Really?"

"Sure. Let's move away from the wagons so we don't get run over." Jacob reined the horse away from the chain of wagons slogging behind us.

"Oh . . . um, what if it bucks me off?"

"I won't let her buck you off. She's pretty gentle. Follow me."

I nodded when William glanced at me. Then he peered over his shoulder at the McNeils, who were behind us. Mrs. McNeil was in conversation with her husband, who used his cow poker as a walking stick while they escorted their team.

"Jacob will take good care of you." Of that I was sure. "He used to ride our ol' Nellie back home all the time."

Jacob led the horse to a clear spot away from the moving train, and William half ran, half hop-skipped behind him.

Suddenly Mrs. McNeil was at my side, panting like she had just sprinted up a mountain. "I don't know about this."

"Don't worry, Mrs. McNeil. Jacob won't let anything happen to William."

"He's such a small boy." She wiped her brow with a handkerchief. "And not very brave."

"Well, Jacob is not very brave either. But he has a talent for reading animals. If he had even an inkling that the horse wasn't gentle enough, he wouldn't let William ride her."

Jacob hoisted William onto the saddle. The boy almost spilled headfirst over the other side, but he clasped the pommel and righted himself. Jacob led the mare by the bridle while William held a white-knuckled grip on the horn. Mrs. McNeil bit her lip and balled her fists at her side. I wasn't sure who was more nervous.

"If William is going to help Mr. McNeil on the farm, it would be good for him to know how to ride a horse."

"He told you that we were going to inquire about adopting him, then."

"He is so excited. That's a nice thing for you and Mr. McNeil to do."

"He's such a good boy and deserves a good Christian home. And you know that Charles and I were never blessed with another child after we lost our Beverly." Her gaze was glued to William while she talked.

"You'll make a nice family." I sighed under my breath. They would make a nice family. I'd never heard Mr. McNeil raise his voice in anger. I'd never seen so much as a scratch, let alone a bruise, on Mrs. McNeil, so he must not hit her. I'd never seen him drunk, or even imbibe in a sip of whiskey. He was kind to all, including the animals. And Mrs. McNeil had a heart bigger than Mount Hood looming on the horizon. I was suddenly jealous of William's good fortune.

But what about my future? An orphaned girl considered to be of marrying age. Jacob could find work to support himself—if he could keep his secret. But I would refuse to marry the first eligible man who came calling just so I could have a roof over by head and food in my belly and be subservient to his every whim. Even Eliot, if that was the life he could offer me. And I would not be a victim of a man's abuse ever again, no matter who he was. Ma would want a better life for me than the miserable life she had with Pa. Of that I was certain.

"Mrs. McNeil, look at me." William's smile was as wide as the Missouri as he swayed in the oversized saddle while he clutched the pommel with both hands. "I'm riding a horse."

"You be careful, William!"

Mrs. McNeil was going to be an excellent, although overprotective, mother.

Chapter 31

D*ear Diary,*

We reached a town. A real town. Not a fort. Not a trading post. A town with real buildings—a mercantile, a saloon (of course), a church, a blacksmith, and some houses. It's called Dalles, and it sits at the edge of the Columbia River at the base of the Cascade Mountains, almost at the foot of the mystical Mount Hood. Jacob said that we just needed to hire a raft to float us down the Columbia River to the Willamette Valley. Our new home. But that was before . . .

"What's the matter?"

While I'd set up camp, Jacob had gone to town to inquire about transportation down the river after we'd arrived and settled in among a horde of weary campers on the outskirts of Dalles. He returned, shoulders stooped and a frown carved on his face. He dropped a burlap sack to the ground near his feet, as if it were an iron ball and chain weighted with his life burdens. He picked up an empty bucket, flipped it upside down, dropped onto it, and rubbed his hands on his thighs.

Scout rested his chin on Jacob's knee.

Jacob ignored the pooch.

"Jacob, what is it? What's in the sack?"

"You want to know what is in the sack? There's a linchpin to replace the one that's cracked, axle grease since we've been out for a week—I'm surprised the wheels still turn—lard because I used all your cooking grease on the axles, and oats for the mules. And I splurged on an apple for each of us since we hadn't had fresh fruit in weeks. I didn't have enough money for beans or bacon. We're going to have to survive on hardtack for a while longer."

I molded my lips into a pout, and my stomach growled. I was sick of the tasteless hardtack. The dry, bland, baked paste of flour and water stuck like glue in my throat and sat like lead in my stomach. But since we had consumed the last of our beans back in the Blues, hardtack and hope had sustained us. Plus the jackrabbit Scout had caught one afternoon, which I'd skinned and fried for supper. "Why did you buy more supplies now instead of waiting until we get to Fort Vancouver?"

"Because we're not going to Fort Vancouver." He stared at his feet.

"But we're supposed to stop in Fort Vancouver at the mouth of the Willamette River to stock up before going to Oregon City."

"That was the plan. But now we need a new one."

"What? Why?" I gaped.

"It's too expensive. We can't afford to hire a raft."

I squinted at him. "Can't we make our own? There's plenty of timber around here. Mr. McNeil and Mr. Jeffries might help us."

"It's not that simple. The river is too dangerous. It's swift and deep, and there are rapids. We'd never be able to negotiate them on our own. Most people hire Indians as pilots. They know the river and can navigate the safest route. And then one of us would have to walk the mules overland on a narrow path anyway. Unless we wanted to leave them here." He looked over to where the team was picketed in the grass a short distance from the wagon. "Or we could leave the wagon here and take the mules on foot, but then we wouldn't have any shelter when we got to the Willamette Valley."

I picked up another bucket, turned it upside down, sat on it across from Jacob, and plunked my chin onto the heels of my hands. "Does that mean we have to stay here? What are we going to do?"

"No. There's another way."

I raised an eyebrow.

"There's a new route. It's called the Barlow Road. It goes over the Cascades around the south side of Mount Hood."

"That sounds okay. Then why are you so down?"

"It's a toll road. Mr. Barlow charges five dollars a wagon to use his trail."

"Haven't you earned five dollars working for Mr. Jeffries?"

"After purchasing these things"—he nodded to the sack near his feet—"I have four dollars and twenty-five cents."

I smiled. "I have a confession to make."

He squinted at me.

"I've been doing some mending for the elder Mrs. May. I've earned a dollar and twenty-five cents. I was saving it to buy some fabric and a pattern for a new dress when we get to Oregon City." I had been trying to devise a subtle way to approach both Mrs. Mays about making new dresses for them when we reached the Willamette Valley. While not nearly as tattered and patched up as mine, they both could do with a new dress—or two.

He grinned and he patted Scout on the head. "Maggie, you may have just saved us. We'll get to Oregon City with a whole four bits to spare."

I frowned. "How are we going to survive on fifty cents?"

"Just like we did to get here. One day at a time. Mr. Jeffries is going to take his cattle over the Barlow Road also. I'm sure he'll need some help."

"So we'll be alone in the wilderness with Mr. Jeffries and his cows."

—◇—

After breakfast I headed toward the McNeils' camp to say goodbye. But then I took a detour in search of Eliot. I'd had a restless night. Eliot floated in and out of my dreams like a hovering ghost who disappeared whenever I reached out my hand or opened my eyes. The burning desire to see him sizzled in my gut. I didn't know why the need was so intense. He didn't seek me out the previous evening. He must have assumed that we had arrived. Or perhaps he was already floating on a raft through the canyon on his way to paradise. My mind pictured Constance tightening the noose around his neck. Would she and her mother rope an engagement commitment out of him before I saw him again? The fire in my belly burned hotter. He was here. I could feel it in my bones.

I weaved through a throng of wagons toward the river. My eyes followed a log bobbing in the swift current. A stiff breeze from the west billowed up the canyon, kicking up whitecaps. I wrapped my arms around my chest and shivered. I was glad we'd been forced to take the land route instead of the river. The image of the man that was swept from the boat on the Missouri all those months ago still burned in my mind.

I stopped on a grassy knoll where some other women and girls had gathered for a better view of the activity on the dock. Sissy and Constance stood side by side near the pier, in conversation. Constance leaned her head closer to Sissy and rested her hand on Sissy's arm. She must have said something amusing, because Sissy whipped her hand over mouth, as if to stifle a giggle. They acted like sisters. Or sisters-in-law. The embers in my stomach festered.

Near the dock, Eliot was one of four men aligning themselves by a wagon, one on each corner, preparing to hoist the bed off the bolsters and onto a waiting raft. The wagon's blue paint, which had matched Eliot's eyes, was now chipped and faded to a dingy gray. It was probably the Samuelsons' wagon. Or perhaps the Appletons'. They had both been painted blue. It was like the two families were united—through thick and thin, better or worse, till death . . . I swallowed the thought. One of the other men was younger also. Not a man, but a boy. A younker, like Eliot and Jacob. I remembered seeing him at Fort Hall and Fort Boise. He must have been Constance's younger brother, Cody. I assumed the fourth person was Mr. Appleton. Eliot and Doc Sam were on the front two corners, nearest the raft that was tied to the dock bobbing on the wind-whipped ripples.

I'd watched four burley men struggle to lift an empty wagon box off the bolsters many times over the course of our journey. But two average sized men and two almost men? I bit my lower lip. Through the din I heard Doc Sam shout, "One, two, three, heave."

The two men and two almost men hoisted the wagon box from the undercarriage. The wagon teetered. The men shuffled—knees buckling, shoulders shifting like see-saws, as they struggled with the heavy weight. Cody stumbled and almost fell, but he recovered. Eliot and Doc Sam scuttled backward toward the raft. Eliot cranked his head to peer over his shoulder. They reached the edge of the dock and were about to step on the vessel. Eliot's boot heel nicked the edge of the raft and he nearly fell, but he regained his balance.

"Easy, son," Doc shouted.

Nearby trees swayed as the wind kicked up a notch. The rippling whitecaps on the river crested higher. The boat wobbled.

Eliot and Doc Sam shuffled backward on the teetering raft. Cody and Mr. Appleton cleared the dock and stepped onto the raft. Just two more steps and the wagon would be centered and lowered onto the craft.

I realized that I was holding my breath.

Cody stumbled and lost his grip on his corner of the wagon. It crashed to the dock. His pa tried to slide his hands from the corner to the middle of the tailgate to pick up the slack, but the weight overpowered his strength and his corner clunked on the boat's wooden slats. Eliot disappeared from my line of sight. Doc Sam teetered. The wagon tongue thundered as it crashed on the vessel.

Splash.

Constance and Sissy screamed.

"Eliot!" I raced from the hill toward the river, close to where Sissy and Constance stood.

Doc Sam leaped into the water.

"He doesn't know how to swim," Sissy whispered.

"He'll be all right." Constance tried to sound reassuring, but I detected the quaver in her voice. "The water can't be too deep. He should be able to walk out."

But he wasn't walking out. Neither was Doc Sam. "Please, Eliot." I held my intertwined fingers against my chest to keep my pounding heart from exploding.

An Indian zipped through the crowd and splashed into the water. After a few high-kneed steps, he dove under the surface.

He resurfaced a moment later with his arm wrapped around Doc Sam. Mr. Appleton and Cody rushed to them. They each wrapped one of Doc Sam's arms around their neck and led the hacking doc to shore. The Indian dashed back into the water.

"Come on, Eliot. Where are you?" My knees wobbled, and I trembled. *This can't be happening.*

Mrs. Appleton moved next to Constance. "What's happening?"

"Eliot fell in."

"He's a strong boy. He'll pull himself out."

"He doesn't know how to swim," Sissy whispered again.

The Indian resurfaced, shook his silky hair out of his eyes, swam downstream a few yards, and submerged.

"Come on, Eliot. You promised you would find me." I didn't know if I whispered that aloud or under my breath.

The Indian resurfaced and swam to shore. Doc Sam and Cody raced down the riverbank to meet him. The Indian stood in the knee-deep current and shook his head.

"Nooo!" I clasped my skirt in my fists and raced toward the bank. Without stopping, I kicked through frigid ripples, my eyes focused on the spot where Eliot tumbled. "Eliot! I'm coming Eliot." Just like William. I'd pull him up by the collar and drag him to shore. Woosh! The riverbed vanished from under my feet and I was sucked under the surface. Panicked, I flung my arms and kicked my legs. Nothing. The heavy wool that I had used to reinforce my skirt weighed me down, siphoning me deeper into the grip of the churning water, its arctic blanket smothering me. Blinding me. I kicked harder and flailed my hands. *Up. Up. Which way is up?* Nothing. *Need air.* Icy water flooded my lungs. I tried to gag it out. *Kick. Kick.* Nothing. Like drooping dandelions at the day's end, my limbs wilted and my body went numb.

"Ma?" She hovered over me like a translucent angel. Radiant. A bright light silhouetted her slender frame. The furrowed lines of worry, abuse, and hard labor were washed from her beaming face. "Ma. You've come for me."

She held her hands out, palms up, as if beckoning me to join her. "My lovely Margaret. What I fine lady you have become."

I reached out my hand. "Ma. Take me with you."

"You can't come now."

"But, Ma, I love you. I want to be with you."

"I love you too dear, more than you could possibly imagine. But you can't come. Jacob needs you."

"But Jacob's a freak!"

She narrowed her eyes and shook her head. "Jacob is not a freak. He is a decent, loving, sensitive human being. I'm trusting you to help him navigate through a world that doesn't understand."

"But, Ma . . ."

Her beautiful figure evaporated into the blackness. "Don't leave me, Ma."

Something snagged my hair and whipped my head back. The world went blank.

Chapter 32

D*ear Diary,*

My soul has been ripped from my being and is submerged in the Columbia with Eliot. He's gone. And I am lost. I was vaguely cognizant of Jacob finding me alone, dripping wet and shivering by the river. Not alone, but smothered in a swirl of activity as wagon after wagon loaded onto rafts and set adrift downriver. But I might as well have been trapped at the bottom of a well shaft, for as conscious as I was of the world around me. Jacob may have gone for Mrs. McNeil. Or maybe she found me on her own. She scooped me up and smothered me in her bosom. William wrapped his arms around my waist. My arms dangled like limp noodles at my sides. The world had become a blank canvas, stripped of its former masterpiece.

We're high in the Cascade Mountains, near the south side of the mystical Mount Hood, but the mighty peak is veiled behind the thick forest. The nights are the hardest. Beyond the flickering campfire, the inky-black darkness smothers me in a blanket of loneliness and unrest. Fear still lingers in the air around us—the forest creatures that hover in the blackness beyond the reach of the fire's glow; Laurel Hill, the last major hurdle between the

Barlow summit and the Willamette Valley; anticipation and trepidation of life in our new home; and the ever-present risk of discovery.

Besides Mr. Jeffries and his cows, our caravan includes four other families whom we've joined up with on the Barlow route. The Fishers, who I imagine will have a lifelong aversion to any body of water larger than a puddle, and three other couples whom we did not know before—one with two children, one childless, and one with a three-week-old baby. It was inconceivable to me how a woman could endure the arduous journey while carrying a child.

Jacob tossed a log on the fire. It popped and crackled and spit a stream of sparks into the dark. The dancing flames painted a golden glow against his face as he reclined against the log that he used as a backrest. We sat on the ground near our wagon.

The other members of our party had either retired for the night or were huddled around their own private fires a short distance away. The men puffed on pipes, and the women sat by their sides, leaning into them for warmth and support.

I rubbed my thumb along the petals of the brooch that was concealed in my hidden pocket as I sat cross-legged and watched the flames dance around the log. I probably should have told Jacob about the pin, but for a reason I couldn't explain, I wanted to keep my last vestige of Ma private. I removed my hand from the pocket and crossed my arms across my chest. I was still wrapped in the foggy numbness of my grief. And from my vision of Ma. I hadn't told Jacob about it. He would think I was crazy. Maybe I was crazy. I felt like the puzzle of my brain was missing some key pieces.

A flurry of sparks spiraled into the air and dissipated in the darkness. "Jacob, what are we going to do when we get to Oregon City?"

He sat up and retrieved the stick he had been using as a fire poker and stabbed the log. The log didn't need adjustment. "Well, the first thing I'm going to do is to find the land office and claim my three hundred twenty acres."

"Then I can claim my three hundred twenty acres at the same time."

"No. Only men can claim their three hundred twenty acres. If a man is married, he can claim an additional three hundred twenty acres for his wife. But an unmarried woman isn't entitled to anything."

"That's just not fair!" I was tempted to spring to my feet and stomp off. But the darkness and the wild creatures beyond the glow of the fire trapped me in place.

"Quiet. You'll wake the baby."

"The baby is clear on the other side of camp. Probably sleeping, you know, like a . . . like a sleeping baby." An owl hooted from a nearby tree. I shivered and pinched the blanket that was draped around my shoulders tighter around my neck. The icy Columbia waters hadn't yet drained from my bones. "Then what is an unmarried woman supposed to do?" What *was* an unmarried woman—an unmarried *orphaned* woman—supposed to do other than live in a cave and beg on the streets? Or work in a house of ill-repute. I buried my head in my hands. I wanted to weep. Then I thought of Ma. She didn't raise me to be a beggar. Or a quitter. *Somehow, Ma, I need to figure this out.*

"Same as back home, I suppose. Live with her family until she gets married off." He leaned back on the log. "I suppose she could get a job in town, but other than the brothel, I'm not sure that anyone would hire a woman."

"Then what am I going to do?" *I would live in a cave and beg on the streets before resorting to a brothel. Besides Eliot, what man would allow me, or any woman, the freedom to be their own person? Eliot, why did you leave me?* There must be something. I thrust my elbows onto my knees and dropped my chin into the heels of my hands.

"I have a thought. But it will mean that we'll have to stay together until you find a husband."

"So that I can be your servant. So far, I don't think I like this idea."

"You haven't even heard it yet. And I don't think you could ever be anyone's servant." He rolled his stick in his palms.

"Nor will I." I leaned back on my elbows. I sounded defiant, but deep down, I knew a woman had no other options.

"Okay. Humor me for a moment. Think of all the women who have traveled two thousand miles to Oregon. What is the first thing they are going to want when they get there?"

I yawned. "To soak in a steaming hot, soapy bath and then sleep for a month."

"Touché. What will they want as soon as they wake up?"

"Someone to cook them a hot breakfast of johnnycakes and fresh eggs fried over easy with a steaming cup of coffee. And then to do the dishes."

"Then what do they want to put on when they're rested and sated?" He poked the log with his stick.

"Clean nether garments, a new dress, and stockings without holes."

"Aha."

"What? You mean you're going to cook me a hot breakfast and make me a new dress?"

"Don't be silly. You know I can't cook or sew." He set the stick on the ground beside him.

"I don't get it."

"Pretend that you have money and you can afford to buy a new dress."

I closed my eyes and tried to envision the impossible. "Jacob, we've never had and extra dollar to spend on a luxury like a store-bought dress, so why should I pretend?"

"But you know how to *make* dresses. And other women with money who are desperate for a new dress will gladly pay for one. Or two or three. And two or three for each of their daughters."

I sat upright and wrapped my arms around my shins. I thought of Mrs. May and her mother-in-law. Could they be my first customers? "I'd need some money for fabric and patterns."

Jacob sat up from the log he was leaning on, picked up his stick, and started scripting in the dirt. "That's where the three hundred twenty acres comes in. Instead of farming it, I'm going to lease it out. Mr. Jeffries will be my first tenant. He wants to grow his herd and will need more pasture. And he'll farm part of it in hay. Also, we won't need four mules, so we can sell Penny and Buck for money to get started."

I frowned. "Hmm. Penny and Buck are part of the family now. I'm going to miss them."

"Yeah. I will too." He fiddled with his stick.

I knew he would miss them more than I would. "And what will you do?"

"I'll run the shop."

"Hmph! So you're going to lock me in a closet to make garments for you to sell."

"Okay, we'll both run the shop. You can handle the customers and make the dresses, and I'll manage the inventory and keep the records. We'll stock other items as well. There's already a mercantile in Oregon City, but in addition to your dresses, we'll carry other items that the newly arrived pioneers will need to set up their households."

"But what about the children I've been teaching? We haven't even discovered if the Swiss Family Robinson gets rescued."

"I have an idea for that also."

"You know what happened to that marooned family?"

"No. You haven't got to the end yet."

"You've been listening."

"Of course I've been listening. Along with Mrs. May and Mrs. Fisher and Tommy."

"Ah yes, Tommy. He needs to learn to read for himself."

"And you can teach him. I suspect that most of the children will need to help their families with their farms and households during the day. So they won't be able to go to school. If there is a school. But you could use our shop for a classroom in the evenings. Maggie's Oregon Schoolhouse."

I almost hugged him. Maggie's Oregon Schoolhouse. I could almost hear the school bells clanging through the trees.

Then I leaned back on my elbows and stared into the fire. I took a few shallow breaths. "Jacob, what happened back at the river? How was I rescued?"

He looked at me. "What were you thinking anyway?" He resumed his scribbling in the dirt. "I heard that an Indian pulled you out."

"Oh." I leaned my chin into my palms. "I was always afraid of Indians. Since I was little, I'd heard they were savages and subhuman. Yet they've helped our caravan in so many ways, I'm not sure if we would have made it without them."

"Well, you certainly wouldn't have made it." He paused. "We were taught to fear them. Because they're different. They look different. They dress differently. They have different customs. The white man believes their ways are best and since the Indians aren't Christian, they must be bad. We never tried to understand them."

Like Jacob was different. *Ma, I get it now.* "Jacob, I'm sorry."

"Sorry for what?" He looked at me.

"I'm just sorry. About everything. The way I shunned you. Because I was more worried about what people would think rather than trying to understand what you were going through."

"I don't know how you could understand. I still don't." He gazed into the smoldering embers.

"I will probably never understand. But even though you just happen to be my brother, you're a good person. A decent person. A decent man." How had I not realized that he had become a man? A much better man than Pa ever was. "I promise that I will always stand by you. No matter what."

He was silent for a few moments. Then he tried to coax another flame from the simmering ashes with his poker. "Do you remember Luke from back home?"

"The kid who beat you up all the time? Of course I remember him. And good riddance that we never have to see him again." I wanted to spit at his memory.

"Did you ever wonder why he singled me out to pick on?" He set the stick down and wrapped his arms around his shins.

"Because you were smarter than he was. Because you were a runt, and he knew he could always win, and so that he could feel powerful in front of his friends. Because we were pikers. Because . . ."

"That's only part of it. Do you remember when it started, early last summer?"

"It started from the first day of school when we were six. When he first saw you. But it did get worse last year."

"It was the last day of school. I was helping Mr. Jones clean the classroom."

I smiled and shook my head. "You always were Mr. Jones's favorite pupil."

"Luke was fourteen then. Do you remember Eddie?"

"That little squat with the perpetual runny nose?" I flared my nostrils.

"He's the one. He was what, maybe nine?"

"Sounds about right."

"Mr. Jones asked me to clean the rags he used to wipe the blackboards. They were extra chalky that day. He had made every kid write a summer message on the board, a goal that each of us would achieve or a lesson that we would learn over the summer break."

"Yeah. I think I wrote something about reading a book—*Gulliver's Travels*—or something like that." I chuckled. "Of course, I never did it."

"I don't think anyone did. Anyway, I took the rags outside and started shaking them out. I wasn't smart enough to stand upwind, and I started gagging on the chalk dust. I walked down to that little stream that flows by the storage shed behind the school. Luke was there." He paused for a few breaths. "He had Eddie pinned to the back of the shed with his mouth over Eddie's. He was kissing him. I was so stunned that I dropped the rags. When Luke saw me, he hopped away from Eddie and kept repeating, 'It's not what you think. It's not what you think.' I didn't know what I thought. I just stood there and stared, stunned. He said that he was just teaching the brat a lesson, and if I ever breathed a word of it to anyone, he would kill me."

"So he beat you up all the time to make sure you kept quiet."

"And to prove that if he wanted to, he could pound the life out of me." He picked up the poker and swirled the ashes—the last of the wood that we had cut for the fire. "I didn't understand it at the time. But now that I have these feelings that I can't explain, I realize that I'm not the only one."

Scout rose from where he was curled up by the wagon wheel and sat next to Jacob and rested his chin on Jacob's lap.

"But I'd never do what Luke did—kiss someone who didn't want to be kissed."

"Jacob, I will never understand what you are going through. And I don't know what's going to happen if anyone discovers your secret. But you're a good person and a good brother. I promise I'll stand by you, just like you've done for me." I'd lost track of how many times Jacob had come to my rescue on our journey. About as many as I'd had to rescue him from Luke.

"Thanks, Maggie. That means the world to me." He patted Scout's head. "And, Maggie, I know you're grieving for Eliot. But you're strong and stubborn, and you're going to find the life you want to live."

I studied the smoldering embers. He was right. There was nothing that would hold me back from living my best life, including the stupid rules that were designed to bury women under rugs and trample their spirit with muddy boots. I'd trekked two thousand miles across the most formidable land, climbed steep mountains, forded swift rivers, and crossed wastelands and deserts. I'd survived a buffalo stampede and fierce storms. I'd suffered through hunger and thirst, unbearable heat and frigid cold. I'd grieved, and was still grieving, the loss of Ma and Eliot. I survived Pa's wrath. And almost drowning. After coming this far, I would not let anyone shove me under that rug or put me in my "place".

The owl hooted.

After a brief silence I said, almost in a whisper, "Jacob, you know you're going to have to marry someday. Find a wife and start a family."

He didn't respond.

A wolf howled. Scout snapped his head up and cocked his ears. The night chill seeped deeper into my bones. "I'm going to sleep in the wagon tonight." I rose.

"Maggie . . ."

I sat back down

"We're going to make it to Oregon City. And we're going to be okay."

Jacob was right. We were going to be okay. Individually and together. But as I endeavored to live my life on my terms, Jacob would always have to hide behind a mask.

I gazed up into the inky sky. No moon and no stars. Something, soft like a feather, dusted my cheek. "It's starting to snow."

Epilogue

*D*ear Diary,

    It's raining. Again.

Downstairs, the front door slammed. Meghan jolted and dropped the book. "Uh-oh. Mom's home."

"And we haven't even started cleaning." Jason hopped to his feet and spun in a circle. His face contorted into a scowl.

"What are we going to do?" Meghan clasped her hand around the brooch resting in her lap, scrambled to her feet, and slipped the pin into her pocket.

"I don't know." Jason scratched his head. "But we can't let Mom sell the house."

"Do you think Maggie and Jacob are our ancestors?"

"It's possible. We need to research our family history and find out."

The twins stared at each other, wide eyed and mouths agape, as footsteps clinked up the stairs.

Aknowlegments

Dear Reader,

I am humbled that you trusted me with your valuable time to read *Hope, Tears, and Dreams on the Way West.* I hope you enjoyed hovering with Meghan and Jason as they followed Maggie on her journey and perhaps learned some intriguing Overland Trail facts. This story is a work of fiction. Although thorough in my research, I am a storyteller, not a historian. Please forgive me for any inadvertent errors.

This book did not come together in a vacuum. The manuscript would be riddled with typos and grammatical errors if not for the detailed eye of editor Dori Harrell, who also offered valuable suggestions that added depth to the characters and story. I am also grateful to the rangers at the Baker City Oregon Trail Interpretive Center and especially Casey Tayler, who treated me to a private tour when I was the only one to show up for the Friday Ranger program. A special shout-out to Karen "Storyteller," a guest performer at the Interpretive Center, for not only her entertaining and informative show but for taking the extra time to answer all my silly questions. My neighbor Dr. June Brendon patiently answered all my medical questions. Thank you also to James and Diane Huckabay of Reecer Creek Publishing for helping me wade through the publishing minutia.

I am indebted to my aunt Janet Gross for her feedback after I "forced" her to read an early draft while she was visiting. She has since visited again (and I'm sure breathed a sigh of relief that I didn't burden her with another manuscript)! Next year. I would also like to thank the wordsmiths from the Reed Building Writers Group—Diane, Jean, Vivian, Christopher, Dale, Mary, and Rand—for their insightful comments when I shared snippets from the novel.

T. Lynne

Thank you for reading *Hope, Tears, and Dreams on the Way West*. If you enjoyed the book and would like to help bring it to more readers, please take a moment to post a short review on Amazon.

T. Lynne

About the author

T. Lynne Jackson holds a B.S. in accounting from Central Washington University and an MBA from San Jose State University. When not crunching numbers or writing, she can be found running and hiking the trails near her home in the Pacific Northwest with her dogs. She is the author of *An Impossible Promise: A WWII Survival Novel*.

Visit T. Lynne at <u>www.tlynnejackson.com</u>.
Facebook and Instagram @ tlynnejackson.author.

www.ingramcontent.com/pod-product-compliance
Lightning Source LLC
Chambersburg PA
CBHW020235010826
48973CB00006B/1520